UNAMBO

UNAMBO

A NOVEL OF THE WAR IN ISRAEL

By MAX BROD

TRANSLATED BY LUDWIG LEWISOHN

THE JEWISH PUBLICATION SOCIETY OF AMERICA

5712 — 1952

AUTHOR'S NOTE

For the factual material used in this narrative I am obliged to those whose accounts complemented my personal experiences, as well as to others who permitted me to cover the battle scenes under expert guidance. I am especially grateful to Lieutenant Zeev Schul, the admirable young author, who permitted me to insert, partly in paraphrase, partly word for word, the description of facts given in his two short stories called "Tales from the Jerusalem Hills."

I have utilized with the utmost scrupulousness all the military and political data based on the evidence of accessible delineations and documents. I have permitted myself a single chronological and geographic shift in Chapter Six. The narrative demanded it. But in this instance, too, I have changed no decisive details of the occurrences.

Tel Aviv, December 6, 1948

CONTENTS

UNAMBO

CHAPTER ONE

In which a strange laboratory in no man's land receives guests for the first time and, in all likelihood, for the last.

1.

The scene was the Café Shalva in the cruel humidity of one of those soaking May evenings in Tel Aviv, in which the air has the disagreeable taste of sifted red-hot sand.

The apparently violent wind from the sea is of no avail at such times. It seems to die a bare pace beyond the balustrade of the shore promenade. There it collapses and does not penetrate to the glowing concrete cubes of the city's buildings. The evenings here are not always so disagreeable and exhausting. But quite often they are, and between early May and late September their numbers multiply.

In that hot Café Shalva we were sitting, each one sipping his *tasas*, the chilled grapefruit juice. Only two lamps burned in the big room and both were swathed in green gauze. In spite of that, a zealous civil guard would appear from time to time at the gaping door and roar in, *"Lechabot eth ha-or!"* ("Put out the light!") The tired waitress would then scold and stamp her feet and exert herself to prove that this ghostly illumination did not exceed the police regulations.

Only a very few people sat at the tables near the radio. The green and yellow panes of the apparatus were dimmed by a covering of old newspapers. These people were evidently such as had no safe *miklat*, or bomb shelter, at home. The Café Shalva, it must be observed, emphasized even in its advertisements that it possessed and placed at the disposal of its guests an excellent one hundred per cent safe *miklat*. And this is a great rarity in Tel Aviv, a city built upon dunes, with few cellars below the houses. And the war had broken out quite literally overnight; there had been no time for preparation.

So there: three cheers for the Café Shalva and its *miklat*! To be sure, when things got serious the inhabitants of the upper stories of the house would protest against the use of the bomb shelter by the frequenters of the café and act in no pleasant fashion toward the "intruders." This controversy, originating in rather ghastly instincts of possessiveness, was far from settled, seeing that the war was barely a week old.

Well, no one paid much attention to the rage of these original inhabitants of the house. One tried to save one's own skin. In addition, the cellar, that rarity, having formerly been a bakery, was roomy enough. It was not admitted that anyone had a right to a permanent place in the shelter. All afternoon, in the course of several attacks from the air, violent and grotesque quarrels had taken place, which had left me half crazy. The inhabitants of the house felt at a grim disadvantage, since, when the alarm sounded, they had to stumble down the stairs, whereas the frequenters of the café were comfortably ensconced on the ground floor within easy reach of the cellar entry. For this reason sundry belligerent individuals among the house dwellers had taken possession of the courtyard. They established themselves on camp stools there in order to be as near to the cellar as the "strangers." Surlily they read books; several ladies took to knitting. Thus they waited for the next screaming of the sirens. It wasn't pretty—this disunity and triviality of spirit in the midst of the warlike conspiracy against the infant state. The sight of these people waiting there in their hate-filled stupidity rather broke me. And I was really too tired to go home and go to bed. I was simply unable to summon the necessary resolution.

To be quite frank, I was rather scared to go to my apartment in the third story right under the roof. It is true that the night attacks of the Egyptian Spitfires had become less frequent. But the moon was nearly full now and was like an invitation of nocturnal attacks upon the blanched city. During the first week of the war, moreover, there had been frequent attacks by night, and the damage done by bombs had hitherto been confined to top-story apartments. Later we were told, to be sure, that also apartments in lower stories, perhaps especially such, had been menaced by splinters and by air pressure. In these evil days one learned a good deal—things of which one would gladly have spared oneself the knowledge forever.

The other two who sat with me at the café table were my friend Paul Helfin, the film director, and his nephew Gad, seventeen and a soldier. Gad Reis had just come from the front; he had brought prisoners to town; at three o'clock in the morning he was to be back in his battle position. He had placed his rifle, his sailcloth ration bag, and his round steel helment on the magazine holder of a neighboring table. He said little. He answered our questions tranquilly, seeming the while to be thinking of something else. The great brown eyes in his thin, tanned face seemed to see nothing nor were they ever raised. "You don't expect *him* to tell us tales of heroic deeds," Helfin said to me. "We don't understand this new generation. Nor does it want us to understand. On the contrary. I have the feeling that it cuts itself off from us intentionally. Yet it was we who, in all the lands of Europe, worked for decades to build up Palestine. We did our duty to the best of our ability and acted by the best light we had. Our aims and the aims of these young people were the same. But they don't want to acknowledge it; they don't like to hear it. Isn't that so, Gad?"

The youth growled softly. It obviously displeased him to be talked about. He put a leather case on the table and took to examining his revolver.

"An estrangement has arisen between our youth and ourselves. I don't know why. Perhaps if I could make up my mind not to direct this film; if, as is proper, I were to enlist—"

"I beg your pardon, but you're at least forty-five."

"Forty-eight. But I'm an ex-officer. I might be useful. And to produce a film at this moment, to run off a shadow of life instead of living life. . . ! On the other hand, it has its uses too. Our propaganda is wretched. Good films are needed. They're pressing me. And you can imagine the tripe they'll produce if I refuse."

Someone at the neighboring table coughed and this cough sounded like the unarticulated word "if." Who was intruding upon our conversation and subtly jeering? The fat pale man who sat alone at that other table had long made an unpleasant impression on me by a strange attitude of bodily deliquescence. Oafishly he had spread himself over two chairs with a sort of ironic shamelessness. He seemed, as it were, meltingly to coalesce with the folds of his wrinkled white suit. I gave him a sharp look. He coughed and turned his eyes self-consciously away. With a vigorous gesture I pulled my chair to one side, as though the distance between him and myself was not great enough, as though I feared some revolting infection. The fat man struck me as extraordinarily disagreeable. One reason was, probably, the penetrating odor of perfume which he spread about him.

Gad jumped up. His face was radiant. A very young girl, almost a child, had slipped in gently. Blond hair waved about her lovely hot face. The girl wore the simple popular costume of the working youth of the land: a plain white blouse, a short blue skirt.

"That is Atida," the young soldier cried delightedly.

"She knew that you were in the city?"

"I didn't tell her. Probably some acquaintance saw me on the open truck. But now you'll have to excuse me."

He and the girl sat down at another table. His determined silence was now changed into eager chatting.

"A thoroughly fine boy," my friend declared. "He simply didn't want to go to see her in order to spare her annoyance. And he was crazy to go. But her parents are bent on making a citified young lady of her."

"You don't mean to tell me that these children have already established a serious relationship?"

"Whatever our young people do, they do with a deep seriousness. They can't imagine anything else. They are swift and strong. They are the contrary of all that we were in our dancing and flirting days. They mature, as it were, over night. Especially in this time of terror. It goes without saying that these two want to marry and found a household. No nonsense about it. They seem to be full-grown at sixteen, and of a purity which is almost frightening."

I was familiar, of course, with my friend's rather one-sided enthusiasm for "our magnificent youth" and didn't contradict him.

He was full of bitter reproachfulness toward himself and toward the world; he offset this by his enthusiasm for the new generation.

"The parents are not worthy of these children," Helfin continued. He smiled approvingly. "It's interesting too, how this generation forms an interconnected whole. Whatever happens is carried by the atmosphere. Take the arrival of Gad in this very large city. Something like magic is at work."

Involuntarily I turned around and looked at those two, whispering together in their corner. A certain shyness created a distance between them. But the seventeen-year-old warrior did not take his eyes from the vivid, lovely girl. Out of her handbag she took a little pamphlet, a copy of one of the familiar miniature scores, and handed the present to the delighted boy.

"Gad is a passionate musician," my friend boasted vicariously. "He will be more than promising if he survives the war."

"What do his parents say to that?"

"Hitler took care of them. Right to the ovens of Auschwitz. Of his whole extensive family on both sides in Austria and Germany not a soul is left. He and I are the only survivors. He came here just in time ten years ago with the Youth *Aliyah*. He is almost a *Sabra*." My friend used the word *Sabra*, cactus, with which the native-born Palestinians seek to point out their rude and thorny toughness. He used it with their own proud matter-of-factness. "Gad was brought up on the pedagogical farm of Ben-Shemen. He had just finished school and had joined a group which was to form a new settlement in Galilee, just north of the Lake of Kinereth, when the Arab attack took place. Nothing is left of the tents or huts or young trees of the settlement. During the reconquest of the mere naked earth ten of his young comrades fell. Later they were forced to abandon the settlement altogether. The Syrians invaded with cannons, armored cars, and tanks. We had just two old machine guns. In the meantime the United Nations at Lake Success sat in council, as they had been doing for months, in fact since last December and most emphatically since May 15, trying to invent a way by which this attack upon us could be defined as being no attack at all, and this war with bomber planes and heavy armor as not a war at all. The hypocrisy involved makes one despair of humanity. Gad hates war, as I have hated it all my life. But what are we to do in this situation? Stretch out our neck for the ax? I don't even pretend that we have done the right thing in every detail. But one thing is certain beyond doubt: we are innocent of starting this war, although I am not prepared to deny the generalization that no one is guiltless. Had we all followed the teaching of Him who once preached in Galilee . . ."

Again it seemed to me as though the fat man at the next table repeated my friend's words "had," followed by a hoarse grunting. Did our conversation make him nervous? Was he projecting his nervousness upon us?

Luckily Helfin did not observe this impertinent jeering. He was caught up in his own ardent reflections. "Yet I am confident that we did no evil in Galilee. Driven from Europe, a tiny remnant of the persecuted, we have dug up the stones, sunk wells, planted gardens on barren cliffs. Gad loves fruit trees above all things. He wants to plant and to build. These youths, who may not have heard of Socrates, have the ideal of a Socratic decency and simplicity. The world grudges us that too. So we are forced to defend ourselves. Ah, if only our *Kibbutzim*, our settlements, had been armed. Then not so many of our best young men would have fallen in those first few days. At the very beginning all they could do was to let the motors of their trucks and tractors run all night and drive their vehicles uphill and downdale with as much noise and glitter as possible. These were the new trumpets of Jericho. And the enemy really believed that we had tanks and did not attack in force. Later on he came with twenty heavy tanks from Samach to the gates of Dagania Alef, the classical settlement, sacred to us all, and was about to penetrate through the wire entanglements into the garden. The work of generations which had engaged the affection of thousands seemed doomed to destruction within a few minutes. For our people had nothing but rifles with which to oppose the heavy armor. At that moment, even as the first tank was crossing it, there arose from the trench two boys, who had recently arrived from Buchenwald, and threw bottles of benzine at that first tank. It burst into flames. The two Syrians in the tank had just been heard laughing aloud over the absurd attempts of the Jews to resist. That laughter had been audible. They laughed no more. The driver of the tank leaped out and was shot. The second tank turned around, which threw the others into confusion. All fled. One of the rescued colonists said later, in the first breathlessness of liberation, that the benzine weapon called a Molotov bottle should henceforth be called in Hebrew *Male-tov*, 'full of goodness.' Yes, it was cruel and horrible, but a blessing for the innocent people who were attacked. It was like a miracle. And the same thing happened in the south, in Negba, where a whole Egyptian battalion, equipped with all modern weapons and trained for years in the practice of war, was dispersed. A man who was there said to me, 'It was really even as it is written in the Book of Judges: "They fought from heaven, the stars in their courses fought against Sisera. The brook Kishon swept them away." *Min-shamayim nilchamu ha-kochavim.* Otherwise we could not have prevailed.' The impossible was made possible. To be sure, we didn't see the stars. The people of Negba fought from bunkers; after all their buildings had been destroyed. But isn't all this courage and this power born of faith more than merely human? Similarly a group of bicyclists conquered the Jerusalem quarter of Katamon and drove off the shock troopers. And I recall the words of a mother at her son's burial beside a row of new graves, 'Do not say that it was in vain. Had these not fallen, who knows how our land would look?' Remember your Simonides, 'Wanderer, when thou comest to Sparta . . .' But now comes the most incredible. The world is taking no cognizance of these mighty happenings, of this heroism as of Thermopylae. It shrugs its shoulders and turns away when it does not utter some cool critical observation. Let's turn on London on the radio."

The news broadcasters' rasping, falsely amiable singsong came over the wires. "King Abdullah emphatically denies that he is waging a war. He is undertaking a police raid against bands of terrorists. At a press conference in Amman the ruler declared that the action would be successfully concluded within two weeks."

Enraged, Helfin turned off the radio.

"I wouldn't get excited if I were you," I said. "Remember your Goethe, 'Baseness is no cause for crying'—and so on . . .'"

"He stills hopes, you see, this ruler of the desert, to turn back into desert all that has been planted for decades at the cost of so much labor and sacrifice. A handsome objective indeed. And in just two weeks! And who is to say whether he won't succeed, whether reality is not concealed within these cynical threats. Because there's no doubt that Mr. Bevin is squarely behind him. And in spite of all our exertions, we are still so weak. You know, I've never echoed the vain and empty boasters—"

" 'For it gets the best of us spite of all denying.' " I insisted on finishing my quotation.

"No, look, it's something different this time; it's not the usual baseness; it's not the average indecency of the world. It's something more. I'm thinking of the shameless lies involved! When Japan also, and quite unblushingly, called its war against China a police raid, it was consistent enough to resign from the League of Nations. Mussolini did the same thing when he attacked Abyssinia. Or was he thrown out? I forget the exact circumstances. At all events, Japan, or so we are told, is today being 'punished' —punished for the very thing which the five Arab states are now undertaking against us under the patronage of Mr. Bevin. The single difference is this, that today all these violators of law continue to sit in the United Nations Assembly, debating and drinking cocktails with everyone's approval, while everything we have built is being crushed. Meanwhile Reuter and the Exchange News Agency carry out a universal and well-planned campaign of lies in order to throw a smoke screen around the simple truth and fact that we are defending ourselves against five aggressors who declared quite openly that they would invade our territory on a definite date. It's no trouble at all to befog everything. Call these planes which bombard Tel Aviv hour after hour—for how long will this lull last?—call them parts of a police raid and at once the impression is created that it is not *they* who attack this peaceful city, but that it is the city which has, as it were, leaped into the clouds and started to fight the Alexandrian bombers. It's an old experience. Remember? 'Jewish peddler bites German shepherd dog.' " He uttered a deep sigh. "Everything, everything in the world can be contorted and befogged. That is the melancholy symbol of our age."

He continued with his great accusatory oration. Alas, it left me rather cold, seeing that I had heard it all before recently, whether in parts or in its totality.

It is a common observation that a specific expression of countenance is a constant characteristic of many individuals. Even when, at times, this expression vanishes, even when the man with melancholy pendent cheeks laughs—yet something of his melancholy peers through his laughter and remains subterraneously there. Other faces always have a touch of gaiety and complacency even when anger or pain momentarily cloud the small shrewd eyes. Thus my friend Paul Helfin was characterized by a very special expression; it stamped him for what he was, even when for minutes or even hours he appeared to escape from himself. And this unforgettable expression which characterized him was that of an affronted astonishment. He was affronted and astonished by what the evil world dared to do and dared to expect of him and others. It is thus that I always remember Helfin when I recall the image of him—his tall, slender figure, his short brown Van Dyke beard—thus, when I summon him up, six months after the improbable things which we experienced together and which began on that sultry night spent in expectation of the Egyptian bombers.

In addition to his Van Dyke, Helfin wore a rather bushy mustache, probably a vestige of his Anglophile period. This growth of hair had something martial about it, which hardly harmonized with his gentle and naïve physiognomy. Indeed I have never known a kinder man or one of deeper good will. But precisely on account of the goodness of his own will he was permanently wrought up over all the wrongs that were done in the whole world. To the world he showed a mask of harmonious self-mastery, even of serenity. Indeed there were many who took comfort in his tranquillity and sought refuge with him in their own difficult moments. But a smaller circle of friends, to which I belonged, knew him better. To us he showed his real self. "As far back as I can think," he was accustomed to say, "everything in the world has grown worse and worse. From year to year.

During the last two decades the dignity of man has been ever more shamelessly trodden under. Often I think that this impression must be an imaginary one, that I fall into the trap of a banal formula of the world's decay, since each one believes things were better in his childhood and youth—or else, that I'm simply crazy. But next something happens under my very eyes; what still seemed impossible yesterday, as too unbelievably brutal, actually takes place today. No one even utters an excuse. And what still seems incredible today will surely be the bestial reality of tomorrow."

Torrents of grief would thus break forth from his rebellious heart. In this respect he was no comfortable companion; he could easily get on one's nerves, especially when one suffered under one's own burden of woe and indignation. Onto that he threw the whole weight of his own depression. But he did not consider that. For hours at a time he would pour forth his reproaches against the course of events, against public and private wrong, and you felt as though he were accusing you who were with him of it all. At last one was forced to rebel. "You don't have to convince me that the British policy is a very net of intrigue. I know it. I am entirely of your opinion. You don't have to address your philippic against me. Don't talk to me! Go to some public forum and declare there what is being done to you, to us. I am as powerless as yourself. And you attack me, as though I had a share in Abdullah's ambition or Farouk's rage to make war, as though I had instigated the bloody aggression of the Arab Legion or could, by a whistle, call it back."

Then, of course, he would stop. He would utter an embarrassed laugh and look more astonished than ever. His situation was, of course, bizarre because he had not meant, needless to say, to accuse his interlocutor. He had merely, so to speak, misused an oratorical device. The whole thing reminded me of a saying of my wise mother with which, at times, she took the wind out of my childish sails when I complained of things which were not in her power to alter. "You go fight City Hall," she would say good-naturedly. Or else, more briefly, "You tell the rain to stop."

On this occasion, too, Helfin uttered his great accusation

against that monstrous crime of which we seemed to him the victims. He played the double part of prosecutor and counsel for the defense. He sought to distribute right and wrong with an even hand. "I do not say that much would not have been different, if we had had the skill from the beginning to establish better human relations with the British bureaucracy here; if our extremists, whose misdeeds I detest, had not hanged those two innocent English sergeants . . ."

"If, if"—now there was no doubt of the echo uttered at that neighboring table.

I felt as though I had been stunned. The sultry night, the expectation of the next air attack, the psychical aggressiveness of that fat man—everything irritated me. Confusion seemed to take hold of all my senses, and Helfin grew more and more unrestrained. He declared that there was nothing left upon which one could place any moral reliance; that the condition of humanity was giving rise to utter despair—above all, truly, the evil that was being done here, in this land of lands, the complete destruction of justice, the unleashing of hell, the indifferent and careless glances of the so-called civilized worlds on both sides of the ocean. "It is beyond all bearing," he gasped. "And I wouldn't be surprised if on this consecrated earth, where prophets and redeemers have taught, now, today, before the end of all, the Devil were to appear *in propria persona.*" The last words of his that I heard were: "I am amazed that God is not ashamed of having created such a world."

"Well and powerfully said," the fat man clearly articulated now, swung himself nimbly about, and slid with great agility to our table, seating himself on the chair which young Gad had left. The sweet, penetrating perfume that had almost nauseated me a few minutes before seemed now to surround us like a curtain. "I'm extremely fond of such powerful expressions. Perhaps you gentlemen will permit me to join your conversation. Involuntarily I caught a few fragments of it; I was especially and keenly interested in the circumstance that in your conversation you employed so many conditional sentences. No, I'm no philologist, as you might think; no pensioned schoolmaster. But the conditional locution seems simply to enchant me."

He fluted the words, as though he enjoyed them, yet with an air of irony. With histrionic emotionalism he raised his right hand and with a shudder I observed that the hand had no thumb. The lack of a limb always presents a slightly uncanny sight; the sight in this case was rendered more painful by the absence of any scar or stump. The skin was as tight and perfect as a new white kid glove. It looked as though this large fat hand had never been provided with more than four fingers.

"Yes, gentlemen, these sentences that begin with an 'if' always remind me of that agreeable operetta of the good old days in which people had such a fondness for naked and well-nourished shoulders, those shoulders which a writer once compared to smooth ice-runs. 'All I did was to kiss her shoulder, you see . . . '" Actually the horrible creature now began to sing in a hoarse, edgy voice. "In that same piece, *The Beggar Student,* you also find it archly said, 'Let me assume that your love were not true . . . ' There we have it again—that charming conditional locution—'Let me assume!'

. "In this connection I would like to contradict one of your assertions," he continued with a laugh and with an access of coughing which seemed to be caused by a horrible smoker's catarrh, as though his voice had to fight its way through whole layers of phlegm. "This, to be sure, only with your permission. If—that word goes without saying—very gay, isn't it? Well, then, with your permission, it is my belief that it would have changed nothing, if your honorable terrorists had pardoned the two British sergeants. Undoubtedly it was a crime, as the saying goes; according to a maxim of Talleyrand, it was worse than a crime; it was a blunder. But it had no effect upon British policy, which is very simply based upon the reports of its Near East experts and founded on the incontrovertible fact that in the territory of the richest oil fields of the world there are forty times as many Arabs as there are Jews. Briefly and unhappily: the sympathy of forty times as many people seems more important to the benevolent government of Britain than that of a small splinter population. What is there to criticize in this calculation? It had been made, gentlemen, long before those two were hanged. Only, without this murderous deed, it would have been harder for the government to arouse, and to betray into the mistakes it desired, a people of such ordinarily sound judgment."

"This people of good judgment seems either to forget or not to have been told that the atrocity in question was in answer to a previous atrocity committed against itself." His ever vigilant sense of justice forced Helfin now to contradict himself. "It was only a few days prior that five Jewish partisans were hanged by the English."

The fat man said, "After being sentenced by a court of legal standing."

To which Helfin replied: "By a court established *ad hoc*, the legality of which the partisans never acknowledged."

From the magnetic drowsiness into which these forever repeated arguments seemed to thrust me and into which perhaps, also, I was escaping the antipathy and horror which seemed to stream toward me from this unknown character—out of this somnolence I was roused, at an indeterminate later moment, by the invitation, or rather the mere question, whether I wouldn't like to drive somewhere—it wasn't clear to me where—in a car that stood in readiness. Quickly I said yes. Just to get out of this hot café seemed a great gain. Helfin's nephew, who in the meantime had taken his girl home and had come back, joined us. For the space of a few hours he had no legitimate shelter. Or maybe it was just the hunger for experience, the joy of living, or mere curiosity that made him tag along.

2.

From the café I had seen no car stop in the rather empty street, although the doors and windows had all been open in order that the heat might be mitigated. Now suddenly a car was there—an amazing enough car, for it was twice as big as even autos de luxe are apt to be. Nor was it streamlined according to the contemporary notions of elegance; it seemed rather to correspond to the taste of some Indian maharajah who had a rather confused notion of the progressive civilization of Europe in his Himalayan wilderness. The thing was broad and square and overloaded with gold ornaments. The roof was supported by narrow black Greek columns of wood into which the panes of glass were set. It reminded me of a hearse. But it was comfortable enough; we sank down on the seats as into deep, broad leather armchairs.

There was no chauffeur. The fat man himself took the wheel and drove with extraordinary ease, almost without looking at the road. He stepped violently on the gas, and since he kept turning around to talk to the three of us, I was afraid we might at any moment either murder one of the many bicyclists, who were using no light, or else ourselves hurtle into some corner of the winding Ben Jehuda Street. But always at what seemed the last moment he kept the car on the road by some gesture of the little finger of his mutilated hand. All the while he kept all the lights of the car brilliantly lit, although we were now approaching the center of the city.

I called his attention to the black-out regulation necessitated by the war. In all the houses there was only here and there a surreptitious half-lit window.

He laughed with intense amusement. "A man has to have a little pull," he observed lightly.

The car leaped and flew, as though there were no obstacles. In its brightly lit interior I now had a complete vision of his face, especially since he kept it turned toward us, seeming to leave the car to its own devices. This face could not really be called homely; rather it was marked by a certain large complacency, like the face of a highly experienced man who had exhausted all the arts of life. It was not homely, yet irritating in a disagreeable way. It was utterly pallid and broad and almost perfectly circular. The eyebrows were sable and thoroughly unsymmetrical. The one was a rigid straight line immediately above the eye; the other had two angles and twitched without interruption and was placed high in the low, furrowed forehead. Very strange, too, was his baldness, which constituted a not excessively broad band between his forehead and his nape. As a rule, men who are very bald wear their remaining hair trimmed short in order to mitigate the contrast. The fat man evidently despised this mitigation. His remaining coal-black hair rose in two thick tufts behind his ears on both sides of his baldness, so that at moments they had the effect of two powerful horns. I do not remember ever having seen before a sight so grotesque and revolting. It was a depressing sight, too; it was like the sticky, raspberry-like perfume which surrounded him.

It was incomprehensible to me that my two companions seemed to be aware of none of this. The young soldier was probably thinking half of his girl and half of his return to the front. But there was not for a moment a rift in his tranquil demeanor, and my friend Helfin was so violently involved in his arguments that he had no awareness of the outer world at all. He was explaining with all his zeal how unheard of had been the behavior of the British government which, on the fifteenth of May, had, as it were, sought to throw us with fettered hands to the wolfishness of the five or six or seven Arabic aggressors (six if we count Saudi Arabia, seven if we count Yemen). For on the fourteenth of May any weapon, a mere rifle or revolver, found in the possession of a Jew had still been regarded as illegal and had subjected the owner to ten or more years in the penitentiary. But on the fifteenth of May we were somehow to defend ourselves against armies which had for years been "legally" equipped with British cannons and British armor and had been trained, and were led by, British officers. This we were to do or die like dogs. "That was the plan. Oh yes, Brigadier Clayton, that was well thought out! To this moment it is hard to understand that we were not annihilated by the *blitz* within forty-eight hours."

The fat man declared that we must leave the car. It was forbidden to drive farther. Technically impossible, too, even "if one has pull."

"Where in the world are we going?" I asked.

"Into my laboratory. You seem to have forgotten."

I didn't tell him that I had been discourteous enough in the café not to listen at all for a while and even to have napped a little in the weariness brought on by heat and excitement.

With steady step the fat man preceded us. I observed only now how tall and powerfully built he was. He was a head taller than the lank Helfin, and the weight of his limbs corresponded to the breadth of his face. He conducted us past the Danziger Clinic and after a few hundred paces we found ourselves on a field covered with ruins which seemed to end only with the horizon. A first glance reminded one of the ruins of Pompeii, for there too one sees the indication of streets and alleys which run not between houses but between what were once rows of houses and are now heaps of crumbled fragments, insignificant, lowly; remnants that reach to the knee. But there was this difference: in Pompeii the rubble has been cleaned up and placed in neat layers. Here, on the contrary, in Manshiyeh, the no man's land between Tel Aviv and Jaffa, where conflict had raged for weeks, no one had yet had a chance to create order. Of some houses a half-wall was still standing; other buildings had been razed to the very earth, so that the flat ground which had once borne these houses was more like the sketch or map of a city than the city itself.

So we went from street to street, past empty shops, past walls of sandbags, past heaps of sand which had run out of such bags, past wire entanglements and ruined doors and window frames. Here and there a wooden hut seemed still inhabited or a balcony showed behind whose curtains a candle began to gleam. Had refugees taken possession of a few dwellings? Or was this but a reflection of moonlight? For thick green moonshine lay over all these ruins. One caught oneself avoiding this sharp light as carefully as one did by day the glare of the sun and taking refuge in the shade. Night had brought little relief from the heat. This happens during many nights in Tel Aviv, when sunset seems to open new sources of heat and when one involuntarily ascribes this nocturnal war to the almost painful radiance of the moon.

It was the remnants of the concrete houses that were most frightening. They did not exhibit the old-fashioned and not unpicturesque aspect of ruins with empty rows of windows. They seemed hammered into fragments to the earth by some gigantic fist, hewn into individual great cubes, which lay in confusion. Chaos was here—chaos for all time, never to return to form.

"What was the score that your friend brought you?" I asked the young soldier beside me in order to divert my thoughts.

"The Fourth Symphony of Brahms."

I breathed more tranquilly at once. There was something

which stood like a green and flowery height among all this dusty desolation.

The fat man told us that he had helped in the fighting here. He pointed to great heaps of rubble. Here in a corner house had been a Jewish defensive position; across the street, Arabs had entrenched themselves and had had to be dynamited out. One could still see the brick wall that had been raised to help fortify this house; one could see the bullet holes; the remains of the wall had been blackened by the charges.

We remained standing in front of a heap of rubble and looked at it in silence. From afar there came to us the street noises of the nocturnal city of Tel Aviv—motor horns, a motorcycle, a whistle, a gay tune. It wasn't so far away. One had only to turn a certain corner and one would be back in the throbbing city. But here there hovered the desolateness of a melancholy ghostly realm, silent, utterly lifeless, heavy as tears. Suddenly a sharp fume came to us from a still smoldering ruin.

A military guard approached us. The fat man evidently exercised his pull once more. He glanced sharply at the soldier, who promptly saluted and let us pass.

"It was from this point," Helfin cried, "that Tel Aviv was attacked daily from the thirtieth of November on, immediately after the decision of the United Nations. Almost daily people were killed in the city, once ten of them at once—children, women, a baby in its cradle. They shot from the Hassan Bek Mosque. Later they used mortars too, so that in the very middle of Tel Aviv houses collapsed and buried their inhabitants."

"We all know that, Paul!" I admonished my friend.

"My point is we had to do something about this attack. We offered to make peace with them. Dr. Heykal, the mayor of Jaffa, refused. You mustn't forget, either, that the owners of most of these destroyed dwellings and shops were Jews. In Manshiyeh the population was always a mixed one and Arabs and Jews dwelt together in peace—up to the very day on which the British permitted the Iraqian so-called volunteers to enter Jaffa."

"Here we are," said the fat man.

"Is it here that you have your laboratory?" Gad spoke for the first time and pulled tighter the shoulder strap of his rifle.

"Why not, young man? I like to work undisturbed, far from the noises of a big city. I don't need the exaggerated conveniences of modern places of research. *Bene est cui deus obtulit parca quod satis est manu*, as you know. You don't? It's a pity that the young here don't learn Latin. A flagrant lack. Nothing wrong with that classical culture with which you, my dear Professor Helfin, have exhibited so happy a familiarity. The Heroes of Thermopylae—'Wanderer, when thou comest to Sparta'—finally, 'Socratic poverty,' not so bad." In this vein of horrid babbling, interrupted by accesses of coughing, he continued for a while. And the astonishing thing was not only that we put up with his impertinent jeering. It was even more noteworthy—as I figured out later when I reviewed the adventures of this ever stranger night—that it didn't occur to us that there was in the whole business a profoundly uncanny element, seeing that the man had not sat near enough to us in the café to be so well informed concerning our names and the intimate details of our conversation.

"What I'd like to know," our young soldier remarked, "is where you get your electric current here where everything is in pieces."

"All the current I want. You'll be able to observe for yourself in a moment. Shall we enter?"

3.

He had brought us to the foot of a stairway which led up to a platform. Here we faced the unharmed wall of a house, in which we observed a little door, ivy-framed and with a neatly engraved brass sign over the door knob. The fat man opened the door. Strangely enough there was no room on the other side of the door. The platform continued beyond the wall. It was empty and surrounded by a low wall of unhewn stones which bordered on rubble heaps. After a few steps we once more reached a stairway, which descended from the platform or, rather, from the deserted courtyard of a destroyed house, and issued in a subterranean passage of solid masonry. Above the entrance to the cellar there was to be seen a horse's head which projected from the wall. It was not of stone but probably of wood and painted in the colors of nature. It could even have been an embalmed authentic horse's head which, according to some barbaric custom, was nailed to the entrance wall of this subterranean passage, a phenomenon observable among the peasants of Nordic countries.

The sidereal firmament, somewhat blurred by the brilliance of the moon, glittered in all its southern splendor. Like a gigantic gate the Milky Way stood in front of its eastern sphere; on the north of this triumphal structure hung, like the measuring rod of the Divine Creator, the double triangle of Cassiopeia. Opposite it to the south swung majestically the titanic constellation of Scorpio, not wholly visible in Europe, but present here in the sky during the glowing summer months and occupying a great portion of the heavenly plain. The heavenly beast spread out its mighty pincers, consisting of innumerable stars, like the wings of a gigantic bat, turning them, like ready weapons, against the much suffering city. On the back of the constellation glowed, like a malevolent red eye, a ghastly giant star, the throbbing rival of Mars, the Counter-Mars or Antares.

At the foot of the stairs we entered a long, handsomely vaulted subterranean passage. The walls were composed of smooth white tiles; here and there an electric bulb glowed; the whole reminded one of a passage in a subway and was similarly curved. The fat man opened a grillwork gate, adorned with Arabic lettering. This gate was no stage property. Beyond it we entered a carpeted antechamber. There were fresh flowers against the walls as well as old tinted steel engravings in narrow gold frames. These seemed doubly homelike after the scenes of destruction which we had just witnessed, even though a few frightened wood lice as well as other vermin hurried across the white walls.

We were politely invited to take off our things. But since, after the fashion of midsummer in Tel Aviv, we had nothing on except short-sleeved shirts and shorts, there arose from this invitation too something of the cheap, disagreeable, slightly coarse irony which the fat man seemed to feel to be obligatory upon him. He himself hung his wide white coat on a hanger.

We crossed two or three dark rooms, in which there was a

21

moist and claylike odor as in a sculptor's studio; then we came into a brightly lit, comfortably furnished room in which, however, that powerful perfume once more exerted its unpleasant effect. Great clusters of grapes as well as bananas seemed to await us on a small white-covered table against the wall. Bottles of wine and brandy were visible; imported cigarettes and cigars lay in heaps on silver dishes. Gad at once sat down at the piano and softly struck certain chords repeatedly and tried his skill in uncommon modulations, tasting a joy he had long missed. Rows of books in a glass-covered bookcase bore witness to the owner's culture. But there were no test tubes nor bottles nor any apparatus that seemed to point to a laboratory in the ordinary sense. The leather armchairs resembled the seats in the gigantic car in their soft luxuriousness. The air seemed pleasantly cool. This was due to two ventilators and to the additional circumstance that a part of the thick ceiling was open, as is the custom in the better film theaters in summer. Here, to be sure, the construction of the ceiling was very massive. We were at least several meters below the surface of the earth. But one could see the stars and it seemed to me that I saw the red master star of Scorpio throb with a tinge of malice.

"We have a bomb shelter here too," said the fat man, perhaps deliberately misinterpreting my searching look. "Here, gentlemen." He opened a small nearby door, from which a stair descended farther down into the earth. "All modern comforts! I want my guests to be thoroughly comfortable. I find in general that people take life far too hard. Isn't a little comfort much better? Let's be a little carefree, a little *sans souci*. It is this very principle which I want to illustrate by the little experiment which I promised to show you. Permit me first of all, however, to explain to you, gentlemen, what impelled me to invite you here."

His zigzag eyebrow quivered more than ever, while the other seemed to freeze into a permanent rigidity. "You, my dear Professor von Helfin, expressed an opinion, in that conversation which I had the honor to overhear, to which I find myself unalterably opposed, the opinion, namely, that in the midst of all the noise and confusion of our time, the Devil would one day turn up in person. It wouldn't surprise you, you said, at all. Now this is an extremely impertinent notion against which anyone at all familiar with the Devil is bound to protest. The Devil doesn't in the least like to destroy, and to vegetate in the midst of suffering. He is partial to superfluity. He is a gay and gentlemanly fellow as I shall prove to you from one of the oldest documents that treat of him. For that document we have to return once more to classical antiquity. But, if you will forgive me, Colonel Gad, one can't get along without it." He drew forth a volume from his large bookcase and opened it. "I have here the panegyric of the Sophist Prodikos concerning Herakles at the cross-roads, as it is handed down to us by the good Xenophon, whom I, myself, consider something of a fool. In this speech appears the symbolical figure of Virtue and promises the young citizens battles, intolerable hardships, and misery. The Devil, however, says —I am quoting it to you now, 'I see, dear Herakles, that you have not yet decided upon the path of life which you intend to pursue. Choose me as your companion and I will lead you along the most charming and comfortable path; you will need to renounce no pleasure. On the contrary, whatever there is of heaviness and pain in life will always remain unknown to you.' Isn't that a handsome offer? And quite unequivocal!"

"So far as I remember," Helfin objected, "the end of the story is quite contrary to this."

The fat man was quite untouched in his crude and primitive superiority. He didn't reply. He lit a new cigarette and eagerly offered us some. Then he went merrily on, "Let's go on, however, to the soundest expert in the whole field, to the Sieur René Lesage. Here I have his masterwork, *The Limping Devil*, in which I like to read desultorily. How does the Devil in this story show his gratitude to the hero for liberating him from the bottle? He regales him with all kinds of gay and scabrous anecdotes. And how does this Ashmadai introduce himself? 'It is I who have introduced luxury into the world, and all excesses, and all games of chance and alchemy. I am the inventor of the merry-go-around, of the dance, of music, the theater, and the latest French fashions—' "

"Possible enough that this Ashmadai was or pretended to be

a relatively gay devil," I interrupted him. "It just happens that I recently reread that charming and informative book and I remember that it contains other and far less appetizing devils. There is Belphegor, who stirs up hatreds among the councils of princes and rulers and incites to insurrections and wars. Next there is Flagell, the demon of the jurists, of their paragraphs and their chicaneries. Why do you emphasize Ashmadai?" And in a sort of rage I took a deep drink out of my glass of the red wine of Richon-le-Zion.

This seemed to shake the assurance of the fat man a little and to irritate him, too. "Ashmadai is more congenial to me. He is, as you know, indigenous to this country. The wise King Solomon himself conjured him up and took rather shabby advantage of him, to the point of chicanery, in the matter of the building of the Temple. Well, let's pass over that embarrassing story, of which the whole diabolical world is still ashamed. What is gone is gone! Briefly and badly: the whole business just happened to be a matter of obvious notoriety in this country. So if you're going to talk about a new epiphany of the Devil, my dear and honored sir, it can't be anyone but Ashmadai or, as the Christians say, Asmodeus, around here."

Helfin, who had rather devoted himself to the brandy, sprang up. "And it doesn't even have to be a limping devil. It would be just as well if he lacked some other bone—a thumb, for instance."

"We'll get to that subject by and by," said the fat man with sudden seriousness. Once more he had a paroxysm of coughing and spitting and blowing his nose, so that he could not speak for a while but by violent simultaneous gestures prevented anyone else from interrupting him. "It is, let me tell you, a mere lay opinion that the diabolical powers are separate and not coherent. In hell, too, there exists a Trinity or a Sevenfoldness or, if you like, a Thousandfoldness. In the last analysis, if one may say so, all the diabolical persons coalesce into a single person, namely, Satan. Whether you call him Belial or Lucifer or Belphegor or Bel-zevuv, illiterately called Beelzebub, or Ashmadai —it is always the same. But let me not forget that what I wanted

24

to show you was some technical experimentation. I didn't mean to lecture on theology."

Young Gad lifted his fingers from the keys. "In our technological period it's natural for the Devil, too, to go in for experiments."

"Bravo, young man, let's drink to that!"

"Thank you, I don't drink." The soldier waved the glass aside. At that moment I was aware of the fact that Helfin and I were both already rather drunk and that it would be senseless to try to follow Gad's good example. On the contrary, I seemed now to be seized by a genuine thirst and all that was from now on spoken and done in our subterranean hiding place and drinking parlor came to me as through a soft, thick fog. The air, too, had grown heavier from the smoke of our many cigarettes and was whirled about by the big ventilators rather than drawn off.

Was it not the theme of the *Chaconne* of Brahms which Gad now played? While these sublime chords resounded, offering in their crystalline purity a vain resistance against the delusions which swathed us more and more, and while they rose in their first and second variations, the fat man produced in the middle of the room, placing it upon a dais, a little marionette theater which, with amazing swiftness, he had brought out from behind a green drapery.

"What first attracted my attention to you, gentlemen, was your laudable habit of using the word 'if' so frequently. *If* Churchill had been in the place of Bevin . . . and *if* I could decide to join the army instead of directing a film . . . And that went on and on. You know, since I've been very frank about it, that I am passionately fond of this locution, of these delicately thought out conditional sentences—I can't make myself heard, my dear Paderewski, over there! Suppose you quit for a while! But you don't have to jump up on that account, as though a tarantula had stung you." Mocking an imagined old whore he chanted the stave of a street song. Then he seemed to return to a more reasonable state of mind and said, "To meet the needs of these conditional concepts I have constructed my little machine. Its purpose is to help people to pass through many difficult hours.

For men continually are confronted by an 'if.' 'If I had done so and so or so and so, then this or that consequence would not have ensued.' You have a friend and he wants a loan and you refuse it. He raises bloody hell. But it's not the first time; whenever he wants to be gotten out of a hole he does that. O.K."

That rather vulgar polygot slang in which the fat man expressed himself, colored though it was by some cultural and ironically courteous pretension, annoyed me like an evil odor. At the same time a mysterious compulsion forced me to listen to him with increased attention. For it seemed to me suddenly as though in this cellar I was about to gain light upon many things that tormented me. Even upon Helfin's habitually astonished face the expression of amazement and tension increased.

"What you forgot was that it might be serious. This time it was. The s.o.b. kills himself. Gone but not forgotten. Now dirty little Mr. Prudence says, 'A-ha, if I had said yes.' If!—Or take another case. A bank director votes against a bond issue. Just to show what a stubborn wise guy he is. Usually no one gives a damn about his opinion. This time he happens to get the better of the others. What happens? His beautiful institute goes into bankruptcy. 'If I had been in a better mood that day and if I had voted for the issue, everything would probably have happened differently.' To the end of his life he will be tormented by this dilemma and yet he never knows how the cat is going to jump or how she would have jumped, if—if . . . Well, I leave you to figure it out. Now this is where my little patent comes in. Our prudent little gentleman and our bank director and all the other guys don't have to make a decision. All that each one of them does is to employ my machine, which I call unambo. Unambo is the patented trade name, and it's going to be called that, gentlemen, that and nothing else. You switch it on, I say. Observe, no mystery about it!" Although he had no shirtsleeve, he made the prestidigitator's gesture of rolling up his sleeves. "And then you simply press the button—"

My eyes hurt me at the swiftness with which several puppets made of cardboard whirred back and forth on the little stage, which was suddenly illuminated by a sharp, pale-blue light.

"Ah, once more I forgot to reckon with the merely fragmentary intelligence of man. And so permit me to explain." The oaf disconnected the machine and began to explain in the condescending tone of a first-grade primer, "What you see here is a double stage. At this point of its center the stage is divided into two equal sections. At first the same play is performed on both sections of the stage. A young man descends the stairs to the dune. He hesitates. He knows that the interview to which he is going will be of decisive significance for himself and for all the rest of his life. Had he better turn to the right, where the fatal woman is waiting? If he preferred to cut and run? *If*. . . ! Such is the simple paradigm. Now I set the wheels in motion. Thereupon you see the same action in a twofold execution. Up to a certain point. . . ." Once more, in order to be able to explain the better, he turned off both the light and the movement. The puppets stood still. "The whole notion came to me from the technique of stage directing. A hit, eh what? Yes, Mr. Helfin, I was your competitor for quite a while and took up play directing; it's a favorite occupation of mine to this day. Now take that little man! We won't let him tremble much longer. Shall he go? Shall he not go? I'm on the side of comfort. Does one always have to confront a rigid 'either—or'? There is a third way, the way of evasion and amenity. What is its name? Its name is "both at the same time." I simply make no more decisions; I live doubly; I live both lives simultaneously. Unambo! *Uno*—one; *ambo*—both! Whereupon I turn my indicator to the proper place and press it down. That will cause you to see how the life of our little man would go nicely to pot if he kept the rendezvous. That action takes place on the left stage. And the entirely different course of his life, if he takes to his heels as fast as he can, *that* we see enacted on the right half of our little theater. This time you are merely spectators. But whoever has the good luck to possess this machine and to project himself properly into it, such a one will have lifted his existence out of the realm of decision by having doubled it. He need be oppressed by no further doubts, since he is equally present in the two lives that are led. He has, so to speak, made a declaration of neutrality. Does all this seem a little confused to you, gentlemen? It's really quite simple. Watch, please. I press the indicator!"

To be quite sincere, we saw less this time than we had done before his explanation. A large number of puppets appeared on both sides of the stage; light and darkness, day and night alternated. The tempo was terrific. There was kissing and whispering and faint screeching. Simultaneously on the other side there were miniature revolver shots and the police appeared and both actions developed rapidly, each one being more than a little complicated and seen thus at the same time the whole thing was inextricably confused.

After his jeering fashion the fat man seemed to grasp our failure to understand. "I see. Hard to understand, eh? You get used to it by and by. Unfortunately you get so well used to it that in the end it's a bore. Take me—I'd like to get rid of the whole trashy business; if one of you wants to buy it or even accept it as a gift—you have only to say so. To start with, what you can do is to let the two plays be played one after the other instead of simultaneously. The stage on the right will present a fragment of the action, let us say the first day. I mean the first day after the decision has been spared one or repressed. That is to say, of this-as-well-as-that, which we have substituted for the either-or. While this is enacted, the left side of our theater is dark. Next we darken the right-hand stage but let the figures and the action remain, while on the left stage we repeat the corresponding day under the contrary condition of action. Time, you see, plays no part in the whole mechanism. You can use any rate of speed you like."

"How about the tempo of nature?" Helfin asked. He seemed to have pulled himself together, while I was overwhelmed by a terrible confusion and hardly knew what was happening to me.

"Certainly," the fat man answered assentingly. "You can have natural size too. Our experiment renders us as independent of space as of time. We have escaped from both. We are free of all relative contingencies, of every 'if.' For we have made a premise of the 'if' and have therefore eliminated it. And so, space, too, obeys our modulation. Oh, did you ever? I forgot the chief thing. It's a very great relief for beginners. Here, each one of you take one of these monocles!"

These lenses were of a greenish substance and looked as

though they were opaque. But you could see through them very well indeed when they were inserted between the lids. We wanted to give the third lense to Gad, only to observe that he had slipped away. Perhaps his limited leave was over or perhaps the whole performance had disgusted him. We didn't know which. He must have vanished after the very first showing of the marionettes. At all events, I didn't remember having seen him or heard his voice since then.

I had no time to ponder on this matter. For now that I had the green monocle in my eye a profound change had taken place. What a magician the man was! Instead of puppets we now saw living human creatures. They were not only life-sized; they moved in a natural manner and spoke with human voices in all the shadings from soft to loud, whereas, before, all that we had heard was a monotonous, low, incomprehensible murmur and a kind of metallic chirping and whirring such as a small mechanical apparatus equipped with many small wheels might be expected to bring forth. At the same time the proscenium arch and the artificial light had disappeared; nor did we seem any longer to be in an auditorium, but in reality upon the sands of the beach of Tel Aviv. And it was by daylight, although midnight now lay behind us. It was thus in the natural light of day and in the open air that the entire inexplicable phenomenon presented itself to me. I really had no means of knowing how Helfin reacted. Not until much later did I infer anything from certain remarks he let fall. My memory is confined to what I myself saw. It was a love story, not even an unusual one, that developed before my eyes: A young man goes to meet a woman. On the parallel stage the same scene was enacted and the young man began to pursue the same path. At a certain point, however, he proceeded in the opposite direction, and there a friend appeared who consoled him. Thereupon the lady in question came up from the beach and created a scandal.

At the point at which this variation of the theme set in my knees grew weak under me. I put down the monocle and struck the table with my hand. Instantly the acting characters shrank back to puppet size. "That is black magic," I cried. "That should be forbidden."

Helfin watched longer than I. Was his interest keener than my own? Or was he simply younger and stronger than I? While I sat down on a sofa, finally half reposing on it, with my head on a soft pillow, I continued to hear the fat man give further instructions: "You can take this apparatus and let it deal with more essential and less private events. For instance, what would have happened if the English had not succeeded in making a mere mercenary of Abdullah with their subvention of two million pounds a year, if the desert despot had instead made a special treaty with us?" And at this moment I was aware of a gigantic crashing, as though all the sand and masonry under which we were hidden were beginning to slide. I dared scarcely trust my eyes. But was what I beheld not the biblical plain of Ajalon, turned today into the battlefield of Latrun with the white monastery and the blue hills of Judea in the background? Tanks rolled forward; the soldiers of the Arab Legion with their red-checkered kaffiyehs swung their rifles and themselves faced fire —and on the other side, in the parallel manner now familiar to me, there unfolded itself a scene in a totally different, wholly peaceful environment. Jewish engineers were chatting with Arab Bedouins and Jewish peasants beside a well, and between them passed back and forth the *findshan*, the shining little Arabic coffee cup of porcelain.

"Are these mere hypotheses or is it reality?" Helfin asked with a remnant of critical thoughtfulness. At this moment his good-natured yet somehow martial countenance seemed to me almost foolish in its vain attempt to preserve at any cost the continuity of a reasonable attitude.

"It goes without saying that I would like to answer your question," the fat man answered imperturbably, "if you would first define precisely (if!) the exact difference between reality and unreality. All that I know is this: the Unambo machine is a success also in those cases where one doesn't quite mean to escape a decision but is rather inclined to make a tentative venture along both paths before concluding definitively. So first —or simultaneously; it comes to the same thing—you adjust the machine to peace; then to war. Or the other way round. At all events, you adjust it to both solutions, not merely to one."

"But in ordinary everyday language you call that evading an issue," I growled from among my pillows.

No one paid any attention to me. I was alone with my deathly exhaustion.

When I looked up once, after a period, the little theater was gone. Once more the fat man stood in front of the bookcase with a pamphlet in his hand. If I rightly understood what was being said it would seem that the entire collection of books was a special one concerned with a single theme. The fat man dominated the conversation. Uninhibitedly he talked in his equable, slithery manner, interrupted by coughs and sneezes, but never at loss for a word, seeking to persuade my friend, who seemed now, as I had long done, to have arrived at the limit of his strength.

"At the very least I believe that I have proved to you," the fat man said to Helfin, "how nonsensical the assertion is that it is the Devil's intention to extirpate the race of man, as the church father Tertullian avers. One might, in fact, assert the very contrary: to act beneficently to the human race, to relieve it of the most unpleasant and painful aspect of life, namely, of hard and sharp decisions—such is the Devil's wish. To blunt the crises that constitute man's eternal suffering. Is that so ungrateful a desire? I consider it the greatest kindness that can be rendered to man. *Sans souci*—that, gentlemen, would be the best of mottos. And who would dare to object if once a human being were to succeed, at least for a period, in living without care?"

"In this best of all periods he has a wonderful chance of doing that," I whispered, to myself more than to the others.

"You're awake, are you?" The fat man turned to me with bitterish friendliness. "You missed the best part of everything. I've been reading to Mr. Helfin from this excellent pamphlet. It was written, as you see, by Professor Franz Spirago, who, as the title page tells us, was a commissioner of education in Prague. The title is *The Devil and His Activity*. Below that we read, 'With the Imprimatur of the Most Reverend Episcopal Office in Osnabrück. 1933.' The very date of the pamphlet assigns it to the rank of a curiosity of my collection. I want you to note, please, the last sentence of the preface: 'I dedicate this essay to the holy archangel Michael, the conqueror of Satan.—Professor Franz Spirago, Commissioner of Education, Prague, P.O.B. 160.' Don't you think it's quite touching that he adds his post office box? He probably wanted the archangel to know the address to which to send his thanks for the dedication. The whole essay is written in that same innocent style. But, as is so often the case in life, the purity is just a little spotty. The author, being a good businessman, is not too careless of his worldly interests. You can gather that from the many handsome things said in the course of the essay concerning his other little tracts, all of which have appeared in many printings. Now this Spirago—what do you suppose the name means? 'Air hole,' perhaps?—isn't perhaps quite worthy of the other authorities adduced here tonight. But like all the others he wants to persuade us that the Devil—or the devils, whichever you prefer, gentlemen—wants to hurt mankind and to obliterate all living things. 'All that exists is justly doomed.' This, you remember, is the saying which another poet and thinker places upon the lips of his jesting Mephistopheles. Well, we have left those stages of demonology behind us. It's nothing but bluff or, as the soldiers here express it in a little word just imported from the Arabic, *Chisbat*. Take it from me, it's nothing but that. It is recognized today that the Devil wants to ease the life of man, who has gotten into such difficulties on account of the development of his so-called civilization, by drawing from his heart the frightful arrow of decision."

"What exactly do you mean by that?" Helfin cried with an acerbity which, at that moment, I did not wholly comprehend.

The fat man laughed impudently. "Nothing that I haven't already said. How false everything is that that schoolmaster Spirago adduces, not only his teaching concerning the enmity to man of the so-called 'fallen angel,' you see at once from his very first words. And with that observation we will close today, seeing that our symposium has worn you two gentlemen quite out. All I want to offer you is that one more bit of *merde*, namely, the very opening words of this excellent pamphlet, with the request not to attribute the rancid hortatory style to me:

" 'Our generation does not wish to acknowledge the existence of the Devil. One often hears the religiously indifferent say, "It's evil people who are the Devil." Dr. Vilmar makes an appropriate comment, namely, that the whole world would be in a different situation if it were only faintly aware of the actual personal existence of the Devil. But the enemy of mankind has no warmer wish than that people cease to believe in his existence and that therefore the sinner suspect no danger from the side of hell. Similarly the dogmatist Klee declares it to be Satan's subtlest diplomacy to persuade man of his nonexistence.' "

"And what exactly do you mean by that?" stupidly I babbled the previous words of my friend.

The fat man grunted but said nothing. He spread out his thumbless hand with a gesture of invitation and led us into the antechamber. Thence he led us through the uncomfortably dark rooms, which smelled of mortar, through the long white-tiled, glittering corridor back to the surface of the earth. He sort of danced on his feet and trilled his favorite comic song from *The Beggar Student*.

We had to pass through two of the ruined streets. At the corner we found a car that seemed to be waiting for us. But this time it was a quite normal Chrysler of the new elegant shape. The car took us first to the center of Tel Aviv and from there to the *Zafon*, or northern quarter, where we both lived not far from each other. When we had entered the car the fat man had left us without a greeting.

It was late night. I hoped now to sleep away my headache and my intoxication. But at five o'clock in the morning all the inhabitants of the city were driven from their beds into the shelters by an air attack. We heard the bombs first, and only several minutes later the sirens.

But in spite of my extreme weariness I could not keep myself from going back to Manshiyeh in the early forenoon. I wanted to see the fat man once more; I wanted to ascertain what part of that meeting was sober, earthy reality, and what part magic and delusion.

By the light of day the ruined streets of this unswept Pompeii seemed more desolate than they had done under the equable glimmer of the moon. The revolting odors of destroyed toilets were more noticeable now. And only now, too, one became

33

aware of many horrible details, such as destroyed furniture and the pools and the spilth of sanitary pipes that had burst, as well as the plundered dwellings, on the doors and walls of which cries for help and mercy had been written in white or red chalk. Again a military guard approached. Manshiyeh, as well as the city of Jaffa, which we had conquered, was strongly guarded. The purpose was to prevent the robbery and theft of suddenly' masterless property. It is a source of deep regret to me that we had just begun to take this precaution. In the very first days after our victory, irresponsible things had happened here. We just had no police force; we had no legal prescriptions to restrain the mob which exists everywhere and always, just as we had no defense against air attack. Whence shall a state which has just crawled out of its chrysalis and which, at that first glimpse of life, is attacked from all sides—whence shall it get at once the organization and the protective measures forced upon it by the lowliness of the world? I was wretchedly depressed and lost all desire for any undertaking or for finding a direction through all these confusions. Turning to go back, I came upon that door, isolated like a stage prop, and upon that empty platform. A stairway led up to it in front and down from it in the rear. But at that place one saw nothing but an old piece of grillwork lying over a hole in the earth. The grillwork was adorned with a pattern of Arabic letters. I tried in vain to lift it up. Moreover, the hole was not even big enough to admit a single crouching man. Perhaps it had been the opening of a cistern once upon a time, or a part of the sewage system.

I've heard of drugs that give gigantic wings to the imagination, evoking visions of mighty mountains and landscapes and clouds or cosy homes or gardens of roses. Perhaps some such drug had been given us with the fruit and the wine of which we had partaken. Thus all dimensions had been confused; the great had seemed small, and the small, great. I was confirmed in this opinion when, next to the grillwork amid all sorts of ruined household gear, I observed the head of a tiny toy horse, of which the colors and wide threatening eyes reminded me of the huge horse's head that had peered at us from the head of the wall.

34

CHAPTER TWO

In which the question "Whither do we go, O Father?" is asked, but will not be answered.

1.

The palatial new building of Habimah, in which the Philharmonic Orchestra was playing, is one gigantic ice chest in the summer months. In the foyer behind the six enormous pillars something of the sultriness of the night was still noticeable. In the auditorium itself, with its excellent air conditioning, the climate was a magnificent and normal one, a European climate, so to speak, bland and refreshing at once. At every intake of breath one was more aware of the delight of inhaling air that was pure pleasure. A little later one forgot that too under the dominance of the music.

It was the Fourth Symphony of Brahms which was storming forward toward that unconquerable wall of the final movement which consists of those rows of sound, each of eight Cyclopean granite cubes, offering their eightfold defiance to fate and chaos; victorious, now through the beautiful power of determination, and again through the simultaneity of power and gentleness.

More than ever were we moved by the living experience of this symphony. For we did not only understand it; we *were* it upon this historic moment.

It was only in the intermission that I gradually awakened from the magic dream of these great identifications. And so it occurred to me then that this brave conductor, Izler Solomon— his name will be preserved in our annals, for he left New York on the very day of the proclamation of the state in order to help with the purity and power of art in this critical historic moment —but no, not upon him was my thought fixed, but upon the connection between him and my friend Helfin. Helfin was to be at the concert; we had agreed to meet here. But his accustomed seat three rows ahead of me . . . I realized suddenly that his seat was empty.

That made me very restless; I felt that I must look him up. I cut out the second part of the program. And, parenthetically, isn't it rather barbarous to listen to more than a single work of the first order on one evening? Ought one not to be so fulfilled by it that there is not the least room left for an additional impression? And is not everything beyond that mischief and snobbery?

From the cool auditorium I went into the tepid foyer and from there, alas, into the hot and sticky night. The sky was overcast. Those were the "kine of the Nile," those clouds which the rising, monstrous river exhales. When the Nile rises, we too observe it here annually at the proper time. The geographical spaces cohere. But these clouds bring no rain. They are mere layers of a thick sheet of mist above the city; in the morning they deceive us into hoping for a cool dawn; from hour to hour thereafter they intensify the heat like the lid over a boiling pot, until in the evening the glow resembles madness. Thus Mizraim sent not only its bombing planes over us but also its unwholesome heat.

It does no good to curse. One goes on into the humidity; there is no choice. And so I hastened toward the well-organized, elegant Liebermann Street, in which Helfin lived.

Helfin and the conductor! During my walk I tried to recollect the exact details of the connection between them which had struck me during the intermission. In March, Helfin had gone to Europe. He had had great plans. His projected film, at which he had been working for some years, was about to be realized. He still needed some international assistance in order to create the embodiment of his vision. He wanted no trace of junk but an authentic, pain-touched representation of our life today with its immense and ever again befooled yearning for peace. He had not left "the land," as we briefly call it here, for almost three years. Europe had done him good. Then, however, the bad news which streamed to Europe from the land began to disturb him. Many of these news items were lies; he knew that, since they were British or Arabic propaganda. He knew it and yet he half believed them. For he made the mistake of subtracting as untrue only one half of what was asserted by the press and the radio; actually he should have subtracted nine tenths. But even the small part of the news which he believed drove him almost to despair. He had a vision of Tel Aviv in flames, his friends dead, Jerusalem dying of hunger and thirst, the land without electric power so that supplies were rotting in the refrigerators. He saw inevitable destruction coming over all that was dear to him.

It has been said that there is no maxim so absurd but that at some time some philosopher has made it a premise or even built the entire structure of his thought upon it. An analogous saying is valid today, namely, that there is no lie, however absurd, which some politician has not occasionally employed and even made effective here and there.

Helfin knew this fact; nevertheless he was victimized by the lies. This did not take place immediately after his arrival in Europe. At that time he still had a healthy foundation of fact and truth, which he had brought from his recent and immediate experience of our land. Gradually, however, in the course of weeks, this foundation crumbled to such an extent that he could no longer resist the systematic intensification of lying and tendencious news. What finally decided him was, however, not the turbid flow of lies but a very special experience in Geneva. He abandoned the very promising negotiations concerning his film which had begun and came back home in May, a few days before the proclamation of the state.

He would often tell how profoundly surprised he was when, landing at Haifa, he saw the first placard announcing a concert and saw the names Mozart, Beethoven, Shostakovich. He thought it must refer to a concert of the previous year. He went right up to the placard. The date showed him that the concert was to take place within the next few days. The announcement concerned an American conductor and his program, everything quite as usual. So all was not lost. Music was being played; the theaters were open; Tel Aviv did not lie in dust and ashes. The conductor, Solomon, had just arrived. A few kilometers from the theaters there was being fought a desperate battle, a decisive battle for survival or destruction. . . . But nothing was being given up that was part of the necessary work of every day, nor anything that belonged to art, to the higher level of life. Even during the most horrible moments this pulse missed no beat.

It cannot be said, to be sure, that this mood of consolation in which Helfin found himself during the early days after his return lasted very long. Everything was better than he had imagined out there in the alien world. Even so it was bad enough. It was full of danger and—this hit Helfin with particular force— full of cruelty and injustice against us. That expression of affronted amazement never left his countenance any more. He fell into a mood of despair which frightened me. Essentially a poet, he had always been prone to imaginative exaggeration. Never, in all the years I knew him, so much as now. He came near to infecting me.

Only the briefest period had elapsed since that night with the fat man. In retrospect it seemed to me a euphoria brought on by some wild poisoning. A few fragments of reality had perhaps really been experienced and seen and touched. But they were without significance. All the rest must have come from some hypnotic suggestion and now seemed wholly incredible. A mass of nonsense? In all likelihood.

Absorbed by the dangers of war, I had scarcely thought of these wild impressions for several days. I had made the appointment to meet Helfin at the concert by telephone. It was his absence that caused me to reconsider the unclarified adventure which we had had together.

I had the feeling that something quite disagreeable might have impinged on Helfin from that quarter. I hastened my step. But even while I hastened on, my anxiety for him assumed still another form. Hadn't he mentioned Bianca Petry, a girl who had been pursuing him for three years and of whom he himself was frightened? I knew it weighed upon him that recently, just before his departure from Paris, she had located him. It was in Paris that they had met three years before.

He knew, or thought he knew, that Bianca had sworn with all her native energy and despite many a vain attempt, to win him yet. With a sense of moral discomfort he told me that she had quite openly lured him, even in letters. She had rationalized by saying that it made no sense to speak anything but the truth. This circumstance seemed to contribute to that crushed nervous state that had fastened itself upon him since the brief lift after his return home. The girl's importunity and the war both oppressed Helfin's soul. Then there were lesser evils, to which he often reacted with a wild rage, such as the heat and the continuous noise on the streets and in the house. The suffering over the war predominated. The other miseries would change and each one would at some time be the center of his constant irritableness.

I was quite prepared to find Bianca, whom I knew only from his description, with him, whether to "annoy" him or to "save" him. He could take it as he liked. He had never confided in me why he regarded this girl as so dangerous. He had always, as was inevitable, been surrounded by handsome women who desired him as their prey, and his position in the world of the film must surely have accustomed him to them and must also, so it seemed to me, have long ago provided him with the appropriate measures of defense against these assaults. But it was clear that he had a quite special terror of Bianca.

To my delight I found him alone and quite well and not in his worst mood. He sat at his desk in front of his tall bookcases. He put into neat order a great number of papers which he had on his desk. It was this bundle of papers, as appeared later, which, after the very worst had happened, was to give me so much food for reflection and for vain speculation. As I came in he had been busy writing. But he seemed not displeased at the interruption. He smiled in greeting and bade his aged, white-haired serving woman, who had opened the door, to bring a second glass. A carafe stood on his desk. He offered me iced coffee. "You may have iced tea with lemon, if you prefer."

"Why weren't you at the concert? Did anything happen?"

"Not a thing. First of all, sit down!"

That "first of all" pleased me but little. Yet I soon found myself in the accustomed mood of comfort which this room always induced in me. Since the Venetian blinds were down and the windows curtained, the tasteful, simple floor lamp with its broad red shade could diffuse its mild light unhindered. From the balcony of the adjoining room a pleasant little nocturnal breeze blew into this upper story. I watched the books in the shadows. He had loaned me many and I had always read them with joy; for Helfin recommended only what had distinction and depth, both among the books of the ancients and the moderns. What a wealth of inspiration had I not received in this room in those better days before the world slandered us as cannibals and barbarians. The lamp, the coolness, the recollection of those better days—all this flattered the senses, which recently had received so many disagreeable impressions. And this mood was sustained by the excellent coffee which the aged Dvora prepared so admirably and with all the affection with which she customarily surrounded her master.

We spoke of the events of the day. They seared our hearts. The news was far from good. Everywhere we held out with our last ounce of strength, with our uttermost exertion. That we did even that was a miracle! But Jerusalem was cut off from the rest of the state and communication between Jerusalem and Tel Aviv was blocked by the Arabs at Latrun. The Old City of Jerusalem was still being defended with epic heroism. But how long could that last without any help from the outside? Capitulation was certain.

"It was our business to reckon with that necessity from the start." Thus I sought to console him. And, after the fashion which is in our very blood, I continued, "Have you heard the latest anecdote? On Rothschild Boulevard, where our elders hold their 'parliament' on the street and debate with each other, one of them reasons as follows: 'We can be saved in either of two ways—by the way of nature or by a miracle.' Swiftly another interrupts him: 'What do you mean by the way of nature?' Whereupon the first replies, 'By the way of nature? It's perfectly clear. The Messiah will come.' "

The anecdote did not cheer Helfin. "Certainly we should have foreseen that. So the Old City, which is our sanctuary, was bound to fall. What distresses me is the circumstance that the world thinks only of the Christian and Mohammedan sanctuaries in the Old City. No one seems to care that immemorial synagogues lie within those walls and are probably now destroyed. And in them were the Houses of Study of the great mystics. All that is gone! And who will protect the new city of Jerusalem? The defenseless are attacked by fire from mortars and cannons. The world is completely indifferent. The two different measures with which our cause and that of the Arabs is being measured—it is that, that simply tears me to pieces."

"We see now," I agreed with him, "how correct we were to have occupied Jaffa and Haifa and Tiberias, as well as Safed, if the report is true, within the past few days. Otherwise we would be surrounded by the enemy in all these cities just as we are in Jerusalem."

But Helfin grew even more somber. "And, alas, alas, on our side, too, dreadful errors have been committed. There was the bloody incident of Deir-yassin, where women and children were murdered. Of course," he added contemplatively after an interval, "the war was forced upon us and one might almost define war as that unnatural condition in which horrors take place because they must take place. We desired peace and peace only and never wearied of offering peace. And a few days after Deir-yassin the Arabs, though assuring them safe conduct, attacked and set on fire the convoy of cars which were driving to the great Hadassah Hospital and to the university. Seventy-nine human beings were burned to death—nurses, physicians, university professors, among them a most distinguished cancer specialist and all his collaborators. All people of the highest intellectual and moral character. And nobody talks about this frightful attack. It is scarcely known. All the greater is the cry about Deir-yassin. And the British soldiers who were still in the country, for it was still under the Mandate, and who pretended to be so profoundly responsible for 'law and order'—they sat there and watched at a hundred paces from their guardhouses how the cars were attacked and how they burned and how the human beings in them were burned to death. They watched from morning until four o'clock in the afternoon. Then, at last, they intervened and saved a few. From that moment on, to be perfectly fair, they risked their own lives. But why did they wait all those hours? The Arab attack on the convoy lasted, with brief interruptions, for eight hours. More and more Arabs appeared on the scene of combat with guns and hand grenades. Yet one shouldn't speak of a combat, for the Jews had no weapons and the English had emphatically guaranteed the security of the road and had forbidden the Jews to bear arms. I imagine that it is a case unique in all history. But the world doesn't talk about that. During all those eight hours we telephoned to every possible British administrative office and delineated the situation and begged for help. The English replied that they were negotiating with the Arabs and that everything was in order. In the meantime, on the very edge of the city, publicly, before the eyes of all, the massacre continued. The English were active in only one respect. Energetically they barred every path to the Haganah, the Jewish army, which was proceeding from various points to bring help. Nor must it be forgotten that the mere appearance of two or three English tanks would have sufficed to scatter the Arabs. For eight hours they let our people burn. In the end there were no bodies left to be buried, only a few limbs and charred clothing and the names of the seventy-nine."

"One simply doesn't comprehend it. It is hard to believe even when the most reliable eyewitnesses make their report."

"There are many other things which my old pacifist's heart cannot grasp." Nervously he tugged his little beard. "For I still believe that in every situation, even in the midst of war, one must and can seek to re-establish justice and that that precisely is a fundamentally Jewish attitude."

"But if, as you said a moment ago, war is itself the very dominion of all mistakes—"

"That doesn't exclude the attempt to strive to reduce the element of error. But there is that other school of thought which argues not only that every barbarity is permitted in war but goes further and says that war without barbarity is a bad joke and a childish game. Others aver that peace is impossible without entire sanctification. One must love peace so totally that one is willing to be destroyed. According to all these people one must take one extreme stand or the other. The choice is between war with all its cancerous lies and bestiality or peace with a halo plus a martyr's death. Try to choose between those two extremes." He stopped abruptly and an expression of cunning suddenly came into his face. He lowered his voice. "Suppose there were something which rendered this decision superfluous. Suppose one could have ruthless war and ruthless peace simultaneously. Would you mind looking around? Don't you notice anything? Not really?"

I followed the direction of his eyes.

2.

By a nail in the wall above the piano, swaying gently in the breeze, hung the little puppet stage from Manshiyeh. It was in fact nothing but a thin little framework lined with organdy. Only the black wall of wood that divided the stage into two halves seemed reasonably solid. All the rest reminded one of a big butterfly net or, rather, of the frame of a mosquito net over a bed. The whole contraption gleamed with a bluish-green iridescence. It seemed to hold in its atoms that intense blue light which we had seen. That light seemed on the edge of breaking out of the apparatus at every moment. What was most emphatically visible was the red switch, hard by the miniature prompter's box, that our uncanny host had manipulated in his subterranean laboratory.

"Where did you get that?" I could not hide my astonishment.

Helfin looked at me with a pretense of gaiety. He prolonged his silence as though he wanted me to guess at what needed no guessing. "You've got to have a little pull," he quoted ironically. Whom was he jeering at with this uncannily sharp and rising tone of voice?

"Your fat friend was here?"

"Yes and no," my friend replied. "Take it as you like. I assure you that he didn't present me with the little theater on a silver salver. I probably would not have accepted it. It found its way into the house by another road. It turned up in our trash can. You wonder how? Well, my good Dvora sometimes tries to save her steps. When she takes down the garbage pail and empties it into one of the municipal receptacles below, she often lets it stand in the garden and does a little shopping in the street, fetching milk or tomatoes. Well, no one knows what may not be surreptitiously slipped into the pail. You would never have thought of that, would you? And the thing has almost no weight. Briefly and not so well, as the fat man was fond of saying, we pulled the machine out of the garbage pail. It was rather crinkled but spotless. Here on the wall its crinkles are coming out as they come out of a suit of clothes when you hang it up. It's practically smooth now." Tenderly he touched the delicate contraption and then looked at me roguishly. "Don't be afraid. I won't press the button. We're not at that point yet and probably will never be."

"Tell me," I interrupted him, "are you dreaming or are you talking seriously?"

As had happened several times on this occasion he seemed not to hear me but continued on his train of thought. "We fished something else out of the garbage pail. When Dvora and I took an extra good look, what did we find? A well-known book. We disinfected it. Doesn't it seem familiar to you?" He took it from his desk and handed it to me.

I read the title on the gray cover: "*The Devil and His Activity* by Professor Franz Spirago, Commissioner of Education in Prague."

"Now, this aforesaid 'air hole,' or whatever this word Spirago may mean, produced a very noticeable whirl in my brain. Judge for yourself. I opened the book, just as you're doing now. Out of it creeps with very long, pendulous, tentatively probing antennae, a certain insect which is sometimes known as a cockroach and which here, in our country, somewhat differently stylized, bears the beautiful name of *dshuk*."

Impulsively I put the book away.

Helfin laughed gayly. "Don't be afraid, old man. Miracles don't happen twice. Because I want you to know that this particular *dshuk* was none else than our fat friend."

My discomfort increased. Perhaps I looked restlessly about me and showed an impulse to jump out of my chair. Helfin was still laughing but in the diminuendo of his voice there was a hint of dread. "Please sit still, my dear fellow. I'm really not crazy. Everything proceeded very normally. It was like this. The *dshuk* ran into the anteroom and hid beneath the red hangings over there, in the direction of the pantry. I was about to follow it when from behind the hanging there appeared, courteously bowing, our fat friend in his slouchy white suit, just as he was the other day. Dvora swore, to be sure, that she had not left the hall door open. But she is gradually losing her wits. She's a widow and her only son is at the front and that doesn't make her judgment very steady."

"Then, if I understand you correctly, the fat man rang the bell?"

"I didn't hear anything. But let's not bother with these uninteresting trivialities. What was interesting was the dispute that I had with him. I can assure you that he talked so rationally this time that he really won my confidence—to the extent, I confess, that I told him various things which usually I refuse to express. About our country here, for instance. How I love it and how at the same time it makes me very unhappy, which is not the fault of the land but is due to the concatenation of outer circumstances. He understood me thoroughly, oh, astonishingly well. He's really a very comforting person, passively as well as actively, and tries to make things comfortable for himself and for others. He didn't, by the way, commend that little device over there by a single word. It must really be comfortable to be able to lead two lives instead of one—in which one is constantly at the crossroads, like that Hercules of old, confronted by a yes or no. But the fat man spoke no syllable about all that. On the contrary, he warned me. He warned me seriously, if you want to put it that way."

"Stop!" I interrupted him and used an emphatic tone, quite different from that of our conversation. I stressed that change of tone by rising swiftly from my seat and striding up and down the room. "Stop right here! First of all I want to make it clear to you that I am absolutely unwilling to be dragged into this feverish nonsense! Tell me, do you really believe what you are driveling here or does it amuse you to persuade yourself that you believe it—an absurdity like this stage with its two simultaneous scenes? All right. We were both rather drunk that evening and we thought we saw something like those two groups of lives. I don't want to insist on the relationship of alcohol and seeing double. It's too banal. So I will admit this much: that

45

this Unambo is a very clever toy. We were rather under the hypnotic influence of that strange person who suddenly emerged from the dimness of the café. I'm willing to go as far as this, that we were subject to an identical hallucination. But not a step farther. The difference between us is that I have liberated myself in the meantime from that slightly diseased condition. But you! Would you kindly tell me, if I may imitate the vulgar manner of our fat friend, did you again eat or drink something that makes you completely *mishugah?* Well, I didn't. Not I. And as for you, Paul, I'm taking you tomorrow to a neurologist to have him take your blood pressure and test your various reactions . . ." I would have gone on scolding for a little while, but I nearly collapsed at suddenly hearing from behind the bookcases and, seemingly, from out of the wall, the hoarse trilling of those verses from the operetta *The Beggar Student.*

"That's nothing," Helfin tried to calm me. Suddenly he seemed to feel that he had the upper hand. "You happened to jolt the phonograph and I had that particular record on. It isn't so strange that I take some interest in that song now. On the other side of the record is another song, which begins, 'Let's take this case . . .' Would you like to hear it?"

I declined with thanks. A little dazed, I dropped back into my seat. It seemed to me as though one had tapped my head with a hammer. I was tempted to go into the anteroom and to look behind the red hangings to see if the fat man in his white, crinkled coat were not lying in wait there. But I was ashamed to show such weakness—I, who had just been preaching dignity and reason.

"I wanted next to tell you about the warning which the fat man gave me," Helfin continued equably and stopped the phonograph which had made me shiver. "I asked him at once, of course, whether the apparatus we fished out of the garbage pail were his property. He looked at me with subtle cunning and let his mobile eyebrow waggle—you probably noticed how he does that—and said breezily it was difficult to tell, seeing that he had several of these devices and that some of those were in circulation and that he kept no books. He wasn't a bit interested in this device, which he had made for fun; it wasn't even patented; if I wanted the thing I might just as well keep it. And the monocular lense too—he had the green thing with him and took it out of his waistcoat pocket and handed it to me. 'Fine, then I'll make a test right away,' I cried and my hand was already on the switch, when I stopped once more and observed, 'But I don't want it to be decisive. It's only a joke this time.' 'You don't have to worry about that,' he replied. 'The machine doesn't function quite so easily. It demands an effort; it demands that one enter into its purposes with one's whole will. Its results depend upon one's fixed intention. One must, as it were, insinuate oneself into it; one must be convinced. That's not quite as simple as you may believe.' "

I had recovered my power of judgment. So, at least, it seemed to me at that time and place. Retrospectively I seemed to notice that I did not introduce a clear order into several items of Helfin's report. Oddly enough I seemed to feel no need to do so. "And is that what you call a warning?" I asked. "I would rather regard what you report to me as a lure and an attempt at psychical seduction."

"Do you really think so?" Now he had again that naïve, child-like expression of the eye and of those handsome, regular features, of which I was so fond, and which were so out of keeping with his pseudo-martial beard and mustache. "Do you really think so?" he repeated slowly. "Well, as far as I'm concerned, I did feel what he said to be a kind of warning; I can't tell you exactly why. And at that moment I was filled with the strongest distaste of both him and his contraption, in spite of the neatness of its appearance."

"And that was a very sound feeling." I tried to strengthen him in it. "When you think of the garbage pail, you are bound to think of the municipal sewage system, which seems very adequately to represent the subterranean character and dwelling of this congenial gentleman. Maybe that accounts for his using so much perfume."

"Well, I really didn't see any relationship of that kind. But maybe you're right." He seemed to reflect for a little while.

"When I think upon it closely I see that both the impression of being warned and the feeling of nausea arose from the next turn which our conversation took."

"And what was that?"

He seemed to drop into so complicated a silence that I had, as it were, to arouse him from it.

"I asked him after the price," Helfin finally continued. " 'There can be no question of a price,' said the fat man. 'This object is ownerless. You found it. Its value is in reality an indeterminable one. This thing has nothing in common with space and time, nor yet with any of the measures or prices of ordinary existence. But I am bound to call your attention to a not wholly negligible, though minor, circumstance'—you see, there was a warning involved— 'namely, that this little stage of mine is not quite safe to handle. There is a little loss that is sustained—something rather insignificant cannot be recovered, something to which one pays perhaps no attention at all, so long as it is in a normal condition.' 'Aha, I cried: Shlemihl, the man who lost his shadow.' His expression was sweet and sour; there was a treacherous irony lying in wait behind it. It was the expression of one who pretends to have been caught. 'One doesn't like to be found out in a lack of originality. But let us tentatively assume that at this point there is a certain similarity, although the arrangements I make with people are essentially quite different from that affair of Peter Shlemihl's. He loses his shadow. I add something to the possessions of him who makes a pact with me. I take nothing from him. I provide my client with a life Number 2; I bestow upon him, if you like to put it that way, two shadows in the place of one. I double his entire being and permit him to fill his allotment of space twice simultaneously. I do not split him into two, as Wagner's Klingsor does his maid servant Kundry. What my man does in life Number 1 need not be paid for by his life Number 2. No, he is effectually in existence twice. For this very reason he can live with the fulness of his heart's desire, without establishing himself stringently either there or yonder. But, as I have said, a small loss is involved. Contrary to the usage of Peter Shlemihl's patron, who takes the poor fool in, I call attention to the consequences at the very start.

48

They are so unessential in character that I can comfortably afford to do so; they have never yet harmed anyone.' 'And what are these consequences?' I asked the fat man with some impatience. 'Let us be calm, master,' he chid me. 'We're coming to it. One thing after another. The consequence of this activity consists in the circumstance that the finger with which one manipulates the switch becomes transparent. Not suddenly but gradually. Until one's thumb decays and falls off.' 'Like yours, sir,' I remarked. That must have struck him as impertinent, for he choked down his anger and it took longer than usual for him to make his way through the hacking of his smoker's catarrh. The one thing had nothing to do with the other, he answered rudely without giving any reason. But without any reflection it was suddenly sun-clear to me that that noble organ, the human hand, would naturally be weakened and undergo a crippling process if one manipulated such devil's ordure with it. 'From now on,' the fat man continued, 'your attention having been called to it, you will often observe in life one person or another, one of whose fingers is translucent—usually the top joint. The process begins at the top and works itself slowly downward. It is like a Masonic sign by which the participants in the phenomenon recognize each other.' He shrugged his shoulders. 'This is a changeless matter. He who employs my conditional machine becomes one of those through whose fingers the light shines more and more. The guild of these, as I have told you, is spread abroad in the whole world.' "

"I can now thoroughly understand the feeling of nausea," I interrupted him. "But how the fellow could at the same time gain your confidence, as you have told me he did, that becomes more and more incomprehensible."

"Maybe I did exaggerate that a little," he said in an affectionate tone of voice. "Forgive me. This sharp definiteness of expression has to do with my discomfort in this world of today, with my illness, an illness induced by this period. The world was not always so evil nor was I always so ill. However, I haven't yet given you a complete account of that interview. Perhaps it's an overstatement to say that the fat man filled me with confidence; he did impress me. He has vast knowledge and is very thorough in all matters. One must grant him that. Even though the whole question is one of a greater ease of life, he treats it with a kind of scientific exactness—oh, to the point of pedantry. He is very strong on the side of logic. He is certainly not superficial."

"He has always been held to be subterranean rather than superficial: the Lord of the Inferno." I could not refrain from this observation.

"He did not, at all events, seek to be elusive when I became searching. His answers were all adequate. I began by declaring that his apparatus was philosophically impossible. If the same human being could experience the same life twice over, not himself split, but genuinely doubled, though both times with certain deviations, would not the whole course of the world soon assume two different aspects which were bound to collide with each other? 'Aha, philosophically impossible!' He smiled. 'I have been waiting for that all the time, my respected friend. But this impossibility which you point out, and which is perfectly obvious, turns out to be a mere optical illusion. The reason is that people don't give a single damn for whatever happens to another individual. The individual imagines that others are preoccupied with him. Whether my breakfast this morning consists of three olives and a crust of bread or of a luxurious meal of eggs, butter, honey, marmalade, fresh fruits, and everything that goes with it—this circumstance will hardly cause a furor in the house next door. And in the next street the life of hundreds of people takes precisely the same course, whether I live in luxury or perish in despair.' 'That is simply not correct,' I interrupted. 'Let us assume that I have turned the switch and, for the sake of an example, made the following assumption: The fellow across the hall all but destroys me with his piano practice. I have sued him as a nuisance; against all probability I have won the case and had him put out. Now comes the second alternative, that, out of sheer nobility of spirit, I renounce the act of aggression. In that case, according to you, in life Number 2, as you called it, that frightful strummer still torments me. In life Number 1, on the other hand, his apartment is empty or has been occupied by a new tenant. In both cases consequences are bound to arise which beget further and contradictory facts; two chains of causality come into existence; they spread out; they can never again be made to coincide; they impinge on ever wider circles of existence not only within me or in my psychical life—that would be tolerable—but outside, in the world of bodies.' 'The circles are neither so wide nor so significant as we imagine,' the fat man answered lightly. 'I told you that before, master. In the immediate environment of a given member of the bright-fingered gentry, a measure of disorder may occur. At some distance from him the world, upon the whole, goes its accustomed path, as uninfluenced as though nothing had happened. The general course of events remains.' I need not tell you that this frivolous explanation satisfied me nowise; I pressed him for a precise answer. 'If, for instance, I change from stage to stage every three days, then I will experience Wednesday first, and only three days later the preceding Monday. That will be, I understand, Monday of life Number 2. And in reality, have three days passed, or twice three days, when I proceed to the next doubling-up period?' 'Just three, of course,' he said contemptuously. 'You haven't grasped the fundamental principle yet.' Once more, then, he explained to me the fundamental principle. His doubling machine withdraws his client from the boundaries of space and time and extends his spatial and temporal realm in the same sense in which one unbuttons a waistcoat. 'What you have done is to adjust the machine to the passage of three days, to the simultaneous passage of two different sets of three days. Hence three days have passed, not six. A child would grasp that. As a rule a client begins with the alternation of longer periods, of weeks. Later he chooses briefer periods of time until finally he proceeds to the simultaneous experience of both variations of his existence.' My head began to whirl and I tried to get back upon solid ground. I said, 'A good deal is not yet clear to me. Let us assume that I have a friend named Max'—forgive me for dragging you into this matter, but I was in need of a perfectly concrete example. 'This friend Max meets me in that existence which is determined by condition A. Next, let us say three days later—for I seem not yet to have grasped the arithmetic wholly—he meets me again in that second existence which depends on condition B. Let's leave aside the difference of days. However, my friend finds me in one of the two lives happier or wiser or richer or in better health or better dressed than in the other, since something different happens to me in each of the two lives: in one, let us say, much that is good; in the other conceivably a misfortune. The difference will strike him.' 'Not a damn thing will strike him,' said the fat man. 'In general each human being is interested only in himself. What happens to his neighbor is a matter of the goddamndest indifference. He doesn't even see it. He pays no attention.' 'There are exceptions,' I protested. 'All right, there are exceptions,' the fat man repeated with irritation. 'Let's stick to the rule. I don't want to be bothered with exceptions. Furthermore it is most probable that you will meet this Max of yours in only one of your two lives. Why in both? One of the two lives can take you into an entirely different and new environment; it can take you to America. There you will meet altogether different people; you will have entirely different interests from those which are yours in the other variation. And if chance were to bring it about that you really meet your friend twice and that on that second occasion he perceives you to be different, he will not hesitate to ascribe the change to your new situation or to a change in his own mood and vision. In brief, don't worry uselessly. It all depends on the arrangement. The power that makes the arrangement or fate—the name is unimportant—will somehow assume the responsibility for the world's offering a reasonably coherent and understandable aspect, sufficiently understandable to satisfy the touchingly sympathetic eye with which a given human being is accustomed to regard his fellows. You will forgive me for not squeezing out a single tear for the great love and understanding with which here on earth one human being follows the life of his fellow. If, by any chance, an unsolvable contradiction between the two courses of life were to arise, a final means remains. The little machine goes to pot and the uniform life is restored. Why not? Even as the glass tube of the homunculus crashes against the sea-shell throne of the sorceress Galathea, even so may our cute little magic bluff or, if you prefer the Arabic word, this *chisbat* with which we are having fun—for what is it other than a little harmless fun?—find its limitation and splinter against some fact of what is called real life. Going, going, gone!' He gave vent to a few further vulgarities, being evidently not pleased by having to imagine a limitation to his devices. But I confess that it was vaguely but genuinely consoling to me to consider that the ruin of his subtle apparatus was definitely within the realm of thinkable events. 'I want to add,' thus the fat man closed his commentary, 'that all this business is only theoretically so complicated; in practice it works much more smoothly than you believe. Do you want to see once more how it works?' I really didn't want to. Or only on condition that it was not binding. Whereupon he explained once more that it was binding only if one manipulated it with conscious intention and the right seriousness and without any desire to be merely entertained. 'As the inventor and constructor I have, of course, a special relationship to my apparatus,' he said. 'I can let it run by a mere touch of the hand just to amuse us. It is different with you.' "

Abruptly my friend fell silent. "But no! He said that in the beginning. The conversation started with that." The threads of narration seemed to have gotten themselves tangled within him. With nervous violence he denied my supposition that the discourse had, at its end, returned to its beginning, like the snake that bites its own tail. "No, no, at the end we talked about quite different things," Helfin said. "I've already confessed to you that I gave him all kinds of confidences. How I love our land and yet am permanently disappointed here too, since here too I am pursued, since here too I am not permitted to live, and how my tranquillity is taken from me by all sorts of irritations and finally by the massive horror of the war—"

"I know this record of yours," I interrupted him.

But he went right on. "And nevertheless I can live nowhere but here; here only am I free; here only I do not have to apologize for being a Jew. Here I am simply a natural human being like all other human beings. And if I speak of this generalized humanity, it is not falsely or beseechingly. It concerns a contribution which I myself would make. The land is poor, I declared to the fat man; it is hard to live in; at the same time it is unconditionally necessary for us. We have no choice: utter destruction—or this land! Thence arises our determination. Many of those who fight here are the last remnants of large families —flames that resist final extinction. Thence comes their magic power; it is the power of the ultimate remnant. The world does not understand that; it does not feel that in each of us there march to combat hundreds of souls who were destroyed by Hitler in Auschwitz. And now comes the incomprehensible bestiality of this British government which desires to deliver unto death these last remnants and vessels of our heritage. The most amazing circumstance is—"

"I know that record too."

"But no, quite new complaints arise."

"Address them to City Hall."

"The most amazing thing was how the gentlemen in the British Cabinet, after the United Nations' decision of November 29, announced that, as loyal members of the organization, they would accept it. On December 11, 1947, two weeks after the decision for the partition of the land, the British Minister of Colonies declared to an applauding Parliament, 'The decision of the United Nations Assembly is regarded by the British government as the decision of international opinion.' And he added, 'Our acceptance of this decision is not, as has been suggested, a grudging acceptance.' These were his words. At the same time this government—and I mean the government and not the English people, which I esteem highly—began to equip our Arab neighbors for the ruthless attack upon us. The operation proceeded according to well thought-out stages. When, on November 30, the Arabs started with desultory shooting, when they attacked a Jewish bus near Ramle and killed three innocent unsuspecting civilians, the Mandatory government declared that it alone was responsible for law and order and that Jews, on pain of the death penalty, must not arm themselves against the attacking Arabs. At the same time, however, it announced that the British army was not powerful enough to prevent the infiltration of Iraqian and other volunteers into the country. This was their masterpiece of hyprocrisy and lying. Next the announcement was made: We, the rulers, will not stop the aggressors at the boundary, the Jordan. We are, if the world will

54

believe it, too feeble to do that. But we will not permit them to proceed beyond the Arabic district of the country, namely, the triangle Yenin-Tul, Kerem-Nablus. And it is quite the same thing whether the robbers and murderers be stopped at the boundary or at the frontier of this triangle. A very few days later the aggressors, of course, infiltrated from the triangle to Jaffa, to the environs of Jerusalem, to Haifa, etc. They destroyed the security of all roads; they interrupted, as was the intention, communication between our settlements, and there set in those attacks, lasting for weeks, upon our cities and villages which finally forced us to countermeasures. Thus, however, the soil was prepared for the legend that we had started the war and that the Arab aggressors who, on May 15, according to the official declarations of Farouk and Abdullah, marched into the land, were not armies, despite the obvious evidence, but only detachments of police. All these filthy goings-on and, in addition, a very special experience in Geneva, drove me forth from my European vacation to return to this poor but unconditionally necessary land. Yes, I also confided to the fat man my experience in Geneva, which I haven't told even to you."

"Well, under the circumstances your conversation must have lasted until morning."

"Not a bit of it. It took hardly a minute."

"All that?"

"All that."

This repetition of my words, which seemed touched by both malice and stubbornness, was accompanied by a diminishing smile which, for the first time, seemed to me like the smile of someone slightly mad.

I pulled myself together. "Either that's a bad joke or you don't want to stick to the subject. That talk took one minute? We can, you know, talk about something else, if you prefer. For instance, how is Bianca?"

3.

"That I don't know. She didn't, thank God, show up." He breathed with relief. "The conversation really didn't take more than a minute. Because I found the *dshuk* in the corner under the hangings near the pantry. I took one jump in that direction and crushed it under my heel. At that moment the fat man vanished."

So it had been a dream, I decided. Or else, the feverish vision of an organism irritated by the excessive tensions of the war. Several details in Helfin's narrative fitted in with this supposition. His whole condition of permanent political excitement may have had a part, all his wretchedness and his dissatisfaction, which had begun to assume a delusional character. One circumstance, however, was not to be brought into harmony with the notion of a dream; the simple one, namely, that over there, a few paces from us, on a nail above the piano, that little model stage made out of tulle and organdy was still swaying—very light and yet nonetheless a tangible, actual object. Later on, on my way home, there presented itself to me a kind of plausible explanation for the presence of this object. To find all kinds of stage models in the apartment of a film director, even one with a double stage, isn't the most remarkable thing in the world. As for the story about the garbage pail—one needn't believe it or take it too literally. Thus I tried to calm myself and to offer a resistance that was both rigid and anxious against the breakthrough of hostile mythical, primordial forces into our world, into my world, which, in spite of my attempts to patch it, seemed to be going to pieces.

I couldn't help thinking of the head of the little toy horse amid the ruins of Manshiyeh, which I had seen after that adventurous night. Perhaps it, too, might in some way have helped me to a rational explanation of these uncanny phenomena. But did this toy sustain any real relation to the horrible, gigantic horse's head above the cellar door?

I had no answer to these questions. But I confess that a further revelation of my friend thrust these questions into the background. At least at that time, on my way home through the night, this revelation, and this alone, occupied my thoughts. It began with an astonishingly violent fit of rage on Helfin's part. I had recently become somewhat accustomed to these cascades of indignation, to these cries that he was being maltreated, that he was being driven about and robbed of all quietude, like this whole period and like the Jewish people in this period. But I had never heard him express himself with such shrill exorbitance. "I don't want to be purified any more," he screamed. "It is enough! I am weary of being a sacrifice. For you must know that among all peoples there are two categories—the one lives in luxury and comfort even in the midst of catastrophes, which are always the catastrophes of the other category. Those people know how to turn even the catastrophes to their loathesome advantage. These parasites, who are well off under all circumstances, still sit on the terraces of the luxury hotels. They are world stars of press or film, or black marketeers, or courtesans, or diplomats, or the backers of all these varieties. Flattery surrounds them even when all about them their fellow mortals die like dogs; to them are given the most complicated dishes and wines, as though this were inevitable and befitting. As to the other kind, they are the sacrificial souls, to put it briefly. They take the catastrophes seriously and are therefore taken seriously, that is, they are tormented by the catastrophes. And if they had the incredible good luck not to be devoted to destruction, then life purifies them and elevates their souls. People of this kind are supposed to be grateful for their anguish. Their agonies are in a certain sense their good fortune and elevate them to a higher spiritual rank. But I declare that as far as my humble person is concerned I have been purified enough. And I remind you of the fable of that antique king Phalaris in Sicily who, to illustrate his tyrant's arrogance, caused a steer of bronze to be cast. Into the belly of this steer rebels against his despotism were thrown and then within the steer a great fire was lit under them. The victims screamed. But a subtle artist had inserted into the steer's belly so many carefully placed convolutions that the desperate screams of tortured human beings were transmuted into musical harmonies. The more desperate and the louder the victims screamed, the nobler was the music, which, like the bleating of gods, rose from the body of the steer and delighted the hearing of the tyrant. Only in this purified form did Phalaris perceive the dying groans of his subjects. The meaning of the parable is clear. It is asserted that pain purifies and ennobles. So it would seem that God has put us Jews into the glowing steer of Phalaris for this benevolent purpose. Well, I am through. With all my strength I refuse to be the subject of further purification. This became clear to me on my journey, and the place was Geneva."

With these words Helfin proceeded immediately to the second part of his confession. In Geneva he had made the acquaintance of a young French-Jewish poet named René. As a matter of prudence he had long used his first name only, and this had become a custom. René didn't talk much. But once over a bottle of wine he had softened and had related half reluctantly how he had fled to the security of Switzerland. "I, as you know, had gone to Europe,"—thus Helfin introduced the story of René— "in order to identify myself for a brief period with the general fate of mankind, which is difficult enough today and stands, as it were, on the knife's edge. As a citizen of the world I wanted to share the sorrows of Europe. Such was my good intention. But the story of René's flight awakened me from my cosmopolitan dream and thrust me back into the old, specific sorrow of the Jewish people, into the belly of the steer of Phalaris. On the very next day I was on my way to Marseille and on my return home."

And this is the story of René:

As it became ever clearer (thus René had begun) that the Vichy government was yielding to Nazi pressure and was delivering up Jews from the concentration camps in France to the Polish death camps and gas chambers, I determined to flee and to make my way to Switzerland. I took the train to Annemasse in Savoy, from where I intended to cross the frontier to Geneva. Had I known how sharply the trains from central France to Savoy were being controlled both by the Vichy police and by the Gestapo, I would probably not have ventured on the journey. As by a miracle I escaped the spies and patrols on the train. But when we came into the station at Annemasse, I saw that it was crowded with officials and guards. I had to get out, for this is the last station. All exits were guarded. I made a quick decision and went up to a policeman and asked him whether I couldn't get a cup of coffee or something else, since I was quite famished by the journey. Strictly speaking he should have demanded my identity papers. I had none. But the man absentmindedly pointed to the door of the restaurant. I ordered a little something. I hadn't much money and had to be careful. Not to be conspicuous, I choked down food and drink. Paying the waitress and adding a generous tip, I asked her whether there was another exit from the restaurant. She pointed to the delivery entrance, which could be reached from behind the bar and through the kitchen. Evidently she had understood me. The main exit was heavily guarded by soldiers. Quietly I went behind their backs. During the whole of my subsequent flight I met a number of Frenchmen who were willing to be helpful and only a few who were malevolent. Not many of them were as willing to make sacrifices as the admirable Italian people who, for instance, at the risk of their own lives, kept hidden hundreds of Jewish families and escaped prisoners of war in the hills beside Lake Como. This was related to me later with many instances of moving heroism. The French were more prudent and sober, but they too were helpful in their way. I recognized their kind of excellence. As the vanquished they were perhaps more frightened than the so-called Allied Italians.

All day long I wandered through the lovely little town of Annemasse, seeking the way to the frontier and, if possible, to an unguarded point of crossing. But where was such a one? I didn't dare ask; I didn't dare enter an inn. There were uniforms all over. Tired to death, I went into a movie theater in the evening. There I could rest my bones and, when the house was dark, even snatch a little sleep. But suddenly the show was over and the hall was bright. The audience started to go. I sat there alone. I tried to make myself as small as possible when a man went along the rows, whether the owner of the house or an inspector, and saw me.

"What are you doing here?"

"I wish you'd let me spend the night here."

He looked me over and understood. "I've got to consult my wife. Just wait here."

Ten dreadful minutes passed. Was he at the telephone, getting in touch with the Gestapo? After a while he came back, tranquil and somber as before. He showed me a partition behind the stage where I could sleep. First I was afraid and thought that he might hand me over later. Nothing of the kind. And soon, after all the misery and excitement, I slept soundly. Early in the morning he awakened me. There was breakfast awaiting me in his office. At parting he pressed 200 francs into my hand. His face remained cold. "You've got to look after yourself," he said with unmistakable determination. He was glad to be rid of the dangerous guest. He was not hostile; he was not friendly; he wanted his own security.

Again I walked through the city and sought the way and did not find it. By evening, hunger drove me into a small inn. At a neighboring table sat two gray-haired men. They soon recognized in me a comrade in fate. "You can go with us; a group of us are crossing the frontier tonight." Perhaps they were *agents provocateurs*. I was too deathly weary to put off the decision any longer. Even destruction seemed better than this uncertainty.

Before we started out, a child of between three and four years old was assigned to each group of us. Somewhere, far away, there was a committee which insisted on this condition; each time a group of children had to be saved too. "You must call the gentleman Father—*Tate*." The children understood.

Our march went across the fields, up a chain of hills, and then through a forest. It seemed to be endless. At last we stood in the fog beside the hut of a lonely, lofty boundary guardroom. The two guardsmen had been bribed. But it appeared that in respect of the sum, which seemed to be monstrously high under the circumstances, a misunderstanding had arisen. A long controversy began. No accommodation seemed possible between the smugglers who led us and the two frontier guards. The quarrel became more and more violent, the while we, its objects, sat trembling on the benches or on the moist forest ground. The hours passed and midnight was approaching. At that hour new guards were to come who were not in on the plot. The negotiations had been futile and we had to return by way of the forest. "Where are we going, Father?" the child I was leading asked.

He looked at me out of his wise dark eyes. He had learned quickly.

Before we came to the city limit we scattered. I slept on a bench in a park. I was minded to return to the hospitable movie house, but it was closed now. I knocked but no one opened. It was evident that I could not go to a hotel, where one has to answer written questions.

Next day I tried to make my way alone. From afar I scrutinized each human being in the hope that he might be willing and able to help. A boy with an honest, red-cheeked face pleased me. I gave him all I had—about 240 francs.

"Please, what is the nearest way to the frontier?"

He showed me a certain house. I was to go through the front door and come out by the garden gate. I would then come upon a brook, on the farther bank of which was Switzerland. I did as I was told. The brook was turbulent but after sundry attempts I managed to cross it. I was hastening to the nearest farm house. A woman stopped me.

"Where am I?"

"Where would you like to be?"

"In Switzerland!"

"Well, this is still France."

I cursed the boy who had misled me.

"You see that lighted house over there?" the woman continued. "That's the French border guardhouse. My husband is a policeman. He mustn't find you here." She gave me milk and a piece of bread and showed me where the fence of steel-wire entanglement was not quite sound. Of course she could give me the directions only vaguely and from afar. By dark I couldn't find the place. I felt my way on and on along the fence and finally climbed over at a random spot. My hands and clothes were in shreds. Through a violent rain I ran across the fields to the edge of a forest. Here there was another wire fence but not so formidable a one. Beyond it was a dark forest from which I reached a road. I shook as with fever and dripped from the streaming rain. An old woman came along the road. She took me under her umbrella. I didn't have to talk. May God bless this simple old woman. It seemed to me as I walked under her umbrella that of all the kindnesses which had been shown me on my flight this was both the most intimate and the most important.

"Where does that trolley go to?" I asked.

"Those houses over there are in Geneva. This is the last station."

I summoned up my courage and asked the kind old woman to buy me a ticket. She nodded and brought forth her big black leather bag. In the trolley car I was surprised to get back a little change from the money she had given me. The rattling of the car sounded to me like the chimes of Paradise. We were in a suburb of Geneva. I soon got out. A tobacco shop was about to close. I put the change on the counter in a pool of water that came from my sleeve. "That will buy you exactly one cigarette," the salesgirl said laughing and gave me a package. I had scarcely thanked her and taken a few steps around the next corner when I heard my name called.

They were friends who had been saved a week earlier by another road. "Come right along to our regular café." They had been in Geneva for a week and had already adopted a café as their habitual resort.

"You want me to go with you in my condition?"

"Of course you'll first go with one of us and get dry clothes." At that I felt that I was at home.

This was Helfin's experience of Jewish need and humiliation in Geneva—this identical experience which had repeated itself many thousands of times on many frontiers with but slight variations. Single individuals are persecuted everywhere. But an entire people! And now our homeland and last refuge must, of course, according to a certain colonial policy, adopted from King Abdullah, be shot to pieces by Egyptian bombers and cannons.

"What saddened me so inexpressibly"—thus Helfin closed his account—"was, by the way, not at all René's fate, but something that you might call an ancillary circumstance. To my mind, however, it was the chief consideration. I asked René, 'What became of the child?' 'What child?' 'The child that you led by the hand and that asked you, "Where are we going, Father?" ' 'I don't know. I delivered it to the pastor of the town.' 'And what happened then?' 'I don't know.'

"This René, you are to know, is a sensitive poet whose verses echo and re-echo the sorrows of our time. He read me many of his poems in Geneva. A deep preoccupation with the future of human goodness vibrated in them. Nevertheless the anguish and the humiliations which he had endured had evidently served to harden a little his own heart. There seems to be a degree beyond which one cannot suffer and still maintain the entire sensibility of the soul. I can explain in no other way the fact that this humane and amiable man never concerned himself with the further fate of that particular child, nor asked after him nor heard at the time the symbolic meaning of that moving question which the child had asked him."

CHAPTER THREE

Which begins with a brief digression on the part of the author concerning the kind and credibility of this narrative and in which the intrusion of a woman, who doubtless represents an ultramodern type, can no longer be prevented.

1.

It is not without some hesitation that I proceed to continue the delineation of the adventures of my friend Helfin from this time on. The kind reader will already have observed that it has been a matter of no little difficulty to reconstruct the recalcitrant events which I, too, experienced. This difficulty increases and oppresses me as I proceed to the point of breathlessness. Precisely because I insist upon the absolute truth of my accounting and desire to hand on nothing but the really experienced, in its totality and without erasures—for this reason I am betrayed into a most harassing situation. Let me explain that situation.

I am obliged from now on more and more to describe events to which I have no key. Less and less have I been able to understand the course of these events as, in however modest a way, I had my share in the development of these strange concatenations or else observe them immediately. So I had better limit myself to the communication of the simple facts which happened around Helfin. I had better renounce the notion of any comment, which would have to be thin enough anyhow. Yet at this point there arises a second difficulty, which increases my hesitation. To most of what I have hitherto related I was a direct eyewitness. Nor did I now lose sight of Helfin entirely. But the record of the war from this point on to the first armistice of June 10 became ever so much denser and so much more exciting that all private happenings seemed increasingly trivial. I saw Helfin only at considerable intervals. Whenever we did meet he told me a good deal, sometimes in his apartment, sometimes in mine, sometimes in a bomb shelter. He had always been communicative and open-hearted, and not a man of convulsive reserves, concerning whose interior life one must venture guesses. Toward me, at all events, he had always been so uninhibited that I was sometimes frightened. To be sure, I think that he confined this attitude to me. To others he was apt to hush with a curious sense of shame whatever was saddening in his experience. In general he complained more of the corruption in public affairs than of his personal fate. What he said seemed to me, I confess, on the edge of madness. But who, during those dreadful days, did not indulge in nonsensical speech? I regret now when it is too late that I did not at once pursue the proof of some of his assertions. I should have checked them up then and there. It would have been possible. Today there is no power in the world which can ascertain whatever part of sober truth inhered in those often wholly abstruse accounts, of which Helfin was full.

There was a clear temptation to consider certain events related by him as, in their totality, the delusions of a psychopath, of a schizophrenic personality. On the other hand, there were so many other living people involved in his experiences that in the end, however reluctantly, one had to speak of at least a core of objective and corporeal fact and not only of the wild fancies of a brain in hypertension. At the time, I confess, I ascribed much of what Helfin confided to me in his excited condition to his shattered nerves, his excessive indignation, and his humiliation. Yet I paid too little attention to what seemed to me unimportant during those days in which Hannibal stood at our gates and had already almost shattered them. The fiery atmosphere almost extinguished my living sympathy with the fortunes of my closest friends. I reproach myself on that account today. Later on, when under circumstances to be discussed subsequently, his diaries and notations were entrusted to me, I was forced to recognize with whatever astonishment, that all which had been the substance of his long nocturnal delineations, wherewith he tortured himself in my presence and concerning which he seemed so eager to learn my opinion, coincided to the point of the subtlest concreteness with what in his most sincere and solitary hours he wrote down for his own encouragement and meditative consideration. Wherever his oral communication had seemed fragmentary, the written word filled in the intervals. The conversations and the few events at which I was present, and the diary accountings in that vast mass of paper which constitutes the dossier of the Helfin case, complement each other astonishingly and almost without a gap.

Now I would, to be sure, seem too much of a pedant to myself if in the following account I were to seek to differentiate the several "sources" and to attempt separate delineations of what I saw myself, of what I observed in him, of what I learned only from conversations and debates, and, finally, of what became clear through his written words. It often happened that the written material furnished the chief substance and the decisive word and came near to solving the riddle. I confess that at first I attempted this separation of sources in my description. But this seemed to result in forming a picture not even reasonably clear. It was not until I determined to use simultaneously all the sources of information at my command, whether they were firsthand participation in experience or direct communications from Helfin or, finally, those based upon his written confessions, that I began to feel that my attempts to render reality to the best of my ability and to do justice to the memory of my friend were not destined to remain an empty gesture and might, indeed, assume the firmness of form and order.

The simple course of events of the days following our late conversation after the concert may, without the adducing of definite proof, be represented in somewhat the following fashion:

For some time Helfin resisted the temptation to turn the fateful red switch, which, like similar devices on a radio, was fastened, ready for use, at the front of the magic contraption and lured him by the naturalness of simply being there.

Doubtless it cost him conflicts. Bizarre indications on this subject are to be found in his papers, although the descriptions in the dossier are far from clear. Nor is this all. The writing on some pages is deliberately erased. Other pages are torn and scarcely decipherable. There are the silent witnesses of an inner conflict preceding a final deed. It would seem as though a comparatively trivial circumstance gave the final jolt. That which induced the dreadful decision was a mere nothing after, for so long a time, the pros and cons had been comparatively balanced.

My first definite information concerns the actual act of manipulation, the fateful turning of the switch. This information does not come from the dossier. All that occurred in these moments and immediately thereafter, Helfin himself confessed to me entirely and with all the symptoms of extreme emotion, in a desperate conversation. This conversation did not take place immediately after the event; it took place much later, near the time of the final catastrophe. It was, if I remember correctly, our last conversation or, at least, among the last. And it was sufficiently mysterious like everything that concerned my friend from a certain moment on, from, one might well say, that meeting in the Café Shalva. Among the curiosities of the situation is this: how late, almost near the end, it became clear to me— for I must finally dare to confess the whole—that he ran about in the world in a double, a twofold fashion. He was not split into two contradictory characters after the manner of Kundry or of Dr. Jekyll and Mr. Hyde, but as twice over the same kindly, almost too gentle, ever accusing personality, each time, however, subject to a different fate, to a different concatenation and succession of vital circumstance and hence, closely looked upon, reacting differently. For it goes without saying that a changed fate will cause definite deviations in the behavior of a human being, even if that human being remains the same at his core. Subtler changes had not escaped me. In this respect the fat man had been correctly prophetic. People's awareness of each other is not very sharp. As a rule no one is so deeply concerned over his neighbor that he is greatly struck with small shifts in the other's way of life, in so far as they do not directly concern his own interests. Yet the shift in behavior in Helfin's case was evident enough. Somehow I always sensed the fact that he sometimes seemed younger, even though his glance was wearier and more exhausted—sometimes, that is to say, in one of the two lives which were granted him after the turning of the switch. For instance, in one of his double lives he had taken a hint from

Bianca Petry and shaved off his little Van Dyke. Thus he turned up sometimes with a beard and sometimes without one. And to my intense shame I must confess that, though I had an indistinct feeling of visual confusion, I had no clean-cut variation of impression. It was not until finally he confessed to me the whole extent of his aberration that it became halfway clear to me how I had long missed a very sensible and visible circumstance.

If in this manner I report a sharply circumscribed experience, firsthand and personally witnessed—even though the actual fact is so insignificant as the presence or absence of a little beard—how much more do I blame myself in view of the difference between the certain evidence of such observed facts and the conjectures on which I am dependent for filling in the picture. Conversations and documents, the entire dossier—is it not all at second hand and colored in all likelihood by the temperament of my friend, for which I cannot in all conscience accept the responsibility?

As far as I am concerned, the fat man had been a bodily presence only in the Café Shalva and next in the car. If I were to be pressed, I would also have to admit that he had been present later that night in a scarcely determinable place. From then on I did not see him again. What marks my conversation with Helfin in his apartment after the concert is the circumstance that the little stage did hang on the wall as an unquestionable corporeal reality. Thereafter it, too, became invisible.

Oddly enough on the occasion on which, later on, Helfin made his complete confession to me, he emphasized particularly the negative circumstance of the nonappearance of the model stage. "It melts into thin air as soon as you turn the switch," he said. "It just melts away. Nothing remains except, at most, a light, sweetish perfume which no one smells except myself." This disappearance of the contraption, leaving no trace, seemed to him later an important element of the entire magical procedure. For this disappearance seemed to signify: you yourself have entered into the space occupied by the instrument and hence it has ceased, as such, to exist. "It has been transmuted into that living existence in which you are now living and being. Its disappearance is a confirmation of the fact that your will had the right earnestness and force when you knocked at that gate. You asked for entry and you were heard; you are accepted and are now absorbed into the mystery. And the disappearance of the apparatus has an additional significance: there is no turning back. The boats behind you are burned."

He himself suspected as much at once when, after he had turned the switch, the little stage had vanished into cloud and fume. For he had observed that only the reddish switch had seemed to float, as though upborn by the air, hovering above him for a little while, before it, too, disappeared; and that its flicker had reminded him with a sense of dread of the star Antares, the red eye of the constellation Scorpio. "At first I kept thinking of the remark of the fat man that the little machine might be shattered, like the vial of the homunculus, if a situation arose that seemed to me quite unendurable and impossible. I clung to that as a hope, as a promise. How often did I pray for the event! In vain. This suggestion of the fat man had been nothing but one of the many tricks by which he placed me in the situation in which he wanted me to be."

Concerning the precise and detailed manner and mode, or the technical magical devices by which the experiment with the little stage was transmuted into a really experienced but double existence—concerning these crucial facts I gathered no more either from Helfin's confessions or from the memoirs he left behind him than what is recorded above. On the contrary, all the human circumstances accompanying the incomprehensible happenings became known to me: all, namely, that took place immediately before and immediately afterward. Hence my next task is the recording and handing on of these accompanying circumstances.

In order to accomplish this task appropriately, it may be well to record here what I learned concerning Helfin's biography, long before this critical period, and what experiences I shared with him.

2.

Paul Helfin was born around the turn of the century in a little town in southern Moravia. Before the First World War the cultural orientation of all of Moravia, especially of the southern part, was toward Vienna rather than toward Prague. So Helfin was sent to high school in Vienna and placed under the care of stingy relatives. His own parents, his father being a scribe in the service of the Jewish community, were inconceivably poor. Helfin's youth was stark and poverty-stricken. This was the first of the untoward circumstances which define his life. Even later, when he had made quite a name for himself in the world of the cinema, he was never, except for a brief period in Salzburg, really free of economic pressure. When he was a student in high school he gave private lessons to stupid fellow pupils to earn a little money; later he slaved as a stenographer and night telephone operator in one of the big Viennese editorial offices. His chief interest was in the history of art. He liked to tell about this period later. "I lived chiefly on crescent rolls. I had discovered that in a certain café near the editorial offices where I worked, the head waiter would sell all the rolls left over from that day at half price at closing time. Now Viennese crescents and other rolls are undoubtedly excellent. But I wouldn't advise anyone to eat them, as I did, by the dozen as his exclusive source of nourishment." He never forgot in later years, when he related these hardships of his youth, to add the observation that, since the period of the First World War, the very notions of need and of want had undergone very powerful changes.

At the university he met a fellow student, a gentle, beautiful, and clever girl, whom he married. His and Stella's marriage was singularly happy. They loved each other and their aspirations took the same direction. Both were equally interested in social and aesthetic problems; both came from Zionist Labor-Youth formations and were at one in their desire to build a better future for mankind and for their own people. They plunged into practical political work; at the same time their professional activities were quite successful. Paul rose to be the art and cinema editor of a great newspaper. He was planning a voyage to India on which his wife was to accompany him and serve as photographer. Just before they were to set out on their journey, Stella was killed in an auto accident. Helfin never recovered from this blow. "Life torments me too much"—this sentence, which seemed later to hover over his life like an invisible motto, was first heard on his lips at Stella's funeral.

For years he lived in solitariness. One never saw him with a woman. He renounced the Indian project. He began to make films and became famous.

I met him in the days of his editorship. He came to my attention the first time when a colleague of his had suffered the loss of all his possessions, including a fine library containing many precious works about the graphic and plastic arts, in a frightful conflagration. We inaugurated a collection in order to sustain the courage of our common friend. Helfin made a contribution, of course. A quite considerable sum was collected. A few days later we learned that, in addition, Helfin had sent his own library, consisting chiefly of books about painting, architecture, and allied subjects, to our colleague's new apartment. His conscience had bidden him to make a real sacrifice rather than to give an alms. With delicate shame he hid his goodness by making fun of book collecting and by insisting that books at home were so much unpleasant superfluity. If you wanted to look up something you could comfortably do so in the University library or the Imperial library. For home use a hundred volumes sufficed. All the while we all knew that he was a passionate bibliophile.

At that time, although a good deal older than he, I sought out his friendship. In contrast to so many people who in the past decades, probably under the influence of Nietzsche, had come to regard as fascinating, colorful, genuine, as the notable substance of life and the world, nothing but the evil, the bestial, the elementary-primitive, the wildly instinctual in its ghastliest forms—in contrast to such, I say, I had remained old-fashioned or, perhaps, decent enough to regard as of more emphatic value the rare phenomena of genuine humanity and virtue. In this respect Paul Helfin became the source of a powerful experience to me, a classic example. He was ready to help by day and by night. It was not a conscious matter with him. He simply followed his inclination, which he sometimes misinterpreted as a mere whim and over which he smiled with embarrassment. Once in a while there would follow some kind of an intellectual substantiation, and a theory of what goodness meant, of what he called renunciation, was explained by him, though without any connection with his own instinctive acts. He was open to every appeal. It was hard not to exploit him. One had to be careful not to impinge on his time and strength. I myself was in the happy position never to call upon him. I would have been ashamed to touch the spring of his childlike trust, of his simple joy in helpfulness. For his response was to my mind almost too facile. So I contented myself with observing him. And so I came to see how whole mobs of suppliants came to him with their varying demands: loans, letters of recommendation, interventions, the reading of manuscripts, the disposal of these manuscripts after they were read. The crassly material demands were the relatively simpler. Other callers had taken to the habit of pouring out their hearts to him, of asking his advice in situations which in all likelihood no advice could affect or to engage him in debates, both sterile and endless. Nor were there lacking eccentrics who kept him breathless with their mad projects. Never did Helfin turn anyone away; he seemed to have time for all. How he managed I never understood. For he was a hard worker, too; he must have been able, aside from his great patience, to get along with very little sleep, in order to satisfy the demands which were made upon him.

In the midst of all this he was not happy. In the very first really intimate conversation which we had, I perceived this not without astonishment. "I am not fond of people," he said. "I would like to love them, true enough, but I don't succeed in doing so. They are too scoundrelly. Now I'll tell you something remarkable. Many feel the way I do. I'm not alone; on the contrary, I probably represent a very frequent variety of character. You see, there is a discord. Many people, revolted by the goings-on of their fellows, turn away from them and buy a dog who is grateful and does not lie. But if so many people have this specific insight, why don't they combine toward a common procedure? Why don't they throw off their vices and seek to lead a simple and pure life, seeking to respect each other, even if they cannot rise to the mutuality of love? And is it not at least suspicious that there are so very many who feign from the high watchtower of their excellence to condemn all others? The vocation to judge mankind from a high vantage point ought, in its very nature, to be rare, if not, indeed, of a strict singularity. It shouldn't seem to be found on every street. False, hollow, too facile and sensual seems to me increasingly this morbid contempt of one human being for another, of one of the sons of Adam for the other, for the whole rest of the world within which those who separate themselves from the mass as being righteous are necessarily present by the hundreds. Well, my dear fellow righteous ones, why don't you find each other and live harmoniously with each other!" Then would come over his face that expression of astonishment and of being affronted and hurt. "I know it's nonsense to talk that way today. A moral paradox is to be seen in these legions of 'Timons of Athens.' Precisely they have no business to turn up in masses. I feel that in my very bones, as well as the atmosphere of the ridiculous that surrounds it all. But these are not our worst troubles today, although, if they were rightly treated, that is, if this problem were solved, it might rid the world of its troubles. However, I'm not so stupid as not to see that the world is not likely to pursue the path of solving difficult moral paradoxes and contradictions, but pursues with primitive stubbornness a path infinitely simpler and coarser, namely, the road to destruction." The rise of fascism in Italy after the horrors of the war, the attack on Abyssinia, the Spanish war, the rise of Hitler to power, not only not prevented but favorably regarded by many once apparently progressive forces, were cases in point. "You have the impression as though it takes complicated thought to hit so unerringly upon what is stupid and harmful and revolting," Helfin used to say. And then he would add, "And it's moving nearer. It will soon be the turn of Vienna and ourselves." He predicted that as far back as the time of the rape of Abyssinia. And all that distant anguish plagued him as though the pain were in his own body. He possessed the unhappy gift of compassion at a distance—not only distance in space but in time. He once showed me a passage in Grillparzer's Diaries. The poet was taking the cure in Sliacs in the summer of 1851: "Although the cure is not, if I am to be honest, doing me the least bit of good, what worries me most is the misery of the Athenians in Sicily. I have been reading the seventh book of Thucydides."

"In my earlier years," my friend once explained, "I had elasticity enough to draw new hope from every defeat that I encountered. I developed within through every misfortune. Even the loss of my wife contained a monition toward a spiritualization of my inner life. And I did not wholly fail to hear that voice. All that is over. I can't go on that way; I don't want to be improved any more. I want to be left in peace, that's what I want!" Poor man. He stood even now on the threshold of his acutest trials. Fate did not ask what he wanted, nor what he was capable of or not. After the great European success of his films he bought a villa in Salzburg. But Hitler was already lying in ambush behind those mountains. Oh yes, a few years were still to elapse. Yet when I went to see Helfin in his new house, it was with strange enough words that he led me from room to room. "Once upon a time I had a beautiful house," he said, and when we went into the next room, "and look, I had a beautiful library once, too."

It was long before I could answer him. From the window we saw the far Alpine peaks melt into the dusk of the pure wind of the evening. Then I brought out something somewhat like this, that, in spite of all, there was an element of cowardice in our readiness to abandon the positions which humanism and a humane life seemed still to occupy.

"I don't see those positions any more at all." He was abrupt and sharp. "And who in the end tells us that we are right? Perhaps we just imagine that we are the forerunners of a better future for man, the first gleams of a dawn. Perhaps we're nothing but the last. Perhaps we are those last red lights of a railroad train which thunders irrevocably out into the night and is lost to view in the impenetrable blackness. Is it so certain that it will be said some day, 'They were the harbingers of light; they announced the beginning of the great peace'? Perhaps the development of history is taking another direction and we were but the obscure and feeble remnants; in us, perhaps, that dream comes to an end which many centuries have dreamed, and an epoch of blood and terror assumes its final and permanent dominance."

"What will be said in the immediate future is not important, for that immediate future will be followed by a farther one. The spirit does not perish. We must not yield to weakness."

Helfin did not, in fact, weaken. In ample time he began his new life in Palestine. Soon thereafter Austria fell to the Nazis.

Let me remember once again the terrace of his marvelous villa in Salzburg. In this landscape in which charm and grandeur are united, he read Swift. He read the political writings, not the Gulliver daydreams. In this clear mountain air he sought no soothing potion but the clear black poison of the man who perished of his misanthropy, of that Irishman who fought throughout his life against British injustice (Helfin called these preliminary studies for Palestine) and who caused to be written on his gravestone that there lay the body of Dean Jonathan Swift, "in the grave, where cruel indignation could not longer lacerate his heart." *Ubi saeva indignatio cor ulterius lacerare nequit.* "What I am afraid of," Helfin once observed, "is bitterness, the bitterness that sets in on account of too many and too vital defeats. I wouldn't like to get to the point at which Swift had arrived when he said, 'What is happiness? To be permanently deceived and so be in the cheerful and peaceful frame of mind of a fool among scoundrels.'"

Then came the Palestinian chapter in Helfin's life.

It began surprisingly well. To fit oneself by reversal into a new order; to begin from the very beginning, renouncing all previous achievements, undergoing a complete change of circumstance—none who has not experienced it can estimate the amount of energy, of concentrated will to life which such a transformation demands.

As a matter of fact Helfin displayed more energy than is commonly expected or demanded. He conquered his new homeland in a euphoric tension of all his powers. He felt the confirmation of a final homecoming. He was well received; a few unselfish souls who felt themselves akin to him received him fraternally. He was now able to emphasize the second half of the inscription on Swift's grave, "Go, wanderer, and seek to emulate, if thou canst, the determined fighter for manly freedom." And, indeed, the first year after his settlement was the happiest of his life. He lived as in a long dream of blessedness. He started all kinds of projects and finally had the good luck, granted to but a few here, to continue what he had begun in Europe and so to take up his profession. He needed not, as happened here to many a former bank director, to drive a taxi or raise chickens or serve to impatient guests the food cooked by his wife. Even such occupations were regarded as not unlucky ones under the hard pressures of a new and poor community. Helfin's luck was better. He was asked to build up an artistic production of films beneath this eternally blue sky. Then came the Second World War.

Helfin's studies and preparations, which were fully under way, had to be put aside. "That's the queer aspect of my life," he explained. "I am not lacking in a measure of practical ability, but fate plays a game of chess with me. If I make a good move, it makes a better one and my defenses crumble. It is as though my ability teased the dark powers. The more spontaneous my initiative, the more powerful is the counterblow. I play quite well and lose every game. I am beginning to cut a humorous figure on my own chess board—the figure of an intrepid little horse which, in my case, turns out to be a luckless little donkey."

Under the most difficult conditions he showed a strange resilience. He volunteered for the British army and later joined its Jewish Brigade. On several fronts, including the battle of El Alamein, he fought against the Nazi monster. His pacifism resulted in no conflict. The two world wars had an entirely different character. During the first, aside from the fact that he had been too young to bear arms, he had felt a neutral attitude, for he had seen the errors and the horrors on both sides in an identical ugliness. The second war signified the saving of mankind from cannibals. Helfin did the little he could. The grimness of fate destroyed all his kinsmen and friends in Central Europe. Timely flight had saved only his nephew Gad Reis and himself. Again the air was black and bitter about him. The news from the death camps broke within him what had begun to assume the form of a new core of vitality. Now sheer despair set in; the entries in his diaries record his nausea and his weariness of life.

And then, as though to prevent any renewal of impulse, there set in, in 1945, what constituted still another war—that wave of restlessness that spread over all the world, which went from Greece to Pakistan, to India, Burma, Korea, Indonesia, of which the conflicts in Palestine were but a tiny, though sufficiently bloody, episode. Were all these the preparations of the third inferno, of atomic war? The politicians seemed quite set upon it, although they were not sparing of a hypocritical, ineffectual whining for peace. Was it a war of nerves? It was assuredly a nerve-destroying peace.

"No one wants to renounce even a trifle," Helfin declared. "The most trivial demand is stubbornly insisted upon—the kind of demand which bears no relation to the threat against world unity. And this unity is prevented by the stubbornness in question. It seems to occur to no one that a relaxation of the universal tensions of this unyieldingness is the first and only condition of any promising negotiations. Everybody is ashamed to give up even the smallest point. Yet precisely such renunciations, smaller and greater, would clear a path. The first demand upon any human being today, whether in public or in private life, is this: you must renounce. Or, to define it more precisely: in the exertion of your measure of power, you must never go the limit. This forgoing need not be permanent renunciation; it need not be the negation of anyone's world or value. He who forgoes advantages desires to enhance the value of the world and of his own life by self-limitation in favor of his neighbor. It is precisely by doing so that he opens himself to the infinite influence of the spiritual world. He wins where he seems to lose. To retrench the boundaries of egoism, not for the sake of self-evisceration but in order to create room for the liberating reality of the spirit, such is the decisive necessity. Of course the adversary will jeer and ask, 'How far can you retrench?' The answer is, 'No generalization is either possible or necessary. The measure will be clarified from case to case, if I permit my pure and tranquil instinct to prevail. It will depend upon that element of quiet veracity in each.' That gives the adversary his opening, 'Then why don't you preach, like Lessing, and say: "Little children, love one another." ' I would like nothing better, were I not convinced that love must be wholly spontaneous, that it cannot be forced, least of all by preachments, which at once bear the danger of a suspected hypocrisy and so are more harmful than helpful. No, we must be strict toward ourselves and eschew any illusion. Love, love among men, must be a pure gift. You are lucky if you feel it. For then you are certainly on the right road, and I would encourage you and fortify you to continue upon it. But if you do not feel that emotion, then your problem begins right there. No amount of talk will help. And that, alas, is the condition of humanity today. It is unmistakable that we do not live in a period in which the love of humanity is active. What remains to be done? That small and modest forgoing of advantage. And this is so important, since people can be persuaded to this act, which is an act of the will, while they cannot be persuaded to love. Hence it should be made clear to men that this forgoing of advantages is the last road to redemption that is open. It, too, demands a complete inward reorientation, a horror of that extreme political arrogance which seems to so many the last word of wisdom. This, too, is almost impossible. But only almost. And so the future depends on that *one* word."

Helfin despised lamentations. I believe that I was the only one whom he acquainted with his experiences and opinions in all-inclusive discussions. The only thing I was to learn exclusively from his diaries was what had happened to him during his first sojourn in Paris.

In 1945, soon after the war's end, Helfin had remained in Europe a few months after his discharge from the army in order to study the methods and the development of the French motion-picture industry. He renewed his plan for the creation of an indigenous Palestinian film. In the course of these preparations he came upon a small Jewish studio in a Parisian suburb where with negligible technical equipment original experiments were being made. Two brothers named Josefovitch furnished the capital; they were actors, too. The driving force of the group was Bianca Petry. It was obscure with which of the brothers her relationship was the closer. Not that Helfin cared. In the very beginning Bianca was merely something like a rescuer to him. And that had come about as follows:

For years Helfin had paid no attention to women. The long restrained ardor of his heart had driven him into a most unhappy and unseemly love affair. He had been enchanted by a handsome Greek woman, by her blue-black braids, by her tranquil brown Olympian eyes, by her symmetrical body. As far as her soul was concerned, she seemed to have substituted her body for it. This, in itself, might have had an element of distinction, had she not sought to destroy this secondary soul too by opiates. Her mind could rarely be counted on; her frigidity was almost constant. In vain had friends warned him against this dangerous woman, who had already ruined several men. In the first passionate urgency that he had known for years, he believed himself strong enough to rescue this lost soul and restore her to the activities of a natural life. He was told that in the conflict between love and morphine, love had no chance. Morphine is irresistible. He laughed at his advisors; he was soon up to the eyes in this adventure; he had almost lost his way back. It was Bianca who took pity on him. She took long walks with him; she persuaded him of the worthlessness of the Greek woman. She reminded him of his obligations to his art and to the land he had chosen.

3.

She talked to him seriously and sensibly, quite as a physician would have done. Energy and toughness were her conspicuous qualities. She had suffered much. Before the war's end she had succeeded in escaping from the camp of Bergen-Belsen under obscure circumstances, of which she never spoke. She had then been active in the French underground. There was no horror of the years of persecution which she had not shared in all its immediacy. She had seen those she loved and valued most die of hunger-typhus, of dysentery, by a salvo of shots at the edge of open graves, or by malicious bullets in the back. It was to be inferred from certain remarks that she made that her final escape had been paid for by the most equivocal daring, that is, she had feigned to enter the service of the Gestapo. She had letters from influential leaders of the underground confirming the reality, if one may say so, of this feigning. But now and then an enemy turned up who accused her of having really acted as a spy and of having betrayed refugees. She repudiated such accusations with fiery indignation. But in all these affairs certain details remained obscure enough, and in the very midst of peace she seemed still surrounded by the atmosphere of conflict. Like everything else she had the ability to put this, too, to a good use. The uncommon and adventurous atmosphere that surrounded her was an additional charm which, if properly exploited, might well prove useful to a young actress at the beginning of her career.

Up to this point, it must be confessed, she had done little to fulfill her ambition.

It is to be supposed that she had begun her career on little Austrian or German-Bohemian stages. So far as could be made out, this had lasted only a year or two when the rise of Hitler had swept all Jewish artists from the theater. Her blond hair and her dainty little nose were hardly those of a recognizable Jewish type. This circumstance had been of advantage to her during her later adventures. But her careful colleagues of both sexes had kept racial lists of the German stages years ahead of time. In addition a well-defined pride kept her from denying her Jewishness. "I never lied," she would explain, and her eyes would glitter wildly. It didn't quite jibe with this that in order to get a minor job on a German stage in those days at all she had undergone baptism. "In one word, you're a pretty cute little article," Mr. Josefovitch had once remarked when this particular episode was being discussed. "I would make any sacrifice for my art," had been her answer. It should be added that she had long re-allied herself with the Jewish religion. At this period she was a Jewish Nationalist of great passion. In the meantime she had been raked over the coals when she appeared in a French film on account of her foreign accent, which clung to her in spite of the almost inhuman pertinacity and conscientiousness with which she pursued her French studies. It is clear that if a special cruelty of circumstance can justify implacable ruthlessness in the pursuit of a certain goal, many excuses can be made for Bianca. She was a creature of her age—of this age and of the yellow badge.

Now she had found out that a fairly well-known film director had come from Palestine to Paris. She reversed herself at once. Within twenty-four hours she cast off Yiddish, which had hitherto prevailed in the studio, and the entire familiar, melodramatic American East-Jewish style. Her strength of character was such that she was able to persuade her colleagues in the studio. She now embraced the task and the ideal of creating a new Hebrew film in a new labor style in a new land. With a zeal which Helfin could not refrain from admiring and which persuaded him to increase his own linguistic efforts, she built up an entire structure on the little Hebrew that she already knew. Since her whole soul was in the enterprise she made the most astonishing progress and her teacher called her a miracle woman.

This common language study to which she was so tirelessly devoted was the first bridge between herself and Helfin. They determined to speak to each other exclusively in Hebrew and under all conditions. At the beginning they both committed such gross errors that people who were really masters of this difficult language were quite speechless. But Bianca's impulse admitted no difficulties. As a matter of honor no German or French word was to be used. When they disagreed, when they quarreled, they did so in Hebrew. Helfin, who had been in the land for some years, had never underestimated the necessity of speaking its language; he had studied industriously and had made reasonable progress in the course of time. But the real passion was communicated to him by Bianca. As an actress she was, of course, far more dependent upon a perfect mastery of word and sound than he himself.

Her vocation as an actress, whether on stage or screen, was the unshakable aim and ideal of her life and her ambitions. All else might change and sway. She made a point of a modest demeanor, of unemphatic emphasis on girlish shyness and delicacy, but behind these shy gestures, which were probably also merely played as part of an admirably executed role, there was hidden a steely assurance of a definite aim and the unshakable conviction that greatness was her portion. In this respect she was probably quite genuine; one felt this regulative passion in her whole character. Her talent, her powerful expressiveness, appeared incontestably in a few scenes which Helfin shot as tests. What made her peculiarity difficult to grasp was just this, that she was not entirely unveracious, that in her reiterated declaration of her will to truth, of her contempt of any impure influence or pull or impure advantage, there was a grain of real conviction, for the reason that the profound inner assurance of her authentic artistic gifts was part of the very vibration of her life. And it was precisely this fraction of genuineness which gave rise to the confusion which her personality created.

No one ever really found out where she had been born or what her name was. It was perfectly certain that she had originally been called neither "Bianca" nor "Petry." Several cities were mentioned as having been the scenes of her birth. When these contradictions became pointed she would explain them in the simplest manner. She *had* been born in Cracow. But when she was two her family had moved to Breslau. Her adolescence had been passed in Königsberg. And so on and so on. Was it, anyhow, so important? And she would laugh. Wasn't truth so mighty a matter that it had reference only to decisive circumstances and not to these nonessentials? In regard to trivialities she preferred to give free reign to her play instincts and artistic preferences. Once and for all she declared, as a reply to all possible future reproaches of giving a false account of herself, it happened simply to be a part of her doubtless not too important personality, but an integral part, that she paid no attention to trivialities and was often unable to distinguish between the realm of the experienced and the merely dreamed or desired. In matters of this kind she did not pretend to be reliable. Whoever wanted to be friends with her would have to renounce this convenience. And she would emphasize the word convenience contemptuously. She was simply not at home to Babbits. There were times when she simply preferred to be silly and to enjoy being silly. Who was going to forbid her that? Life was poor enough without a few jokes and a little flexibility. She would adduce the example of her mother. "My mother was the simple wife of a small merchant. But as clever as possible. And good as gold. When she came home from the annual fair she would tell us children stories of the unheard-of things which she had seen in the county seat, like a giraffe with two heads and a calf as big as a house, and all kind of rarities that we didn't dream of in our village." (Village? Helfin would reflect. I thought the line was Cracow, Breslau, Königsberg. . . . So this is still another version!) "My father was strict and he would cry out, 'But Chaye, there's not a word of truth in all that!' My father was a very pious man; he disapproved of lying. Then my mother would weep and lament, 'I'm not even permitted to use my imagination.' She always thought that that was bitter wrong done to her. And I agreed with her."

It is not to be denied that there was something very attractive in her cynical way of making a public show of all the lying, inconstant, fugitive, uncontrollable elements of her temperament and thus to seem to give herself the framework of an illusory veracity. There were, in addition, her great, gray, innocent eyes which, to be sure, were so harmless only on a superficial view of them. In their depths there was a very feline sparkle and glitter. Oh, the eyes were beautiful; conspicuously so was her entire slender figure, especially her long and shapely legs, which she liked to show. One had to get used to her pallid face which, considering her size, was rather small. It was a narrow face; the nose rather protruded but was blunted at the point. The bright-blond, soft hair and the firm and youthful bosom gave to her entire, rather etherealized appearance something immediately captivating.

Actually, her hair was tinted. But, said Bianca, it was a legitimate tint, because the artificial blondness went with her eyes and her complexion. Thus she would analyze herself very frankly. She also told Helfin during their very first conversation that she had had some plastic surgery done to her nose. Originally she had had a horrible hooked nose. She had begged a famous surgeon for a long time until he had consented to trim this frightful obstacle to her career. He had done it twice. The first time the result had not satisfied her. She never explained how all this had been accomplished, for she had never had any money. And oh, the pain she had suffered in the hospital, and what the determination to have the whole thing done over again had cost her!

The secret of her extraordinary energy marked every circumstance of her career. She had the highest opinion of the artistic transformation of human appearance and of the entire technique of cosmetics. Furthermore she complained that she had not been born a man. In her childhood she had still hoped that she might become a boy. "We women are so badly off; it is disgraceful how dependent we are on our looks. I would much rather stand or fall by achievement. But who will let me?" Whenever this subject was discussed she would become crudely aggressive. "A woman must cheat men and make fools of them. Nothing else works!" She would frankly add that she was much older than she seemed to be. And it was evident that she had had many experiences. In spite of that, she had indubitably the charm that arises from freshness, from the appearance of unspoiledness by the world, of a simplicity of soul which had no foundation in the facts of life.

What she offered Helfin as the bond between them was a community of interests. He certainly needed her, that was clear enough—if only on account of his catastrophic Greek. As for herself, well, she was even fond of him. Of course, her interests were involved; it would be silly to deny that. Her attention had first been attracted to him by his professional eminence. Later on she had observed him as a human being and had begun to grow fond of him. It was evident that he was different from the men she had hitherto encountered, the mere brutal, bestial exploiters. She told him that she loved him with the same quiet objectivity with which some day, if it came to that, she would tell him that she had had enough of him. "I cannot deal in half-measures." There was no use trying to be subtle about that. But she was pretty sure that she never would want to get rid of him. She was not disposed to explain that either. This was the way it was. Concerning all that which, according to them, needed no further discussion, they talked a very great deal, although they were both on their guard. "Don't let's *talk* things to pieces." Yet it was so tempting to peer into the abysses of their incalculable instincts.

You couldn't ever reduce Bianca to a formula. She would glide from clever, edgy observations unmotivatedly to quite tender and feeling ones. Such emotional moments were precious in proportion to their rarity and brevity. A sudden pressure of the hands at their common perception of a fine passage when they sat side by side in a theater—that was a kind of consecration. They never mentioned such things in words.

The Greek was still an obstacle to their union. With scientific objectivity she told him that he was still in bondage to the woman. After a pause she would add, "What a pity." They even developed a little secret language.

One evening she stayed rather longer than usual in his hotel room, in which they often chatted. Unmotivatedly she put a shawl about the shade of the floor lamp and said gaily, "This is to create the right mood." She told the story of one of her girl friends who once said to her that the great and famous lover, the handsome actor X, was not all that he had once been. You had to drape the lamp in a thick silken swathing. "He is at the point where he needs the right mood." While she was talking she slipped out of her dress and out of her chemise and lay naked on the divan. Helfin kissed her forehead and eyes. His desire turned into hostility against himself. He had a vision of the wholly different conformation of the body of the Greek woman. He felt a strangeness here, and an alien perfume. Bianca glanced at him. "I don't please you," she said calmly. "Oh, but you do," he hastened to say courteously and guiltily. "I've been very much admired," she replied and closed her eyes. She lay still for a little; then she got up and put on her clothes again. Not for a moment had she lost an air of careworn, unselfish seriousness. Her dignity had remained perfect—a statue with a gesture of helpful friendship. "Your bondage to your Greek is deeper than I thought," she said without a trace of irony or of being hurt, in the level tone of a diagnosis offered among colleagues.

Several days later the group of people in the studio began to quarrel with each other. Hitherto Bianca had worked devotedly at the scenarios, at trial shots, at tests of all kinds. She had been the first to appear in the studio in the morning and the last to leave it at night. Helfin, who had interested himself in the experiments of these fine young people at her insistence, was utterly astonished. "I've got an offer from René Clair," Bianca told him. "All these idealistic attempts take years and leave us in the same spot."

"How did René Clair happen to come to know about you, if I may inquire?

"He saw shots from our studio. I sent them to his secretary. They are the scenes with me that you shot."

"Is that the extent of your loyalty to the Hebrew film?"

"Loyalty is the excuse of weaklings."

"If that is true then there was nothing wrong with Hitler's method."

"I was always convinced of that. Only he was not intelligent enough to use his own method."

Helfin at once discontinued the discussion. Several times before, they had reached the point where any understanding was impossible. But Bianca restrained him. She had only made that observation because it always infuriated her to have anyone attempt to lay down the law to her. In fact, she wanted to continue to work with him as well as with René Clair, but not in this foolish collective enterprise with half-baked plans, rather in some important, leading role according to a definite system, with the proper financial backing, "as is the case everywhere and as it must be."

"Our way is different. We're just beginning to build," he said. "Each of us must serve as a pioneer and sacrifice personal advantage. Our law runs: Only if we achieve the impossible can we exist."

They had discussed that a hundred times. He reminded her of their shared Hebrew studies. "Watch out, you're on the wrong way," he warned her.

"Or else you are. But I don't mean to give you up. You have great inspirations. You should come with me."

They had lost the common ground which had served to unite them. Nevertheless she seemed seriously to desire not to break with him. For it was immediately after that controversy that she made her special effort. She came to him again that evening. Once more she stripped. This time it was no statue that approached him but a woman full of passion. She played upon him with every sensual device and thus surprised him into giving up his psychical resistance. She overcame him and their union took place. Afterwards a sense of revulsion struck him. She, however, declared with a satisfied sigh, "Well, we fixed that."

From then on he avoided her and tried not to be alone with her, though when they met socially he conversed with her readily enough. He had no desire to hurt her, although he himself felt profoundly affronted by her. Bianca had evidently no ill intention toward him; she simply didn't know the difference. Life had taught her one single lesson: force prevails everywhere.

That nocturnal scene, however, had one happy consequence. The influence of the Greek woman over him was broken. He was rid of her. "You ought to be grateful to me," said Bianca, who had found out that he saw the Greek woman no more. "Maybe for a while—how shall I explain that to one so innocent? —maybe for a while you're fed up with that whole line of goods." Her laugh was obscene. "You *have* got the horrors. Well, my remedy was rather like a horse's bolus."

"I'll credit your account with the fee," he said angrily and turned his back on her.

He had a much clearer vision of her than before. There are people whom we do not properly see until we have had to turn our backs on them.

What made him most indignant was her behavior toward the young enthusiasts in the studio. They had had faith in her; they had seen in her the leader who would make any sacrifice for the organization of a Jewish film art. They now tasted the bitterness of disappointment. Helfin tried to console these desperate young people who had suddenly lost their way. Hitherto his contact with them had been almost wholly through Bianca. He now talked to each one separately and saw that among them were individuals of admirable character and talent who really possessed that intrepidness and sacrificial ardor which Bianca had only cleverly simulated.

The only disturbing elements in the group were the two brothers Josefovitch. They had earned money on the black market—not enough money to produce films on a grand scale but too much to put their hearts wholly into the efforts required by an artistic experiment. These two somber creatures were always close-shaven and yet with darkly shadowed cheeks. This, by the way, was their only common characteristic. In all other respects they were quite unlike. The older was plump like an Italian baritone, the younger thin and short. These two leaders suddenly lost all interest in the development of Jewish or Hebrew art the moment that Bianca left the group. All the others, the young people, who worked in factories by day, continued to come in the evening. Helfin promised to try to take the talented ones among them with him to Palestine as soon as his own plans matured. For others, too, for all who harbored a real determination, an attempt would be made to find decent provisions in other callings. None would remain excluded. The young people came to have confidence in him. Now only was he told about Bianca's unclean intrigues. She had always been an object of suspicion. But she had always talked herself out of everything. She was reproached with quite coarse and dangerous practices, with slanders against a possible rival, with acts of surreptitious vengeance, above all with machinations which had to do with political and criminal intrigues. Of course there was no factual proof of these serious accusations. But they whirred in the very air. Those who had known her here considered her capable of any enormity, so that Helfin concluded that he had gotten off rather easily and cheaply. Once he confronted her seriously with a whole register of lies which she had told him. She now had a contract with Pathé and simply laughed in his face. Was he, she asked, really so stupid or did he merely pretend to be so stupid as to have taken all her tall tales at face value?

It was at this time that a call came to him to return to the land. His friends wrote him that one, at least, of his old plans now seemed to be most promising and that his presence was necessary.

Since, moreover, he had collected the necessary material and had completed all the preliminary sketches, he did not hesitate to take the next plane. The last news he had of Bianca was that the older Josefovitch had shot at her and that she had sustained a slight and superficial injury. The Boulevard press printed her picture and a biography which was, of course, a brand-new one.

A brief sketch found among Helfin's papers seems to render the vision he had of Bianca immediately after his first Parisian sojourn. The sketch is headed "An Interesting Type of Female." Somewhat abbreviated, it reads as follows:

"One often hears this woman or that woman say, 'I rely exclusively on my feelings.' As a rule, women seem to think that that settles the matter. Who is going to be so sordid and prosaic as to adduce reason when the heart has spoken? Closely looked upon, however, that appeal to feeling doesn't solve the problem but only poses it. For now the question arises, 'What kind of a feeling is this feeling on which you depend? It may be a high and noble one; it may equally well be a coarse and common and malignant one. Maybe you're only bent upon your career, upon some sordid advantage. And you call that your feeling.' True enough, the depths of the soul are not accessible to the reason and at the core of life a mystery remains. The peculiar characteristic of the calculating woman—not of every such woman, but of a certain variety, which I am here rather scientifically analyzing—lies in the fact that she uses the noble and incalculable as a mask, behind which she pursues her advantage and her gain in the soberest and most businesslike fashion. She obeys her instinct. So she says and so it is. But whither has her instinct led her? Into some abyss, into the realm of tempests or misery or solitariness or despair? Not a bit of it. When the clouds have vanished we observe that our lady who has obeyed nothing but the instincts of her nerves and of her blood is suddenly in that precise situation in which she would have landed if she had plotted and planned with cool objectivity and precise foresight.

"Let us take an example. Enthusiastically this lady allies herself with a collective undertaking. Oh, it was her instinct that bade her do so. Everything connected with the collective is now sacred to her and every detail of the highest import. She makes something like a cult of it. The observer or contemporary would never understand why the woman in question spends many hours over memoranda and takes part in debates which have to do with the undertaking only quite indirectly or peripherally. And you will be answered that it is an irrational impulse, beyond all calculatedness, which binds this woman to a group of young people intent upon the pursuit of an artistic ideal. If one of the young people must buy a hat or has a slight cold or has some task to perform, the lady in question will find no way too long, no day too weary, to co-operate with this special preoccupation of her friend. She is the best of comrades; she strives zealously for the common goal, until . . .

"Oh yes, until, through the activity of the collective, her private aim has been attained and has been solidly founded. From that moment on, in which the collective enterprise can no longer serve her private purposes, it ceases to exist for her. It is completely blotted out. Other factors have now become more useful. And so the moment has come in which her feeling tells her that her path and the path of the collective diverge. And who gives you the right to assume that every step has been calculated? At one period her feeling told her that the collective was her place. Now her feeling tells her that she should be elsewhere. And feeling is inconstant, isn't it? Isn't that the very essence of feeling, that it is changeable, unaccountable, not subject to reason? Only trivial souls regard loyalty as a real value. Loyalty, duty, obligations—are these not stuffy moralistic notions? Is one really to force oneself to a task from which delight has fled and to which no powerful and genuine feeling impels one? Can you expect that? Not possibly! Nothing that is good, nothing that has integrity, can be brought about under external pressure. Do you want mere feeble attempts? Do you want mere pity and its empty phrases? And so, coolly and firmly, our strong and sincere woman says goodbye. Maybe you think that she used to give her whole energy to the collective because it was useful to her? Or that she leaves it now because it has ceased to be so. You could assume that, if she were the calculating type. But she never makes a reckoning; she follows her feelings, though it lead her to destruction. Is it her fault that, as luck would have it, she was not destroyed, that her personal advantage happened to coincide with her inner monition? That's accident, pure accident. And it's really rather a pity.

"This states a special case. There are ever so many people who plan their unclean plans. But to do that and at the same time to exclaim, 'Look, what an instinctual creature I am, what a second Villon I am—bursting with dreamy monitions and irrational instincts—a very nomad upon the earth, like Li Tai Pe, an adventurer, my whole heart one vague caprice'—to utter such cries and simultaneously to have nothing in mind but the mathematically accurate calculation toward the attainment of very mundane advantage, *that* is profoundly shameful and also not a little farcical.

"But if the woman in question is really skillful and knows how to play the role of innocence and feigns successfully to have no traffic with reality and to follow only the inner voice, there will always be simple souls who believe her and who whisper to each other, 'What a sensitive creature she is, so delicate, so full of mystery, so vulnerable.' They have no notion, these simple souls, what a brutal beast of prey their sensitive plant really was. Until they themselves feel the fangs. For it is each one's turn who has ever had any close relationship with the lady.

"One of her skills consists in what I should like to call 'simulated sheet lightning.' This irrational lady who is so proud of never following anything but the voice of her soul, whose monition coincides only accidentally with her personal advantage, this lady is the mistress of a very specific trick. She warns you against herself. Since she is so terribly devoid of reason, she beseeches you not to count on her. 'I am so whimsical, so changeable. Do not rely on me, my friend. You might regret it.' When you hear the lady talk that way, you think she must be a very monster of honesty and decency. You don't suspect that these occasional cries of warning are part of her well-tested and calculated system. Precisely because she warns you, you are rocked into security. 'I'm really not a bit of good. Be warned!' And you think, Someone who speaks so cannot be evil. And there you are —in the trap! 'Don't believe me,' says the sensitive plant, 'I'm fond of lying; I don't myself know where day ends and dream begins!' and you think, Dear harmless, poetic soul; the lies will of course concern trivialties—old, forgotten things. Then you are surprised when the lies ooze from the center.

"Fundamentally this is the Fascist method. Fascism, too, appeals to feeling and operates with filthy calculation. Fascism, too, can't get along without lies and acts as though it only occasionally toyed with them. And it is also particularly revolting when fascism pretends cleverness and warns of its own lies. Then arises that 'false sheet lightning,' like that of the female Fascists of the art of love and which is false because there is nothing genuine about this type, not to the very marrow."

To this notation Helfin had added a later marginal note as follows: "Perhaps too sharp. Perhaps even not wholly just. Disregards, perhaps, her subjective sufferings, her vain attempts to make a genuine talent prevail." A still later note in more recent ink adds: "Very difficult to judge—all that."

4.

And so Helfin returned to the land of Israel in 1945. A company was founded which acquired some well-situated lots on the dunes of the coast, south of Bat Yam. Here studios were to be built containing all the latest apparatus, in order that they might also be temporarily leased to foreign film concerns. The profits could then be used for the native films, which would admit of no compromise, which would have to unite documentary value with fresh and original delineation of life. And Lerski would magnificently do the photography.

The trademark "Palestinefilm" (there was no Israel yet) was to be the sign-manual of beauty, power, and profundity.

It was a great joy to Helfin that he could take with him to Palestine the best of the young people who had worked in the Paris studio. Of course they could come only as so-called "illegal" immigrants on wretched ships, with hunger and delay and heartache as their companions. This was all that Mr. Bevin permitted. But they did come, and the Haganah, the defense troops, brought them on boats to the coast by night, after they had slid down ropes against the sides of the ship.

Sincere efforts now set in, lacking Bianca's subtleties and striving for mere effect. Little Nechama with her touching childlike blue eyes; Zvi, the rather morose athlete (the comrades knew each other by their given names only); the curiously melancholy comedian Jonah, the sight of whose pitifully hollow cheeks evoked a lyrical laughter that was really a gentle compassion; and the uncomplicated, pure, carefree, gay Baruch (who could be confidently cast in the role of wise and dignified old men, precisely because his heart was so transparent)—these four indefatigable young people formed the kernel of the company with which Helfin began to work. Employment for their daily bread they found in the building trade, in tailors' shops, in a *Kibbutz* not far from Tel Aviv; but in all their free hours they gathered about their leader. They began to rehearse single scenes and actually to film them, these being scenes which followed the organic development of Helfin's scenario.

This scenario and its continuity was influenced by the developing events of the time. It portrayed a young man who begins as a friend of the English and who is decisively in favor of coming to an understanding with the Arabs. He is progressively forced into an anti-English attitude. For British policy tended more and more to be not only criminally selfish but also illogical and plainly foolish. To every sensible proposition of the Jews the Arabs replied with a brusque "No." No compromise. Everything! But this attitude was not native to them; they were incited to it by the British politicians. What those politicians had not foreseen was that the Arab League would, as it did, increase its chauvinistic demands to the point of danger to the whole empire. The Jews were ready to be Great Britain's reliable friend. It took a long time for the pro-British Jewish masses in the country to realize that they were being betrayed. And it was reserved to a British Labor government, which the Jews had enthusiastically welcomed, to deepen and sharpen this betrayal. The whole political cunning of British policy seemed to consist in the sly but stupid notion of leaving Palestine through the front door of Haifa, in order to re-enter it through the back door in Transjordanian disguise. Hence the abundant military aid that was given to Jordan; hence British officers openly led Abdullah's legion. At the same time the utterly shameless and not altogether unsuccessful attempt was made to persuade the world that England was neutral and had no desire except to establish peace. Obviously a bloody farce. The real state of affairs was unequivocally transmitted to Helfin through a minister of one of the British dominions who stopped one day in Palestine in the course of a flight over Asia and then told his story to an intimate friend of Helfin's in a distant land. The admirable High Commissioner Lord Gort, the hero of Malta, had invited him to dinner and told him sadly he would have to leave this beautiful country; he would have to resign, seeing that everything that he tried to do to exercise justice was countermanded from London with direct and open hostility to the Jews. The untimely death of Lord Gort who, like other just Englishmen, such as Commandant Wingate, had won the respectful affection of the Jews, prevented his issuing an open protest against the policy of London.

All this provided the background of the film. The hero himself, deeply attached to a beautiful Arab lady of noble birth, and a determined proponent of world peace, finds his wounded heart driven more and more toward war and the inhuman logic of war. His soul is torn asunder. He would like to lead two lives (the manuscript of the scenario bears at this point a more recent scribbled note consisting of the word "*Unambo*")—each the contrary of the other, yet both times lived by himself in a double corporeality, in order to avoid the conflict which he is unable to resolve within himself. One life is to be loving and upbuilding; the other is to be destructive. One is to be in the arms of peace; the other with a Sten gun in his hand. For both courses seem necessary to him. He sees no other way out. It is necessary to extend himself by doubling himself in order to have to forego neither eventuality. And all the while he knows that renunciation is his portion.

What was now needed in the plot of the film was a redemptive event which would permit the protagonist to return from this riven, twofold inner contradiction to the unity of nature. But Helfin could find no such event. And hence for the time being the story could not be brought to an end.

During this very period, while Helfin was working with his little group, discussing his notions with them, comparing one notion with another, the conditions in the country deteriorated day by day. The English foretold that the moment they left the land it would disintegrate into bloody confusion. It was easy enough for them to make this prophecy. They left no stone unturned to make it come true. It happened that Helfin was not entirely a novice in this matter. He had witnessed the establishment of a new state once before. He was capable of drawing comparisons. As a lad of eighteen, in 1918, he had been present in Prague when the Czechs established their new republic. The English could not persuade him that the transfer of a governmental apparatus, even an involuntary transfer, must needs issue in disorder and confusion. How nobly had the old Austrian Empire made the gesture of resignation. In completely good order and perfect condition it had placed in the hands of the revolutionary Czechs the offices, the railroads, the public institutions, so that the new masters were able quite comfortably to move into that complete dwelling prepared for them. The British, on the other hand, had the open intention of shattering everything before they left. With certain conspicuously honorable exceptions, the official British line was: We are arranging chaos. We'll show them how well off they were with us. For this purpose, months before the withdrawal, the London government carefully excluded Palestine from the sterling bloc in order to ruin the currency, shut down the postal service and all communication with the world by paralyzing the airports and air lines. At a later period we discovered that the captains of all British trading vessels had been forbidden to touch at Palestinian ports. On a single day twenty-two ships left the port of Tel Aviv. There was to be no food, no gas, no fuel. But promptly at the termination of the Mandate, on May 15, there was to be the invasion of five Arab armies, glittering with the latest armaments, against an unarmed people who had been able to do no more than improvise a feeble and supposedly illegal defense. Such was the plan. That Jewish intrepidity and self-sacrifice would conquer all difficulties and rout the plans of the cunning and build a state out of nothing under hostile bombardment and defend that state against a prodigious superiority of power—this is a historic event to which but few contemporaries beyond the land have yet ascribed its true measure of memorableness and human dignity.

In retrospect, history has an elevating aspect. It's quite another matter to be on the spot when the thing is brewing. Helfin, who had to undergo all these miseries, was not among the fearful ones, but he was equally far from that exorbitant confidence which acknowledges no obstacles. Moreover, the malice of the English politicians wounded him very intimately. For he had been a passionate lover of English culture, both older and more recent; he was devoted to the poetry of Donne and Blake and Eliot and to the art of the great British novelists.

Nor were there lacking sharp personal annoyances. A quarrel broke out in the film company on which any further realization of his plans depended. A real-estate man, a Mr. Schäftel from Petah Tikva, began to intrigue and wanted to get control of the whole business. This led to law suits, of which the end was unforeseeable. Everyone seemed to try to be more recalcitrant, more malicious and hostile, than the next one. Everyone was facing the war in common and the front against the enemy was solid and closed. But behind the lines things happened analogous to those later events in the courtyard of the Café Shalva where, in the midst of imminent danger, the tenants of the house and the guests of the coffeehouse fought each other over free entry to the bomb shelter.

There were things worse than such trivialities; worse evils raised their ugly heads. Helfin witnessed the upsurge not only of that heroic youth but of all in the land whose hearts had remained young. But he could not close his eyes to the old, old evil impulses which even at such times vegetate in the existence of a people. While the sons died on the fields of battle, there were those who speculated in hidden food stocks. It was incomprehensible; it was difficult to make these two elements converge into the same picture.

In the face of these painful experiences, too, Helfin would have preferred to be split into two separate beings, one of whom would have tasted to the full the pure ecstasy of witnessing the deeply proved moral power of his people, the while the other would have been glad to wend his way through all the dark alleys of national selfishness and to take upon himself and to consume all this moral soilure in order later to be the scapegoat which, driven out into the desert, purifies those who have been impure.

The acrid annoyances rose in his throat. He gasped for air. It is melancholy when a man like Helfin, who wants to love his fellow men, is recurrently faced by phenomena—such as the eternally debating, legally intricate, thievish Mr. Schäftel—that transform his feelings into a contemptuous hostility. There were moments when he wanted the whole thing to blow up. He was at times amazed at the coarseness of his own reaction to coarseness and vulgarity. He was frightened at the thought that low things could make him fall so low. He came to the conclusion that men of good will might easily harbor the evil of the evil within themselves.

Added to the real obstacles which blocked his path, like the intervention of the jovial, disgustingly healthy Mr. Schäftel, there were less serious disturbances which annoyed him within the framework of that crisis of the world and of the land which had been visibly approaching since 1946. Some of these little private disturbances had their slightly comic shadings. In his better moods he would laugh at them. But in his worse moods, although each in itself amounted to little, they seemed to add up to a burden to which his nervous system was no longer equal. There was, for instance, a little, currish movie critic named Siegmund Zemanek. Years before, he had done this man, as so many others, very considerable favors. He had worked his way through long, dull scenarios which were of no use at all and were still lying in the original drawers. He had done his best to improve and advise. Nor was this all. The then young man had been in a state of moral collapse. Helfin had lent him his support and had had to listen to his confessions, which were so turbid in character that he liked to forget them and had left them for years in the twilight of the subconscious. An insufferable moral decay had risen to him from Zemanek's talks which had filled him with vicarious shame. But since it seemed to ease the man if he could talk about these things uninhibitedly, he had let him go on; he had tried to conquer his own disgust and had even attempted to create some order within the disgusting confusions of this existence. He had, of course, kept the man's secrets strictly to himself; he had never betrayed him by the slightest indication. With a certain degree of satisfaction he had seen that the curative measures proposed by him had not been wholly in vain. Zemanek seemed to be able to enter upon a healthier and better life. Then he succeeded in escaping from the Hitler persecution. Like everyone saved from Europe, Helfin received him with sincere pleasure. And the first thing that called attention to the presence of Zemanek in the land was a furious attack upon Helfin. The latter was really surprised. He didn't expect this cur to use the little job of film reviewing, which he had dug up for himself, for a series of insults against Helfin and his whole career.

These poisonous attacks continued from week to week. They didn't hurt Helfin's reputation because they were too stupid. A stuffy pedant blew himself up and made a public show of his mixture of malice, ignorance, and frivolity. He was intoxicated with what a great artist has called "the stinging delight of knowing better" and characterized thus as the chief vice of the polemic critic. What was really interesting was the insolence and arrogance of the little "yapper," as he soon became currently known, since he voided his wild malice not only upon Helfin but upon a number of other men who had accomplished serious things. He was laughed at; no one took him seriously. When, at a meeting of the board of directors Schäftel once pointed out the attacks of Zemanek against Helfin as a motivation for a budgetary reduction, he was met with the observation that to be attacked by Zemanek was in the nature of a recommendation. So it wasn't any practical hurt that got under Helfin's skin. He also saw the psychical mechanism. Here is a young man who all his life has had the feeling that he was underestimated, neglected, maltreated. Finally he has a tribunal from which he may vent his stored-up bitterness. He has been irritated to the point where he desires to irritate others. You can't expect him not to take advantage of this opportunity.

"But why should he make me the target?" Helfin wondered. "Does he not owe me some gratitude? Is this it? He knows that he need not fear me. He knows that I am, if you like, too decent to betray any of his secrets in order to revenge myself in turn. Yet, although he knows that, he attacks not only my artistic ability but my character. Ought he not, at least, to refrain from that?" Stella, his wife, had often warned Helfin to have nothing to do with these distracted souls. His laughing answer had been, "But the others don't need me." But that had been in the days of his youth and freshness. Now the battle of life had somewhat wearied him and he saw that Stella had been right. And it was a fact that it was these unstable creatures who thrust themselves at him and gave him no rest—it was they who later on, under the most extravagant pretexts, would, so to speak, explode in his face. It was obvious that his helpful and at least apparently well-balanced and self-controlled character attracted them at first; later it became a veritable red rag. They arose against him under the sway of some hysterical rage. There seemed to be no exception to these disagreeable surprises. Zemanek was but an example of many.

What was the substance of the fellow's reproaches? That Helfin's films, which he examined pedantically from the beginning, from the early Viennese successes, were all of them too "slick" and pretty for the reason that Helfin, in his human capacity, too, was inclined to an "indecent prettification and obliteration of conflicts"; that, for this very reason, he was incapable of creating a contemporary work of art. He had no eye for evil. He was the untiring mediator, the builder of bridges across abysses which he had refused to examine. Objectively Helfin thought the accusation wholly groundless. Of course, every accusation, whether made by others or by oneself, can be morbidly read into some feeble element of any text or work. For we are none of us without faults. But that he was oblivious of the abysses toward which our age is rushing—that accusation could not in common honesty be aimed at him. To suffer under the injustice that prevailed and to foresee a fate even more evil—was this not the entire content of his life? Precisely this suffering and this foreseeing stamped his existence and gave his careworn countenance that permanent expression of affronted amazement. "Why, the damned man might as well accuse me of stealing silver spoons! When I consider what it costs me to sustain even an unstable equilibrium when from all sides the grimaces of historic horrors are turned upon me. . . . He ought to know that, the little cur. All those years ago, when I dragged him out of his catastrophe, he should have been able to perceive it." That very

99

catastrophe, which Zemanek thought he was confronting, Helfin had considered as not fateful or necessary but half a matter of mere words. For that reason the man had been rescued. His revenge now sprang from that whole source. At least subconsciously he was now ashamed of the fact that Helfin had been right and had been able to help him because the conflicts involved had been endurable. Therefore his polemic now declared that Helfin had no eye for the depths, that he was superficial and frivolous . . . Was he, Helfin, now to bare his breast and like Coriolanus show the wounds which bear witness to an inner torment in order to legitimize himself before this currish attack and to gain from somewhere his justification as a modern artist? Critics do from time to time harbor the illusion that they have the right to make such demands, and it was one of Helfin's deepest and sincerest sorrows that the Jews are a people of critics. Much as he loved his people, he saw a fault at this point which it would probably take the cleansing air of Palestine to remedy. "There is no other community," he used to say, "where polemics are so highly respected as among us. All one need do is to belittle everyone else and to represent oneself as the sole bearer of a fundamental sincerity and at once one has won the first skirmish for public respect, even though one's positive merits are indiscoverable. 'He is a sharp critic'—that suffices as a mark of praise for an aspiring writer or politician, irrespective of the justification of his criticism, or the lack of it. Quite so, amid primitive peoples, no one asks the head hunter on his return home whether he has acquired the scalps of his rivals in honorable conduct."

5.

In himself the yapping critic had no importance. He represented one of the minute details in Helfin's life. But taken in conjunction with other phenomena that accompanied his days the shamelessness of the weekly animadversions of Zemanek made their special contribution to the myth of our time—the myth of real or feigned ruthlessness. And Helfin had the feeling that he himself became more and more centrally and unescapably involved in this myth.

A delightful nine-year-old child, Dani L., gifted, amiable, handsome, had been killed by a fourteen-year-old ruffian. The thing had happened not far from Helfin's apartment. He had known the dear little boy; he had seen him grow up. . . . Once, at dusk, Dani had been humming a tune to a game which he had invented and which irritated the ill brought-up ruffian. "Shut your mouth!" Dani saw no reason to stop. A hurled stone struck his temple. A few hours later he was dead. . . .

There was brutality all over the world. But in Israel—at the least in Israel—unkindness of any sort should be taboo. Here should be offered an example to all the communities of earth. This should be the first step. And now in this state of war, in that inevitable coarsening that war induces, from the imitative games of children on, it could not be said that reality was even foreshadowing Helfin's ideal.

A motorcycle rattled by. Helfin, irritated to the core, concluded that the new myth of ruthlessness had no better symbols than two which were so frequent here—the cypress tree, which gives shade only to itself, keeping its coolness within and, on the other hand, the motorcycle, which makes a hundred times more noise than a single human being has the right to make as his contribution to the total noises of a given street. And no mechanic had yet tried, as had been done in the case of the typewriter, to diminish the racket. Obviously there was no financial incentive toward this mitigation. People seemed quite unconcerned as they operated these thunderous nuisances and struck by no shame when they broke down and stank and screamed with redoubled force.

For one who has not experienced it, it may seem strange to say that street noises or the noises occasioned by neighbors can become a desperate, vital problem. And yet it is so. It does no good to put cotton in your ears. The noise penetrates the cotton. Now there is in Tel Aviv no ordinance, as there was in the old Austrian Empire, which forbids or limits intrusions into the private domain of reasonable tranquillity. No attempt has even been made to formulate such an ordinance. Nothing has been done, in a word, to compensate for the notorious mistake of the Creator in that He gave us lids with which to exclude undesirable impressions from the field of vision but gave us no corresponding devices with which to close our ears. Well, a great many people in our land are blessed with such strong nerves that the yelling of children, the roaring of radios, the beating of carpets at any time of the day seem not to disturb them. And the mythic ruthlessness of our time renders them careless of the sensibilities of their neighbors.

Helfin knew, to be sure, that there was one way of protecting oneself from the noise, namely, to make oneself like it. Not to try to protect oneself at all. To accept it as an expression of the Mediterranean temperament, to regard it as justified, perhaps a little funny in its naïve arrogance, to make one's peace, with a sincerely smiling countenance, with the hostility which seems, but indeed only seems, to accompany the waves of tumult, seeing that it is actually true that the people who caused the noise desire no evil. They don't in the least desire to shorten your work or to destroy it. They are gay and simple souls. It is one's duty to determine to forgive them. They know not what they do. Wads of cotton and little stopples of wax cease to help; love and insight never cease. They affirm the evil and thus wave it away as with the gentle gesture of a magic wand. In the early years of his residence here, Helfin would have been capable of such an attitude of all-embracing love. Nowadays he was too weary, too exhausted by too many combats.

There was the trumpet tone of the uninhibited motor horns; there was the penetrating scream of little girls after their *Ima*— each little girl screaming peremptorily after *her* particular *Ima* until the *Ima* in question appeared at the window. (One of these little angels, having been shown a photograph of the skyscrapers of New York, demanded in amazement, "But how do you get your *Ima* to the window?") Above and beyond all these terrors there were, as far as Helfin was concerned, two very special ones. There was the thin man who kept hammering on the balcony to the right of him, and the other man on the ground floor across from him who maltreated a piano. He refused to call him a pianist. He called him the piano-er. The hammerer and the piano-er constituted a diabolical duet meant for his destruction. He tried for a long time to regard the phenomenon humorously, inventing still other names for these pertinacious ones. He hadn't, at first, wanted to make them elements in his myth of ruthlessness. The annoyance seemed too unimportant and too commonplace for that. He had thought this for a long time and he continued to think so when the duet became a trio and the critical yapper joined the hammerer and the piano-er to form a chorus as from the infernal regions. He had still laughed when he spoke of this new troika of Satan. His laughing mood had overlooked the circumstance that annoyances do not dull us but exhaust us. He came to see this; he came to see that the jeering masks of the goblins that surround us do not dissolve in mist. Time, on the contrary, lends them an increased corporeality and palpableness.

The hammerer seemed relatively harmless. He was an elderly man, a pious man with a skullcap on his head. The house next door, with its many apartments and many, many children, belonged to him. But on account of certain tricky paragraphs in the regulations concerning evictions, this poor man, who had arrived from America too late, was permitted to occupy only a single room in his own house. This single room and the balcony that belonged to him were separated by only a sort of air shaft from Helfin's apartment. Under these circumstances the pitiable landlord had determined to turn his balcony into a model balcony, into the balcony of all balconies, into a substitute room which would make any other dwelling superfluous. For this purpose he had erected a roof over the balcony, made partly of wooden boards and partly of rough sailcloth. At the sides he inserted glass windows into the new wooden walls. At the front, one half was left open. The balcony was to have all the advantages of a room, partly, indeed those of a kitchen, and yet remain a balcony in order to admit the air so necessary in Tel Aviv. At the same time the man erected projections reminiscent of dovecots to increase the available space. To the balustrade there was nailed a flower box, which was, however, not used for planting flowers but for storing cooking utensils. Round about the balustrade, storage cases were hung; in one corner was placed a folding chair.

These arrangements seemed to be endless; the old gentleman

was of a very inventive turn of mind. No sooner had one improvement been completed when he had a bright new idea. He executed all the work himself under the admiring and approving glances of his wife. Now he would be sawing and now he would be hammering. His own technical skill and his spontaneous delight in it spurred him on to ever renewed effort. It must be confessed that from the street the whole contraption made the impression of something botched and grotesque and could hardly be called agreeable to the eye. In fact the whole result was pitiful enough, measured by the expenditure of daily effort. It is likely, on the other hand, that the advantages and practical usefulness of the undertaking could be appreciated only from within. Moreover, the man was a perfectionist. The work was its own reward. Its inventor strove not after completion. His ideal was one commended by the loftiest thinkers, namely, the striving after a goal in infinity which one approaches without ever hoping to reach it. Was not the man a happy one? Sometimes when he saw him so zealous and so absorbed, Helfin was tempted to envy him. The only pity was that the enterprise involved so much noise. He did sometimes stop for a week or two. But then he started again with renewed enthusiasm, for hours at a time and inevitably during the period of the siesta. The blows of the hammer came in series and each series rose to a sharp crescendo. Then there was a pause. And again another series, beginning with a light tapping and increasing to a very thunder. There was no protection against this.

The case of the piano-er was essentially a graver one. Unless he happened to be out of town, he strummed from 7 o'clock in the morning until the evening hours, interrupting himself only briefly at noontime. He practiced; his industry was of a horrifying consistency. He was a powerful young man, but one of his legs was shorter than the other. Consequently he had been trained to be a music teacher in his *Kibbutz*. He was destined to this calling by no talent, but by his crippled condition. The *Kibbutz* was situated at the front. Hence the children had been evacuated and the young man conscientiously used his enforced holiday for his self-improvement. How could one bear to object to this situation? If ever Helfin complained to a neighbor that this kind of noise poisoned the very air, he received the tranquil answer, "What would you have? The man is trying to improve himself in his profession!" What could he do? Move? There were no available apartments except for millionaires. But the wrong notes struck again and again in the same places, both in the exercises and the sonatas, were literally unbearable. If the man were to practice for a hundred years he would not play a single page correctly, not to speak of expression or feeling. It was hopeless. At first Helfin thought that a whole school of music had moved into that ground-floor apartment and that several pupils were practicing in alternation. He could not believe that a single human being could make so many mistakes. It was for this reason that he couldn't possibly call the creature a pianist and invented the word piano-er. A very factory of cacophony had come into being over there. It was an abysmal misery. And the man was so serious in his efforts. If he couldn't manage a passage at all, he repeated it ten times, fifty times. There was something animal in this pertinacity. A fine notion of music this creature will communicate to the children! Helfin thought, and something flamed up in him. The gnawing worm! He should be obliterated! He will disgust his pupils with the very notion of music. And then there was another chain of feeling; for this, for this did Mozart, Haydn, Bach write; for this did their creations arise from gracious mood or holy dedication, that they might torture to death a sensitive ear with these tattered, riven fragments of their well-built forms. Music for home use—music for home misuse. Ought that not to be a punishable crime? Alas, it was clear to him in addition that his enemy had not scaled the heights of ruthlessness and meant, in fact, to be considerate. For, quite aside from the fact that he probably had no notion of the measure of Helfin's desperate situation—quite aside from that, he actually played softly. Well, this had its favorable aspects but also its unfavorable one. The favorable aspect was clear. The unfavorable aspect was this, that it prevented Helfin from crossing the street and begging for the cessation of the practice during a few hours. It prevented him from taking this measure. For how easily could the piano-er thereafter, out of spite or defiance, make the keys thunder. He was strong enough to do so. Thus a part of his power to hurt lay in his very reserve. It would be dangerous to issue a challenge. Unhappy experiences which Helfin had had in Vienna in similar cases made him extremely cautious. And so he saw himself perpetually caught in a very spider's web of eternally repeated and featureless tones. "I am being tickled to death by music; that's what's happening. That doesn't seem too bad in a mere description. But one must bring home to oneself the uninterrupted character of the tickling impingement on the nerves. Uninterrupted!" The thing made him ill; it gave rise to hallucinations. The hideous sounds arose in his soul even when the teacher did not sit at his horrible untuned piano. The merciless irritation of the nerve assumed the nightmare vision that the piano was playing on all by itself. It was so saturated with cacophony that it oozed it out continuously into the circumambient air.

And yet—there was a moment in Helfin's life in which he had welcomed the man's playing of scales as something beneficent.

When he came back from his second sojourn in Paris and his taxi turned the corner into the familiar street and stopped and out of that ground-floor cavern those dreadful hesitating scales resounded, as though nothing had happened, as though nothing had changed, Helfin was, for the minute and the hour, tempted to press to his bosom this caricature of art as a symbol of security. He welcomed the old piano-er and melted in tenderness over his stubborn industry. For had not the European press stated that the city was surrounded, encircled along the line of Ashdod-Lud-Nathania, and was being reduced to rubble by bombs and mortars? And now all was normal, including his tormentor across the street.

Next day he hated both him and the hammerer as he had always done. And hated them more from hour to hour.

In addition the kine of the Nile were again swathing the sky, squeezing out one's breath, cooking the blood in one's veins as well as the sweat which seemed to flow uninterruptedly from lip and nape, turning the brain into a kind of paste, of which the odor seemed to hover over the weary senses.

Early one afternoon Helfin came out of a very exhausting meeting of the directorate of his film company. He had had to fight senseless and unintelligent objections. He needed repose and lay down on a sofa in the dimmed room. Mr. Schäftel of Petah-Tikvah, the owner of the majority stock, had preferred not to come to the meeting at all. He had been represented by his manager, a quite elegant gentleman named Goldgarten. The latter had merely shrugged his shoulders at everything. It was a deliberate maneuver to waste time. And precisely on this occasion Helfin had wanted to have a serious private conference with Schäftel. For the eventuality that the conference might last late, he had even reserved a room in the hotel Armon for the man and had expected him with assurance. And Schäftel had seemed to promise. Then he had failed him. Ah, he must rest and forget everything for at least half an hour! Bang-bang-bang-bang! The hammerer was at his crescendo. And immediately thereafter the piano-er began.

There had been four air-raid alarms during the previous night. Each time one had to be vigilant for an hour or half an hour and wait for the hits, the farther, the nearer, and encourage the frightened people in the shelter. Fine. That was one's duty. But now he was worn out and needed a little sleep. And just that was impossible.

The excessive weariness oppressed him and pumped up melancholy thoughts with every heartbeat. Was it not lamentable beyond all measure, the story which a musician had told him today? The musician accompanied a singer on the accordion; they were both being sent from hospital to hospital to cheer the wounded. One of the young patients had said in the seriousness of his honest enthusiasm, "I'm so sorry I can't applaud. They amputated both of my hands."

The musician, who saw how deeply Helfin was moved, had felt called upon to give him a pleasant piece of news: "Have you heard that we now have a secret road to Jerusalem? Across the mountains, starting from Hulda! Every night our army is taking foodstuffs and fuel to Jerusalem. Even cannons. Our soldiers call it the Burma Road." Helfin didn't believe it. It belonged among all those rumors with which people tried to ease their lives. Alas, Jerusalem was surrounded, cut off from Jewish territory, lost. Jerusalem was starving and had to fight without artillery and was thus condemned to a kind of suicide. The enemy could crush it with impunity. This was the fourth week of the war and the horrors were increasing. The hatefulness of war! And yet we could do no other; we had to defend our lives. Four weeks and the United Nations in faraway "Lake Unsuccess," as we now called it, had not been able to bring themselves to stamp the Arabs as aggressors, although nothing in the whole world could ever have been clearer. The British government invented new trickeries daily to keep this declaration from being made and thus to protect the murderers of the peace from any sanctions. What were they waiting for? A cease fire within twenty-four hours had been commanded for both Jews and Arabs. The Jews had obeyed. They had obeyed before the necessary hour; for it had turned out that the telegram had been circuitously sent. It had been idiotically relayed via Cairo. There it had been kept. Was that really a mistake or an accident? It became clear too late that the U.N. had asked only for consent to a cease fire. So the Jews said yes and acted upon that assent, which caused them first of all to lose several important front-line positions. The Arabs, of course, didn't give a damn for the monition of the U.N. They answered with extreme coolness: No armistice until the Jews are destroyed. This was the moment, then, to apply sanctions, was it not? Not a bit of it. Instead there came a feeble question from the U.N.: What did the Arabs really mean and what had they meant to convey by their refusal?

Was it not evident that all these juridical contortions encouraged the aggressors and caused the death of hundreds of young men on both sides?

A soft sizzling noise, as though far in the sky something were being cooked, say, a soup—we know what kind of a soup. During his errands in the forenoon Helfin had had to plunge into shelters twice and at the very last moment. The bombs were already screaming.

At luncheon he had read in the paper the following report from London: "To an interpellation in Parliament, Mr. Bevin replied that he did not believe that the recognition of Israel on the part of England would diminish the tension in Palestine. He added that England was still working at a peaceful solution of the Palestinian question which would be equally satisfactory to Arabs and Jews."

Well, what did they really intend? England is still working: Peace, peaceful solution, satisfactory. Soft, gentle words, and it's nobody's fault if meantime a few hundred more of these magnificent young people fall and others can't applaud because their hands have been amputated.

A nausea had risen in him. He pushed his food aside.

His vitality seemed utterly consumed. His always too sensitive ears seemed to hear the continuous purring of planes. Were they hostile planes? Were they *shelanu*—our own? Difficult to distinguish, or quite impossible, except by night when our planes flew low with red and blue lights. The sound of an approaching motorcar can be easily distinguished from that of an approaching plane after some practice. It approaches rapidly and flits swiftly by. On the contrary the noise of a plane increases very gradually; often one hears a plane but sees nothing. It is a steady steely shrilling, to which is added, as it approaches, a dark, deep, powerful contrapuntal bass. If the bass approaches baritone range the danger increases. As the plane withdraws the bass sinks chromatically. Expertness is needed. But there are other cases in which a plane which is directly above your head emits a sound so gentle as though it were far away and harmless. The point is that it's very high up and that you were never nearer death. "In this war," Helfin reflected, "I haven't experienced death, but certainly the beckoning of many little deaths." Strictly speaking, he did not fear death, but this constant tension of the expectation of death was a kind of torment to which he was scarcely equal any more. Added to all this was the coarse irony of false resemblances. There were so many motors about. The approach of a car often resembled a siren; the hateful motorcycle rattled like antiaircraft fire. In addition, children had invented a very clever way of imitating to the very point of deception the rising and falling howl of sirens. It made one shudder to the marrow. In reality you should have been smiling— if you could still smile.

The same paper in which Helfin had read the report of the session of Parliament had served up as a kind of dessert Zemanek's tenth or eleventh article against Helfin and his art. At this time he wished he had that fellow's troubles. He didn't even read the article. He was too sad. Usually, such was his experience, people have no conception of the state of mind of anyone with whom they have dealings. Dully they assume that the other one is serene and therefore vulnerable. No one imagines that the other's soul is seething, that he may be fighting to keep himself from the extremity of despair, that he is avoiding an ultimate crisis by the breadth of a hair and that one additional drop of poison may suffice to make the pitcher of his wretchedness overflow.

Nevertheless, on the way home, Helfin had smiled to himself, reflecting on the saying of one of the latest humorists, "I haven't done you so much kindness yet that you should treat me so maliciously."

Now he had a headache. Now he wanted to rest at home. And now those two raged—the hammerer and the piano-er.

The mail lay on his desk. Out of the first envelope he took the article of Zemanek marked with a red pencil. That was the last blow, that amiable attention on the part of an unknown correspondent. Trivial as the bit of malice was, it led to an eruption. His three tormentors in close co-operation! Couldn't he get rid of them? Couldn't he grind them into the earth with his heel? His hand twitched toward the red switch of the puppet stage. Perhaps there was a way out. One ought really to try it. Perhaps one could annihilate the tormentors round about.

He approached the little stage. "May they all be buried six feet deep!" He really articulated the imprecation, and that seemed to ease his heart.

He stopped, somewhat ashamed of himself, trying to curb the unworthy impulses. Frightful how angry and evil I, too, can be. And then I complain of others? But why should I alone always be the considerate one? Such was his next thought. It is I who make myself ridiculous. He thought of the wretched currish critic. He blames me for being too tranquil and well disposed—of being so to the point of indecency. He'll find out that I can be quite as tumultuous as he if once I cease to resist. Without half trying I can be as common as he. He'll find out. I'll destroy him. A black mist rose before his eyes. I can recall to this day how he used to try my patience all those years ago. "I know I torment you, Mr. Helfin. You're so kind. You forgive my importunity." Instead of simply *not* being so importunate, not tormenting me, keeping his mouth shut, he emphasized his importunity by babbling about it and making it an even heavier burden to bear. "You're such a good man." How I detested this line of talk. With it he burrowed into me. "There is chaos in me. But you, with your well-tempered view of things . . ." The scoundrel! The louse! I'll teach him to know how good I am and how well tempered!

He admonished himself to further reflection. The fellow isn't worth my anger. And in the last analysis he may really believe that he is right, that he is being objective and merely showing me my place. Do I expect him to praise faults which his lack of understanding seems really to reveal? Do I expect praise as a matter of gratitude? Certainly I don't. All that I demand of gratitude is a decent tone.

The worst of it was that, of all the painful blows of fate that he endured, it was the most insignificant, relatively the most unimportant, that was to persuade him to seek refuge with the Unambo machine as a last resort. It was not, alas, the political situation with its naked force and its lies that brought him to this point but the private attack of a seventh-rate scribbler. That was unworthy of him; that was contemptible. He must not fall so low.

He found himself growing calmer.

He didn't like that either. Tranquil and harmonious again. Thus he reproached himself. Suddenly he stood still in the middle of the room. Other reflections pursued him. "Let me suppose . . ." He had forgotten the real significance of the apparatus. He had forgotten the "if," the yearning conditional propositions of which the fat man was so fond. At this bar one could drink the waters of two variations of life. One needed not to decide. That was the great thing. *If* I wish death and destruction to my enemy, if once I imitate the badness of his heart and do not curb my tongue at the last moment—then so-and-so will come about. I will overthrow him and plunge him to the earth. If, on the other hand, I restrain myself once more and keep my mouth shut and undertake nothing against him—then I am once more a gentleman, one who does the right thing, one who doesn't over-emphasize his own importance. . . . But I can do a third thing: I can turn the red switch. Then I'll have both lives. I'll be attuned to both and experience both. Life will be played on both of the stages. That is Unambo, a sure-fire hit, as the fat man insisted. Then I don't have to choose. The painful contradiction between yes and no is spared me. I can yield and not yield at the same time; I can be indecent and decent too. I don't have to go on sitting in the red-hot belly of the steer of Phalaris and roar and be purified. Let the others be roasted now—those who have always tormented me. . . .

And Helfin grasped the switch, which seemed to grow round and smooth in his hand. Hidden wheels were set in motion and began to whir and executed with great ease and swiftness the complicated notions which Helfin had in mind.

Simultaneously with the rattling of the little machine there came to his ears the loud ringing of the bell of his apartment.

It was as though, by pressing and turning the switch, Helfin had also set in motion the ringing of the bell at his door. The gentle whirring and the far, shrill bell melted curiously into a single vibrating noise.

In his excitement, moreover, he had forgotten to use the dark-green monocle. But this trickery seemed unnecessary. For already the little model stage rose as though on wings. It floated upward and seemed to melt into thin air. The meshes of the fabric dissolved into foam. Nothing was any longer visible but the red switch, the eye of the constellation of Scorpio.

Helfin was shocked and raised his hand to his forehead. It seemed to him as though his finger gleamed red. He looked at it closely. Had it become transparent already? Did the magic work so swiftly? No. It was a mere visual delusion. Stupid of him!

The outside bell continued to ring. Dvora opened the door, though she had orders to admit no one at this time of the day.

The sound of Dvora's calm voice eased Helfin's tension. He was imagining all kinds of nonsense. He had better see a psychiatrist. Of course, it was true that the little stage had vanished. Probably the strong breeze that blew in from the balcony at this hour had lifted it from its nail on the wall above the black piano and blown it into the garden. There was nothing much to that. He chid himself for letting this kind of fantastic nonsense add to the necessary and unavoidable excitement of life.

In the anteroom he heard a second voice, a deep, very resonant, well-known voice.

He opened the door of his study. "You might as well come in, Miss Petry."

A reproachful look informed Dvora that his command was not all-inclusive.

He greeted this guest in a more friendly fashion than he had decided to do in the eventuality of her appearance. He knew that she had arrived in the country. Sooner or later she would try to see him; there was no surprise in that. Now, at this moment, it almost seemed to him as though her coming relieved him of a certain anxiety. Possibly he had feared that the accursed little theater or, rather, the use of the switch, would entail some fatal consequences having to do with one of his three tormentors. He now thought he saw how stupid and superstitious his suspicion had been. Bianca Petry's visit had, quite obviously, nothing to do with the three trivial devils. Foolish as he at once judged his illusory notion of the magic influence of Unambo on the fate of irrelevant people, indeed of any influence, to be, yet he breathed more easily.

"How are you? When did you get here?" Easily and firmly he uttered the conventional phrases.

Somewhat later Dvora brought in the iced coffee and two cups. Helfin and Bianca were absorbed in their conversation. Dvora, having deposited the tray, asked for the afternoon off. Her son was back from the front for a brief furlough; a neighbor had just conveyed the happy news. Gratefully she took her leave.

When the door of the anteroom was closed, Bianca pressed Helfin's hand encouragingly or even challengingly. As one can fail intentionally to see or to hear things, so one can also fail to feel them. With a courteous gesture Helfin bade Bianca sit on the sofa. He himself remained at an appropriate distance from her in his chair.

CHAPTER FOUR

In which the Unambo machine fails to bring all the expected easements; in which, on the other hand, the "Burma Road" proves to be more real than had been assumed.

1.

Without any preliminary nonsense, Bianca informed him that all her Parisian plans had ended in complete bankruptcy. "An incomparable fiasco," she called it sincerely. Nothing at all had come of her contracts with Pathé, with René Clair, or of any other opportunities. "You are my only hope—as in reality you always were. I simply left the right road. Will you be able to forgive me?"

"You mean you are returning to the Hebrew film. How patriotic! Three cheers!"

"It's not handsome of you to make fun of me. What more can I do than say that I committed a folly as big as the Eiffel Tower?"

"A little *puncher* as we call it here," he observed. And he couldn't refrain from adding how curious it was that even the screaming publicity and the pictures in the Parisian press occasioned by the assault of Mr. Josefovitch had been so brief in their effectiveness. "That's the way it was," she agreed sadly. She didn't pretend at all; she confessed her entire disappointment. This pervasive minor mood suited her very well. She had on a dark dress and a swaying little black hat on her blond hair, which had recently been done. Her cheeks were pale. She was stylized a little like a young widow who doesn't want to seem to be gay too soon. Helfin had to admit that she didn't make a bad impression.

He had never underestimated her acting talent. Certain plans that he had would be more easily realizable with her than without her.

With her unerring instinct she read his thoughts in his eyes. "I know you'll understand. Oh, I did annoy you. But you will not take it out on me. What I'm afraid of is that young crowd in the studio. Wonderful people, I always knew that, but quite unforgiving, I am sure."

"You don't have to worry about them another minute."

"But I know they won't want to work with me. Frankly, I'd feel the same way . . ."

"The four of them have long been mobilized."

Bianca's face showed amazement. Something of the old comradeship seemed to awaken in her. "Where are they?" she asked solicitously. "Do you know anything exact about them?"

"Not very much. It's forbidden, you know," Helfin replied. He was constantly corresponding with his young friends but saw no reason for passing on superfluous information. "Nechama works with the Women's Battalion. Zvi is a *chablan*, a sapper who places mines and blows up Arab fortifications. He is as intrepid as ever. Baruch is with my nephew somewhere around Latrun; the melancholy Jonah is helping in the melancholy task of defending Jerusalem."

"Why so melancholy?"

"Because it's hopeless. I'm afraid Jerusalem must be given up. It is sealed off from the world. Help cannot reach it. Our friends are starving." His sorrowful excitement, momentarily repressed, or at least diverted by Bianca's appearance, rose within him again to the very brim of his being. "What is worse, at this season of intense heat they have a single liter of water per capita per day— one liter both for washing and for drinking. Try to imagine that. And no electric current. It's easy to say the words. But imagine the long evenings and not being able to read. But there are more tragic consequences. The bloodbank in the hospital cannot be refrigerated; the wounded die because transfusions are impossible or because splinters from grenades wander about in their bodies since no X-rays can be taken. Consider how many young lives could have been saved. Well, what follows from all that? The teacher's place is in the school. I am enlisting within a very few days. My mind is made up. I can't endure being an onlooker any more."

"You'll do no such thing," she exclaimed and arose from the

sofa, as though to diminish the distance between the seat assigned to her and his armchair. Was it her intention, he wondered, to throw herself with this cry upon his neck and ask him to let bygones be bygones? His cold eyes, keeping her at a distance, warned her not to attempt to exploit the apparent appropriateness of the moment. She stretched out her beautiful slender white hand for something. Then she sat down again on the sofa, moving back and forth with almost a touch of awkwardness. Her face had flushed red. Involuntarily he accepted that as a kind of tribute. I did put you out of countenance a bit, you little bitch, he said to himself. I don't care whether you've been play acting or not. Even if it's pretense, it still shows that I forced you to use the most violent means. An awkwardness on the part of Bianca Petry! What sense does that make? I could simply say to her, "Why do you pretend excitement, solicitude, almost love, when the thing is so simple? You need me in order to go on working at all. Of all your opportunities I represent the only remaining one." Nevertheless he knew that this conception might not cover the whole case. There had always been an element of natural liking for him at work in her. Not a great deal. But this very parsimony of feeling had its own attractiveness which he rather enjoyed. This blending of a sparing element of affection with so powerful an egoism was perhaps her most personal note—the last result of her spiritually frozen state. "Don't you want to have some coffee?" he asked her, pointing to the little table that stood between them. He lifted his own cup to his lips. "It's ice-cold," he said with a shadow of pride in Dvora and his well-ordered household, surprised all the while at the temptation to express anything so trivial.

"Are you still so fond of playing the piano?" she now asked with a glance at the black instrument.

She restrained herself and became objective. That was part of her technique. He, too, had said something tranquil and remote. But he had done it involuntarily. Bianca's principle was never to let the other person exceed in coolness; it was herself who, being the cooler, retained the upper hand.

An obscene thought occurred to him. On that occasion when she had gotten the better of him sexually, she had made something like a scientific observation. Pseudo-science at so burning a moment. Very stimulating. Revoltingly stimulating. "Among the Chinese, the woman takes the initiative," she had whispered on that occasion. He didn't know why just that occurred to him at this moment when she tried to ease the tension between them by her remark about his fondness for the piano. That had certainly been calculated too. Whether she suddenly burst out into passion or unexpectedly poured ice into one's veins, everything was calculated. At the same time she was not wholly wrong when with her own kind of frankness—a strange and not easily definable variety of frankness—she often insisted that she was quite uncalculating, that she always did the next best thing that popped into her head. "You yourself are not calculating," he had once said to her. "But something in you, something like a mechanism, calculates uninterruptedly in its own frightful way." Ah well, he had been warned long ago. He knew that he must be on his guard.

"Oh yes, I've recently practiced from time to time," he replied. In order not to hear the piano-er who, by the way, didn't permit the rival playing to disturb him at all, he had stormed through the two Chopin études in G major. "Would you like to hear?" She nodded. He played about twenty measures.

At this moment the outside bell rang.

In spite of everything, this seemed to him an interruption. Bianca's visit had, evidently, not displeased him.

He went to the anteroom and opened the door. At the threshold stood his nephew, Gad Reis. He had on his steel helmet; he was lowering his knapsack from his back; he was one mass of sweat and whitish dust.

"I can hardly. . . ." Helfin was in some confusion, although he was delighted to see the boy. "I am at an important conference. Can't you come back tomorrow? Are you staying for a few days?"

"Staying till tomorrow night," Gad replied without a trace of surprise or irritation. He smiled and showed his handsome white teeth.

"Go to the Hotel Armon. A room is reserved in my name there. It was to be occupied by Mr. Schäftel from Petah-Tikvah. Tell them at the Armon that Schäftel isn't coming; you are to occupy the room. Right?"

Gad nodded gaily.

"Room with private bath," Helfin added cheeringly. "And tomorrow morning you'll turn up here, won't you?" Quickly he took leave of the boy. He saw how Gad readjusted his knapsack on his shoulders.

"Who was that?" Bianca asked in a rather disturbed way when he re-entered the room.

"Nothing. A registered letter." An inner voice bade him not to permit the slightest contact between Bianca and his nephew. Then he returned to the subject of their talk which hung in the air between them. Gad's turning up had thrown a renewed and powerful light upon it. Closing the piano, he said more to himself than to Bianca, "The time for being an observer is over. One's duty admits of no question. Whoever can still fight—his place is on the field of battle."

"Provided that there are not more important duties behind the lines."

"Oh yes, I know this talk about art in general, and art for our boys. I hear it all day long. Are these things really important at this moment?"

"Absolutely," Bianca cried.

Helfin was amused by this cry of hers. It was the self-defense of the little bitch. But quickly he returned to his point of view. "To tell you the truth, it's not only a question of one's duty. Life is full of horrors. What meaning has it that makes it worthy of being guarded? To what end? It should be thrown away and one should be glad to be able to throw it away for a great cause."

That was quite after her taste. It reminded her of that poem of Li Tai Pe which she was fond of quoting: "A human being who, in this life, wavers between yearning and fulfillment cannot do other than throw himself into the boat of his destiny and, the while his hair streams in the wind, give himself up to the whim of the elements."

"That, really, describes you very well," he observed. She did not perceive his irony. What disturbed him ever so slightly was that this irony, thoroughly understandable as it was, had yet a small element of the unjustifiable. For in reality it was not to be denied that Bianca had something of the true adventurer within her and that, at times, lashed by her own strong temperament, she went ahead regardless and did indeed yield herself up to the whim of the elements. More than once this had landed her in utter misery. However much might have been invented in her various stories about herself, the situation in which she had gambled away everything was too recurrent not to be genuine in character. Nevertheless, to name in one breath this attitude and the poet Li Tai Pe—there was something positively indecent about it.

Bianca's latest story from Paris had to do with a wealthy Lesbian, a rich woman, a painter by profession, who had used her as a model. The Lesbian had fallen in love with the model. She had ended by keeping her imprisoned in her villa in Passy. Bianca had been watched by three female guards. "But you know what I'm capable of, when I put my mind to it. I pretended to try to seduce one of the three. That's the way I got out." Helfin seemed vaguely to remember that she had once told him a very similar story in connection with a count, the ancient lord of an estate somewhere in Italy. It was the same plot of imprisonment, love, and flight. Perhaps the two fables, variously adorned, could be traced back to a single experience. In the case of Bianca one never knew. "But I talk about myself the whole time," she said. "How about yourself?" He had nothing of equal picturesqueness to report. His three tormentors were rather colorless and trivial. He made brief mention of them. Mr. Schäftel, too, was probably an ordinary shabby speculator.

The little that he told her she absorbed with delicate sympathy, with genuine comprehension. She had the right sense of its inner structure. He could not deny that this did him good. After all, here was someone who knew his sorrows; who remembered the pattern that he was accustomed to make of them, who, in a word, took his suffering seriously. An accurate memory is sometimes more characteristic of the inner interest which one human being takes in another than all the ephemeral assertions of sympathy, however kindly or even passionate. Bianca remained quite objective. "There is that game of chess which fate plays against you. How well I remember. You never make a false move; nevertheless you lose every game."

"How strange. I thought of that symbol just the other day," he admitted.

"It is a powerful image. You used it once to me in Paris. I've never been able to forget it." Her appreciation was frank. "The image fits me too, you know. But one shouldn't talk too much about these things. Self-analysis robs one of the last vestige of health."

"The whole most modern school of psychological thought affirms the exact contrary."

"Well, perhaps I don't mean it quite as I expressed it." With her own characteristic uncertainty she glided, elegant as a will-o'-the-wisp, across depths and abysses. "Sometimes one resists something in order to exhaust its pleasures or advantages thereafter. In spite of all precautions, we did analyze each other a good bit. I do still think it rather unwise to get too intimate either with one's self or someone else. It's the same thing; it's really not good for much. It's so misleading. Don't you think so too?" She looked at him as though in need of help; she had an air of humility. "I prefer the notion of two constellations, each having its inner movement. But their course is parallel; their aspiration is so too. But neither impinges upon the other and neither hinders the other. Don't you remember that is what we two once desired? We made a compact of that kind at the time when I began to talk you out of your infatuation for your beautiful Greek. By the way, did you ever hear from her again?"

With a good conscience he could say no.

"I suppose you've had many other experiences?" she asked with a sigh of curiosity, not untinged by irony.

He didn't think it necessary to answer. As a matter of fact, during the three years since Bianca had broken the ban, he had honored the memory of Stella abstractly but not physically. At this moment, however, he did not regret his incontinence, though he had often sorrowed over it and felt it to be a weakness. For at this moment, in contradiction to his frequent moods of regret, the experiences he had had with women gave him a sense of security in the face of this dangerous female and erected, so to speak, a protective wall between himself and her.

With penetrating intelligence, the while her gray eyes glittered like two fiery jewels, she repeated to him that conviction which, as he had told her in Paris, he had drawn from the deepest strata of his life, namely, that the world tormented him too sorely. She repeated his analysis very accurately. That flattered him. And she spoke tenderly. Her deep voice seemed to weave a web in the space between the sofa and the chair. And this dark voice had often an element of gentleness even when its utterances were reserved, moderate, thoughtful. Indeed, it was at such moments that, in contrast to the content of its utterance, it sounded so gentle. And Helfin had been so wounded by the infuriating annoyances of recent weeks, he was at so low a state, that he needed desperately a strengthening of his ego. It was this that she offered him. He had not sought it, but he could not now refuse it. The weariness which made him yield to this lure was neither wise nor good. He was aware of that and yielded just the same.

Very carefully Bianca repeated what she had heard him say on other occasions: "Most people who suffer shipwreck or, at all events, endure unusual difficulties, carry the enemy within— throwbacks to unresolved conflicts, to old, half-forgotten fissures of the soul. The remarkable thing about you, Paul, is the fact that you have made your peace with this inner enemy. It took you long years of difficult struggles. But you did succeed. You have fewer inner conflicts than anyone I know. Energy and decency are well balanced in you. There is no excess of energy, as, alas, in me. But there is no mere drifting either. Awareness of mind and imagination are in equilibrium."

"Stop, stop. Don't exaggerate!" He was irritated. It occurred to him how just a little while ago, before he had turned that switch, he had discovered a very contemptible characteristic in himself. Not the great sorrows of the time, not the world crisis, a small and private annoyance had given him the final impulse. . . .

"Wait a minute. I'm coming to the chief thing. I'm not in the least trying to pay you compliments. On the contrary! The chief observation to make is this—that you are nevertheless unhappy. That's it. Fate tries to take away from you by outer circumstances the rewards of your spiritual triumph. There they are— the game of chess, the hammerer, the piano-er, the yapper—these are all symbols of one and the same state of affairs." She spoke weightily, calmly, seriously, like a physician who explains a diagnosis.

"And why should that happen to me?" he asked almost fearfully. It was as though an echo was expected to know more than the voice which it mimicked.

"The objection is obvious. To seem so excellent to oneself, so flawless, just that is the sin of self-righteousness to which the most cruel punishment is meted out." She had gotten all that from him too. But she gave it back to him cleverly and at the right moment.

"Precisely. One always sees oneself falsely. In his confessions Rousseau accuses himself of all kinds of horrors; in the end he represents himself as the best of men."

"Who is Rousseau?" Bianca asked.

"Don't you know?"

She laughed heartily. "No." Her lack of education was astonishing. He remembered that, of course. Proudly she waved her ignorance like a banner. What she valued in herself, as in others, was the power of presage, of sure intuition, of instinctive understanding. Not education. Sometimes she would explain that very convincingly, with an insight akin to genius. He was not unaware of the extreme fallacy of her attitude. But this thing was so complicated that it was difficult to put into words. In order to recognize it clearly one would have to descend very profoundly below conventions of both thought and fact. Once, in Paris, when he had found out that she had not the slightest notion in what continent Capetown was situated, she had said, "We didn't study geography in Bergen-Belsen." The thrust had gone straight to his heart. She liked to twist the arrow in the wound. A lot of learning made people superficial, she would say. She was fond of five or six writers—Villon, Rimbaud, Li Tai Pe, Lawrence—"because they are intertwined with my very life. What do I need the rest for, or any additional knowledge?" For the moment in question there would be something convincing in those words of hers, especially if she let her eyes glitter. On this occasion she was not in one of her arrogant moods. "I just happen to be stupid," she declared. And that, as he knew, was the worst lie of all.

He had the impulse to complete his condemnation of her. "A distrustful observer," said he, "would conclude that this, perhaps, is your fundamental fault, the empty fiction of your life, that you seek the source of all your failings and failures outside of your self instead of within you."

"But since you yourself are this observer," she replied skillfully, "you allow for this fundamental error in your accounting of me. You correct it and so you render it harmless. But even this does you no good. The old, old riddle remains. The whole world is in a conspiracy against you. Why?" She fell silent. And as though she had only now realized the fact that the space between them was the only thing that separated them and that it was, so to speak, only the broad carpet which seemed to have transformed itself into a source of division between them—since she seemed to perceive that suddenly, she came quite frankly over to him and sat on the arm of his chair. She took his hand between hers. "Poor Paul!"

That was exactly what he had wanted to hear. Or so it seemed to him. He was more grateful to her for these words than for all her analytical exertions, although he appreciated those too. He kissed her hand. He did not speak.

"If you knew the devastations caused within me by all the outer misfortunes," he said after a while. "I am disgusted not with the world but with my own miseries and my own errors." His eyes were moist while she stroked his hair. "I have become a horror to myself. These eternal repetitions. A blow falls. You resign yourself; you pull yourself together; you get the better of it and re-gain your equilibrium. A new blow falls. You run through the same moral gamut on to the next blow. How sterile that is! And what an unbearable bore, once you know how it will continue. This everlasting seeking of consolation or consoling oneself—just that constitutes the inconsolable. To be pursued by misfortune as I have been—and our entire generation—that shoots beyond the boundaries of the moral."

Her comment was that she did not only understand him thoroughly but that she shared his feeling.

His mood became more and more drenched in woe. He uttered all his lamentations. He told her of the events of the past few weeks. "Just think of those ten or eleven articles that man has written in abuse of me, so poisonous and so wholly unprovoked. At this time, of all times, when one needs every ounce of strength to keep oneself going. That wretched creature!" How good those caressing fingers felt on his hair. Thus does a mother console her child, not asking after right or wrong, loving the child in either case. He cast aside his last reserve. He told her the story of Zemanek—how, years ago, in Vienna and Salzburg, the man had been a burden and he had not been able to get rid of him. In his high, hoarse, excited voice the man had confessed to him his state of moral decay. The reason was a strange one. For years he had been living in a sexual union with an elderly woman who was next door to a moron. But he had not been able to disentangle himself from this relationship. He had bought a revolver—for himself, for her, for both. He could no longer endure this obscenely unnatural situation which was both curse and shame. Helfin had tried to mitigate his despair. In true pastoral fashion he had made practical suggestions. He advised him to leave the woman's house, to move to another city. Zemanek had resisted this advice with a mixture of stubbornness and whining. But he had come back for the advice which seemed his only source of help. Even then Helfin had not lost patience, although Zemanek's behavior had, at times, been insufferable. He had once explained that the titanic darkness in his breast rendered of no avail the pale street lanterns which Helfin's second-rate understanding tried to light. Well, all this big talk was useless. He had had to leave Vienna; the hook that finally hooked him was an extensive Italian journey, such as he had always dreamed of. It was Helfin who had procured for the eternally grouching "Pocket Byron" a job as companion and tutor to a young nobleman who was going to Italy, Spain, and Greece for a year. Zemanek had returned from this journey thoroughly recovered. As he himself said, he was sound as a bell. There was no more talk about the woman. Quite normally he had married a good-looking young girl and produced healthy male twins. Yet scarcely had he arrived in Israel when he began . . .

"That's an extraordinarily good story," Bianca said meditatively. With a little rhythmic motion she struck her ring repeatedly against the metal base of the floor lamp. And she repeated, "Extraordinarily good!" Next she added in a decisive tone, "We'll publish that; we'll spread that bit of news; we'll have a little broadside printed. The man is done for. Just leave it to me!"

"What are you thinking of?" He jumped out of the chair. "That would be a filthy trick. He told me those things in confidence. Moreover, you don't use heavy artillery against a bedbug."

"He hurt you, didn't he? All right. Then hurt him! And twice as hard. That's the only way to get along in this world. Go him one better."

"That's not for me. That doesn't go with my principles."

"Your principles? Any new ones?"

"Not new but more clearly compelling."

"How would you formulate it?"

"The necessity for renunciation."

"Frightful!" She played a whole tune on the lamp. "Weakling! You're going to give up a weapon which is in your very hands? You're fighting against your very instincts. And that is the worst of sins—the sin against the splendor of life."

"On the contrary. Our instincts must be restrained and domesticated."

"Like gentle little animals, eh? To hell with that! That would be filling the world with sickly, pallid, spineless creatures. Who would want to live in such a world? It would be a bore!"

He moved the lamp out of her reach. Her drumming was getting on his nerves. "That brings us back to our old, old dispute."

"At this point we don't understand each other," she cried to him with the gaiety of combat in her voice. She had ensconced herself comfortably on the arm of the chair. "And never did."

His answer was not angry, nor was her tone as hostile as it had been in Paris whenever, in one form or another, they had fought out this particular battle. All he wanted her to know, since he despaired of convincing her, was this: he differed from her radically in the given matter and would yield under no circumstances. At the same time he was aware, as he had always been, of the erotic element in these disputes and enjoyed it. They were undoubtedly two people divided by fundamental characteristics. In this there was a repellent element, but there was also a binding one. Nor could he hide from himself the fact that at this moment it was not disagreeable to him to know that this enchanting, glittering woman was bound to him, however banal her ultimate motives. They were motives having to do with her career; they were quite transparent; they nevertheless dressed themselves up in philosophical contradictions which needed to be resolved and were themselves embodied in a skin so white, in curves so rhythmic, in an atmosphere of such delicate fragrance.

"No, at this point there is no compromise," he said emphatically. "We simply don't understand each other."

His last words had been accompanied by the shrilling of a siren. An air attack! He was tempted to say, "There you have an example of your unbridled instincts!" But the desire to speak had faded. So one would rush down the stairs in a hurry and seek shelter. The same old thing. First you thought that your ears had deceived you. For a moment the world stood still. You asked yourself: Again? Not possible. But with its horrible rise and fall the whistle repeated its insistent warning. It left no room for doubt.

Bianca threw her arms around his neck.

"The *miklat* is downstairs at the landlord's," he managed to say. "Come on."

Abruptly she pulled him back into the deep armchair. He almost stumbled. "We don't understand each other a bit," she whispered hissingly and kissed his ear. "Let's stay here," she breathed. "Why drag out life with all its ugliness? You said it yourself. It is too revolting. Let's stay here! Are you afraid? What is there to be afraid of? The worst that can happen is that we're killed and have this whole business definitively behind us."

The siren had fallen silent after its upward and its downward shrieking, which, though meant as warning, had sounded rough and inchoate as the wildest threats. Shudders quivered along the skin to the roots of the hair. Have we reached the threshold of death this time? he wondered, Are we about to cross it? I, and you, of all people, with me? The enemy seems now to have gone over to the use of fiftypounders. The bombs were lighter before.

Complete calm spread in the street. The enemy planes were still inaudible. The alarm signal had been correctly timed.

Soon thereafter the accustomed street noises arose, the signal cars of the Civil Guard and the motorcycles were rattling back to their posts. The cars of the Fire Department and of the sanitary service of the Red Magen David were all taking the course prescribed by the organizers. All members of the Civil Defense were at their posts, if not to prevent disaster, yet to meet it and to reduce it within the smallest limits. Now another trilling whistle. Another, dying away, answered from the distance. Then calm again followed by the salvos of the antiaircraft guns. The moment was serious!

At the end of half an hour it became evident that this time the Egyptians had not succeeded in getting over the city. Explosions, to be sure, were heard faintly from afar. Sometimes they were not heard at all, which did not mean that in some distant suburb frightful damage and loss were not being suffered. At all events the immediate danger to the city had passed. The siren uttered a long, liberating trumpet blast; its triumphant glissando cut through the air.

The mood between the two had changed. Then tension had been released. More than that—Helfin was now slightly embarrassed, and Bianca's mood was dry. The transformation pleased neither. Involuntarily they strove to restore their previous situation. Inevitably in vain. To conceal his embarrassment Helfin made a little joke; it came out frostily, almost morosely. Bianca wanted to appear tender, for a certain element of barrenness in her nature, which now made its appearance, seemed to her out of harmony with her purposes. So she repeated her words, "Poor Paul," which she remembered to have impressed him. But now the words made no sense, or else what they meant was no longer desirable. She made up her mind to be practical. "When does your domestic dragon return? Before supper?" He admitted that this was probably so. "What a pity," she continued coolly and, as it were, scientifically. "We could have had a beautiful night." She proposed that they go to the shore promenade. They could have supper together, perhaps in the Hotel Layla. Josefovitch would turn up there too.

"Which of the two?" he asked acridly.

"This time it's the younger one," she answered, frankly accepting his malice. "The older one is in the country too. But he doesn't concern me any longer."

"I take it that the younger one does?"

She contorted her mouth.

"And how do you expect both of them, or either of them, to concern me?" he insisted.

She was perfectly willing to inform him. "After all, they're in the film business too. They have extensive plans. At all events, Philip, the younger, has. Maybe you can remember their names by now. You used to confuse them. Philip is interested in your company, too." He would have preferred to sweep all this talk aside as one sweeps a heap of useless papers from one's desk. But that seemed no longer possible. He did not feel as free as he had done an hour earlier.

Neither did the refreshing breeze from the sea, which they now enjoyed on the promenade, change his mood. On account of the frequent alarms the promenade was almost empty. They sat down on a bench. "Day after tomorrow there is to be a four weeks' cease fire," he said. "But it looks as though the Egyptians wanted to do their worst up to the last moment." He spoke mechanically. His thoughts pursued another direction. How odd that Bianca was so well informed concerning the film company with which he was having so much trouble. Just today an important session had ended in nothing. Maybe she knew that too, although she had been in the land only a very few days. But it corresponded to her immense and practical vigilance. She always found out at once and accurately all that was within the circle of her interests.

She didn't stop. "Philip has the highest opinion of you. If he were to acquire the greater part of the stock in your company, it would be wholly on your account. He esteems your work highly. He would provide money and you would provide art."

"The stock is not on the market," he answered sharply. "It's not for sale. I'm sure of my people. They're not thinking of any change."

"Are you so very sure?" She emphasized every word. "Well, that's fine. I was just thinking that in case Josefovitch takes the matter up, you might welcome being able to count on me, just as I could count on you."

"You don't expect me to betray my young associates?"

"Who talks about betrayal?" She tried once more to be quite gentle and amiable. Nevertheless he refused her invitation to sup with her and Josefovitch. There was no further mention of the night. Of course she had made excuses to her friends; she was inexhaustible in excuses. Helfin made no move. To do so would have placed him at a disadvantage. She considered herself skillful in the tactics of love. "The one of two lovers who cannot live without the other is the underdog and the slave." To be sure, that was not true except in the most banal sense. But he knew that Bianca pinned her whole faith to this maxim which she had once read in the pages of a seventh-rate scribbler. At any cost he meant to maintain his independence of this woman, whose ruthless ambition was transparent to him. Therefore, too, when she proposed that they meet the following day, he said that he had, alas, not a moment to spare. It wasn't true. But tactics must be met by tactics. "Maybe the day after tomorrow then?" She agreed calmly and, for any eventuality, gave him her telephone number and her address. She was at the Pension Rotfisch.

He was forced to call her number on the very next day.

Leaflets began to circulate in the city toward noon. They dug up that old, shabby scandal of Zemanek. One of the many afternoon papers next printed the news that the "yapper," to whom Helfin would now have gladly given another and more honorable appellation, had not been willing to survive the shameful exposure. He had hanged himself in the laundry room of his house.

To call the criminal woman to account, that was Helfin's first impulse. He called up the Pension Rotfisch and asked for Miss

Petry. She had gone to Haifa. Should he follow her? Wouldn't that be senseless? Yet he felt suddenly welded to her, being the accessory to her immitigably horrible misdeed. There was no excape from that. True, he had forbidden her to take so revolting a step for the hateful purposes of vulgar revenge. Yet within him, without the information given by him, she could not have taken this step. Her intention was clear. She was utterly indifferent to the scribbler's fate; her aim was Helfin. To draw him into an indissoluble bond with herself, to make him her vassal and victim forever—that might be of real use to her. To cause measureless devastation for the sake of a small advantage—he had always known how thoroughly capable of that she was. When she had rung his bell, when he had released his good old Dvora from his command, he ought to have known what kind of a creature he was admitting and to whom he was giving his confidence. Now it would be necessary to unmask Bianca publicly as the betrayer of confidences and thus draw the sting from her permanently. Yet that would introduce a new element of destructiveness. How was he to start? Was he to accuse himself and beat his breast in public expiation? Yet expiation must be accomplished, even though ruin resulted from the process. His heart seemed to beat in his very throat and his head was feverish. He needed desperately to have someone's advice. As his only friend he sought out his nephew Gad. The latter had come to his apartment in the morning. Too late, alas. Helfin had already gone out. So they had missed each other. As though by magic everyone had disappeared. For the first time Helfin saw the gleam of the red switch in the whirl of his dispirited thoughts. All these confusions had begun with it. They led from the trivial to the important, from awkwardness to error, from small mistakes to bloody catastrophe.

Nor were this day's confusions yet at an end.

A day comprises its night. And during that night the Egyptians arrived. They utilized the final hours prior to the armistice that had been imposed upon them. This time the bombs reached the center of the city and fell on a purely residential quarter. (In the cold-blooded military news of the Egyptians one could read, of course, that "hits were made on important military objectives.")

In Helfin's immediate neighborhood, walls of fire rose and splintered stones flew. A yellow tornado of rubble floated in the air. The moaning surface of the earth seemed to pant like the heaving breast of a sick man. Helfin had taken refuge in the bomb shelter. When he emerged into the smoky, dust-filled night, he perceived that both the house next door and the house across the street had been hit. Both were almost entirely destroyed. The dead had already been removed except for a few who were said to be buried under the ruins. Shaken by sudden fear as by an evil conscience, Helfin asked after two names. Yes, both had certainly been killed, the old hammerer as well as the piano-er.

Perhaps they were buried under the collapsed stories. Helfin made his way in among the working debris teams. He himself grabbed a crowbar. Since the regulation to dim all light had to be strictly observed, all that one saw here and there was a shaded blue lantern. At one point the half-broken stones at which he was working gave way at once. A stair opened before him, filled by a brown fog. A half-rotten bridge of wood seemed to sway above an abysmal cellar. Helfin leaped from the stair to the swaying bridge. Subterranean torrents roared. The bridge seemed to jump to meet him and to hurl him forward, even as a bowstring hurls an arrow. He was crushed against a black wall and struck his forehead against it. His forehead hurt and seemed to contain a dull rumbling, which next entered his throat and continued to fill his whole being. He groped his way in the darkness. Through a door he entered a long corridor. The roaring in his head turned into a feeling of utter faintness. For a while he lost consciousness and collapsed like a bag.

He didn't know how long he had lain beside that subterranean wall. When he recovered consciousness, daylight glimmered along the corridor which, it appeared, had been built below the foundations of the houses. Helfin pulled himself up, crowbar in hand, and wavered forward. He knew now that he was lost. Quite at random he wandered hither and yon; he had no notion of the direction in which he was going. What drove him forward was the weariness that threatened to overwhelm him. Sometimes he thought that he was wandering over the bottom of a deep well; again he thought he was in the midst of an extensive quarry; now he seemed at the bottom of a steep ladder and climbed up along a wall of square stones. All this was subterranean, though in some places more light penetrated than in others. He was on the point of fearing that he would never find his way out of this labyrinth of cellars, when he observed at his side a grillwork gate with ornaments in Arabic script and immediately thereafter entered a flight of dark rooms which smelled of mortar. Next he was in a winding corridor, in the white tiling of which was mirrored the light of single electric bulbs. These bulbs appeared at regular intervals, as in a subway station. Then a short stairway led upward. Above the exit through which he emerged into the light of day he saw a shadow. He turned around and looked up and saw the opaque, ungleaming eyes of the huge horse's head that had been fastened to the wall above the cellar door. There was no further room for doubt. A few steps more and he reached the empty platform surrounded by rubble and stray stones. He descended a few steps and passed through the ivy-covered wooden door with its knob above the engraved brass shield. He was in the midst of the vast ruins of Manshiyeh.

2.

To judge by the position of the sun, it was early afternoon. He was still tired, but with a kind of somnolence. The painful roaring had vanished from his head. In spite of the noonday heat, the way from here to his house had seemed strangely short. Now he stood in his room, which was pleasantly dusky. He laid his hand against his forehead and it seemed to him as though a kind of web and a bright-red patch were flickering along the wall and floating out of the window. He didn't perceive clearly what was happening. But he knew precisely what he had just been thinking. He was repelling and repressing something. He didn't want his three tormentors to be annihilated. Definitely he retracted this desire; he condemned his bitterness and his rage not only as unseemly but as clearly contrary to his character. He expelled from his lips the vulgar imprecations he had uttered. And at that moment he was astonished to see one of his finger tips invaded by a ruddy glow. Was it imagination? From his forehead he drew his hand down to his eyes. At that moment his doorbell rang violently. The echo of a light whirring was still in his ear. Oh, his poor overstimulated, unprotected ears, how had they recently been tortured!

Now the doorbell rang clear and without accompanying sounds. He heard Dvora's slippers cross the anteroom. She was opening the outer door. The tones of her calm voice quieted him.

He heard the answer uttered by that other voice, that deep and resonant voice, well trained in articulation.

The two voices contradicted each other. The deep voice demanded admission immediately, no matter what had been ordered. Calmly Dvora refused. She repeated the same words, that her master was not be disturbed at this hour.

Helfin tore open the door. Bianca stood in the anteroom, her small black hat on her blond head, pale-cheeked, dressed in an unobtrusive dark frock. Helfin stared at her as at an apparition. "You heard that I don't want to be disturbed." He slammed the door in her face.

He flung himself on the sofa. He wanted to sleep. He heard the door to the hall close. The woman was leaving. "I did that well," he said to himself and gave himself up to the first comforting waves of slumber. Suddenly he heard: "Bang-bang-bang." Then a pause. Then the hammer in its usual crescendo. The hammerer! And immediately thereafter the notes of a concerto of Bach over which the piano-er had worked for weeks in vain.

What was that? Had these two arisen from their graves among the ruins?

He sat up and stared wearily about the room. Impossible to rest. Softly Dvora knocked at the door, bringing in the iced coffee. He looked with curiosity at the tray. Only one cup. Well why should there be more? He was alone. Why was he surprised?

The old woman repeated her well-known request. He shivered. Did the Unambo machine begin only now to unfold its power of duplicating life?

Dvora had put the tray down. Her son was here on a brief furlough from the front.

"Again today?" he cried.

"Yes, he came today," she said without any sign of surprise. "I haven't seen him since he joined the army. That was in March.

There was no national army then. The boys were all partisans and each one was at his post. God be praised! Except for them we wouldn't any of us be here any longer. The Arabs would have cut off our heads. Well, so that was in March. And now"—she counted on her fingers—"there's been April, May, a little bit of June—it's three months and a half. And now my big son is back. He's two heads taller than I." She rose on her toes and lifted up her arm as far as she could stretch it. "That tall he is."

"And just now . . ." Helfin put the words in her mouth.

"Just now a neighbor brought me the news. And now I'd like to be off until evening and go home."

She had her own dwelling in a suburb. Only during the day, as is customary in the country, she took care of Helfin's household. "I'll look in this evening to see if you need anything, sir."

Sometimes she would stay overnight. There was a little bedroom for her to occupy. If he seemed particularly nervous, as had been the case in recent weeks, the good woman had not had the heart to leave him by night without protection and help. But this day was exceptional. The old woman's heart was full of joy and his own began to vibrate with hers. He gave her what there was in the house—cake, chocolate, cash. For her child she took it all gladly and thanked him and took her leave.

The outer door fell to with a bang. Of course, the old woman's hands had trembled. That was the impression. . . . And yet it wasn't. . . . Helfin meditated for a while; he stared into the void; he tried to gather his thoughts. There was no point at which he could begin to reason. It seemed to him as though he were plunging into a veil of clouds.

He did his utmost to pull himself together. He lifted the coffee cup to his lips. The beverage always gave him a small renewal of energy. He inhaled the agreeable aroma. "Ice-cold," he said appreciatively, proud of his well-ordered household. He stopped. How like an echo those words seemed. Within them was audible the lifeless, puppetlike sounding of an icy flute.

In order to get rid of this ghostly echo he sat down at the piano and began to play a Chopin *étude*. The swift and tiny configurations rang and glittered.

It was not long before the doorbell rang twice.

Was that importunate woman not to be turned away? Had she come back?

He passed through the anteroom and opened the door and met a pleasant surprise. There was his nephew Gad. The steel helmet was on his head; he was letting his knapsack glide from his back while he loosened the shoulder straps. He was covered with dust and his shirt was wet. Out of his thin, sunburned, unshaved face his handsome white teeth gleamed. He smiled a broad smile.

"This is wonderful," Helfin said. "Of course you'll stay with me and lodge here."

"Till tomorrow night," Gad announced.

"Come on then. Why do you keep standing there? Give me the knapsack and march yourself straight to the bathroom."

Gad started to move about. Whatever he touched showed signs of the dust of the battlefield.

"Go to the bathroom as I told you!" With the tips of his fingers Helfin pushed him in. Soon one could hear the merry plash and rush of water. Helfin was happy to have that dear guest; between them, in spite of the great difference of their ages, there existed a kind of friendship, a friendship as between father and son but wholly untarnished by compulsion or command. Gad had had a very strict father and a weary, overworked mother. Even in his childhood he had escaped from his cheerless home and had gone to see his uncle, who always had so many books with beautiful pictures in them. Also the uncle told him stories, which never lacked wildly imaginative elements. It all started with the illustrations in an old edition of Shakespeare; from there it went on and on. To the child, Shakespeare was but another word for fairy tale. He had no sooner come in than he would beg, "Tell me more Shakespeare." So in the following years he heard the stories of *King Lear* and of *Othello* and of *The Tempest*. So, delicately and unpedantically, Gad continued to be educated by his uncle. As he grew older the attachment between these two grew ever clearer. At the first favorable opportunity Helfin had sent the boy to Palestine, where he had followed him six months later. The parents of Gad, who had morosely refused to go, disappeared in the Nazi ocean of blood. Those were days in which small errors and delays were tragically expiated.

From the bathroom arose the sound of Gad's singing:

> *"Through the chill of the night the wind blows,*
> *Thrust the logs on the fire that it glows!*
> *Bring the ax and at once it is done;*
> *Red warmth for the watchers is won!*
> *The flames, they shoot higher,*
> *Our songs, they aspire,*
> *Pass around, pass around the* findshan!*"*

It was the new Hebrew song whose vigorous waltz rhythm was being heard everywhere. A soldier, Chayim Feiner, had composed the melody and written the verses. At the front and in the streets the boys were singing it all over the land. Helfin was grateful that Gad had been rescued. Now, of course, he was exposed to danger once more. It must not, must not be, Helfin reflected, that I lose him too.

The splashing of the water from the shower was accompanied by the singing:

> *"The fire—see it whisper and burn,*
> *While the logs to a scarlet mass turn,*
> *When renewal for warmth must be drawn*
> *From the groves and the forests of dawn,*
> *Then every log sings*
> *As the fire upsprings,*
> *Then pass on and around the* findshan!*

> *"Remember no praises to move,*
> *But brew us the mixture with love.*
> *Sweet and coffee mix up,*
> *Fill with water the cup,*
> *With the water that's seething*
> *For the brew that is breathing,*
> *And pass on, pass around the* findshan!*

"Recall when the battle was o'er
How with hearts that were riven and sore,
Motke, the djinji, *began;*
'We miss that dear friend, that brave man.'
Our tears—they were gleaming,
But the brew, it was streaming,
For we still passed around the findshan.

"Generations—they pass in a night,
And the fronts and the guards and the light!
Why this ditty took hold of us so,
There's no stranger that ever can know.
The reserves and the flier,
All let it rise higher,
While they still pass around the findshan."

Oh, merry tones of youth! Oh, cleansing water as from the sky! Helfin had a vision of a group of soldiers in the shade of ancient gnarled olive trees. Among them from man to man was being passed around the burnished little coffee cup of porcelain. These Jewish heroes were acting according to an excellent Arab custom. Could not these two worlds come to a final understanding and peace?

Now there was silence in the bathroom. Had Gad vanished? Anything could happen today; nothing that was thinkable was impossible. Helfin approached the door and heard the familiar sound of a tranquil activity. The boy was shaving. Suddenly during the ensuing silence, which was broken again by the running of the water from the faucet, Helfin became aware of his paternal delight in the boy. Only now was his life reaching a final development; he felt that he was setting out upon another path by virtue of the fact that Gad was important to him and not some illusory female in her tempting frippery. The ingratiating image of Bianca's fatal form faded. As though to convince himself and prove the unbelievable to himself, he cried through the door to Gad, "I suppose they sent you home on account of the armistice?"

"I beg your pardon?"

"Well, didn't the cease fire take place at 10 o'clock this morning according to our time?"

"You're dreaming. The date set is Friday, June 11. That's the day after tomorrow morning. And it isn't at all certain that the cease fire will become effective. I rather imagine not."

Helfin's heart throbbed. "But today is Friday, June 11."

"Maybe on your calendar," Gad laughed within. "To the rest of us it's Wednesday the ninth."

"Well, I must have gone mad." Helfin trembled and hurried to the window. There he would find the indubitable evidence.

The house next door stood as it always had; so did the house across the street. The old man with his black skullcap came calmly and unsuspectingly out on his balcony and began to hammer at one of his boards.

And so, it went through Helfin's head, I know the future. In the night between tomorrow and the day after tomorrow, that is, during the last night before the armistice, there will be horrors! All about me will crash. Only this house in which I live will remain. Now I ought to run out and warn those people. I should cry aloud, "Get out, save yourselves. Take refuge with friends or relatives. What you are about to experience, I have already been through. I am only recapitulating and repeating these days, which you do not yet know. I already know them, or at least parts of them, fragments of them. No, I cannot foretell everything. There is no changeless fate. Nothing is predetermined. The free will of each human being can change one thing or another and thus transform the whole. Yet it is most probable that tomorrow night . . ." But they would consider me a madman if I began to prophesy. And indeed I can predict only half the future. . . . And which of the two futures is the really real one, the actually true one? That which is already completed behind me or that which we are all approaching together? Everything within me is like an inextricable coil. I lose the thread and the connection.

These contradictory thoughts were at the point of breaking him when, fresh and radiant, Gad appeared. That other life, the one which had already run from the spool of fate, the strand of yesterday and the day before—all that now lost its importance in the face of this corporeal reality. It did not vanish; it receded into a shadowy background. There it faded more and more. And when Gad stirred the thing up once more, saying, "Whatever made you think it was Friday?" it seemed to Helfin that he was about to find his way back.

At the same time a small jealousy began to stir in him. "Naturally you will now go to look up Atida."

"Is it really so natural?" The soldier grinned.

"Why not? Or is it over?" He would have been sorry for that. The girl had pleased him; it was obvious that Gad had chosen well.

"Why should it be 'all over' right away?" Gad rather jeered. Alone with him the boy was much more frank than if even one other was present. "You older people do have the funniest notions."

"What do you mean by funny?" He really liked to be set right by this youngster.

"Because all you can think of is what you call love. We call that the romantic involvement. Undoubtedly that too is a part of life. But there are far more important things. Atida is in Galilee helping to rebuild the *Kibbutz*. It's immediately behind the front at Mansura-el-Cheit."

"That sounds Arabic."

"It is an Arab village. But the Arabs all ran away. Not from us at all. They ran away from their Arabic neighbors in Tuba, their mortal enemies and competitors in cattle theft. When the general disturbances set in they began to be frightened on account of an old blood feud between their tribes and so they ran across the Syrian frontier. We moved on after them. We took over the fields from them. But it's just a waste without our cattle and our houses. Of course, we have some new land. We sowed that to grass and the harvest must now be cut. So hands are needed."

"And Atida's parents permitted her—"

"She ran away." Think of that well-behaved, charming child, Helfin thought. There is no end to surprises. Whenever he had seen her with Gad, her behavior had been so gentle and modest. "I wouldn't have given her credit for it," said he.

"You're right," Gad said dryly, yet with a perceptible undertone of triumph. Proudly he continued, "I did, you see. Still waters. . . ."

Helfin thought that the boy used this proverb in a purer and better than the usual sense. "You'll go up to see her?"

"For the present I see no chance."

"And why not?" Suddenly he remembered that he was the boy's host. "I can't give you coffee in the *findshan*, but I can guarantee its quality."

Gad sat down. He devoured the rest of the cake. "We haven't got such good things in Mansura. But for the present I'm here on a special mission. Going back tomorrow night."

"Don't tell me except what you want to." Helfin knew that the young people of the Land disliked curiosity and hated to be questioned. Sometimes they would condescend to give information. "The less I know about the war, the better it is for me." Helfin slid into his accusatory tone. "Do you imagine that we don't feel the effects of the war here? We even had a little naval battle outside of Tel Aviv. I saw the very last phase of it myself. Prior to that an alarm confined us to our houses. But finally a few of us did manage to get out. There were four Egyptian ships— a corvette, an armed freighter, and two landing boats of the British type. They approached the coast. Our three tiny naval vessels attacked them. At a distance they looked like sewing machines. One of our planes made a direct hit on the freighter; another one pursued, swooped down and was met by a deadly salvo. Two sons of our most precious citizens were killed in that plane —a Sprinzak and a Sukennik. But they fulfilled their mission. Within three hours the enemy was put to flight. So we created a navy out of nothing. And planes out of nothing. One of them we call our Primus, after the little kerosene cooking stove. Yet we're glad to see it in the sky. Everybody says, '*Shelanu*, that's ours.' It looks as though it had just come out of a retrospective exhibition of prehistoric airplanes. I believe it's a double-decker, totally antiquated. Somehow it works. The whole thing is marvelous. One would like to embrace in gratitude every one of those who had the right forethought and prepared what could be prepared, despite the hypocritical moral preachments of Bevin, of which the purpose was to make us drowsy and deliver us unarmed to the mercy of the well-armed enemy. It is all magnificent and yet it is sad, too."

"Why sad?"

"Because, in spite of all our acts of bravura and intrepidity, like this naval battle, we achieve pretty pitiful results."

"Why pitiful? Who says that?"

"Everyone who is not dazzled by our own propaganda."

Gad was all aflame. "That's the talk of Tel Aviv. We at the front use a different vocabulary. And we know the facts. We have won the war."

For the first time Helfin heard a victorious word uttered by sincere young lips rather than by official-toned newspapers which always impressed him with the contrary. "Won?" he asked incredulously the while he clung to the word itself. It was the first gleam of light, of hope which, as far as he was concerned, shone above these last insane weeks. "We have won? Surely you exaggerate." His voice shook.

"No. I mean it." Gad was calm. "The six Arab states have a population between thirty and forty times greater than ours. Nevertheless we drove all their irregulars out of Jewish territory at the end of the Mandatory regime. During the official war, that is, since May 15, we have protected the boundaries of the State of Israel, with the exception of four or five tiny settlements and the Old City of Jerusalem, against all the invading forces. That's bad enough! But in compensation we have occupied 400 square miles beyond the state, and control the entire coast as far as Isdud in the South, the Arab border city according to the partition plan. Is that not victory? At all events, you must admit that it is at least an unexpected success, even though it cannot yet be called a final decision." He had weighed his words carefully.

"But Jerusalem is lost to us," Helfin cried with pain in his voice.

"Who told you that?"

"Well, we can't hold it."

"That may be the opinion in Tel Aviv. In fact, I am told that in Tel Aviv, Jerusalem has been despaired of. But Jerusalem does no such thing and nobody dreams of doing so."

"How do you know that?"

"Well I happen just to have come from there."

"You're joking. Jerusalem is cut off. Oh, maybe you took a plane."

"No, I came by the secret road."

"Now you too annoy me with this silly rumor. Burma Road, eh? Patriotic gossip."

Helfin's skepticism, which must have seemed most unreasonable to Gad, provoked the boy to say more than he had probably intended. "It happens that I just came along the Burma Road in which you don't believe. I helped to build it, too. So did your pupils, Baruch and Jonah. They'll turn up quite soon. I invited them here; I hope you don't mind. They will confirm all I say, if you don't believe me. And the special mission in which we are all three employed has to do with this very road, which does indeed rank with the most fabulous things that people have ever achieved."

"But I do believe you," Helfin murmured. He got up from his chair and paced up and down the room, quite prepared to be full of astonishment and admiration. Suddenly he stood still, "I can put up those two boys, too. I have a folding bed and the other can be bedded on the floor. It's wonderful that you brought them."

"I thought you would agree." Gad smiled. "As a matter of fact, four of us were supposed to return in the jeep. But at the last moment the fourth man was ordered elsewhere. I suppose you would have put him up too."

"Certainly, certainly." Helfin was slightly distraught; his attention had shifted to another matter. "On the return trip you will have an empty seat in the jeep, I take it?" It seemed to be so. Now he seemed suddenly gayer than he had been for long. I've got to go and forage for you people. Those boys will be hungry. Where are they keeping themselves?"

"They're on a special mission, as I told you. They are assembling a convoy. They let me off for this afternoon on the condition that I do double work tomorrow. At sunset tomorrow we're going back."

"At sunset tomorrow," Helfin repeated thoughtfully. "That is well." He became very much alive. "Help yourself to cigarettes out of the box. No, sit still; I'll fetch them. And here, to begin with, are cookies and brandy."

Somewhat wearily Gad had stretched himself out on the sofa. "Thank you! We really don't have cigarettes enough in Jerusalem. Everything else is pretty good."

"The worst thing must be the water shortage," Helfin said, moving a little table nearer to the sofa. "One liter a day per capita."

"Now who told you that story again!" Gad was positively hurt. "There are ten liters a day for every inhabitant. For the moment it's only cistern water, because the British-Transjordanian general has occupied the pumping station near Latrun. But we'll change that too. And the water is chemically treated, so that we haven't had a single case of infection yet. That speaks well, doesn't it, for our medical organization."

"To hear you"—Helfin could not resist the gentle jeer—" one would recommend Jerusalem as a health resort."

Gad stretched himself comfortably. "That I wouldn't recommend. Resorts under constant artillery fire are hardly the ideal thing."

Helfin tiptoed to the door, for the lad had sunk into deep slumber.

When Helfin returned with his purchases of food and entered the room the shrilling of the siren arose. That was to be expected, he said to himself. Exactly the same hour as the day before yesterday . . . that is, it wasn't the day before yesterday at all. Yet the "then" corresponded to the moment which now, *now*, palpably enters my experience. It was the anticipation of this moment, or else its image projected into the space of my "now" from another space. Or, if one prefers, it was a variation on the same theme. Into what dark mystery have I entered?—He felt himself steeped again into all that misery and misfortune out of which he had been pulled by the vigorous personality of Gad. He leaned against the arm of the sofa and regarded the sleeping boy. His brown, wavy hair covered his forehead; his breathing was calm. Helfin said to himself, we'll stay here; we will not seek refuge. To what end? To run after life and its horrors? It is so revolting and so senseless. Why should one fear? One should be glad to get the whole thing over with. . . . In the street below, the defense guards and the police were at their posts. The noises of the city had fallen silent. All that one heard were the signals of the official cars. A distant, dying siren answered. What was it that had happened simultaneously with these noises the other day? Or ought one rather to say "now, at this moment"? Helfin was forcibly reminded of the identity of the noises. But oddly enough, Helfin accomplished this act of memory unemotionally, coolly. This was not like the old operatic, magic device of a "philter of forgetfulness" which causes all that has happened to be obliterated. The past remained; only he was indifferent to it. It seemed devoid of significance and somehow not pertinent to him. It did occupy his thoughts somewhat as our mind is momentarily taken up with an alien landscape which suddenly arises before us. From the window of a railroad car such an image will suddenly arise and occupy our attention, only to lapse back into the indifferent monotony of the journey.

Gad awoke. One of the whistles had done that. He immediately recognized the character of the uncanny silence which was so strange at this hour. It was the silence between the shrillness of the signals. With the active instinct of the front-line soldier he got up swiftly. "That's an alarm!"

"Certainly," Helfin said indifferently.

"Let's get downstairs then! Quick! Where is your shelter?"

Helfin laughed. "Where is your courage?"

"You call that courage? To be butchered senselessly? Come on, come on! There is quite a different place for me to risk my skin. Not here in Liebermann Street." He pulled Helfin toward the door. They hurried into a ground-floor apartment of the house. No better protection had yet been provided here. Gad was vividly indignant over this; he threatened to report such damned negligence.

When they went back upstairs, Helfin's two pupils turned up. This time the alarm had been followed by no audible attack.

Helfin was not surprised. He was in no mood to emphasize his prescience. He didn't value it in the least. But he couldn't repel nor avoid a certain painful prefamiliarity with what was taking place. This feeling, mixed with both slight horror and shame, filled him for a little while during the trumpeting of the all-clear signals.

Soon the ghostly impressions left him. It was long since he had seen his pupils. How changed they were! A bitter determination and new tragic experiences had chiseled new furrows into their faces. They were mirrored unmistakably even in the crystal-clear being of Baruch—that being which had, to his regret, always caused him to be cast in the parts of serene old men. This trait in him, as of a natural innate wisdom, had remained. But it seemed shattered against a feeling of the ineluctable, which had once been foreign to him. Compared to him, even Jonah, the melancholy comic actor, seemed stirred and vivid. And indeed it soon came out that Baruch was suffering from a frightful impression which he could not get rid of. One of his friends had been an officer in Nizanim, one of those tiny settlements in the extreme South which preferred to perish to the last boy and girl rather than give up to the Egyptians. This resistance, normally speaking, would have seemed senseless; yet on account of it the lightning-like attack of the Egyptians had been blunted at the start. The officer in question had accomplished one of the maddest acts of this memorable action. With his last few men he clung to the completely surrounded hill near Nizanim. By telephone he ordered his own battery, which had already withdrawn, to lay the heaviest possible barrage upon this hill. Together with him and his few companions, hundreds of the attacking enemy fell. "Let me die with the Philistines!" Thus out of the dark abysses of a people's destiny the words of Samson re-experienced a wild rebirth. Now Baruch's best friend was no more—and he had been a member of the battery which had carried out his friend's command.

No one gave a thought to films. Jonah alone had preserved a measure of his lyrical flexibility, of which momentary gleams, whether of melancholy or of gaiety, shone on his face. Contradictory moods succeeded each other within him; the swift changes were sometimes almost gruesome. Quite as though Jonah had no entire control over them; as though they alternated despite himself. An involuntary clown plagued by an ultimate insecurity. A profound distrust of all human affairs seemed to fill him and was kept in balance only by military discipline. "They sent us around from one office to another today," he said. "But I wouldn't give in. In the last place you would have expected them to have sense—bang, there they granted us the trucks for the convoy."

"You don't have to be mysterious in Paul's presence," Baruch interrupted him. "Day after tomorrow, immediately after the cease fire, we will issue a communiqué about the substitute road to Jerusalem."

"I'm flattered that you give me credit for being able to keep a secret for two days." Helfin bowed ironically.

"No quarreling! No room for personal feelings!" Gad's tone was sharp. "Military orders."

It annoyed Helfin that precisely his little nephew was so stern with him. "I don't even want to know anything. What I want to do is to co-operate. I've been thinking of it for days and weeks. Now that I have you fellows here, I see it more clearly than ever. This is no time to make films. Maybe next year or the year after. Tomorrow I'm going to join the army, in spite of being almost fifty. I'm a former officer and they'll put me to use somewhere."

No enthusiastic scene ensued. No glasses were clinked, if only for the reason that, in Gad's opinion, an army in which the use of alcohol was unknown was a uniquely desirable phenomenon. All the soldiers agreed that an army which prefers coffee to whisky is unconquerable. Not that they refused the brandy now. But immediately afterward Jonah went in to the kitchen to substitute for Dvora and see to it that coffee was plentiful, even though its quality was below the usual standard.

But, though there was no outbreak of enthusiasm, the young soldiers began eagerly to discuss where Helfin would be most useful. Each demanded him for his arm of the service; each found qualities which destined him to special effectiveness either as a sharpshooter, like Gad, or as an artillery man, like Baruch. "It's a good thing," said Gad, "that Zvi isn't here. Then you might have become a sapper."

"The thing for you to do is to be an aviator." Instructively Jonah lifted his index finger. "My tortoise has been sniffing at you this whole time. She doesn't make friends with everybody." Jonah always carried his pet tortoise with him; he declared it to be the proper mascot for an aviator.

Since they now regarded Helfin as one of their own, they discussed the matter closest to their hearts—the "Burma Road" and the relief of Jerusalem. It now came out that, especially in the past few days, Gad had worked to the very limits of his endurance. For this reason his friends had forced upon him the repose of this single afternoon. But this was mentioned only in passing. Their real theme absorbed them. "*Al pachad*," Baruch began, "no fear!" And "*yihye tov*, everything will be all right." After these introductory words which had become magic formulae, they went on (in Hebrew, of course) to describe the condition of the city, in which in fact there was a lack of all things, especially of munitions and food. Since there was neither electric current nor kerosene, the housewives were forced to prepare primitive meals on hearths built of bricks in the courtyards. They seemed to themselves like cave dwellers. Covered with soot they went a-hunting for fuel wood, university professors competing with Bucharin porters. There was a period during which it was discovered that a well-known insecticide contained a high proportion of petroleum and was therefore combustible. The news went around and soon the supplies in the drug stores and pharmacies had been exhausted. Then blank need set in again. Even the bloody conquest of the village of El-Kastel had helped little. Now, to be sure, the whole road which led through the deep valley uphill to Jerusalem was in Jewish hands. But the entrance into the valley in the plain, starting at Ramle and Tel Aviv, was still blocked. The Arab Legion was stationed near Latrun in the vicinity of the biblical Emmaus. Upon their withdrawal the British had made a present of the fortified police camp to the Legion. From there it commanded the highway. Now the commander of the *Palmach*, the shock troops of the Haganah, who was responsible for this highway, sent for historical atlases from various libraries. He studied them day and night. Not he alone, of course. The same notions arose simultaneously in sundry minds. The Romans, to whom the name of the Arabic village El-Kastel (Castellum) directly points, must have known of additional roads through the mountains between their fortified places. And the Arabs—were they not wont to drive their camels across the desolate hills of the Judean desert, the landscape of Samson, across Zara and Esh-Taol through the dry bed of the brook of Sorek which they call the Waadi es-Srar? Of course, these sandy roads would hardly be adequate for the motorized convoys necessary to supply the needs of a large city. Nevertheless, nevertheless—

"Wait a minute, Baruch." Jonah waved his hand. "The way you tell it, it conveys nothing." He placed his hand upon his heart like the harlequin in the old comedy and shook himself a little. They smiled while a deep melancholy, itself quite fleeting, passed over his face. "Gad ought to sit down at the piano and illustrate how that story is to be told!"

Gad sounded the eight chords out of the Fourth Symphony of Brahms to symbolize Jerusalem's stonelike endurance and resistance. What needed next to be conveyed was the mood of that *Palmach* commander and of those commrades from Hulda and Kfar Uria who became research students and in pain brought forth the solution. Gad played the first of the piano pieces of Schönberg's Opus 11. It is full of a consuming passion for the news; in it are the Dürer-like melancholy and inner darkness of the man of knowledge who, releasing himself from old bindings, seeks new paths of cognition. The two other lads immediately grasped the connection. The thought leaped for a moment through Helfin's mind: Our youth is by no means as uncultured as Bianca wants to make it appear. At the next moment his imagination was back in Hulda.

Time was pressing. Thus Baruch continued. And so, during the very next night, two friends, taking a jeep (which had been, so to speak, "borrowed"), looked for the road across the mountains. The adventure was dangerous. At every cliff one might meet Arab sentries. The whole front was still fluid. In the moonless night, too, abysses and the steep sides of mountains were to be feared. Now the jeep had to leap over boulders and now to plow through deep sand. From a distance answering signals could be heard. And now Gad played the first night music out of Mahler's Seventh Symphony. In all likelihood Mahler had thought of a troop of marching medieval mercenaries, of which the songs are to be found in *The Boy's Magic Horn*. But at bottom the mood of danger and of the intrepidity of man was the same.

The road which, with some repair, was found to be the best was that which led across the recently conquered Arab villages of Bet Susin, Bet Dgis and Dir Muheisin. This road could be prolonged up to the old Jewish colony of Hulda, provided one had workers enough. Along this detour it was possible to by-pass the fortifications of Latrun. It required, to be sure, the tracing of the new road for more than 30 kilometers by the use of narrow footpaths through impenetrable hill country.

And now they set to work by day and by night. Children and old men and women helped. It was clear to them all that here was a possibility of bringing medicaments to the sick of Jerusalem, to supply the defenders of its threatened positions with arms, even to transport light artillery in order to bring to an end that intolerable situation in which the enemy could with complete impunity cover with artillery fire the university buildings, the libraries, synagogues, the hospitals, the dwelling places of peaceful citizens, whether rich or poor. In other words, Jerusalem had to be rescued. And this was the only way. The extraordinary thing was that the Arabs took not the slightest notice. They had evidently not dreamed that there could be any means of frustrating their hunger siege. Under their very noses the road was built—only by night, of course, and to the accompaniment of occasional exchanges of rifle fire. Our people overheard the conversation of Arab sentries; they heard British commands. The action which the enemy took for mere reconnoitering was part of an all-embracing plan which finally pushed him out of a broad corridor. Through the center of this the road continued to extend. A single vigorous thrust on his part could have caused the enemy to recognize what was going on in an unprotected terrain, for our work of fortification had to be very gradual. But, whether to the right or to the left, our foes sat as under a magic spell. And we worked on between. Ravel's mysterious "Forlana" was used by the pianist for delineating the background of this action with its magic circles and witches' leaps and petrifying incantations.

Baruch hastened to end his report. The Jewish attacks against Latrun had no purpose but to divert the attention of the enemy from the building of the road. The maneuver succeeded. Finally there was but one hill left, so steep that no jeep could climb it. You started the car, and dust and sand and rubble flew. The car did not move. Everywhere one made one's way in zigzags of needlesharp turnings. Every driver that got through was completely encrusted in mud. But at this last point none got through. Yet this piece of road was but three kilometers long. To by-pass this hill would have meant a prolongation of ten kilometers. Our strength, despite any excess of sacrifice, was not equal to this task. Yet Jerusalem—its 100,000 souls—was bound to be starved out tomorrow, day after tomorrow, in the face of this supposedly humane century with all its fine phrases, if this obstacle were not conquered. Meanwhile they saw at the end of the road from Hulda the beginning of the road to Jerusalem. No obstacle was left except this hill.

Cars filled with flour sacks rolled up to that last obstacle. Here 600 riflemen were waiting. Each one took a bag of flour on his back. They climbed up the hill and then descended again to meet the trucks on the other side which had come empty from Jerusalem and were waiting here. No word broke the silence of the night. No cigarette gleamed. Where machinery was powerless, human beings took its place. They looked like human ants, for when each had the sack of flour on his back, the whole procession had the aspect of a procession of ants.

Gad asked to be forgiven that at this point he had to play the hackneyed *Prelude* of Rachmaninoff. There was nothing more appropriate to such situations. But this jest served to restrain the emotion which vibrated in them all.

Helfin found for once that he didn't even dream of the steer of Phalaris, nor of his complaint against these fated acts of wild courage. It didn't even occur to him. He embraced Gad who was about to delineate the arrival of the first convoys in the jubilant city of Jerusalem. He did this with the smiling, lighthearted strains of Stravinsky's *Petrushka* and the triumphant song from the *Semitic Suite* of Boskovits. "Let me go with you tomorrow," Helfin cried, "no matter whether they accept me or not. You've got to take me along in your jeep. I confess that when I asked just now whether you could spare me a seat, I still had the additional notion of doing some photography. All I want to be now is one of those human ants. That's all. You can't refuse me that. That's the way out, for which I've looked for so long: to take the war upon myself and still to remain loyal to my peaceful stars. There can be nothing more blessed than to bring food to the hungry, medicine to the sick, and liberation to those in danger of destruction. Nothing in me rebels against such military service. I will myself be among the rescued."

On the next night, when the jeep with its four passengers left Tel Aviv on the road toward Rechovot and Hulda, the great symbols of Divine Justice flamed in the heavens—the two triangles of stars which seem to sustain the equilibrium of the sky, like the two balances of a scale. Or, perhaps, they are like two trowels which the Divine Architect used in the work of creation and then hung up by two nails in the firmament in order to have them ready to His hand if it were to please Him to improve or to complete His work. Or else, create one figure of these two triangles and there results another symbol, one of peace, which brings healing and blessing to all men. This union in the sky has not yet come to pass; perhaps it will remain for the days of the Messiah.

At the steep hill of Bet Susin, Helfin, like the other passengers, was given a sack of flour to carry. Others were laden with weapons, tins of gasoline, parts of machine guns. Strict regulations prevailed. The entire effort was for the moment first aid. Soon the hill was to be conquered by a serpentine road. Also a third road was under discussion, an asphalt road, as well as a pipeline, inaccessible to the enemy, for the purpose of piping fresh water to Jerusalem. All plans were in readiness.

3.

On that same night, the last night before the four weeks' armistice, Tel Aviv was bombed from the air with singular violence.

Only confused rumors of the details came to Helfin's ear. Immediately, too, he had no way of informing himself further. The papers published no details. His enlistment had been accomplished. He had passed the medical examinations the day before the night in which he became one of the working ants. A day later he found himself on the way from Jerusalem to the northern extremity of the country in upper Galilee, in one of the advanced positions, which was called the "Little Forest of the Fifty." The place had not yet an official name. It was just a grove in the plain of Hule near the Syrian frontier. It had a view of the forested slopes of Mount Hermon which now, in June, had lost its cap of snow. The military camp was in the midst of greenery. There was no village, no habitation, nothing but this camp in the openness of nature. Hermon lay beyond the frontier. But much nearer, from the slight elevation of the naked grayish-yellow foothills beyond our new settlement, Kfar Szold, one had a view of the Syrian military positions, the trenches cut into the cliff-side. The enemy troops had moved from Damascus to the frontier without penetrating our land. Thus, even if it had not been for the armistice, they would probably not have interfered either with the life of this camp, which took place calmly under the smooth leaves of the shadowy sycamores. The heat of summer was quite bearable here. Helfin couldn't help thinking of an observation of Gad: "In our country the heat is no enemy. Nobody has ever died of a heat stroke here, as people do, for instance, in New York."

Gad was far away now, as were his other young friends. Torn out of his usual environment, Helfin had to work hard at the training of volunteers who had come from Canada, the United States, and England and who spoke only English. Consequently the paper fastened to one of the tree trunks and composed on the model of the British regulations bore the title "Training Syllabus." It was an extensive program: reveille, the reading of charts, the use of weapons, gymnastics, etc. etc. He taught and learned simultaneously; he recovered what he had learned as an officer. Moreover, this was quite a new world, new faces, new people. Here it turned out, too, that not the whole army confined itself to coffee. Some of these young men drank their beer directly from the bottle. Each day passed like every other, except occasionally when there arrived one of the big transport trucks on the way from Rosh Pinah or Kfar Giladi and was surrounded by everyone as it stopped in the cool shade of the trees.

Several days later Helfin got news from Gad, whom he had begged for information. Two houses in Liebermann Street had actually been hit by bombs. They were in Helfin's immediate neighborhood. But no one had been killed. It was only in the first confusion that some people had not been found. They had, in fact, taken refuge in shelters. The half-ruined houses were being torn down. Gad had heard nothing about the suicide of a journalist, nor had anyone in Tel Aviv been able to inform him concerning a malicious broadside. Anyhow, Tel Aviv was hardly in a mood to pay attention to such things. The people were happy enough that the cease fire gave their nerves a vacation. For the present no one thought of anything else except a little recovery and the practical work that had to be done in the matter of rebuilding.

So Helfin, too, took courage and completely repressed those somber memories. Happily he strode between the tents of the camp. The Jordan River, here near its source and the hills of its homeland, murmured by in the form of a pure, swift, narrow brook. Precisely at the camp it made a sharp turn so that it appeared on two sides of the forest ground. The murmuring of the brook blended with the cries of command. There were in reality only a few tents, one quite large and serving as a council chamber. Farther on, at the edge of the grove, there was a kitchen barracks with storerooms. Most of the soldiers camped in the open. All they needed was a mattress with white mosquito netting draped above it. This netting at first reminded Helfin disagreeably of a certain little model stage. But he forgot that too. He felt himself to be a free man. This simple life agreed with him. To one of the tree trunks was fastened a tiny mirror, the only sign of urban comfort here.

Daily he rode out on reconnaissance into the hill country up to the settlement of Dafne in the land of Dan. Not far from there but beyond our boundary lay the ruins of the old city of Caesarea Philippi, with its long-ruined grotto of Pan. There in the midst of forests is to be seen one of the clear springs of the Jordan.

153

Pan, Daphne—echoes of antique song and harmony. Yet here in the valley there grew now only the prosaic eucalyptus trees, the willow-like giant trees which looked as though nature had for once done something quite wrongly and superficially, for the trunks, from which the rind, as it does in birches, peeled off in rather coarse pieces, showed gray, red, lemon-yellow, blackish tints which seemed to have nothing to do with each other. As though they had just been splashed there, Helfin thought, and then reproached himself for the jest. The time would come when he would understand this apparent dissonance too.

In reality this was not the kind of employment that he had wanted. Had he gone to war to take horseback rides for pleasure? A silvery airplane cut the sky at an unimaginable height. Hardly visible, hardly audible, a bright fleck in the blue. No bombs.

Shelanu, our own? Or perhaps a peaceful passenger liner? So the armistice was really effective. There was some talk that the Supreme Command was planning a combat to recover Mishmar-Hayarden, that settlement which the Syrians had taken by a surprise attack immediately prior to the cease fire. But it wouldn't come to that. The ranking officer of the camp, a tall, thin American, who weighed every word, explained carefully that no breach of the conditions of the truce would be contemplated on our side. "We're sticking closely to the regulations of the U.N. In this particular, as in the war in its totality, we base ourselves upon the moral and legal fact that we respect and carry out the decisions of the corporate body of civilized peoples. Everything that we do is founded on the partition decision of November 29. The United Nations simply did not have the courage to put into action what they decided by a two-thirds majority. Hence we jumped into the breach. We are the executor of that world will which, in this exceptional instance, was briefly a reasonable will. According to it we are establishing our rights."

"Very fine," said Tom, a young fellow who had come from Melbourne and who was riding beside Helfin. "I just love our commander and his clever speeches. But it was much more fun when we wore our nightcaps and when '*nachshon*' was the password."

"What is *nachshon*?"

"Don't you know?" Tom wrinkled his freckled nose. "You

haven't been around long enough. 'Operation *nachshon*'—that was the secret name for the storm attack on Kastel. There wasn't much organization at that time. The officers had no gold braid on their shoulders and no one had any stripes. We all slept in the same tents, when we had tents. And also in actual combat there were no differences. We were guerillas. And that was our best time." In vain Helfin tried to demonstrate that the "illegal" period had to be followed by one of discipline, that otherwise no decisive victory could have been achieved. Tom shook his long reddish-blond hair. "Each one wore his woolen nightcap with a difference. One would have its two ends on either side; another would twist it so that it looked like a slanting brown sporting cap; a third would fold it up like a napkin and use his shoulder strap as a napkin ring. Doubtless our big caps with the large visor which protects your eyes are more practical. But the nightcaps were more fun."

"Why did you come here to volunteer, Tom?" Helfin asked him.

"Why, why? Why do you ask?"

"Well, Australia is far away."

"Not as far as you think. In the Jewish world, what is 'far'? I was born in Berdychev. My original name was, of course, Tevye. I meant to send for my father and mother and sister and four brothers to follow me to Australia. I'm an electrician. But down there they have funny little regulations in the matter of immigration. They told me to wait. They told me that it might be done later. But the others, the party of the murderers—they didn't wait. They were in a hurry. On the very first day on which the Nazis entered our town my four brothers were shot. They branded my sister's arm with the words 'Officer's Prostitute.' She had hardly known what a man was. During the first night, so my mother wrote me, she cut the veins in her arms. I never found out what happened to my mother, and that's probably the worst of all. I did get some indirect news of my father. A man told me—one of those who escaped after many adventures. He saw him in Auschwitz. This man was forced to work for the Nazis. His work was very easy. All he had to do was to sort out the garments and the gold teeth and the cut-off hair of those who had been burned to death. Everything was put to use. 'How did you stand that?' I asked the man who was from Berdychev too. 'You get used to everything,' he said, 'It just depends on whether you have the will to live or not. If you have it, you survive.' Now I never did understand that fellow, not even when we were at school; for we attended the same school. He was a very silent and reserved boy. He, too, is somewhere around here now among the foreign volunteers. Not a bad fellow. But what impressed him most about the Germans was the agility with which they executed their intentions. He used to say that with a kind of admiration in his voice. Those who were destined for the gas chambers were taken by motorcars to the trains. Scarcely had the trains arrived in Auschwitz when the prisoners were divided. It was so organized that Jewish guards, speaking Yiddish, demanded their garments of them. And it was during such a procedure that this boy from Berdychev met my father. My father was a very pious man. After he had given up his clothes he still clung to the bag of red velvet which held his *tefilin*, his phylacteries. 'What shall I do with my *tefilin*?' he asked an attendant. And my schoolmate heard the ruffian answer: 'You won't need those any more. Don't you see the smoke over there?' And he pointed to the solid black smokestacks above the ovens in which the people were being burned. Others who had arrived at the same time chid that coarse fellow. They asked him why he wanted to frighten the old gentlemen with his stupid jokes. None of the new arrivals understood that the man had spoken the truth and was not joking. They simply couldn't believe it. My schoolmate told me that to console me, I suppose. But all I could see from that moment on was the image of my pious father, more embarrassed than frightened, holding the old, red *tefilin* bag in his hand. And so I came and joined the Haganah. You do see, don't you, that Melbourne isn't as far away from here as one might think."

Tom fought down his tears and was embarrassed at having to do so. Tom, the *djindji*—as people with red or red-blond hair are called in Israel, not jeeringly or mockingly as in other countries, but with a certain tenderness and even a certain curious appreciation (for they are usually very sincere and energetic people, these *djindjis*, even as King David was, as the Bible explicitly states)—this Tom, this usually somewhat noisy Tom, had the embarrassed feeling that he had told too much and had too freely communicated the mystery of his life. Helfin hardly knew how to console him. He still had a piece of chocolate in his saddlebag. He gave the chocolate to the boy. And Tom took it, gave one more dry sob, and then bit into the sweetmeat. Helfin considered whether he should also tell a story, the story, for instance, of the extermination of his own family with the exception of himself and Gad. Would that be a consolation? A piece of chocolate made no sense either. But *mele*—it's all the same thing. There's nothing you can do. *Mele*—it's all the same thing; let things be as they will. It's a good word. Often it's the only word worth uttering. It's like the Arab idiom *fish kalam*—let's not say anything about it. Tom's story and many thousands of such stories would be recorded in the same gigantic volume in which would also be written down the story of the flight of René to Geneva, the story which drove Helfin from Switzerland. Six million Jews were thus hunted down and murdered. No people on earth has been so deprived of its rights and so hunted down as we, he thought. And now they grudge us even our last right to live in our homeland.

"I'm bound to tell you that I had very little to do with Zionism formerly," Tom continued more calmly. "I was a Socialist and I am one still. I want help extended to all people, not only to Jews. That's banal enough but it is an important truth. Nobody ought to suffer. That is the last word of wisdom. I don't want a single Arab to suffer either. But the Arabs have space enough. Abdullah's kingdom is extensive and underpopulated. Iraq is vast and relatively empty. They have land reserves for centuries to come. There is no necessity to restrict immigration here. It is only we who would perish if one doesn't let us come in. That's the reason why I came to fight in this war. It is a just war. Nevertheless," he ended with a little expression of stubbornness, "it was more fun when we wore the nightcaps and the officers had no insignia."

The answer which Helfin revolved in his mind was no longer an answer to his belligerent young friend but to himself. It wasn't fun that counted any more, nor the satisfaction of the individual.

It was a question of serving. That was the meaning of mobiliza-tion. Of course, he had had a better time during that one night when he dragged the sacks of flour. He had had the feeling that he, personally, was being useful. Now there had come the higher wisdom of the stripes and the insignia and had placed him here. This was the reward for his long love of English civilization. They wanted to put to use his knowledge of the language. And it was his simple business to obey—not to ask questions, but to do as he was told. One had now to approach one's duty with a certain hardness. This was quite different from the hardness of a certain handsome lady who came into his mind. One must now be hard toward oneself, not toward others. Toward oneself—that's the whole point. And there is happiness in that. It is a serene renun-ciation, not one dictated by satiety. Was not this what he had always desired? Or did he only understand now what had been the aim of his desires?

Toward the south extended the bare, sun-scorched hills right up to Lake Kinereth. These were not the rich forests of Syria mounting up to Hermon. These hills were naked. That consti-tuted, too, the contrast to Europe and its beautiful forests which he had loved so much. But things can hide in the forests —evil things that hide there before man and God, or, at least, the evil can think that it is invisible to the eye of judgment. Here, on the naked soil of our country, one is lifted toward the Eternal Eye as on the flat palm of a gigantic hand. Here there is no branch nor leaf between oneself and God. Here one must stand on the naked earth and give an accounting. "Where art thou, my serv-ant?" Thus thunders the voice of the Judge. "Hope not to hide your secret from the light of heaven!"

Suddenly it came over Helfin with great power: Our new state will be a state in all purity or it will not be at all.

And I, too, I will be pure or not at all.

At this point, surely, power had been taken from the Unambo machine. Or had a special grace been granted him? He could not entirely repel the thought of the red switch. But he took hope. What especially encouraged him was that that first variant of life with its evil occurrences and the three murders committed in his thought, had lasted only two days, only to the armistice. And ought it not really to have lasted a week? For he had set the apparatus to the space of a week. And he had now been living for nearly a week the second variant of his life, consisting of the two days prior to the armistice and the almost five days which he had spent here. Thus, perhaps, the dreadful rhythmic magic had faded. Perhaps the life that he was now living was his real and integrated life. Perhaps it had been given back to him and he was meant merely to have been taught a lesson.

He reflected that he had turned the hand of the dial to the line which marked the space of a week. By doing so he had indicated his desire that the alternation of the double stage should take place at weekly intervals. Perhaps he had made a mistake of manipulation. Perhaps his handling had been invalid from the beginning. He was convinced that he had passed only two days in scenery Number One which had, as one might say, the Bianca Petry note. Or perhaps he could change the arrangement even now! This life, which was being granted to him now, his right life, his active life, he would have wished to prolong, to prolong to the very boundary of extinction.

He could not fail to remember, however, that the apparatus had melted into thin air, or else had been blown into the garden. He determined to write Dvora and ask her to look for it. So far he had only briefly announced to her his departure and enlistment. How was he to change the pointing of the apparatus when the thing itself had vanished? Perhaps it could be done by a process of thought. Perhaps if he imagined vividly turning the red switch, he would really be turning it. But it would have to be done with the summoning of every ounce of will power. Otherwise it would not be valid. Probably, he thought, it was so. For it must have made some sense when the fat man had said that one could change the dialing of the machine later on and adjust the simultaneous unfoldment of the two variants of life to periods of two days or three, or to an immediate simultaneity. What one could not do, according, at least, to the fat man's silence, was to discontinue the operation entirely. The only exception to this rule was that the apparatus might crash against an insurmountable obstacle. But at once Helfin chid himself for following these mad ideas. The thing to do was simply not to give in to them.

Revolving such thoughts he reached the kitchen barracks which he had never yet entered. Behind it, in the glare of the sun which pierced even through the tinted glasses, there stretched out before him the illimitable plain. There was more greenness here than in the rest of the country at this time of the year. Alas, some of this greenness was that of swamps. How much work there was still to be done! Even malaria had not been quite extirpated in this region. After sundown the mosquitoes swarmed and stung. Well, the days of peace would come in which the work of sanitation would be continued.

The kitchen was empty. Tin boxes and bottles were ranged against the wall. A-ha, so there were *dshuks* here too? Had they been brought along? The rear wall of the kitchen was pierced by a single door, which was ajar. Immediately at its threshold there was a trench. How odd that, although he ought to be familiar with the entire camp, no one had yet shown him that trench. He clambered down into it.

A greenish pool seemed to put an end to the trench. The famous reeds of the Galilean plains surrounded it. Two *djamussi*, small wild swamp buffaloes, with glistening, fat, black little backs, paddled out of the water. Flights of birds rose. Carefully Helfin pursued a narrow path along the pool. The wind made rings in the water, in which the clouds were mirrored. The path continued past a thickly overgrown hillock. Several times he seemed to be sucked in by the wet, soft brown earth but managed each time to disentangle his soles. He wanted to complete his inspection. Later on he meant to point out rather sharply to Tom and to his other comrades that this aspect of the fortification of the camp did not appear on the maps.

In the midst of the reeds he found the entrance to a second and deeper trench. It was well built; even masonry had been used. Suddenly the ground gave way. A hole in the earth opened, but crossed planks were visible. The planks swayed, yet one could grope one's way across them. They seemed to lead to a labyrinth of dark passages. How could he turn back now? How find the way? For a while he wandered on through catacombs. Then a stair led him back to the surface of the earth. A platform with an ivy-framed door met his eyes. A metal knob. The courtyard which Helfin entered seemed to him like the platform on the Place de Grève, on which the guillotine, the beheading block, did its work. And here, too, were the stairs that led downward and the well-known entrance to the cellar from the wall of which protruded the gigantic horse's head. This time the head seemed alive. It made a grimace and laid bare its huge teeth. It made a biting gesture toward Helfin, who almost fainted at the sight. He fled along the gleaming, white-tiled passage with its vaulted roof and its many electric bulbs along the walls. For one moment he still beheld those two rows of lamps. Then they were extinguished for him in a flood of darkness.

CHAPTER FIVE

*Which shows how strong one can be out of sheer weakness
as well as how, under certain given circumstances, the undermost can be turned into the uppermost.*

1.

He regained consciousness in his own apartment, in his own bed.

On the edge of his bed sat Bianca Petry in the coquettish garb
of a nurse, white as innocence itself, with the red Star of David on
her cap. She begged him to remain calm. For five long days she
had been waiting for this moment. He had gone through a period
of high fever; he had talked a lot of delirious nonsense. He would
have to be most careful now and, above all, not talk.

He didn't feel ill in the least, only a little weak, which was
natural enough after a prolonged illness. Neither did he understand how he had come here. He could hardly trust his eyes. He
looked round on all sides and surveyed his books. Yes, they were
undoubtedly his own and over there was the black piano with
the bound scores. He indicated to Bianca that he would like her
to go on talking. He lifted his head from the pillows. No, he
mustn't do that! Bianca was in her proper element; she could issue
orders. It was becoming to her. She had always had something of
the clear vigilant manner of the physician about her. That
stood out now.

She told him how he had been found in the ruins of the house
next door. He had fainted. There had been a crowbar in his hand.
It was over there now in a corner of the room.

Now he recalled the black wall against which he had been
hurled like an arrow propelled from the bow. With a painful roaring forehead he had been catapulted against the wall. Later he
had collapsed at the turning of a subterranean passage. Now he
remembered. He was told that he had been unconscious for five
days. He grasped the situation. Those were the five days during
which in his "beyond," in that other life, no news had reached

him. And these five days made up the week, the same week which he had passed first with Gad in this very room, next on the "Burma Road," finally in Galilee. The accounting was precise. The apparatus was functioning. "No grace has condescended to me," he articulated sadly, almost solemnly. But no one could understand that except him alone.

"You wanted to help in the rescue work," Bianca explained to him.

This indication restored his consciousness completely. "What happened to the house next door?"

"Bombed out. It's in ruins. The house across the street too. It's a perfect miracle how this house wasn't even touched. But please, you mustn't talk."

"Nonsense," he almost yelled. "Tell me quickly, was anyone killed?"

"A few were wounded; no one was killed. They had all gone in time to the *miklat*."

He wanted to go to the window and see the ruins. She forbade it and insisted that he stay in bed. Finally he fixed his eyes upon her. "You have the cheek to come into my presence after what you did? For it must have been you who had that wretched slanderous broadside circulated. That was a filthy thing to do!"

Suddenly she dropped out of the role of the tender nurse and defended herself. "I thought I was carrying out your own intention; I thought I was doing you a favor."

"A favor? Didn't I definitely forbid any such thing?"

"I don't remember anything of that kind."

"Didn't I say that I would never betray a confidence that had been given me? Didn't I tell you that one must not use heavy artillery against a little worm?"

Defiantly she tossed her head. "You must have been dreaming all that." Obviously she recoiled from no lie. He understood her motivation, too. He was not to escape her any longer; he was to be forced to be a member of her gangster group; their complicity was to unite them.

He made a final attempt to defend himself. "In connection with that I explained to you that one must forgo revenge as well as many other things. Don't you remember that? And I explained to you what I meant by forgoing things, since this matter seems so important to me. And you, as you always do, defended the rights of instinct. And I ended by saying that we would never understand each other on this point. Don't you remember that either?"

"Oh yes, I seem to recall a sort of academic discussion. What did that have to do with Mr. Zemanek? We used to have these discussions in Paris and yet we had a very fine time." She took his hand, careful of him, apparently inspired by affection. "In fact, we had an extremely good time." Her gray eyes suddenly glittered while she thrust the fingers of her soft hand between his own fingers. "I believe that in the end we came to a very good understanding." She closed her eyes and gave a soft sigh.

He was lost! He knew now that he had returned to his former life. He was no longer a training officer in Galilee. How far away it seemed and pale—his ride through the mountains and Tom, the *djindji*, with his freckled nose. They didn't utterly fade, these scenes, but had suddenly become in some manner unimportant and insignificant. "Our state will be a pure state or it will not be!" What did that mean to him now? Other things thrust themselves upon him and needed to be answered. "What became of Zemanek?"

"It didn't really hurt him."

"What do you mean by that?"

"His foolish attempt in the laundry was discovered in time. He's in a sort of hiding now. He has had his warning."

He saw what she meant. He owed her a debt of gratitude. As had been the case with the Greek woman. But it was a question whether the Greek woman had been as much of a menace as she. Maybe it would have been better if she had not "saved" him.

"I want to be alone!" he cried. She left him but only to go into the next room. He felt that she would never leave him again now that she had caught him. Murder or intended murder —there was no difference. The blasphemous thought and wish to annihilate three human beings burned itself into his memory and weighed down his conscience not less than an actual killing would have done. The evil which had broken forth from him was a living proof and witness against him. It had assumed a firm, corporeal form; it represented an iron chain which welded him and his co-conspirators into a mass without a will. Ah no, not without a will, either. But the animating will was no longer his own. It was the will of this woman. He began to weep. But only a few violent sobs were torn from him. They gave him no ease.

Perhaps the thing to do now was to be stone-cold, to yield not the slightest advantage to the adversary. To recede not a single step. He began to dress himself. He decided that he would defend himself, that he would fight. The fact that he felt perfectly well physically gave him confidence. As far as Bianca was concerned, he had hitherto always had the upper hand. More curtly than he had intended to do, he called into the next room, "You had better stop your masquerading!" After a while he said more calmly, "I'm hungry. We might go and eat together somewhere. What time of the day is it? Is it evening? Very well, then we can sup." While he opened his clothes closet, he half quietly, half surreptitiously, drew aside the hangings of the window. The ruins of the two houses stared him in the face. They were like two heaps of broken, white skeletons, like a coil of bones.

2.

The first matter that he readjusted was the matter of Dvora. While he had lain in fever, Bianca had picked a quarrel with his faithful old housekeeper and had simply thrown her out. So soon as Helfin had learned of this from Bianca's own lips, he forced her to drive out with him to the suburb of Abu Kebir and solemnly beg Dvora for forgiveness. Immediately, even before dinnertime, it was settled that Dvora would take up her duties again on the following day.

Bianca accepted the humiliation in good part. "All right, you mustn't be excited; the child must have its way." She smiled as she said this and added with a certain gentleness and quite good-humoredly that she really didn't care about such uninteresting trivialities. It was most becoming to her to play the part of the well-balanced woman who, lovingly and respectfully, yielded to the man who had been placed in her care.

It became apparent that Helfin's anger and combativeness were both almost exhausted by this first victory. What was the use of making a noise anyhow? At supper in the Bridge Club Hotel Layla and afterward at the bar he was told a whole series of details which seemed to exhibit the matter of Bianca and Zemanek as having been somewhat less gross and vulgar than he had supposed. He made his inquiries not only of people whom Bianca introduced to him and who might have had their instructions. He turned his conversation to the matter with people who had not been influenced and with whom he had been genuinely friendly. So he questioned his photographer Recheimer, who was particularly glad to see him recovered and out of bed. He hadn't even heard of a broadside against Zemanek. So Bianca's assertion that she had had only ten copies printed in order to frighten the fellow took on additional probability. The American war correspondent, a Mr. Crooks, whom Bianca brought up to him hadn't even heard about the thing. That, to be sure, was comprehensible for other reasons. All that Crooks ever wanted was an appropriate story for his paper. He wasn't notably interested either in the war or in local conditions. What he needed was something which could be tricked out as a readable story for his audience, something strange, exciting, something that combined Oriental coloration with some feature that might touch the common heart. He liked stories about parents who by accident were reunited to their lost children on the very field of battle, or strange rescues, or noble or else completely mad actions. Now that the armistice had come, there was nothing left for him to write about. Crooks was in despair. He had imagination enough to exaggerate his anecdotes, not enough to invent any. Moreover, he was restrained from sheer invention by a certain primitive notion of honor which, according to him, belonged to his craft. He had never heard the name of Zemanek, since his field of vision was entirely limited by the cable service. The photographer Recheimer thought he had heard that an editorial writer named Zemanek had tried to kill himself. He had been depressed by his extensive debts. He had been saved in time. "So it was a question of financial difficulties?" Yes, he was sure that he had heard that.

Helfin considered that these were all mere rumors and that therefore he was worrying unnecessarily. Meanwhile Bianca was drinking whisky with Mr. Uri Waritzki, who owned extensive refrigeration plants. Waritzki had heard nothing of Zemanek. He was far more interested in Miss Bianca, he declared, and put his hand on her slender waist.

Helfin watched those two dancing in the twilit room. The black-out had now been discontinued. Bianca danced very gracefully. Helfin thought that he ought to be juster in his attitude toward her, less resentful. It was evident that the things that tortured him were less notorious and less well defined than he had imagined. It would be absurd, for instance, to try to white-wash Zemanek now. It would only serve to call attention to a matter which had apparently made no impression at all. He wouldn't help the man; he would injure him. The same would be true of Bianca. And she deserved it. But how senseless to kick up the dust. No use pretending to himself that he had never before wished to send his adversaries to hell. And finally, summing it all up, very little had happened even this time.

"What will your Philip Josefovitch say?" he asked Bianca when she returned to the table flushed from the dance.

"Say to what? What do you mean?"

"Why, that you let this swine-snouted Waritzki maul you like that."

She laughed. "Are you jealous?" And then she added, "It wasn't for very long."

It was not until this night that he found out what an agreeable, indeed, what an enchanting, mistress she could make. They had decided to use for their own purposes this night which was the last night before Dvora would return. They would have to make other arrangements for the future. Well, that would not be too difficult. In the meantime they had this one tranquil night. The other two times, in Paris and in Tel Aviv, had been in the nature of assaults rather than of quiet hours of love. He observed now that Bianca was not passionate in the sense in which he would have inferred her to be after those two experiences. But in those other cases it had been, doubtless, the peculiarity of the situations that had aroused her aggressiveness. Her demeanor now had elements of reserve and modesty. The light had to be extinguished and her tenderness had about it something well considered and conscious and wise which made her doubly desirable. It was passion which had been, as it were, deliberately cooled. In all this a not inconsiderable area had to be assigned to the play of unconscious forces. And that was quite natural. And one is not ashamed of the natural. Yet there appeared an invisible but unmistakable boundary which was not to be crossed. Only under the surface of calm and apparently spontaneous restraint, accompanied by few words or by silence, was the searing flame to be suspected. To let this flame flare up would have been indelicate; worse, it would have been absurd. Authentic emotions are rare. Bianca had announced that conviction of hers in Paris; she had familiarized him with it. Now it needed but the slightest indication to remind him of the mood of her first assault on him in his hotel room. Nor could he deny that he liked that mood to be recalled; it had something ingratiating for him, although its consequence was that imperceptibly he lost the upper hand.

In the course of this single night he was deprived of that imperceptible superiority. The thing was not obvious at once but essentially irrevocable. One element in the situation was probably the dim guilt feeling which the affair of Zemanek had left with him. This guilt feeling prevented him from rebelling against the methods which Bianca imposed on their relationship.

Why should she be the one to set the mood instead of seeking to discover what was appropriate and natural to him? This question was not even asked. All things took place as though there were no such question; as though everything had to be as Bianca desired and as though nothing else could even be thought upon. It must be admitted that her ways pleased him, delighted him in a pain-touched manner not commonly characteristic of him. Fundamentally he was a man of heart, even of a certain simplicity and of a spontaneous goodness of will. And now if there was communicated to him not verbally, not tangibly, but unmistakably, the following message: "We are strangers and will remain so. It would be both illusory and stupid to expect anything else of any human relationship. At this moment we are well disposed toward each other and each will strive to give the other pleasure. Very well. But that constitutes no metaphysical bond.

"There is indeed no possibility of a metaphysical union between two human beings, even though there is something sacred in sensuality. It is nothing but the sacredness of the naked instincts. I hope you understand that thoroughly and have no illusion about the swindle of a 'higher union.' There is nothing between any two people except sensuality and the further fact that, as circumstances vary, they can help or harm each other. Therefore let us guard a certain reserve and even at the seething climax a decent objectivity. It is well just like that. You will come to see it. It is like two constellations which go through their parallel gyrations, each preserving its own course and remaining within its destined orbit." Such was the communication which was held during this rich and exquisite night in a language different from the speech of man but in one which at rare hours and in exceptionally illuminated spirits arises as an equal rhythm, communicating itself from one to the other and penetrating both with its waves. These psychic waves are waves of an unknown nature, differing infinitely from the rigid grammar of words and sentences.

When morning came Bianca was both agreeable and gay, both housewifely and girlish. Since Dvora was expected momentarily, they had to get up early. They strolled through the streets and looked for a café open at this hour.

The air was delightfully fresh; it was not the sultry air of a summer in Tel Aviv. The two lovers seemed to themselves ever so young, like students in the Latin Quarter of Paris. "I'm a pretty old student at forty-eight, I must say," Helfin observed, "and I've been flunked out often enough." Her answer consisted of the obvious and massive obscenity. Curiously enough this did not seem to jar with her pseudo-virginal behavior and ostensible modesty. At least, it didn't break the framework of the mood. Helfin wondered how she did it; it seemed mysterious enough. He glanced at her sidewise, at her silken blond hair, at her arranged profile. He came to the conclusion that her entire behavior was precisely as lacking in authenticity and in the same way and with the same mystery as her tinted hair and her reshaped nose. Nothing about her is genuine, and she is perfectly frank about this lack of genuineness and the final result is, in spite of all, a charmingly harmonious one. And even while he came to this conclusion, he also saw that it offered no explanation at all. Yet so it was. And that was all that one could comprehend.

"Now how are you going to explain to your Mr. Philip Josefovitch where you spent the night?"

"It's pretty late for that to occur to you," she laughed. They were sitting in a *tnuva*, one of the many milk bars in the city. They were drinking coffee and spooning up their yogurt, which is called *lebben* here. It turned out that Philip had, in that sense, not been her "friend" at all. Had she ever told him anything like that? Or even indicated that? He had quite misunderstood. All she had said was that the younger of the two brothers meant more to her nowadays than the older. The older evidently hated her since his attack on her on the boulevard. In true Paris fashion he had been condemned to only two weeks in jail for carrying a weapon without a permit. The two weeks' deprivation of liberty had, however, resulted in the failure of an important business deal. It was this, probably, for which he could not forgive her. So there was nothing to be done with him. *Mele*—no use talking. Now as for the younger one—not much to be done there either. He, too, really hated her, though not so pronouncedly. Now and then he had given her signals of a certain interest. Well, she hadn't behaved too well toward him either. It was a pity, because it now actually pleased him to leave her in the soup. "It's my unfortunate style," she said in comic and self-ironical lamentation. And she went on, "My unhappy style which lands me in the soup, because the guy is filthy with money."

"It is rather remarkable," Helfin agreed with her, "that whenever you break with a man, it is always in a spirit of hatefulness."

Bianca was in a gay mood. One could almost imagine that she was giving herself away more than she had meant to do. "Well, that's the kind of a bitch I am. Someday I'll write a book about it," she said. "And I assure you it will be a most interesting book. Its subject will be how I have gotten the better of all the men with whom I've ever had anything to do. They resist very bravely; in the end they come to grief. Of course they're furious. It hurts their vanity." She continued with a pseudo-scientific analysis of herself. "In reality I am masculine. I should have been a man. Something got addled in the good old egg. How would I know! Male superiority is a completely unjustified phenomenon. I destroy it whenever I can. I have an unanswerable drive toward that end."

Somewhat taken aback and somewhat amused he looked at her. So that was her famous frankness. Maybe she had given herself away too much this time.

She observed his glance and naïvely and with well-imitated "womanly illogic," and even using the usually abominated emotional method and eloquence of speech, she continued, while, as though involuntarily, she drew up his hand and held it against her deliciously small, firm breasts, "But you're different. You are an exception, the great exception in all my experience." Her beautiful eyes were alight and were slowly lowered. He reflected that, though she admitted the artifice of her hair and of her nose, one had to admit that the total impression was excellent. Also one had to watch her like the very devil. A single false step with her and one was likely to end in the gutter.

It didn't occur to him at this moment that not only a single false step but a whole series of them already lay behind him.

Her present situation was the following: She didn't have a penny left. It had taken her last savings to come to the land of Israel. Since she arrived she had been living on loans in her wretched, hideous Pension Rotfisch. Distant relatives of hers in Tel Aviv, themselves poor enough, had at first advanced her small sums, the return of which they desperately needed. It amused Josefovitch vastly and obviously to see her involved in this sordid struggle. He positively jeered in open joy at her humiliation. But this fine gentleman would change his attitude the moment he was told that Helfin was writing his scenario around her as the only acceptable star.

Amusedly Helfin tugged at his little beard. "The other day I had the impression that you wanted to tempt me by the influence you had with Josefovitch. In fact it's the other way around. You want now to persuade Josefovitch to finance you because you're in a position to bring me in as your dowry. That makes me laugh."

"Don't laugh too soon," she said with a shadow of severity.

"He'll finance us both, you as well as myself. You don't seem to know the chief circumstance. I haven't gotten around to telling you." What followed was in fact a great surprise to him. It was the last thing he had expected. Behind his back Josefovitch, the unscrupulous speculator, as Bianca called him with something like tenderness, had acquired from Helfin's company the lots at Bat Yam and the studio that was being built.

"But that's impossible. According to the contract they have to consult me."

"You probably didn't read the contracts as closely as is necessary in this country."

Helfin disliked it intensely when anyone denigrated the country and its people. There were certain circles in which it was the habit to emphasize criticisms of this kind. "In this country as everywhere else in the world," he interjected.

"All right. Then let us say that we have among us lawyers of a singular acuteness who are able to nose out the weaknesses in the formulation of a contract. The members of your company are wonderful idealists. In consequence they did not formulate with the right precision and with the proper assurance some hidden, apparently unimportant provision of the contract. Idealists always act that way. Wicked people are always more exact; they are a hundred per cent and therefore have much more effectiveness. In a word, Philip Josefovitch, or else his lawyer, discovered some gaps in the contract, in the entire structure of the company. By the way, what is your opinion of Mr. Schäftel?"

It turned out that Schäftel had sold his shares to the younger Josefovitch. It had been no accident, the absence of that red-cheeked, apparently jolly gentleman from the meeting the other day. He was already in touch with the speculator. It was now evident that, by the purchase of this share, Josefovitch had been able to influence the company and to have an insight into its structure, and both of these factors he had utilized. "You can't imagine how quickly Philip acts. That accounts for his success. Uri Waritzki gave me some details yesterday while we were dancing at the hotel. By the way, he is a partner in the Josefovitch enterprises—import, export, exchange, gold; above all, foodstuffs and military supplies. Those fellows make a little fortune every day. No trouble for them at all!"

Helfin pondered: Is this the same land whose youth is silently sacrificing itself at the front? It almost seems as though there are here two entirely different countries, even as I am, alas, doubly within life and endure a wholly different existence in each of those two lives, without any fundamental understanding of how these simultaneous happenings can harmonize or are even possible. Take this woman Bianca. From the aspect of one of my lives I detest her. No, she is utterly indifferent to me; she is as far from me as though she did not exist. But today and at this moment I feel drawn toward her and it is this attraction which, at this point of time, while I am thinking these thoughts and letting this spoonful of sugar melt in my coffee—it is the delight in this attachment which now, precisely now, rules me almost exclusively. How is that to be explained? He who could explain it might rescue me from the doubleness of my earthly presence and bring me back to a simple and normal way of life. If I desired it to be so—ah, there's the rub—if I really did. But I myself chose this division, in order to make things easier for myself. And yet in the last analysis perhaps it is this thing that has made life so heavy and so contorted. All is obscure to me and withdraws itself from my understanding. I cannot yet penetrate what has happened to me and what will still take place.

It was over—the moment during which, as rapidly as the dissolving of the sugar in this spoon, he had been given a conscious view, in a sense, of both of his courses of life, and which had served to throw light on both.

He was immediately thereafter hurled back upon the actual ego which was now experiencing life. And that ego rose in a flame of rage. He was now to permit himself to be cheated by that unclean pair, those Parisian black marketeers who, when the French ground had become too hot under their feet, had planned to transfer their operations to our holy land, and to do so now, during the war, during this tension of all our energies, when there was least need here of such riffraff. Had they, by the way, arrived together with Bianca? Probably before, and she had followed them in the hope of ingratiating herself with them again. So far her plan had failed. And now—how did she come by this exact information? It was possible that she was the active factor within the plot; that she herself had thought of it, that she had instigated Josefovitch and persuaded him to plunge his hands into Helfin's undertaking. Or had she only acted the spy from the point of view of an outsider and knew all these things only at second hand? Maybe Waritzki had told her. Or the American correspondent. Or the photographer Recheimer, who had recently been spending a lot of money without doing any work. Threads evidently went back and forth. There must be an entire *knufia*, a band of bandits, who consorted together in that Hotel Layla as their headquarters and who were in cahoots with others in similar hostelries, of which there were many along several streets of the city. It was probable that the same kind of business was being transacted in them all. What was needed was a gigantic iron broom. For the hour and day he must embrace a smaller aim; he must fight for his share, for his work. He must outface this Josefovitch! He must take the bull by the horns. "Where does this Josefovitch live?" he asked suddenly. She didn't know. That seemed incredible. But she insisted. All that she knew was where one might meet him. At the Gold Exchange in Lilienblum Street.

"Where is that?"

"It's just in a little café. The café has no name. I'll take you there."

He said he didn't think that they needed to go at once. He would prefer first to investigate further and to consult the other members of his company.

She didn't agree with him. "You mustn't think that you're the only one concerned. We've got to hurry. Other film directors are running around in Tel Aviv. Nobody else in your class. No, I'm not just complimenting you. But Josefovitch is capable of hiring a third-class man. What does he know about art? But rich men can afford mistakes—that is, if they're rich enough."

Even so they had time to spare. The big man wouldn't arrive at the Exchange before eleven o'clock. The quotations were not published until noon. She seemed to be informed on that point too. So they went first to her pension. This pension Rotfisch, on the borderline of Jaffa, was, indeed, extremely shabby. Perhaps Bianca had invited him to go there only in order to illustrate to him how impossible it was to let her go on living in a dark little hole of a room which was almost wholly occupied by the bed. Everything around was dusty and worm-eaten. The moment one entered the place one had the sensation of withering and rotting away. Helfin decided at once to pay whatever Bianca owed in this hellhole and to take her to a good boarding house of which he knew the owner.

They drove to this pleasant place, which was called "The Imperial." They made their appearance together as though they belonged to each other. After their business was transacted they sat contentedly on the balcony and, instead of the foul air of closed-in rooms, inhaled the fresh wind of the ocean. Tears came into Bianca's eyes. "You're really a hell of a fine fellow, Paul, really," she said. "I am grateful to you. And you did it all so nicely." Touched by her emotion, which seemed genuine to him, he also took it upon himself to pay the debts which she owed her relatives. His kindness and immediate helpfulness exceeded her expectations and confused her for a moment. But after that moment of inner uncertainty she recovered her entire composure and immediately and swiftly explained the plans which she had, quite evidently, long prepared and carefully thought out. Josefovitch wanted to engage Helfin to work for the new company. She besought him to accept the job only on condition that she play the stellar roles in the first three films.

Now the point had come which she had foreseen. Helfin needed Josefovitch if he wanted neither to renounce the whole plan nor start all over again on the annoying search for capital. One more thing he decided to do, namely, to inquire of all the appropriate experts whether Bianca's news concerning the redistribution of power within the company was correct. Unfortunately there was little doubt. It would have been senseless for Bianca to have dished out false statements. He considered her quite capable of it, but only when it was to her advantage. But her advantage in this instance was certainly upon the whole on the side of truth. For, under the circumstances, he was really dependent on the speculator as the latter was equally on his collaboration. And Bianca was part of the arrangement. Why should she not be? Her talent was certainly an estimable one, and there was no reason why it should not develop further under his direction.

"But I won't give up my young friends," he said. "They have been my most loyal assistants."

"I haven't a thing against them." Since last week the relationship, according to her, was already reversed. When she first came to see him the question had been whether those young men had anything against her, not what her attitude would be.

"It's not an immediate problem," he said as though to console himself. "They're all in the service and cannot be counted on for some time." Had he thus in a sense abandoned them? he asked himself. No, at the proper moment he would see to it that the young people whom he loved were well treated. He would keep them all.

Just now, to be sure, his own position was far from secure. He would have to establish it, surrounded by sly enemies.

3.

The coffee house to which Bianca took him around noon was not essentially different from many others of the simpler kind which exist in Tel Aviv. Only the fact that there was no sign over its door could be attributed to disorder or neglect. A moment's observation also revealed the fact that in the glass cases around the buffet the supply of pastries, chocolate bars, and cigarettes was low. In other, similar places there was always a great plenty. The small amounts of merchandise here displayed seemed meant only to preserve the ostensible character of the place. Both of these characteristics, the absence of a sign and of merchandise, seemed to belong together. It just wasn't a regular café, although it rather looked like one. It obviously cared little for customers to come in and chat and drink coffee or tea or orange juice and quietly read their papers, as was customary in similar establishments. No, interest here was fixed on other matters: on making money, on a sense of haste, excitement, competition, even though here, too, guests sat in two or three dim rooms, and waiters with trays of steaming beverages went back and forth. This, too, took place here. But it was a secondary matter. One would have been tempted to say that this place was a façade for the Gold Exchange, which was located somewhere in the depths of the building.

On the other hand, the word "façade" was not the right one either in so far as it expresses a mystery or an attempt to hide something or to point to illegality. The Gold Exchange was an official, legal corporation. Maybe somewhere, in some other street, in some other rooms, there was a black Gold Exchange. Maybe. This one was perfectly open and aboveboard. Above the door which gave on the second room there was a little signboard which announced in Hebrew: "Entrance Permitted Only to Members of the Society of Dealers in Precious Metals." Of course no one paid any attention to this sign. Small crowds of people went in and out. But the sign proved, if it proved nothing more, that an institution approved by the authorities existed here.

Yet what was the reason for this air of mystery or, to express oneself prudently, this emphatic unobtrusiveness, at least, this quiet and apparently indifferent building up of a false front? And why did one keep reading in the papers a constant complaint over the rise in the price of gold, concerning speculations which unjustifiably undermined confidence in the economy and the monetary system of the young state? Why did one read concerning measures which the Ministry of Finance was bound to take and yet did not take? Helfin had very little insight into these complicated matters. But he made the observation that here and now he came for the first time upon a strange mixture, the existence of which gave him no peace thereafter—a mixture of something that was public and obvious and generally known, and at the same time not quite canny, even injurious to the common weal, a mixture of whispered conversations concerning what was not forbidden and which nevertheless was somehow foul. This last element in the mixture quite occasionally got the upper hand, the while everybody continued to act as though everything were harmless, or at worst an amusing impertinence not really disapproved by anyone and not possible to be blamed seriously.

Bianca remained outside. There were no women here. This, too, constituted a difference between this place and the gay, mixed company in the cafés of the city. The presence of men only reminded one of an Arab café. Bianca asked Helfin to go through the various rooms to the inner court of the building. There he was to call Mr. Josefovitch's attention to himself and bring him out.

In that courtyard about a hundred men raised their voices indistinguishably with or against each other. In this courtyard, under the shadow of broad old trees, there existed a wildly modest as well as, in a certain sense, shabbily improvised stock exchange. It was an amazing sight, if one remembered the great stock exchanges of the old and the new world, which exhibit their solidity and legality by means of pillared halls, of gigantic clock towers, of oaken wainscoting, of parliamentary auditoriums, of symbolical figures and allegorical pomp in the form of marble statues with such inscriptions as "Trade and Industry." No vestige of any such thing was to be seen under the green trees between the simple brick walls which enclosed the courtyard on three sides, while the fourth side was constituted by the open terrace of the café, above which rose the frontage of an ordinary apartment house. Behind the walls were other gardens, other dwelling houses, the boxlike structure of a warehouse. The nervous clamor—this noise alone reminded one of the interior of other stock exchanges all over the world—seemed to cover the whole place, including the very trees, as though a pasteboard box had been placed over the entire scene. Yet here, under an actually open sky and in the green shade of the trees, it was not as hot as it would have been in a small or medium-sized hall. A very large hall had not been available for this purpose. Hence a garden, a courtyard, had been chosen. In the center of the courtyard there stood a longish table of stone, such as one sees on the operatic stage at the representation of drinking bouts or students' taverns or knights' assemblies. Here, to be sure, there were no knights. Tightly packed on long benches sat agile little men, many of them elderly and bearded. Behind those who were seated there were ever-moving rows of those who stood. Sometimes there were two rows and sometimes there were three. Now some arose from the benches and others took their places. Being seated there was evidently no permanent privilege. All that was permanent was the tumult. Blending into a single tone all one heard was such words as "One" . . . "one and a half" . . . "two." Only an initiate could perceive who was addressing whom or who was completing a transaction. Some of the men remained calm; others gesticulated and waved notations, pencils, blank books with greedy open eyes. One man stood out, seeming to direct the scene. Though others arose by twos or threes and made some announcement and sat down again, the director remained the same. Yet it was all confusing in the extreme. For later on he who seemed to be directing sat down too and seemed singularly unconcerned with what went on around him. But perhaps he was only tired.

Even in a less confused scene Helfin would probably not have recognized the man he was seeking. The fellow who addressed him with a "Hello, Helfin" was a kind of moving mushroom. This appearance was intensified by a broad-brimmed tropical helmet made of cork. Josefovitch was one of those people who not only adopt the customs of an indigenous population but doubly insist on the use of them in order to seem at home. The tropical helmet, light though large, didn't suit his frail, small figure. "Hello, Helfin, what brings you here? Are you studying scenes for your next picture?" Josefovitch introduced him to some of his business associates. It was difficult to make him understand that someone was waiting for him outside. When he was told that it was Bianca Petry he received the information with a contemptuous wave of his hand.

Nevertheless he said, "I'll be with you in a moment," and seemed to desire to be courteous.

Before they left, Helfin took another look around. It was a madhouse. Madhouses, too, are under the supervision of the authorities. Obviously madhouses must exist; man cannot dispense with them. Tables had been set up along the bare walls of the courtyard as well as on the terrace. At certain tables men sat writing; they had opened great ledgers. At one table a trader took out of a paper roll, which he tore up, many gleaming gold coins. Another counted them, or perhaps accepted them without counting. The brilliant reflection of the metal shone on the fingers of the two. Perhaps, too, Helfin thought, those fingers were transparent. And soon it seemed to his frightened eyes as though others in that company had transparent fingers. He stretched out his own hand. It seemed to him that something was wrong with his index finger. It seemed a little withered and pale. Swiftly he looked up. Had someone observed his gesture? He took a few quick steps toward the exit, which led back into the café.

"Well, my boy, did I bring him to you or not?" With her eyes on Josefovitch, Bianca received them thus. In spite of an irritation between herself and the speculator, she tried to preserve a frank and pleasant mood. The man himself declared that at this hour he was extremely busy. He would be entirely at their disposal that evening in the Layla bar.

"I know that trick. You don't keep your promises."

"Perhaps not to you, but always to Mr. Helfin."

"This is the only place where you can pin Josefovitch down," Bianca calmly insisted for Helfin's benefit. "Everything else is a swindle. Either he has become completely unreliable recently, or he is really busy up to the eyes."

"I've already told you that I am always ready to meet Mr. Helfin," Josefovitch said coolly.

"It may be just as well that we postpone the discussion until tonight," Helfin said. He reflected that he had better first be calm and think the matter over and get more information. Was he to consent to get the capital for his honorable, decent, clean undertaking from this shady character with his resources coming from such madhouses as this? The other members of the company were good, honest farmers or people who had founded their industries here in a pioneering spirit in order to build up the country. They were sound people or they were the representatives of labor unions. And now he was to co-operate with a class which he had always kept at arm's length. Whither was he drifting?

"You did that wonderfully well," Bianca exclaimed when they were alone again and were strolling down through the vivid traffic of Allenby Road. " 'It may be just as well that we postpone the discussion until tonight.' " She had imitated his voice and expression exactly. "Oh yes, you gave it to that fellow who is so vain of his filthy money. You made him feel that money isn't everything. That's the way we'll get what we want." Uninhibitedly she kissed him there in public and pressed his arm, into which she had slipped her own, to her side. Somewhat later they sat in a tiny public park, on one of the few green benches which line the short Bet-Joseph Street.

It was a sober kind of neighborhood. There was a little foliage and a patch of lawn. One could hear and one could see through the branches the big shops and the many cars on Allenby Road. Bianca, as though lost in dreams, as though out of the depth of a common solitariness, said in her low, musical, dark voice, "To have you is to have everything in the world." For a moment she laid her head gently against his cheek. He felt the warmth. And on that nearby street the roars and cries continued. Then came the shrill clamor of the newsboys. The afternoon papers had appeared: *"Yediot Achronot! Yediot!" "Maariv!"* ("The Late Intelligencer!" "The Evening News!") This was the moment which, in retrospect, seemed to Helfin the culminating point of their love. In the midst of this prosaic environment, within the framework of newsboys' cries and the rattling of vehicles, to have heard these profoundly felt and tender words. "To have you . . ." Often at a later period he recalled these words and the silent minutes, never to return, which succeeded them. And he remembered, too, how on that day, in that poor little garden of Bet-Joseph, around the corner from Allenby Road, he had reflected with great happiness and with a deep seriousness whether he could not, in spite of all, make a true comrade and friend of her and had hoped that she might change and develop her soul and be capable of an authentic union. It was a swiftly passing moment of true happiness.

Then he took his leave of her. But one cannot lightly say farewell to a woman who has made one happy. They were to meet again for supper.

He wanted to make inquiries. For this purpose he called on several people, who told him contradictory things and pushed him farther into doubt. At home he took the volume of Scripture, the *Tanach*, out of his bookcase. He was overcome by presentiments, both dark and hopeful, by desires and fears. More for the purpose of liberating himself from trivial circumstance than in order to seek counsel, he turned the pages of the volume. He came upon the Prophets and read in Zechariah: "*Va-ashuv va-essa eynei* . . . Then again I lifted up mine eyes, and saw, and behold a flying scroll. And He said unto me, 'What seest thou?' And I answered, 'I see a flying scroll; the length thereof is twenty cubits, and the breadth thereof ten cubits.' Then said He unto me, 'This is the curse that goeth forth over the face of the whole land: for every one that stealeth shall be swept away on the one side like it; and every one that sweareth shall be swept away on the other side like it. I cause it to go forth,' saith the Lord of hosts, 'and it shall enter into the house of the thief, and into the house of him that sweareth falsely by My name; and it shall abide in the midst of this house, and shall consume it with the timber thereof and the stones thereof.'"

And again he read in the book of Yeshayahu, who has been Latinized as Isaiah: "Woe unto them that join house to house, that lay field to field, till there be no room . . . God will enter in judgment with the powerful of His people. Ye have plundered the vineyards and the spoils of the poor are in your houses."

And ever again he came upon that passage in the fundamental teaching: "They practiced evil and the land became unclean. Beware lest the land spew you forth."

The land will spew them forth. This phrase passed through his mind again and again.

Whatever the inquiries of that afternoon had not revealed became patently clear that evening in the Hotel Layla. As though there were no war in the land, as though there were no nearby battle, this room and the people in it were sunk in the intoxication of gaming. In a second room comfortable meals were being consumed; there was drinking and conversation; from still a third, one could hear the sweetish whining of a saxophone and the dragging feet of dancers. The cynical tone of the conversation into which Helfin was drawn against his will was quite in accord with the slothful mischief which took its ease here, and confirmed it through the greasy matter-of-factness of the assumption that only complete idiots would not be in agreement with it. Once more a prophetic word arose in Helfin's soul: "Woe unto them who call evil good and good evil." But that was the last monition that came to him under the pressure of this immediate environment.

Bianca was more amiable than ever, and the proposals of Mr. Josefovitch seemed to leave nothing to be desired. Helfin had been prepared to offer resistance. Nor did he blankly agree now or sign anything. He simply promised to turn the proposals over in his mind. And when Bianca's shimmering glance, the pressure of her soft hand, her agreement, her slightly emphatic praise of his prudence and skill, which were designed to flatter his vanity and make him yield, though she was not sparing of irony toward the frail millionaire ("You've met your match, my boy. We don't give in so easily.")—all this neither influenced him nor changed his mood. The only vulnerable point in his position which hurt him or, rather, which could have hurt him, if he had had a complete view of what was here being planned, was the circumstance that he was having any dealings with this pack of wolves at all. That he was not in full control of the situation became clear even to him for a fleeting instant from the fact that he did not get up and leave the little cubicle in the bar when Mr. Schäftel came in and joined them at the circular table and started, as always, to tell his uninhibited jokes. This wretched double-crosser had sold the buildings and the lots to that unscrupulous speculator and seemed quite unaware of the shamelessness of his actions. He was as gay and red-cheeked and jovial as ever. You perceived at once that robust health which caused him to blame neither himself nor others for his scoundrelly actions—not even others! That showed how good-natured he was, for most people find it especially difficult to forgive those whom they have bedeviled and betrayed. Bela Josefovitch, the older brother, came, too, and displayed the massive gesticulations of a fat Italian baritone. He paid little attention to Bianca, but did not at all seem to regard her with hostility. Uri Waritzki, the refrigeration magnate, on the contrary, was very attentive to her. He invited her to dance and afterward whispered to her in a dark corner of the cubicle and approached his swine's snout as close as possible to her décolletage. He as well as the photographer Recheimer were in khaki, but neither they nor several others at the table seemed at all incommoded by their military duties. They chattered with uninhibited arrogance and laughed. Others exchanged insolent glances with them and only now and then interjected some spicy observation. All, that is to say, except Goldgarten, the very elegantly attired manager of Schäftel. He did not join in the conversation. Now and then he seemed to indicate his disapproval of what was being said by a slow rubbing together of the palms of his hands. Helfin had the feeling that this man appeared to greater advantage than the others. He liked the calm expressed by the man's carefully combed and parted hair and his greenish, expressionless eyes behind the American polygonal lenses. Helfin thought that one might conceivably trust this man. But that was only perhaps because he was like one looking for a point of refuge upon a distant shore.

He himself confined himself to observation. That seemed equally true of the manager, and this circumstance approached the two to each other, though they exchanged no word. What was it that Helfin observed? What was it that one could learn here? Oh, quite a lot of curious details. First of all this, that here, where the war seemed so far away, all the barbarities which combat among men entails were uncritically and even gaily approved of. At one point, at which the discussion included the question of some conquered Arab villages, Helfin made the observation that excellent care should be taken of the property of the inhabitants who had fled. "And what would the Arabs have done to us if they had penetrated Tel Aviv or Haifa?" the Josefovitch brothers yelled as from a single mouth. "What did they do at Gush-Ezion and at Mishmar-Hayarden? Happily they didn't get that far." Helfin contradicted them in vain. Only Goldgarten quoted against them a Yiddish proverb: "If I am like such a one, I am no better than such a one."

Another cliché which commanded universal assent here was the following: "After us comes the atomic war!" In other words, "What we do doesn't matter in any event. We're just one little pawn in the great game between the Eastern bloc and the Western bloc. The Third World War is unavoidable. And then the destruction will be universal. And we'll be done in first of all." In the miasma of this passive and fatal pessimism which devaluated any effort toward better things, there flourished the numerous anecdotes such as Schäftel's report of a dialogue between two immigrants: "You came on account of Hitler, too, eh what?" The other in a rage: "No, I came to enjoy the climate!" Or the question and answer: "How do you manage to make a little fortune in Palestine? By importing a big one."

It was astonishing how everyone in these circles disliked the Land or else criticized it with an air of superiority; how they made fun of its upbuilding and fundamentally made everything the object of their malicious irony except their own well-being and their own money making. Occasionally there was hoisted the little banner of some patriotic phrase. But it made a poor appearance here and seemed to obligate no one to anything. More and more Goldgarten seemed to find it necessary to rub his palms thoughtfully against each other. The glance with which he regarded Helfin across the table was almost melancholy.

There was another curious thing here, namely this, that all the languages of the world, including Balkan and Levantine, were indiscriminately spoken. Only not Hebrew. Hebrew was evidently unpopular here. Nor was this all. In addition to these languages, and in addition to occasional intrusions of French or Yiddish or Magyar, there seemed to be in use a sort of secret language, from which Helfin felt himself wholly excluded. They talked about snowstorms, about coal, about art collections. They used these words in the most improbable combinations, quite aside from the fact that snow is excessively rare in this country and coal not frequent. Yet they mentioned both as everyday matters. The conversation finally became so obscure that Helfin looked around in utter boredom.

It was at this moment that Goldgarten addressed him. "I saw you once before, today, Professor."

"Where? By the way, I'm not a professor."

"At the Gold Exchange. I want you to be careful!" He beckoned to Helfin and they retired into the dusky corridor of the hotel. "You can lose a lot there. Winnings are trifling. If you really want to earn money, go in for marijuana! It is smuggled out of Lebanon to Egypt by way of Palestine."

"You're joking! How can it get through the military fronts?"

"Oh, as to that—"

"At the front any attempt to pass through is answered by fire."

"There are ways and ways." His face was full of pain and disapproval. "Take it from me, these Jews are capable of anything."

"Many of them. That is unfortunately true."

"Fronts!" Goldgarten murmured once more. It sounded like diminishing thunder. "Try to buy English sovereigns or Mexican pesos on the Exchange here. All you can buy are coins with male heads stamped upon them. You can't buy a coin with Queen Victoria on it. Why? Because the Koran forbids the faithful to possess the picture of a woman. Therefore in the Jewish state 'men's heads' are sold at a discount of ten per cent. Now I ask you, what sense would that make if there were not some communication with Beyrouth, or Amman? Right across the military fronts. It is scandalous, but it is so."

"But who would—?"

"How would I know? In Haifa and other places there are all kinds of people with international identifications, diplomats of all ranks and kinds. I accuse no one in particular. But the smuggling of gold is a fact."

"If I understand you correctly, then the harm is done by the smuggling and not by the Exchange, although it makes a bad enough impression."

Angrily Goldgarten clenched his fist. "These Hebrews!" He used the English word. But on his lips it sounded as though he spoke of some primitive tribe of savages.

Helfin kept calm. "I understood Josefovitch to say that the Gold Exchange was trying to keep gold at a low rate."

Goldgarten laughed acridly. "It may even be so. Without the Exchange it might be worse. Nevertheless it's a fact that in Paris and Cairo gold is one-third cheaper than here. Look at the price of food. That is the consequence! The scoundrels!"

Helfin felt as though God himself had sent him this man. He didn't want to go back into the bar. He was tempted to flee and have nothing more to do with the people in there.

"I don't even say that there isn't some good in it," Goldgarten continued, moving his sharp-edged lenses up and down and thus making a shadow flit across his face. "Suppose you have black-market dollars in Italy or in America. You heard the talk about art collections. Those are dollars abroad. You take your dollars and buy gold outside of the country where the sovereign is from one and a half to two pounds cheaper than here."

"Then, I suppose, 'coal' and 'snowstorms' are business terms too?"

"Those are different aspects of these Hebrew wiles. 'Coal'—that means unauthorized slaughtering, the special realm of your Mr. Schäftel. Now and then, to be sure, his henchmen are caught and a truck with a few head of cattle is confiscated. He goes free. 'Snow'—that means the illegal supply of mills with flour. That is Waritzki's territory. The Josefovitch brothers specialize in gold and foreign currency. They are accomplished virtuosi in these manipulations; they are not simple-hearted souls like the others, who bring in illegal gold and hide it in their mattresses or bury it in their gardens."

"Instead of delivering it up to the government, as has been ordered?"

"Correct!" The manager bowed as though before some unseen high tribunal. "The brothers Josefovitch sell the gold at a high rate for Palestinian pounds. With these pounds they once more buy dollars abroad. That's a fine business, because with these black-market dollars you continue to buy cheap gold abroad and thus the circular movement continues after the well-known manner of the endless screw."

"I assume that you tell me all this in order to warn me."

"Against my boss? What are you thinking of!"

"Well, then, what for?"

"I saw you on the Exchange, Professor. I thought right away you might have some plan. You probably want to make a picture in honor of these Hebrews. Well, it seemed to me that an artist ought to have some correct information. I'm a simple trader, an honest one, to be sure. For that reason I'm very nearly down and out. You need iron elbows in this gang. . . . We can talk again some other time, if you like. One more thing. I wouldn't exactly publish the content of our conversation if I were you."

"I quite understand."

Bianca had come out of the bar into the corridor. She put her arm around Helfin's neck. "Why do you leave me so long with those frightful bores?" Thus sang that deep, soft alto voice, that viola in her throat.

"I don't want to go back in there. I want to get away from here and go home," he said with disgust in his voice.

Her agreement was unexpected. He had feared that she would beg or try to force him to sign. Or else try to do so and not let him go, at least without his being involved in a tiring and fruitless discussion concerning the new contract. She seemed not even to dream of such a thing. What a relief! His eyes must have brightened, for she continued at once, "We don't even have to say goodbye to them. They seem, in any event, to have quite other concerns and to be riding high. They won't notice that we're gone. Come on, let's go!" With affectionate energy she took his arm. Her tread and her every gesture affirmed the agreement between them.

4.

Why was he so amazed to have her make common cause with him, to attach herself to him ever more closely? Should they not, being both artists, naturally present a common front to these unscrupulous chasers of the dollar? Why did he distrust her? Did he not, by doing so, create an obstacle to her by no means impossible change of mind? He reread the little statement describing the negative side of her character which he had written down in Paris as a warning to himself. Perhaps he had judged her unjustly at that time on account of her desertion of the studio. Perhaps she wanted now to prove to him her reliability and unselfishness by being to him the woman who understood him, loved him, considered his needs. Or was it simply that for the course of a few days she was still impressed by the circumstance that he had helped her so decisively, that he had liberated her from intolerable conditions and had released her from trouble and from care? Yet he thought he knew her well enough to be clear on this point: transitorily she might be grateful; she might quite melt in silent appreciation, seeing that glances and charming and attentive behavior could convey far more gratitude than mere words. As a permanent thing this rather idyllic condition could not satisfy the passion of her ambition.

Whatever the reason, a few days of silent happiness, such as he had not had for long, were granted to him. The armistice, moreover, although it was to extend to only four weeks, also meant a release from the instant pressure of political misery and indignation. Nor can it be denied that Bianca, though yielding enough, and glad to be led, remained a demanding woman who kept one in a state of tension by her partly intelligent, partly strangely eccentric notions. Being allied to her meant not having much chance to think of anything else. This, too, he knew: sooner or later, the negotiations with Josefovitch would be taken up again. For careful inquiries established the fact that the man did have a commanding position in the film industry. In this respect he had made a clean sweep. Helfin still hesitated. It was a good thing, at all events, not to press the matter. Bianca thought so too. He also intended to have incorporated in the contract a complete autonomy of artistic decision for himself. Nevertheless the day would come on which one would have to sit down together. But there was no hurry. Yet a strange idea employed his mind whenever he thought of the approaching moment. Even now—thus he meditated with a kind of altruistic anxiety—even now it isn't easy for her to prove to me that she really loves me and isn't just grateful as a matter of duty. Of course, she never talks about that; she never expresses her feelings frankly and unequivocally. She thinks that unrefined. How many disputes we had on that subject. And it's my opinion that feeling, true feeling, is careless as to whether it's distinguished or merely powerful, whether its expression is curbed or overwhelming and wild and immediate. She would never agree with me. To her morbidly delicate perception any unmistakable word is intolerable. Contemptuously she refuses to say what might conceivably go without saying. Whatever is not divined nor manifested through the mystery of silence seems worthless to her. This is certainly a deep and right cognition concerning whatever passes back and forth between two mortal souls; it is a correct view, if it is not pressed too far nor exaggerated. Well, that happens to be the way in which Bianca feels and thinks and in reality lives. For it is true that, even without any direct expression, she manifestly displays to me her tenderness, her special icy sweetness, her spare and prudently appearing spirit which never, consequently, ceases to be a surprise. Even now it is hard for her to keep her love in relief from the banal sentiment of gratitude which unfortunately she owes me for commonplace enough reasons. What a horrible situation! How is so exquisitely delicate and mysterious a soul to separate gratitude from the more precious groundwork of love when, in addition to everything else, I insist that Josefovitch agree to her being cast for three successive stellar roles and thus succeed in initiating her career? He was actually sorry for Bianca when he thought of her happy future and of the blind alley that would issue from that future for her complicated soul. The only thing that comforted him was the teaching of experience to the effect that unexpected and hitherto unseen paths led one forth from new labyrinths—real and not imagined ones—into which one's feet had strayed. And the solution was usually quite sudden. It was this teaching which helped him to conquer his melancholy thoughts.

They had days of quiet happiness. They would wait for a good excuse to send Dvora on some errand, inventing pretexts which would prevent her returning for the evening and the night. Bianca stressed the necessity for prudence. Very earnestly she explained, "You can afford to be careless. If a director has an affair with an actress, it does not reflect on him, only on her. People forgive him; he is considered all the more of a man. The woman loses in value because her success is no longer attributed to her talent but to that relationship." He could have criticized this far too broad generalization, but he preferred to enjoy their platonic intervals. Bianca would pace nervously up and down near the house; any coming or going drove her off again. She waited for entire quiet. All the doors had to be closed, with only the door of his apartment slightly ajar. Then, at last, he would hear the soft tapping of her heels. To disguise herself she would wear a red headkerchief which made her resemble a Russian peasant. Finally, excitedly she would slip in, still lamenting her daring. Each time it took a little while before his affectionate solicitude could calm her. A little surprise, a rose or a bit of good news, would then establish harmony. Then she would be gay and confidential and, at times, of a childlike frankness. Then all the torment was forgotten which had plagued him in the loneliness of his icy tension. Indeed, the contrast between the two conditions served to heighten the warm delight of their being together with a gleam of rarity, of the adventurous, of what had been wrung from fate. The hours passed swiftly. Almost immediately it seemed to be night. At first the hours seemed long. Listening for steps on the stair, peering through the blinds into the dark street, where nothing was to be seen—this, as well as the noises without, of the wind, of the voices of passers-by, fulfilled the time and held up its smooth passage. All things seemed to contain a message from her. At her approach the room itself was mysteriously changed; a soft and festive radiance filled it. Simple things, such as flowers in a vase, an open book, coffee and its fragrance, the black sheen of the piano under the lamplight—in every detail of the room there was a delicate vibration which yearningly manifested itself so soon as the hour of her return approached. And its vibrancy in things grew ever stronger and tenderer. It was so audible that one wondered how one could have failed to hear it amid the preoccupations of life's common day. But now its music arose, varied and many-voiced, now jubilant, now melancholy—that music of life itself to which so incomprehensibly a deaf ear is commonly turned.

Yearning continued to remain the kernel of this love. That was implicit in Bianca's stimulating reserve and in the rareness of their meetings. He was not permitted to call on her at all; that would have been too conspicuous. Also, she preferred restaurants on the outskirts of the city and her prudence grew morbid as the moment approached in which the final contracts were to be signed. When Helfin considered how, with little or no motivation, she had assaulted him in Paris, how she had run after him in Tel Aviv and kissed him on Allenby Road in the midst of the traffic, he was bound to look for an explanation. Well, in those days she had been the huntress; she had followed the laws of the chase. Now the game had been caught and killed. He thought of a more tolerant explanation. In those days they had both been unfettered. Now they were about to make a compact, both professional and artistic. It was not to be denied that it might be reasonable not to flaunt their personal relationship. Commercial managers always treated couples badly and paid them low. Yet at bottom such considerations should have had no weight with a woman so exceptional, so exalted above all common prejudices, a soul, as she herself defined it, which throve on its own wildness. He was more and more convinced that something was wrong here. Yet the more he felt the discomfort of this fact, the stronger seemed the bonds between him and Bianca to grow; the less did he desire that now, when the matter was being clarified, a change of his form of life, a break in it, or a transfer to his other existence, should take place.

The transference had long been due. There was no doubt about that. It was ten days ago, no, twelve, since she had turned up in her nurse's costume on the edge of his bed. How was that possible? How could the period have been extended? Had he hampered the rhythm of the machine or brought it to a stop? What he had not accomplished in the purity of that other life—had strength to accomplish it arisen now for him out of weakness, yearning, desire? How shameful that would be! . . . And more closely looked upon, he was living even now in Galilee as a training officer; he was riding down those distant mauve-gray mountain terraces—all these twelve days. He was here in only one of his two forms of existence; the other variant or obverse of his life was taking place far away. He knew not what was taking place there. One thing he felt distinctly, that yonder, in that other sphere, the second film, so to speak, of his life was being released from the reel. And both reels were simultaneous. It was only his inexperience, his lack of adaptation to the Unambo mechanism that caused him to perceive the variations as successive instead of simultaneous. He was walking around in Galilee—and also here. His existence was twofold. In a certain sense he was borrowing the days which were simultaneously passing in his other life and contained him. But he had liberated himself from them, especially from the eighth day on, from that awakening on. Now he was living anticipatorily and would have to make up for these days;

he would have to pay back these four days which he had borrowed.

While these dark voices hummed in his head and heart, voices which he could not interpret more clearly as they continued to sound, he had the feeling for the first time as though one of his legs had been amputated and as though he dare not sustain his equilibrium by tripping on the other. And to stand up in this mutilation of body and soul against another human being who, despite her delicate and manifold attractiveness, or even because of it, was, at bottom, of so robust an energy, of such singleness of purpose as Bianca, that task now seemed to him doubly difficult. He felt that it became ever more impossible to resist the impending change, the change which was, indeed, overdue. It seemed to him that he was trying with all his might to hold open a door which had the tendency to slam.

From day to day he felt more keenly the exertion that was necessary to keep that door open by sheer force. A curious weariness crept over him; it was like a faint mist that gathered over his eyes without enfeebling either his reason or his imagination. Indeed both faculties seemed to be stimulated to the point of morbid activity. What visibly diminished was his power of moral resistance, his hopefulness, his pleasure in the accomplishment of anything that he was doing or planning.

This diminishing resistance seemed to create threatening visions which suddenly overcame him, especially when he first woke up in the morning or late at night. He saw himself standing in the Layla bar behind a door of frosted glass which led to the dance hall. On that pane he saw the silhouette of a couple— Bianca and the eternally light-footed Mr. Waritzki. Whispering, he had thrust forward his swine's snout. Suddenly someone opened the door halfway. The silhouette on the glass was lengthened so that the snout protruded monstrously, took on for a moment the form of a gigantic horse's head and precipitated itself upon the girl. He knew this horse's head well enough. It was the boundary signal between the areas of his two lives. No doubt about that. For the same brown horse's head leered between the swaying curtains of his room on the next morning while he was still half asleep. He looked at the creature in questioning impatience. Even upon its last appearance it had been no more of wood, but a living creature of flesh and blood with a malicious grimacing expression. Now, of all things, it began to talk. Helfin seemed to himself to hear reproaches out of the vibrant neighing and out of the far, dull repercussion of hooves. This horror came back daily. But there were always new and increasingly irritating variations. At one time the horse's head seemed dead and empty, a hunting trophy against the wall. Another time there were two heads, one peering in at each window in the morning. One neighed; the other opened and closed its eyes and winked them with an expression of devilish understanding. Another time the fire-eyed monster peered out from under the bed, so that Helfin leaped from among the covers with a cry. Instantly the beast had vanished.

These terrors faded as the business of the day set in. Then no trace remained. It was worse that sometimes, in the midst of his waking hours, that second life of his made itself known, though it was not supposed to have anything to do with the life actually being lived. It was as though a coin were suddenly to become transparent so that the stamping of the obverse and the reverse were simultaneously visible. Or, else, it was as though one were reading an ill-printed book, and the letters on the reverse page glimmered through the thinness of the paper so that, between or even over the lines one is reading, that misplaced text makes its ghostlike appearance. What is separate should remain so. Here, in contradiction of all order, divine or human, the frontiers of things flowed into each other. The whole thing would come over him during some animated conversation with Bianca. He would ask himself why he was explaining his notions? Of what concern could they be to her? How could she know when he was serious? For convictions could arise only from the dignity of freedom and not from such a minus existence as he was leading.

Before this inner doubt struck him he had just been discussing an ethical phenomenon: the special kind of Socratic renunciation practiced in Israel by the young people in the colonies. They did not use the words. Indeed, their words were often intentionally hard and irreligious, as though they were shy of all things sacral. They practiced the spirit. They wore the same garments summer and winter; they were hardened and reduced their necessities; they were careless of sleep and nourishment; they were a living sacrifice to their great cause. . . . Suddenly Helfin wondered to whom he was saying this—to this spoiled little worldling who contradicted or agreed simply to seem bright and original? Sometimes she agreed, because that was her whim at that moment. But her yes and her no were equally worthless. In spite of her affectation of a mystic depth, was she capable of thinking anything through? What did pioneering, either the word or the thing, mean to her? To her everything was a spectacle, a showpiece, just as her love of truth was only an instrument of her ambition. The whole thing was a caricature and he, indeed, was no better off. For every word that he spoke concerning things of import was falsified in his mouth when it was addressed to her. And did he still have the right to take anything seriously? Had he himself not desecrated everything and betrayed his own soul?

He was compelled to re-examine his spiritual situation. Just what had happened to him? Was he split into two halves, a good one and a wicked one? No, it was not that at all. He was in existence twice over. But in each of the two forms of his life he was exactly the same, the same kindly, amiable, rather weak person who felt that he had been tried beyond his strength and who therefore, like many others today, had given up his resistance against the harsh facts of the world. These facts were of a different order in each of his two lives. The chain of cause and event which proceeded from his first mistake changed with the circumstances. This, naturally, had its gradual effect upon the inner attitude of the individual that he was. But in both forms of being he remained the same individual, only a doubled one, and thus exposed to other external influences which were sometimes favorable and sometimes overwhelmingly menacing. What he saw very clearly was that he was exposed to the menace now. How am I to resist? he asked himself. For is it not a characteristic of our age that environmental circumstances, the stratifications of society, the power of the state, have grown so massive and so powerful round about us that there is no possibility of resistance. We blame ourselves in vain. Not ours the guilt, but that of the historic process. It has grown too rough and evil in our days.

Counteraction is of the feeblest. At the uttermost one can overcome death, as Socrates did, and thus set the example for the ages. To resist subtle tortures is another matter. The Fascists and the Nazis rediscovered the usefulness of torture as a political factor. The moment that happened, the Devil had regained the rule of earth in the midst of a cloud of terror. Torture is stronger than death. Especially when it is so used that the refuge of unconsciousness is blocked. Who can endure that? The strongest go to pieces. From this cognition there arises a new and modern bitterness, far sharper than the bitterness of Swift. The world has glided away from the leadership and direction of God. And it is His fault. His fault—not ours. "Forgive us, as we forgive Thee."

Thus he came to the end of his heaven-assaulting blasphemy. But had he not once proceeded from the very determination to escape the guilt of blasphemy? . . . And my people, of whom I am an obscure symbolic abbreviation—my people is no better off than I. Israel is shaken. It is making an attempt, never before so sharply made, to rebear itself as a people out of the womb of its own self. And now it sways between this not yet quite accomplished birth into the light and the dark residues of the many ghetto centuries which it has not yet stripped off.

I had imagined that I could be simultaneously the old Jew and the new, the incarnate human being and the bright human portent of our future. Now I see whither this simultaneity has led me.

I can get rid of neither the one nor the other. The twofoldness will not fade. In the midst of that happier life the other is like a shadow on the horizon. Or it might be likened to the diminution of light in the enlarged images of a telescope. It obviously remains. Precisely as now in this minus-life that other, that good life, continues its demand upon me. But on my lips and at the moment of expression it degenerates to hollow declamation, unworthy of that youth to whom I would address it. I am separated from it by an impassable abyss.

Even my beating my breast is a kind of hypocrisy. What do I do except use all that as a theme of conversation to bridge the time between acts of fornication? A philosophy in bed is no philosophy. It is a caricature. If the good to which I aspire would at least leave me in peace and not try to blend with my vices, then these vices would at least be respectable ones. . . .

He was frightened. All this reflection was false. It showed the influence of Bianca, against which he had hitherto defended himself.

Nevertheless it was troublesome to observe the marks of that other shadowy life of his break in so often upon his present existence, whether it was by a recollection of Socrates or the vision of a horse's head with red, rolling eyes.

It came in more sober guise one day when Bianca said to him quite unexpectedly that she would like to make the acquaintance of his nephew. "I'm curious about Gad."

"Why curious? Is that the right word?"

"It is, because you hide him, because you make a mystery of him."

"He is never in Tel Aviv. He is somewhere near Bet Susin around the 'Burma Road.' "

She was amused. "Don't you suppose I knew he was here the other day?"

That troubled him. "When?"

"Wouldn't you like to know how I know? What upsets you? Very well, I'll tell you. It was the day I first called on you, when I had finally found out where you lived. The bell rang. When you came back you said simply, but obviously lying, that it was a registered letter."

He reflected that he had been quite right to do as he did. Gad was a part of the plus-life. He had nothing to do, and must not have anything to do, with that negative existence into which he had slid under the patronage of his perfumed, worldly doll. He had done a thousand times right to keep the two strands of life as far apart as possible. He prayed for the strength of an Atlas to continue to do so.

But Bianca went on, "Don't exert yourself. Baruch introduced him to me in the street yesterday. I just forgot to tell you. We're going to the movies together this evening."

"I forbid that," Helfin almost shouted.

She looked at him in astonishment. "What do you mean—forbid?"

He thought he had gone too far. "All right, I beg of you to renounce this meeting. I don't like it. It would be most disturbing to me."

Hesitatingly she consented after long persuasion. But she refused to spend the evening with Helfin. "I'm annoyed by your littleness of spirit," she said.

"You lay yourself open to the suspicion that you want the evening to yourself to do as you like in spite of me."

Her eyes were very wide. "I gave you my word. Either you trust me or you don't." She was seriously affronted, or pretended to be. It got to the point that he had to agree, as a proof of his confidence, that he would not inquire into her doings of that evening. This corresponded to her favorite principle of preserving her personal freedom entire and of creating about herself at the same time an atmosphere of the uncontrollable, elementary, uncertain, unfathomable. He felt that she ought not to have put him to so painful a test. And anger against her arose within him.

And while the red star, the treacherous cyclopian eye of Scorpio sparkled at his window, he began, with the stubbornness of the sleepless, to compare the ultimate malice of her craftiness with the little good that he owed her.

5.

He didn't inquire after Gad on the following day. His pride was hurt. He perceived within him a gleam of jealousy, of which he was as ashamed, or more ashamed, than of the circumstance that, a few days before, he had had his pointed little beard shaved on account of a few gray hairs. His jealousy was more a jealousy for Gad than of Bianca. If only she had chosen someone else. He had never been jealous of her and Josefovitch or Waritzki. Of course both were very unsightly—one like a mushroom, the other like a pig. Gad, the young, fresh, pure, was too good for this woman. He belonged quite organically to the childlike grace of his Atida. He was unwilling to name these two beautiful children or to think of them in connection with Bianca.

So he didn't ask after Gad. He limited himself to the actor Baruch. But he couldn't help wondering why Gad hadn't looked him up, if he had been in town. Helfin pondered the matter. Perhaps, from Gad's point of view, he was in Galilee and not in Tel Aviv at all. From Gad's angle his life was being lived on another level. Possibly this was the right explanation. At least, it consoled him for the moment. So he had been robbed of none of Gad's affection, nor had their pure relationship been poisoned. To Baruch, too, he was the officer serving at the northern frontier. Both had failed to call on him for the same reason. He asked Bianca, "How do you and Baruch get along? Have you made it up? Are the Paris sins forgotten?" To leave behind him the complicated trains of thought induced by Unambo, and to address this relatively simple question to Bianca, seemed to him a kind of relief.

Bianca's gaiety was very marked. When she seemed truly merry all that was corrupt seemed to be drained from her. One would become lighthearted under the influence of her maddening charm and girlishness although one knew—knew it without perceiving it—that this girlishness was a piece of stage property which had been raised into timelessness and rendered rigid there by cosmetic art. But in spite of all one's better knowledge, it was an improbably slender, elastic and girlish body from which breathed a magic and aromatic vital energy. It sparkled before one's eyes even during the exorbitant and accursed eccentricities of her thought, even in the face of her unrevealed secrets, even in the presence of her falsely blond hair. Here was a caricature of love. He knew it beyond a doubt. But he was caught in its net. And he remained so, in spite of everything. At the moment she was telling with tranquil serenity how she had renewed her old friendship with Baruch and persuaded him to introduce her to Gad. "Baruch is *so* naïve." She confined herself to hints. A letter had played a certain part in the matter. "I can imitate handwriting extremely well. Baruch had a sweetheart in Paris. I couldn't bring him greetings from her. Instead of that I transmitted as from her a little love letter that was a masterpiece. Why does your high and mightiness look so serious?"

Helfin tapped his chin as he used to tap his beard. "I'm just wondering what unexpected forms your famous passion for truth may yet assume."

"Oh, this is just a fantastic little game. What has it to do with truth or falsehood? I like to make up little romances. You make them up for your scenarios and I just tell them. What's the difference? Do you know the story of my mother?"

"I do, I do. You've told it three times. Agreed. I just want to nail down the fact that your principles admit of too many exceptions."

"Quite right. Otherwise they would not be principles. Only exceptions admit of no exceptions."

This merry controversy continued for a time. All the while he was thinking that she might well call young Baruch naïve, otherwise he would not so easily have torn down the wall between two worlds which he had so carefully built up. He wondered how his brave warrior, Gad, would stand the test. If he could not trust him, then there was no one left on earth. But he would stand the test. Helfin determined to be firm in that faith.

"So you and Baruch are reconciled? I'm very glad. Because it means that a certain paragraph in the contract assumes a different aspect. Or it could even be eliminated."

"So you have the contract?"

He hadn't signed it yet, but he had been on that very day in Josefovitch's office, which was situated in the highest story of one of the new and magnificent office buildings of Tel Aviv. A long discussion with the mushroom man had taken place. Now he had the contract in hand.

He spread out the contract in front of Bianca. She sat, as she was fond of doing, on the broad arm of his chair, using it as a side saddle and letting her beautiful slender legs swing free.

"Don't you eliminate that paragraph," said she, "I made a point of having Philip include it. He doesn't understand such things."

"The paragraph says that roles shall be assigned only to professional actors. So that was your notion? And how would you define a professional actor?"

"One who has worked with the big firm companies, not merely in an experimental studio."

"So that point was deliberately aimed against those comrades of yours?"

"Doubtless," she said coolly. "At least it can be so interpreted. But you will not have overlooked the second half of this paragraph, according to which the director, in agreement with the stellar artist of the film in question, that is to say, in agreement with me during the first three films, may disregard this ruling and engage a limited number of nonprofessionals."

Helfin got up. "What, as a matter of fact, were you aiming at?"

"At just what you have in mind. Your suspicion is correct." She didn't avoid his eye; her reply was cold and decisive. "I'll have my revenge on those scamps; I've trembled before them long enough." Immediately Helfin remembered the wild accusations flung against Bianca in Paris. Nothing was ever proved. But an unclean atmosphere of spying, of treachery in service of the Gestapo, had oozed from these suspicions. "I'll take it out on that little hypocrite Nechama, and that fool Baruch, and that scoundrel Jonah who pretends to be so righteous. And Zvi, too . . ." As she gasped forth each new name, new volcanic springs of hatred seemed to open which would not permit her impulses to cool.

He shook his head. "Perfectly frightful! Of course, I will refuse to sign such stuff." At this moment he was sure of the unconquerable oneness of his being. He was the same character in both of those lives. He could defend himself and stand fast.

Bianca hissed, "Don't carry on so! You'll lose your halo. As if you didn't know about revenge. As if you didn't know that sometimes one needs it more than bread and can't go on living without it. Do you happen to know, by the way, that Zemanek died yesterday?"

He hadn't known. He had, on the contrary, quite enjoyed the fact that the other day his yapper had again written an article abusive of himself. It showed him that the man was well again. Now Bianca sent Dvora for the morning paper. There it was. A stroke. "The result of long excitement resulting in angina pectoris . . ." The colleague who had written the obituary had spoken of the late writer's "foaming temperament . . . *De mortuis* . . ."

Bianca observed the impression on Helfin of the unexpected news, how it shook his firmly held security. Skillfully she turned the spit around. Now it was she who moaned with pangs of conscience. She put on a big scene. "I am so sorry—so frightfully sorry—now that it is irrevocable and too late." She wept in her handkerchief. She did not omit to point out that it was Helfin himself who had instigated her and who had therefore indirectly occasioned the journalist's attempted suicide. "It is I who will never get over this . . ." That was just like him, she continued, to start things, to incite others, to do nothing, to send those others out into the battle and to remain safely behind the scenes. Another instance was that of the contract. She would be compromised now; the whole structure would begin to topple if he let the whole thing slide on account of one stupid paragraph.

Her raging brought him to his senses, because in this mood nothing that she said sounded genuine. And when she got back again and again to the pitiable death of the journalist and tried to heap coals of fire on Helfin's head: "What did the whole thing matter to me! For your sake and for your sake alone I went in for something of which the consequences were dark to me." At that moment her expression of pretended innocence was so spectacular that he laughed in her face. "All you have to do is to give up that single silly paragraph, as you yourself called it, and everything will be fine."

She stared at him with hot eyes. "I'm not giving it up. I'm simply not. That's your way—to forgo, to give up. At least, you pretend that it is. It's not my way. I'm sincere. I tell you how it is and what I think and feel. I will not give it up, simply will not." She stamped her feet and went out. He reflected that she had forgotten to go on weeping.

That evening she turned up at the accustomed hour. Her tone was milder. She was tender, although the conflict still echoed in her tenderness. But she presented it now in the form of a philosophical paradox and did not refer it to the immediate reality of the signature of a contract. "I hope it is clear to you," she said coquettishly and in a tone of humorous depression, "I hope it is quite clear to you what a thorough bitch I am? Let's agree on that, at least. Of course, it's tough on me that my lover is a dreary moralist. If you were the man you ought to be you would esteem most highly what the beast within me demands. You ought to be charmed by my very brutality. What I really need is an entire man, a young roughneck! He would like me better than you do. And I would like him better than I do you. It's just my pattern of ill luck that I had to get mixed up with you."

"I'll never be the kind of person whom you are imagining," he answered with that utter tranquillity which is unique and final.

Nevertheless it hurt him that she didn't come the next evening. For the first time he waited for her in vain. This time the icy tension of peering out of the window, of listening for her step, did not issue in the warmth of contentment. The slow hours of waiting did not give way to the swifter ones of her transitory presence.

This experience dealt him a blow which he had really not expected. It gave him a painful feeling of anxiety which seemed to make itself at home in his stomach. It was a physiological process, inaccessible to reasonable management; it was there, impervious to any argument. He said to himself that he had been too rude, too proud. What did he want of her? Had he not always known that Bianca and he were at opposite poles, that in all important matters they represented divergent views, that this was so of necessity, that agreement was not possible, but that for this very reason their conversations had never wanted interest or tension? Thus her partnership in the life of the mind had become almost indispensable to him. He was not thinking of the other aspects, for which a substitute could always be found. But was he sure even of that? He was willing to assume this in order not to make the whole matter more intricate than it already was. There seemed to be no end to these reflections. They absorbed him more than Bianca's living presence. How annoying! He would have preferred to have her here, if only to be less obsessed by her. In brief, he wanted her. He jeered at himself. If this is only the caricature of love, it seems to show unexpected force.

Next day she met him coolly. She said she had quite consciously absented herself. Dispute was so futile. It merely excited her and robbed her of the strength she needed for her studies. She was concentrating on the language, on the correct accentuation of Hebrew. That was now her chief concern. She used that dry, objective scientific tone of hers, the same tone under which she was accustomed so artfully to hide her vaunted emotions. The question at this moment was, what of this kind she had to hide. She indicated that there was nothing of the sort, that this was no time for the cultivation of emotions.

The conversation stirred him very deeply. He barely possessed the strength not to show this too openly. He did not want his defeat by this experienced tactician to be too patent. "I happen to be on my way to Josefovitch," he said restrainedly. "It's rather a pity that you have no time for me. There are still several things for us to think over."

"Among them, I suppose, that one paragraph?"

"That, too. I have been thinking of a formulation which might satisfy us both."

Thus he forced her to come to him. Shamelessly enough, her behavior corresponded exactly to what he had expected and reckoned out. Perhaps she did not think it worthwhile to pretend. Perhaps he was no longer important enough to her. In addition, it was perhaps natural that the dispute had left a residue of coolness between them. For in the main point he did not give in. He refused to betray his young friends. Bianca's coolness on this occasion differed from her usual kind; it was clearly distinguishable from that other, as it were, medical cooling off, meant especially for him, lovingly prepared and initiated by the sober tenderness of their earliest period. This time it was a more general coolness; it was cursory, meant for everyone, meant for the whole world.

He accepted what was offered him. Better than nothing. It did not mean that an arrow did not remain in his heart. Upon the whole he found that he had by no means come off well in the matter. One must never say, "Better than nothing." One must never sell oneself so cheaply. It was humiliating.

In history books there is often to be read the record of long battles in which fortune sways from side to side, in which victory seems to smile now upon one side, now upon the other, before the goddess Nike finally awards the palm. Thus for days on end the waves rose high between these two human beings in a state of combat. Neither admitted defeat. Each withdrew after having gained some small advantage. But Helfin's line of battle remained in disorder by virtue of a single important circumstance. He knew that his days were numbered, that time was pressing. He would have to interrupt this period. The thought was unendurable that this must be so at a moment which he considered especially unfavorable. If only he had been able to draw that arrow from his heart, which grew ever more anguished as the meetings with Bianca increased in iciness. That kind of climate might have been appropriate to her nature; it was not so to his. And to go away now? To feign no longer to misunderstand the invitation of the horse's head which now even in bright daylight protruded its cruel teeth and blinking eyes from the wall, even as a barometric puppet shows the state of the weather, or as once upon a time the puppet figures of the apostles came out of the tower of the city hall of Prague! It had to be! The transmutation was not to be restrained. Ever more compellingly the rhythm of the machine made itself felt. Invisibly it ruled his life; it was not to be violated and he resisted it with ever smaller confidence. Audibly the wheels of Unambo whirred beneath the surface of events. They seemed to cause an unnatural tension in the integument of things and to cause them to vibrate. This tension was like a bodily hurt. It would have been easier for him to have left Bianca in the most tranquil days of their love than now when misunderstanding and ill will prevailed between them.

If only he had the machine! Perhaps he could reset it and thus prolong the present epoch by a week. The armistice had almost expired. In a few days it would be known whether the Arabs desired to renew the war or not. That troubled him but little. He was much more concerned with Bianca, whom he wanted to win over, with his young friends, whom he would not betray, with the accursed contract and Josefovitch. If he could only gain a single week for quiet negotiation, for the re-establishment of equilibrium, to avoid bad bargaining and the making of mistakes. One needed time for such things. And to gain time he would have had to recover the fateful machine. This had been the most unexpected of the fat man's tricks, that at the moment of manipulation the little stage disappeared, never to be seen again. But wait! Had he not always nourished the opinion in the secret chambers of his heart that the apparatus had not vanished at all, that it had been blown out into the garden and might still be hidden in the shrubbery? Now he remembered. He had written to Dvora from Galilee, asking her to search in the garden. He wondered if she had received the letter. But the doubt arose whether a correspondence, a reciprocal connection, was possible between the two realms. A grotesque question. You write a letter from one place to an address in another place. The letter needs a definite division of time. But here the situation was different. You were writing from one time reel to another, the two reels being simultaneous. Was it possible to establish communication between two simultaneous stages of a, so to speak, dialectic existence? Someone more mathematically gifted than himself could, he supposed, have a clearer notion of the matter. There was something in science, he remembered, which dealt with the projection of one plane upon another. Well, luckily, he had no need of complicated theories. As he told himself, he could simply ask Dvora whether such a letter had arrived or not.

He called her in and asked her, looking at her expectantly. Her answer would even be a kind of proof as to whether the whole thing were not a dream; whether he was not imagining this double life; whether he wasn't quite simply crazy.

No letter had arrived.

The postal service in the country had not been of the best. And now, during the war, when everything had to be built up anew, seeing that Bevin and his minions had deliberately created disorder, Dvora's answer was not at all decisive. In addition, it was not out of the question that Bianca had received the letter during his illness and had suppressed it.

He went into the garden himself. He frightened a couple of stray cats who had been stretching themselves comfortably in the sun. He ducked under clotheslines. There was nothing. Noisy children at their play looked in surprise at the intruder. For a moment they interrupted themselves. Next they went on as before.

Very well, then, the apparatus was lost. It could not, in any event, be procured now. All that was left for him to do, if he wanted to persist within this aspect of his life, if he wanted to arrange a peaceful agreement with Bianca before he took his leave, which would now probably be for three weeks—all he could do was to be careful, to avoid the horse's head wherever it emerged or broke forth. Every stair near it was to be treated with suspicion, as well as every door. Either could so easily lead into the well-known white-tiled corridor with its double row of electric lights. He thought it strange that he had never seen the station with its tracks, to which the corridor was bound to lead. It must be a station where one changes trains. For there, evidently, he changed from one life to another. Harshly he laughed at this notion of his which, in spite of its plausibility, seemed also grotesque and uncanny. At the same time he recalled those dark chambers through which at each transmutation of the form of his existence he had to pass. He could smell that smell of mortar as in a sculptor's studio. He thought he understood now. In those halls he was himself remodeled each time; here moist cloths were wrapped about the wet clay. His companions in destiny and he (for there were thousands, hundreds of thousands) were remodeled into new forms under these cloths before they passed through the customs barrier. What, then, he had to guard himself against was that customs barrier which was distinguished by the symbol of the horse's head, the animal escutcheon, and, indeed, against all that was dark and moist like those chambers. Especially did one have to avoid anything subterranean, if one wanted to remain where one was. For the realm of the fat man was a subterranean realm. That much he knew. This was what he had now frequently experienced, not only at that first acquaintance but on the occasion of the repeated transferences from one world to another. The fat man belonged to the chthonian powers and principalities whose dwelling place is beneath the crust of the earth. Therefore it behooved one to be wary of all stairs and descending steps, of all cellars and of whatever lay beneath the surface of the earth.

On the day on which he had agreed to meet Josefovitch, the horse's head multiplied a thousand times and hovered about him from early morning on. Everybody with whom he spoke seemed to have a horse's head, even Dvora. At the next moment this symbol, which made one think of the ass's head in the *Midsummer Night's Dream*, had already vanished. All one had to do was to look at the ghastly thing steadily. It vanished—and at the next moment it reappeared on the next person whom one encountered. On the street whole herds of horses seemed to trot past him. They raised their heads, as one raises one's hat; at the same time horses' heads were placed on other people who turned the next corner. Helfin knew that this could not go on; he was at the end of his string. He would sign the contract today and have the matter brought to an end. Bianca might as well gain her point. He had no fight left in him. Later he might try to abrogate that vicious paragraph aimed at his pupils. At the moment, seeing they were at the front, it could do no harm. What he needed was rest. He wanted at least one other interview with Bianca in order to re-establish harmony between them. Afterward he would vanish for a period. Closely thought upon, it was really no disappearance, no interruption. Only his limited power of comprehension perceived time as at a standstill here. It went on over there in Galilee, in that Galilee which at this moment interested him so little. But to his way of feeling, inevitably tied, as it was, to his small power of comprehension, there arose a hole, a vacuum, which frightened him. So the thing to do was to complete the contract and to create order between Bianca and himself. Then he would see what happened next.

He caught sight of the tropical hat. Philip Josefovitch met him at the office building. "Won't you please wait for me upstairs?" He was courteous as always. "I'll be back in a few minutes. There's just a little preliminary conference." The mushroom man entered his long, pointed private car. Softly it glided away. Helfin had no objection to waiting upstairs. High up he felt safe. High up nothing would happen. Anything was all right that was not subterranean. And with a kind of delight he rode the elevator to the topmost story of the office building.

Here everything was bright in the best American style. Nothing but nickel, steel, and glass. No damp darkness nor mortar smell nor horse's head nor danger. He entered an office in which an elegant female typist was at work. Without interrupting herself, she pointed the way to the reception room next door. When he opened the door of this room it was evident that he had entered upon the long white-tiled corridor with it rows of electric bulbs. *Hic et ubique?* He was evidently being moved along as on a conveyer belt. The undermost had become the uppermost. An order evidently prevailed which was different from the human order. In the background where the corridor made its turn, there grinned—not this time above a cellar door but fastened to the interior of the passageway—the infernal horse's head. "Walked into the trap." This is what the grinning horse's head seemed slowly to grind out from between its long teeth. Then his shrieking neighs burst out into invectives. Curses coruscated. The walls burst tumultuously.

CHAPTER SIX

In which, among other things, the reader receives sundry bits of information concerning the combat of armored cars, as well as concerning the behavior of little children who are being evacuated and, at the very end, also concerning the fodder harvest in Galilee.

1.

It was imperative to save the settlement of Zur-Yaakov, that is to say, of the "Rock of Jacob." For the rock seemed to be shaken.

The last convoy had arrived three months before. This was still under the Mandatory régime, during which the English had energetically insisted that they were "responsible for law and order." Actually they had done nothing to prevent the siege of this little settlement in the hills around Safed. The foodstuffs, meant for two weeks, had had to suffice the settlers to this day. Now, although the armistice was supposed to have set in six days before, the Arabs didn't dream of interrupting the encirclement of Zur-Yaakov. The so-called "Army of Liberation" of Fawzi Kaukadshi, the gang leader, was assigned to the category of irregular troops. At the beginning of the armistice the republic of Lebanon had, indeed, assumed a quasi-juristic responsibility for his gang. Actually this was not put into practice. These bands with whom there fought not only Muslim but also international Fascists, as well as Nazis and Yugoslavs, were daily receiving reinforcements from the villages around the holy city of Safed. They abounded in promises to the "observers" of the United Nations to withdraw and to abandon their positions around Zur-Yaakov. They repeated these promises daily. Quite similarly the Arab Legion at Latrun promised each day to open the pumping station which supplied Jerusalem with water. These various actions had been agreed to in the conditions of the armistice. But the enemy didn't for a moment intend to perform them. So Jerusalem still suffered from thirst, since the volume of water carried by our own supply line was still small, and, by the same token, the people of Zur-Yaakov were in danger of starving to death. In their state of deadly exhaustion they could so easily have been overrun and massacred by those gangs.

In consequence there was being assembled a convoy in the "Little Forest of the Fifty," and Lieutenant Paul Helfin was to accompany the convoy in an armored car marked "number two."

This undertaking was based upon that small country town which has proudly for generations called itself Rosh Pinah, the headstone of the arch. It is situated on the high road in upper Galilee, at the foot of the mountain on which Safed is built.

The city of Safed, or, to be exact, its Jewish quarter, had been liberated. For weeks it had held out against an enormous superiority in power, after the English (in breach of all agreements, as a matter of surprise, in the middle of the night, and prior to the promised date) had left and had handed over to the Arabs all strategically important points. Then, soon after the termination of the Mandate, the Haganah had arrived and had rescued, at the very moment of utter destruction, the inhabitants starving amid their ruined houses and repelling attacks with their last rounds of munition. The Arabs fled at once. Since then the Arab quarters had become a ghost town, silent and empty. There was something solemn about these dispeopled streets. It was as though under this burning sky we had entered the cathedral of the Devil. The echo of a hollow, ironic, grimacing solemnity was returned by wind and stone. During the bright hours of day, too, a dark stillness hovered uncannily over the thickly built-up mountain and on those slopes of a once abundant life. This stillness was like the stillness of places which had been the scene of some frightful crime. Who had committed this crime? In the first place the invaders, the alien volunteers who, as they had done in Jaffa, had begun to cover with artillery fire the narrow streets of the Jewish quarter, an immemorial settlement of the pious of our people. The Iraqis beyond, at Merom, the neighboring mountain, had actually had heavy artillery. The English did not prevent them from firing on the Jewish quarters, and no one had interfered when the Arabs had blown up eleven Jewish buildings. Later all had changed. Open war set in. This was in certain aspects much more favorable to us than the days when the British police held our hands which yearned to take up arms in our defense. It was native Arabs, the inhabitants of Safed, who had to pay the reckoning. It had been planned that they should prevail. They were to storm the Jewish street from both sides— this street which is hedged in between two populous Arab quarters, which is commanded by the old fortress and the police station, and which, at its highest point, measures scarcely 200 meters. It is only down the slope that it spreads out more spaciously and comfortably. As by a miracle, or in a manner wholly unforeseeable, by such a blending of human heroism with divine providence as took place everywhere, this plan was brought to nought. One hundred and twenty Jewish fighters successfully protected their aged, their women, their children against two thousand volunteers, to whom had been added seven hundred regular Iraqis, not counting volunteers from the towns and villages round about who had taken up their rifles in the pursuit of booty. Doubtless, many of the indigenous people had been forced to join the volunteers; others did so out of their own impulse, though they had dwelt in friendly neighborliness beside the Jews for generations. Below the thin educated stratum the Arabs are passionate and primitive. Now they had all fled, the guilty as well as the innocent, all deluded by that native Arab propaganda which persuaded them that these hitherto peaceful Jews would turn out to be intolerant. They all fled into homelessness, leaving their houses and lands behind them. Assuredly, many of them did not deserve this cruel punishment of the refugee, so familiar to the Jew. And now there hovered over these empty houses the dull silence of war—of war which is never anywhere anything but crime, the chief crime and sin of man.

Now Jewish Safed breathed again. People began to talk of rebuilding, of new industries which were to fill the always rather weary streets with life and with immigrants. In the environs, however, the poison of war was still brewing. Separated from Safed by but a few hilltops Zur-Yaakov was still being throttled by a siege.

Meanwhile new literary styles were being discovered in Paris. In America pains were being taken to introduce subtle improvements into the refrigeration methods used in the kitchens of the middle classes. Zürich was radiating the very glow of wealth and splendor, while the newspapers of Sweden, and not only of Sweden, waxed eloquent in announcing that "Universal Festival of Peace," which would be represented by the Olympic Games in London.

Simultaneously in the desolate hills around Safed things took place, things unnoted by the world, which a cold-blooded government had arranged and which man should not suffer, dare not suffer, lest he cease to be man. An unacknowledged war—murder denied while it is committed, hidden from the eye by nebulous phrases—murder as though it were taking place in some dark back room, in some obscure courtyard of the world's life. Such was the tragedy taking place obscurely in the hills of Safed. And a second tragedy, of which the cultural radiance of Europe was equally oblivious, was even now in preparation. In Zur-Yaakov one didn't, you may be sure, take any great interest in that new concept of Existentialism which was to be expressed in a tenth independent periodical. In Zur-Yaakov the children were crying. They were hungry.

And it was for this reason that a consultation of staff officers, at which Helfin was present, took place at Rosh Pinah.

The day before, he had come back in a rather confused state of mind from a tour of inspection in the environment of the "grove." Near the kitchen barracks he had almost sunk into lime. He had managed to pull himself out. "If my nephew Gad were here," he had said that evening, "such things wouldn't happen. He is an excellent cartographer. Our sketches of the terrain would be sounder." The consultation had soon passed on to more important matters. The Zur-Yaakov radio announced the untenable and ever more critical situation of the settlement. At that point Helfin had volunteered to accompany the rescue expedition.

At the break of dawn six trucks had started out from Rosh Pinah on their way into the mountains. They passed the last houses and the forests and proceeded to the treeless slopes. Sunburned grasses and underbrush breathed in the wind. Everywhere the stone skeleton of the earth burst from its skin, whiteness alternating with the dimly colored, with long rows of earth bumps, of craggy rocks which form the stony, scaly armor of the earth. Heavy, broad vultures hovered two by two above the austere landscape. The road turned off from Safed and entered upon a wild territory delimited only by tall hedges of cactus —by veritable walls of these green and prickly plants. Otherwise there was only naked stone.

The convoy consisted of three trucks loaded with food and munitions. These were protected by three armored cars with eight to ten men in each. The convoy was led by a so-called barricade buster, an abnormally massive armored car with a pointed nose of steel, commanded by a highly experienced fighter who bore the nickname of Keren-Or—"Wealth of Light." In this leading car there was also to be found Tom the Australian, Helfin's rebellious young friend. He himself sat in car number two with his Sten gun in readiness. Helfin's name, Paul, had been turned back into the original Saul. Consequently here, where all were called by their given names, he was known exclusively as Sha-ul—in two syllables, with the accent on the second syllable, even as it is written in the Scripture.

Armored car number two was followed by the three precious trucks which were carrying the desperately needed food and weapons to Zur-Yaakov. The end of the convoy consisted of armored car number three.

Into the swaying brownish darkness of the armored car, which was proceeding with its hatches closed, there rattled the last message from Rosh Pinah into the earphones of the radio operator: "Happy Journey." The *mefaked*, the commandant of the expedition, passed the message on to the comrades, each of whom repeated the good wish to himself. The girl who was accompanying the expedition gave a bright laugh. She cried toward a no longer visible background, "A happy stay, rather!" She was as heavily armed as the others, being a member of the *Palmach*, the shock troops which had been the original kernel and élite of the underground army. These divisions alone had retained the privilege of having women as front-line fighters. Whenever a window was opened for a moment and sunshine gleamed into the darkness of the steel walls, one could see Rina shaking her black locks, with the clips of the hand grenades sticking out of her pockets as though they were the tops of fountainpens. Across from her sat the rather pallid *mefaked* whose first name was Arye, "The Lion," and had probably been Leo formerly in Lemberg. A full blond beard framed his young face. He had fought in the Negev, the South. Down there there was never water enough for shaving. So the soldiers were bound to let their beards grow, which later became emphatic adornments. Most of them looked as though these thick beards had been pasted on their young childlike faces for a masquerade. That's the way they looked, these rudely defiant *chayot ha-Negev*, or "Beasts of the South," as they called themselves.

Arye, young as he was, enjoyed the unlimited respect of his men. He had given proof of ability, courage, and thoughtfulness.

It was long since Helfin had sat in such a vehicle. It had been during the Second World War when, under Montgomery, he had shared the attack on Senio, north of the Apennines. In those days the Jewish Brigade was a unit within the British army. Later the British were to arm the enemies of Israel and to incite them against the Land. Rapidly enough Helfin recovered the technique of these vehicles. He leaned against the wall with his hand on the trigger of his gun. He regulated his movements in this box of steel which reminded one of a vehicular prison or gigantic coffin and out of which one would perhaps never again emerge. It all depended on surprising the Arabs. They were depending upon two road blocks, which had, however, been removed the night before. The convoy proceeded as rapidly as the bad road permitted. The enemy was to be given no chance to block the road anew.

But they were keeping a sharp lookout, these enemies. At the end of the first half-hour a bullet whined sharply against the wall of steel. The wagons climbed and coughed. One of them seemed to incline sidewise, as though in its haste it were about to fall into a ditch. But it regained its equilibrium. There was no joking now; there was the ultimate attention of eye and hand. For that first bullet had been only a signal. Dense salvos now resounded from both sides of the cliffs. With these was blended the evil stuttering of machine guns. Who cared what happened obscurely here in contravention of the solemnly accepted terms of the armistice? To whom, in the days to come, would Jews again complain of their suffering and of the wrongs inflicted upon them? There would be no more complaints. It was a question of depending on one's own weapons. Yet no command to fire had yet been issued. There was great prudence in the use of ammunition. At this point one would simply have fired at the naked rock. Onward, then! Undeterred, the barricade buster continued on its way, as though the noise did not concern it. The other vehicles followed at precise intervals. For the time being the action was that of a maneuver.

The road became narrower and the cliffs taller. Next there was a crash. The barricade buster had struck a mine. A dazzling blue-white flame arose like that of a flash bulb. A cloud of dust left a residuum of heavy black fume beneath. The air pressure had also caused the second car to sway for a moment. An unnatural silence fell. It was not a real silence. The sense of hearing was in abeyance, paralyzed by the explosion. Now there was heard a rattling, a rain of small stones falling on the cars after the explosion. And how was it with the victim? The front wheels were jammed; the tires were useless, and the leading vehicle slipped slowly toward the right into the ditch. At the same time a second rain of bullets resounded. Several penetrated the roof of the second armored car. The men all ducked involuntarily. Helfin too. They opened the slits and returned the fire. Next a cry was heard. As Helfin's hand was fetching new ammunition from his belt, he saw that it was suddenly covered with blood. It was not his own blood but that of a wounded comrade. Though his pulses throbbed violently, he aimed his gun, as calmly as possible, at a steel-like gleam in a crack in the rock. Arabs had stormed the first car. They were repelled, leaving several dead behind them. But the combat was on and the convoy had to stop.

Soon—or perhaps a good deal later, for the perception of time was in abeyance, as the sense of hearing had been—soon, then, there came a word of command from the car that made up the rear and was in charge of the second senior officer. Again there was a rattling in the radio, whose antenna rose in the middle of the car and protruded through the roof into space.

Arye transmitted the command. No one stirred; they peered and listened. The command was as follows: The three trucks must return with the rear protection in order to fetch reinforcement from Rosh Pinah. Car number two was to remain to cover the damaged blockade buster, which it would try to tow or else go ahead alone to Zur-Yaakov.

It was the model of a highly responsible order. Yet they all grasped instantly what it meant for car number two and for Arye, as well as for their friends of the group Keren-Or in the ditch. There was barely space enough here for the cars to turn around. Four or five kilometers nearer to the settlement it would have been impossible; the road became narrower and narrower.

Soon thereafter one heard the whir of the reversing motors. In a cloud of dust the three trucks with their armored protection proceeded toward the valley. In the rushing of the mountain wind two cars remained alone amid the wild firing of the attackers. One of them was damaged. There were eighteen men in all. They had eight rifles, ten Sten guns, two light machine guns, as well as hand grenades. In Arye's car up to this point only one man was slightly wounded. His pale face gleamed from a corner.

Again the radio spoke: "Keren-Or calling Ayre. What the hell are you waiting for? Hurry and get reinforcements."

Arye put on the earphones: "Arye calling Keren-Or. Will try to tow you to Zur-Yaakov."

The armored car hugged the very edge of the road while rifle and machine-gun fire increased. It was as though in the midst of the hostile assaults, friendship drove the two cars nearer to each other. From the rim of the cliff above came the enemy's howl of joy. The victory seemed complete; the joy communicated itself from gang to gang. Meanwhile Arye's car slowly approached the other one. They opened the slits in their windows. They greeted each other and smiled at each other and even lied a little. "Everything is going all right," they said, although they were quite aware of the situation. Helfin caught sight of Tom and tried to stretch out his hand toward him. Tom took it through the aperture and pressed it warmly.

Once more Keren-Or's voice was heard. "Fasten the rope inside and then throw it out of the back door. I'll come out and fasten it."

The man in Arye's car had already taken the thick rope from the tool chest. The car moved forward a little and stood still. They opened the steel door from within. At that very moment a bullet crashed noisily against the door and closed it. They opened it again. A soldier jumped out and tied it to the rear bumper of his own car. Hundreds of Arabs from the nearer and the farther heights fired at him. Happily he was not hit. After a few endless moments he climbed back into the car and grinned.

Arye announced himself and Keren-Or's unwavering voice answered, "All right. Now give them every ounce you have."

The machine gun and the rifles in Arye's car fired like mad. The floor of the car was covered with smoking shells. The space within was filled with stinging, suffocating smoke.

A slender figure leaped from the first car, climbed from the ditch to the road, bent down and tried to pick up the rope. It never reached the rope. One saw how the body rose to its entire height and stretched itself before it collapsed in the dust. Before anyone from Arye's car could rush to give assistance, two of the officer's own comrades were on the spot and pulled him under the car, where he was somewhat safer. Thereupon another one of Keren-Or's men crept forward. He tied the rope to the bumper of his car and crept back, the while a very rain of bullets came down on the road. Breathlessly those at the spy holes had watched each of these movements.

Again the radio spoke.

"Keren-Or. . ." there was a pause. A different voice came over the microphone. "Hello, Arye. Keren-Or is wounded. So is our radioman. Get on!"

The driver had not stopped the motor. Now he started the car slowly. The rope grew taut. The heavy blockade buster began to rise, reaching the level of the road. But the damned front wheels wouldn't work and the rope snapped. Swaying like a drunken creature, the gray car slid back into the ditch. Arye rubbed his eyes. "The smoke!" They all knew what he meant; they shared his feelings. No excuses were needed.

Arye's car backed up a few paces alongside of the stranded vehicle. The Arabs now risked coming closer and fired harder. It was impossible at this point to leave the car and rescue the wounded from the other. The rescuers could not have gotten alive through that storm of bullets. They would have saved no one. Through the spy holes they passed over into the other car almost their entire reserve of ammunition. Perhaps help from Rosh Pinah would soon be here. Arye signaled, "We are off to Zur-Yaakov. We'll fetch everything they have left, including a chain. *Chisku ve-imzu*—be strong and hold out."

They shook hands again. "Goodbye, Tom," "Goodbye, Shaul." And Arye's car groaningly and gaspingly climbed the next hill. They all knew that those who were left behind were lost. But Arye's men were not saved either. Turning a corner the car came upon a new road block. Immediately after the first shots were exchanged Arabs must have rolled the huge boulders onto the road from the heights on either side. An obvious trap. And from all the hillsides rattled the rifles. They had all the ammunition in the world, while the men in the car had given theirs away except for what they had in their ammunition belts.

There was no time for reflection. Two of Arye's men crept under the car while the bullets whistled past their ears. Hot oil from the machine dripped on their necks and arms and faces. They heaved at the boulders as the car pushed against the barricade. It protected the backs of the workers, who, alternating by twos, shoved away one stone after another. If the Arabs approached too closely they were met by hand grenades. Finally the road seemed reasonably open and the car went full speed ahead. Luckily no land mine had been laid. But two more had been wounded and lay between the walls of steel rattling and vibrating in swift motion.

Again the crackling of the radio: "Hello, Arye. Tom calling Arye. We have to give up the car. There are only six of us left. We're destroying the car. We'll make a sortie at the next height."

"I hear you, Tom. Help is on the way. You must hold out. Help is near. Do what you have to. Try to avoid further losses."

"Tom calling Arye. Abandoning the car. Will try to talk again in ten minutes."

From their car they could see the black oily smoke rise from the burning lead car. The hills between hid the friends from their eyes. They peered back. They listened. The firing had not ceased. So they were still alive.

"Tom calling Arye. Do you hear us?"

"We hear you distinctly."

"Ephraim speaking. Tom is badly hurt. Only four of us reached the rim. We have a machine gun but not ammunition. Will hold out as long as possible."

"Arye calling Ephraim. Hold on by your nails and teeth. Let the swine have it! We're only three kilometers from Zur-Yaakov. We'll be with you with reinforcements in fifteen minutes. You must hold out till then."

Next came another, strange-sounding voice. "Moshe speaking for Keren-Or. Please repeat back. O.K. I believe we can hold out fifteen minutes longer. After that ask for me in my professional capacity of a choir leader in heaven. They may let me practice my old profession, although I've been just a *kibbutznik* recently." The voice was gone.

But there was silence also in Arye's car. The motor had stopped. He tried to start it. No good. The driver shook his head. A bullet had hit the water tank. The water was running out.

But Zur-Yaakov was now in sight. They had heard the firing there and had sent forth a truck with soldiers. But before he leaped from the car Helfin once more took up the earphones and listened. "Chayim speaking for Keren-Or. We're both wounded but pelting the enemy with hand grenades. Have a few bullets left, too. Am destroying the radio. *Chisku ve-imzu*, hold out and be strong."

Arye's men had put their machine guns in position. With their last ammunition they were repelling all attacks. Then, suddenly, the truck was upon them and received them. The dimness within contrasted with the horrible blue of the radiant, cloudless sky. Each one was tempted to wish himself dead, for that black cloud which lay behind them on the rim of the hill was the last greeting of their best friends. No, it was not death that was in their thoughts; it was revenge.

2.

There was no such thing as rest. Neither had they come here to rest. They had come here to help. It was bad enough that they had brought with them nothing but their good will and their unimpaired energy. Neither weapons nor food—and it was precisely these which were at a low ebb in Zur-Yaakov. Under cover of night the armored car was dragged into the settlement. It could not be repaired. Not even that was possible in this poverty-stricken place. So they had brought nothing up these barren hillsides but their naked strength. They therefore undertook sentinel duty, one or two men occupying the small exposed cement structures known as pillboxes. By the rays of the searchlight from the half-splintered water tower the new men at once assumed their duties. This meant a measure of relief to the utterly worn-out settlers.

Helfin's round began at midnight in the little olive grove in front of the village. With infinite patience the settlers here had blasted away the rocks. They had built terraces for tree nurseries. Low stone walls had been erected not so much as defenses against a possible enemy as to protect them from the spring rains which threatened ever again to wash the topsoil into the valley. A work of peace. Now, too, these walls of field stone served as their protection in war.

An old man, rifle in hand, stood behind one of these breastworks and peered into the darkness of the now wholly tranquil night. The rattle of firing persisted only in Helfin's ears; actually a ghostly silence hovered over the hilltops. The moon emerged from rows of tiny, yellowish bands of cloud. The landscape might, ironically enough, have been that of a picture postcard with the legend "Peace." But Helfin was aware of the vultures with their far-spread wings circling over the hills.

He was to have slept until midnight. In spite of his weariness and the fact that the hours of repose were few, he had been unable to find rest. Horror seemed to lie over all things—over the coarse covering of his couch, over the shelf of modest, tattered books which were the special pride of every settler here. It lay over the dark niches of a cupboard in which toys had been left, although the children of the settler Rosenfeld, in whose simple room he was sleeping, had long been evacuated. This horror lay beside Helfin on the couch, like a neighbor, like a strange old woman, like a mist constantly transmuted in form, momentarily assuming a different visage, among them again and again the visage of one of those ten whom he would never see again. Those brave boys, those good boys in the car, in the dust of the road, on the lonely hillside, next to the radio apparatus which the last of them had dutifully destroyed. What had happened to their bodies? There were the vultures. . . . There were barbaric hands to mutilate . . . Helfin dug his fists into his eyelids hoping not to see the cruel images which arose. He forbade himself to think any further. He owed it to his military duty not to enfeeble himself by the excesses of his imagination but to save his strength for next day's conflict. But thought leaped across these commands. It was with him; that was all. He was about to repeat a poem to divert himself, when Tom opened the door—dear Tom, the *djindji*. Of course Helfin knew that he was only dreaming when, next, he had a vision of Tom's father with the red *tefilin* in his hand; it looked as though he were carrying his own bleeding heart on the irrevocable way toward the black, smoking tower of the crematory. It was a dream as of lead. It was only a dream, yet Helfin cried out aloud in horror. He leaped from his couch and kindled a light. He could not and would not sleep. The last rescued descendent of a numerous family had come to Israel. Here, in the homeland, a bullet had hit him. The family came from Berdychev. Its last gleam flickered from Berdychev to Australia and thence into the hills of Zur-Yaakov. What strength that took and what suffering. And here the gleam was extinguished. Who will say *Kaddish* now? When a whole family dies out and is extinguished, perhaps a very special sort of *Kaddish* should be said. For it is something like the end of a whole people. No, not that. Thank God, not that. *Am Yisrael chai.* The people Israel lives on. Night and cold horror round about—but it lives on. Only ten of its most faithful sons are no more. They lie in the dirt of those hollows in the hills, mutilated, disfigured, there in the ditches or there in the bushes of a hilltop.

If that was possible, what was there left in the world that

could be called impossible? Nor could vengeance extinguish this nameless horror, this sense of being lost, this meaninglessness? Why strive against the final cognition that this was a wound which could know of no healing? Why take the trouble to strive? Was the immitigableness not woe enough? Helfin knew sufficiently well who would suffer that entire woe. Another. Not he. He had arranged it so that it was not he.

He was glad when he heard a knocking. He was being called to take his post. And now he was standing there with this old man among the well-spread-out olive trees by the side of this low protecting field-stone wall. "*Ma shlomcha*, how are you?" Helfin asked. He was glad to talk to someone.

The old gentleman introduced himself courteously. "I am Reb Eisik." Good manners had been preserved in these wild hills. "And you, sir, must have arrived during the night with the *giborim*, the heroes?"

Helfin bowed. "My name is Shaul. And you can go to bed now, Reb Eisik. The morning is cold. I'll take over the watch."

It turned out that the old gentleman would by no means agree to this. He had kept watch here every night; he knew the region thoroughly—every path, every rock. He knew exactly where the Arabs had their advance positions, from which on occasion they shot with incendiary bullets. His familiarity with the strategic situation would not permit him to remain idle; not, at least, until he had communicated the entire content of his knowledge to his successor. His explanations took in every lonely tree on the chains of the hills that stood against the sky. Reb Eisik's head was curiously round and very mobile; his gray hair was cut short. It was the head of one who listens and is perceptively aware of every current in the air.

"Were you in the army?" Helfin asked.

"No, I was in the coffee business," the old gentleman explained calmly. "I am the father of Rosenfeld with whom you're staying. I saw you right away yesterday at noon in the *Chadar ha-ochel*, the dining hall. We older people sit on two benches of our own at a table in the corner. But we see everything that there is to be seen." He laughed comfortably. Helfin was glad to be able to chat with him. Over there, at a distance of a few kilometers, the landscape was weighted down, like the balance on a scale, with the heavy bodies of his comrades. Behind one of those innumerable curves of hills the whole wide landscape was filled with heaviness. Therefore it did him good to be in the company of an old man who gave his tongue free rein. And there was another thing, of which Helfin only gradually became aware. But this awareness increased; it was that of a curious resemblance. At first it made no impression on him. For the present he listened quite innocently to the old gentleman's report. "I am one of the Shanghai people," he began. And this curious expression, which Helfin had not hitherto heard, seemed at once quite visibly to blend that far and glittering metropolis into the destiny of the Jewish people, into which it had, as a matter of fact, been drawn by the process of events. For thousands of Jews had fled from Hitler in all of Central Europe to this single Asiatic city, of which the gates were open for a time to those who had passports. Who among all those thousands in Cologne or Brünn would ever have dreamed that fate had in store for them a place in that inconceivably distant Chinese city? "There are two other Shanghai people here in Zur-Yaakov, a couple. I, alas, lost my wife in China. But our angelic children, God reward them, did not tire in their efforts and so, after ten long years, here we are."

Helfin reflected that being starved to death by Arab gangsters was a fine ending for these aged parents and their angelic children. "Where do you really come from, Reb Eisik," he asked in order to avoid his old litany of accusation.

"I ran a café in Vienna, a mighty nice one in the ninth district. None of these little holes-in-the-wall. No, twenty tables in the main room and an additional room and a garden. We served warm suppers, too. I may say that I knew my business thoroughly. My customers were happy and so was I. Very fine people, apparently. Later on they suddenly turned into anti-Semites. I have no idea why. In Shanghai I went into the same business. It was a nicely furnished room; it was clean; there was even a water closet. There was a little side room, too, and again I had good customers.

"You must realize what a filthy place Shanghai is. Oh, these Chinese. The mud of the courtyard is covered with a layer of filth.

And on this bare filth, without boards or anything, they clean their fish and prepare their meat. Open buckets of ordure abound. Millions of flies first settle on these and then on the vegetables." The old man closed his eyes in disgust. His lax mouth, showing only a few yellow teeth, was open and his lips quivered. To this day he could not get over the uncleanliness of Shanghai. When he opened his lids again, Helfin observed that one of them was paralyzed, that he closed it only halfway and that it trembled. Something in this aged, weary face never ceased from trembling, and yet the old man did not once loosen his tight grasp upon his rifle. "So, you see, people were glad to come to me, because my place was clean and pleasant. And the Chinese are a kind people. When we Jews were interned in the French school building, it was the Chinese who daily sent us baskets of egg cakes. Yes, the Chinese were kindly. To begin with, the Japanese, too, behaved very decently. I am told that Japan is a very neat, clean country. All in all, there were 16,000 of us Jews in Shanghai. Two Japanese majors frequented my little establishment. One of them knew a little German. I suppose I happened to get a good impression of the Japanese, too." He cried that last sentence emphatically out into the air, as though he were defending the Japanese against invisible accusers.

"It was not until a German delegation reached us from Japan that things got bad. The Germans insisted that the Jews be deported to a dirty suburb, into a regular ghetto. So I had to sell out my little coffee house and its furnishings within four hours for what I could get. There was a Japanese high commanding general—Goja was his name, and they hanged him at the end of the war—who was very cruel to Jews. The beginning of any interview with him was that he slapped your face. Or else he kicked you in the belly. Unfortunately it was always necessary to have interviews to get permits from this man. You want a permit to bury your wife; you're kicked in the belly. You have a certain job assigned to you and are about to begin, you get a kick in the belly. That's the kind of swine this Goja was. Then the Germans told him to build an 'electrical plant.' But we knew that it was meant to be a crematory. The Emperor of Japan refused his consent to the undertaking. And before anything else could be done

225

the war happily came to an end. Otherwise we would all have been murdered, as in Poland. As it was, Goja was hanged and that whole German delegation too."

A report sounded in the distance. The old man put his rifle to his shoulder but did not press the trigger. Ammunition was being saved. "We shoot only when we have an aim," he explained. "They've got to be within clear sight. Three times, already, we have driven them off with hand grenades. They've tried to storm the settlement because we were so quiet. They believed we were done for. We inflicted heavy losses on them and so they didn't come back a fourth time. Well, as I was going to tell you," he reminded himself stubbornly, after the manner of the aged, "it was the Joint Distribution Committee that brought us from Shanghai to Marseilles. It was a long voyage. They told us that we would not have to spend a centime and that we would not have to carry our own luggage; all was to be taken care of. There were almost a thousand of us on that ship. In Marseilles I had quite a dispute with a lady, a very fine girl. I wanted to carry my trunk up the stairs of the hotel. She wouldn't let me; she scolded me. 'You put that trunk down right here, Mr. Rosenfeld! I'll be angry if you don't!' And she dragged it up herself. What do you say to that, Mr. Helfin? I can't ever forget that. A girl of good family; you could tell that. You see, that's the way the Joint operates. It's magnificent. Same way in Shanghai. The Americans began to bomb the French school building. Of course it was an error. It didn't take an hour for them to provide lodgings and warm food for us. Nevertheless it was on that occasion that I lost my last savings. Here, God be praised, I need nothing. My son takes care of me." He shook his gun in his hand. "I've learned how to shoot, too."

Now Helfin knew of whom the old man reminded him and what was the meaning of the resemblance which obtruded itself upon his consciousness. These types with yellow teeth and slack eyelids—he had seen them in Vienna cafés, where they played cards uninterruptedly and told each other indecent stories: those card parties of cynical memory in which a dying people sought to ironize its own lamentable estate and succeeded only in doubling its degradation. The intellectuals of this group got drunk on the stench of decay; they repeated the same jokes over and over again and raised a cabaret performer to the rank of Shakespeare. Jewish salons were capable of applauding when one of those intellectuals declared, "The very sound of the word courage makes me shit in my pants."

Here in the clean, keen air of the hills of Zur-Yaakov, there was no room for any trace of that decay. No memory remained of that whole period of the self-destruction of the Jewish soul. Only, strangely enough, the expression had remained—the expression, emptied by feebleness and too much experience, had remained in the similitude of a mask. It was like a deceptive façade behind which a new house had been built, or like the tattered curtain of a theater behind which a play of an entirely different character was being rehearsed. The old man with the stubborn round head and the short-cut gray hair—too much had happened to him in recent years for him to have found the time to acquire a new expression.

3.

In the morning Rina came to relieve Helfin. The old man had gone to bed. Rina, the *Palmachnikin*, as the female members of the shock troops are called, addressed him. He had not talked with her before. Amid the shooting in the armored car, he had now and then at quiet intervals been struck by her dark beauty, by her great black eyes, melancholy not with a sadness of the soul, but rather as a physical characteristic which resulted from the color and the shape of these rather long, mild, warm eyes under the shadow of the long lashes. Sometimes the glance of those eyes from under the lashes had been as gay as the sunny surface of a lake seen through the willows that hang into it. The full mouth with the red, curved lips seemed equally to be regarding one, but austerely, as though it were desirous of denying its soft and sensual splendor. The tall figure with its long legs clad in tight military breeches vibrated with the elastic tread of youth. This strong and yet delicate daughter of the South vibrantly trod upon her native earth.

"We hardly know what the war is like," said Rina. "The settlers in Zur-Yaakov, they know it. They're hungry."

"We'll share their hunger," Helfin replied, as though he had to justify himself for some omission on his part.

"They've been hungry for many weeks. They have scurvy among them. Their teeth are falling out. Do you know, Shaul, what was told me by the *chavera* with whom I am staying? The cook put grass and roots through the meat grinder and baked the product in oil. For they have some oil left. But the people got sick from these baked balls. Others still insist that there exist edible herbs and grasses and they continue to gather them and bring them to the kitchen. They still have a few beans and some soaked herrings. But they can't bear those any longer. Their last supplies consist of some macaroni and tomato paste. Their fuel oil is also low and they need it for their electrical plant and for the water pump. For a month now they haven't been able to wash properly. They sleep in their clothes and their stockings are falling to pieces. Their feet are covered with wounds and blisters. Their old physician says he can't endure to see it any longer."

"We had medicaments in the trucks too."

Rina was angry. "They should not have turned back."

"They took all the risks possible."

"They think they're wise guys," the girl cried, brushing from her forehead the locks which, despite the careful part in her hair, continued to fall over her eyes. "On that principle we shouldn't have risked founding our state."

Helfin felt worsted in the argument. Actually he was annoyed at the girl. Her words were always bitter; she seemed to be incapable of approval. But he was grateful to her, too. It was the right tone for a conversation here. In some mysterious fashion it re-established an equilibrium here, as the hand of a beautiful woman might well do, though here it was the hand of an Amazon, clasping the Sten gun. And once more, as in the case of the old man, a recollection arose within him. Rina looked quite like one of the proud queens of the balls of his youth. At the ball of the lawyers or the radiant and elaborate ball of the engineers there had been a few girls of just such Oriental grace whose words, however lightly uttered, had the effect of juridical opinions when one asked them for the next waltz. But what a difference between that empty past and this living, breathing present with its austere necessities. In that old world nothingness and boredom were under the sway of shifting whims; here a single goal shaped the oneness of life after the manner of an antique work of art. Only the façade, only an expression was similar; the content had changed wholly. The content was now a reality which one respected in deep seriousness with hard precision; it was not the flush which came upon a cheek at a dance.

"One lucky thing was that, just before we came, an airplane dropped vitamin tablets and a few other most necessary things. Now you'd better go and sleep, Shaul. I'll keep watching the sky for the next plane."

"You just keep looking and it will be sure to come." He shook her hand. She smiled a little. He went and he was happy to have reached the age at which one can perceive the beauty of a girl as part of the beauty of the world, comparable to the beauty of a well-grown tree or of an accomplished verse, without wishes and without desire.

Then, during his walk, he caught himself trying to plan that Rina should relieve him again at his next watch, or he her.

A second plane did indeed appear in the course of the day and dropped bags of munition and canned food. The plane flew low. The Arabs fired at it. It circled about and rose again and the last sacks fell beyond the perimeter assigned. At the risk of their lives people went out to gather them in toward evening. Fusillades were exchanged.

A radio message indicated that one bag was still missing. It had probably fallen into the chalky dry bed of a stream whose steep banks offered the defenders a good frontal position toward the north. That night old Rosenfeld awakened Helfin with cries of joy. He knocked at the window to awaken his son, with whom Helfin was lodging, and announced that the last sack had been recovered. The long-haired Dov Popper had clambered into the *wadi* in spite of all warnings and had brought it in, although the enemy had been madly wasting his tracer bullets. An intrepid fellow, this Popper from Vilna! Later on Helfin got to know him better, though from a somewhat different angle.

"Your father is an unusually good host, isn't he?" Helfin asked Rosenfeld when the old man had gone.

"Yes, he lays great stress upon order and neatness."

"I inferred that from his stories about Shanghai."

"The thing has become a kind of avarice in him," the son said calmly. "It is not surprising. Remember that twice over he lost all he had in the world, first in Vienna, next in the Far East. He keeps saying that he doesn't want to face it a third time. And, indeed, he has saved a little already. Untiringly, in spite of his years, he used to go to Safed and hire himself out to work with the road builders. So he has been able to furnish his little room nicely. He has a bookcase full of books as well as a radio which our relatives in Chicago sent him." Helfin quite understood the younger man's anxiety. The whole settlement of Zur-Yaakov and all the equipment which the industrious settlers had built up and earned during long years, was it not once more in the utmost peril? Was there any hope for the old man to save his possessions for a third time?

Several days later Helfin conversed on this and other matters with Popper in the *maskirut*, the secretariat of the *Kibbutz*. It was here that Popper had always done the necessary bookkeeping. Now there was nothing left to write down. The life of the settlement stagnated in monotony. It was using itself up, feeding upon itself, spiritually too. And nothing came from the outside. What remained was slowly consumed. No increase to place in any department. What was the use of keeping books? Hence in his leisure hours Popper was writing a history of the Galilean settlements from the period of Josephus Flavius to our own day. He had a great accumulation of notes, so great that the work was swamped by an excess of material. Recently he had had no time. Since the beginning of the siege everyone had been absorbed in guard duty, sentinel duty, active fighting. Popper had no leisure any more. But as a matter of habit he would often go to the office before going to bed, weary to death though he was. Here in this council room which, now so silent, had been built into the buttresses of the half-ruined water tower of concrete he felt snugly at home. He had very old newspapers stacked along the wall, and cartons of blue pasteboard which contained the materials for his history. He was a bachelor. He could rest and brew his tea just as easily here as in his hot wooden hut. He had long been promised a room in one of the field-stone houses, but the promise had not been kept. Helfin called on him frequently and drank a glass of hot tea with him. "You've got to have a napkin to drink tea properly," Popper explained to him. "That's a Russian proverb. The purpose of the napkin is to keep wiping the perspiration from one's face. The process is very healthy, dear Shaul."

The life of the settlement—if life it could still be called, this minimal and narrow vegetating—proceeded monotonously. The Arabs risked no further attack; they depended on hunger. Nor was any attempt at relief made after the failure of the convoy. The besieged people contented themselves with letting their searchlight play over the landscape and with an occasional powerful salvo. In addition to rifles and hand grenades of both the so-called Polish and the so-called English types, the settlers had two mortars and an old machine gun which used nothing but Italian ammunition and unfailingly broke down after two rounds. The only purpose of shooting now was to convince the enemy that one was well supplied with what it took to defend oneself and thus to dissuade him from a visit. "But this thing can't go on much longer," said Popper. "They used up the last pound of flour in the kitchen today."

"Nevertheless we must not hoist the white flag."

"Two are in favor of it; seventy-five are opposed. Of the two, one is a diabetic who lacks his daily insulin. He used to be a brave man. His illness has made a coward of him. He prefers an even more wretched death to the wretched one that faces him. For he would be shot. None of us will give ourselves up alive. We'd rather perish, as they did at Massada. Luckily we evacuated most of the women and children long ago. Only two small children are left here and a few older ones, a very few old men, and three sick women and one in the sixth month of pregnancy. Those few we could not send off; the road was already blocked. Very well then, another Jewish island will be overwhelmed, like the four villages of Gush-Ezion, like Nizanim and Yad Mordechai. That will not alter Jewish destiny in the larger sense."

"But did we not come here in order to alter that destiny fundamentally, once and for all? Is not that the meaning of our labor?"

"Not exactly," Dov Popper answered hesitatingly. "The meaning of our work is the attainment of justice. Justice alone. Whatever Jews do must have that single meaning. All else would be an aberration from the historic path prescribed to us. On this point a little strictness does not suffice; the strictness must be boundless; it must reach the limit of the possible."

"So you do not think it just that we find a refuge here?"

Classical Hebrew uses only the familiar "thou"; it has no formal mode of address. This circumstance eases mutual understanding among men. Attempts have been made in modern Hebrew to find substitutes for formal modes of address; ancient formulas have been adduced. But upon the whole such attempts have met with no success. People have instinctively rejected them.

"We are certainly justified in possessing a refuge. But we must not neglect to ask ourselves whether any Arabs are displaced. For that would diminish the rightness of our cause."

"Are you talking about the fugitives? We are guiltless in that matter. It was the Arabs who caused the villagers to flee. They used persuasion and even force. The contrary was our policy. Again and again we insisted upon good will and neighborliness and showed by our deeds that we wanted to be friends. The enemy plan was to incite against us the whole of the Arab world. The wretchedness of the fugitives was artificially created in contradiction to our expressed will. Now, retroactively, an accusation is leveled against us. As things have developed, we must now wait until peace is established. We must not permit ourselves to be talked into harboring a fifth column during the war. It will be time for generous concessions later on; today carefully selected exceptions must suffice."

"I don't mean the fugitives; I don't mean the war. It's quite obvious from our total lack of preparation, that we neither willed nor wanted it. I'm talking about the whole undertaking, the development of the past fifty years. We didn't come into an empty land; the Arabs had been here for generations."

"And we didn't mean to displace a single one. The camels and the goats of the Arabs grazed a fruitful land into utter barrenness. Next, rain and wind turned it into desert. To make the desert fertile was our desire. Twice and thrice as many Arabs as before would have had living space at our side. So long as the Roman Empire restrained the nomads, both the Negev, the South, as well as the land of the Nabateans were densely settled. There were five populous cities. They have vanished. Wherever the Mohammedan conquerors came, the desert spread. I'm not even talking about the enormous land reserves of the Arabs in Iraq, in Trans-Jordan, and in Syria. Empty empires. Trans-Jordan alone has an area twice the size of our whole state and is fertile and yet has not more inhabitants than Tel Aviv. And this same Trans-Jordan, unable to utilize its own land, now demands more."

Dov Popper was not convinced. "Yet our claim remained questionable. One should have used the extreme of generosity—"

"It was said of one of us who spoke as you do that he was no longer a Jew but a moderate Arab—unfortunately the only moderate Arab." Thus these two contended concerning justice and injustice; they repeated that old, old debate, the while the two triangles of the divine scale inclined their silent constellations over the ruined water tower.

In an interval of their conversation Helfin asked Dov what personal experiences had made him so wise and so tolerant. These experiences were hardly of a character to render a normal human being at all conciliatory. A special temperament was needed to draw some honey from so much bitterness. Helfin had, indeed, observed at once an uncommon element in this lonely scribbler. But the first manifestation of this uncommon element had been rather displeasing: Dov Popper was well built and powerful, perhaps a little too plump, yet of a good and sturdy build; but his homeliness was extraordinary. At the sight of this blood-red, broad face one was taken aback initially, not knowing how to range it with any observed category of the human countenance. One had first to pass in review many other, equally unpleasing faces one had encountered, before one was able by some analogy to find a place for these actually absurd individual features which Dov Popper displayed without self-consciousness. There was that thick nose—if one could indeed call it a nose or some object never seen before. Viewed from the front it was so unnaturally broad that the face with its protruding scarlet cheeks seemed to be separated into three almost equal masses. It seemed, this face, to consist of three bunchy cheeks without a nose or, if one preferred, of three noses without any cheeks. The symmetry of this partition was badly disturbed, however, by the fact that the back of the nose was twisted leftward at its middle. Thus, whether seen from the front or in profile, this grotesque semblance of a nose protruded like a grasping finger. The whole countenance was like the nose in this respect, that everything about it was excessive. There was too much hair and it stood up recalcitrantly in wiry bunches. The ears were too big. Even the fine, high curve of the forehead was of gigantic dimensions and seemed to weigh down the lower part of the face. In conversation light came into this face. The large bright-blue, almost whitish eyes were far from gentle. They reminded one of white-hot steel. They were the eyes of a wild enthusiast; their utter purity insisted on an element of the beautiful in this disproportioned face. That radiance appeared not only in conversation. Also when the little blond Chaya, the neighbor's not quite two-year-old daughter, toddled in and trustingly laid her little head on Dov's knee, an expression of tranquil goodness smoothed the excesses of this screaming physiognomy in which so many contradictions were assembled.

Dov's personal fate, which he related with entire simplicity, exhibited a similar structure. Here, too, a first glance showed the most disparate elements. Upon closer attention one got to the point of seeing it all guided by a great, pervasive honorable aspiration. Dov Popper had been a journalist in Poland and had devoted himself to the service of the Revisionists, the right-wing extremists of the Zionist movement. The assassination of Arlosoroff had disillusioned him. Like not a few others, he despaired not only of the radicals but of the whole Zionist will. The attempt on his part to live as a Pole was a grotesque failure. The Polish government sent the young reporter to Spain. But since at that time the Polish régime of Colonel Beck had recognized the Franco party in Spain, Dov Popper was obliged to serve on the Fascist side. That revolted him. He fled to Italy at the first opportunity. In 1939 he returned to Poland and was sucked into the current of the beginning World War. He was picked up by the

Germans and used by them as an interpreter for Polish prisoners of war. This experience was equally horrible. He fled across the frontier, where the Russians took him prisoner. After mistakes and mad wanderings of all kinds he joined the Polish regiments at Tobruk, who were this time fighting on the right side, against Rommel. With them he came to Palestine, where, for the second time, he discovered the blue-white ideals of his youth. He went to work on the land as a settler. His scribbling became an avocation. He had helped to make arable the hard soil of Zur-Yaakov. Contentment came to him. But he had never really settled that old, interior conflict. Something seethed within him. Some time ago, just before his settlement was cut off, he had read an article by a leader of the opposition in Jerusalem whom he greatly admired. This article had stirred him deeply. It contained the following statement, "Let us stop this babble that we are carrying on a defensive war. Our papers try daily to assure us that we have been attacked. How long are we going to talk ourselves into these lies? Away with these illusions! Some of us actually believe the slogan of our defensive position."

"I thought we all believed that! Illusions? Did he really use that word?"

"I still have the paper here." He took it from its holder in the wall. Hitherto he had quoted from memory. Now he read the text to Helfin. A deep sorrowfulness made his strange and grotesque countenance seem less unbeautiful.

" 'It is not to be denied that we came into this land in which the Arabs dwelt. We *had* to come, we had to settle here; we had no other choice. Prophetically Theodor Herzl foresaw our disastrous destruction in Europe. This fundamental position of Zionism is unassailable, even from the Socialist angle. For the extermination practiced by anti-Semitism marches more swiftly than Socialist redemption. Hence the mere difference between these two tempos would have sufficed to seal our doom had we not as a people proceeded to an action of our own. But we must be aware of the fact that this action is tragic in character. We must grasp this fact and not imagine that we are morally in the right. We are obliged to settle here and the Arabs are obliged to resist. It is they, not we, who are on the defensive. The conflict is insoluble. For we may turn and twist as we will: ultimately it is we who drive them from their soil . . .'"

"Quite wrongheaded! It is we who create the very soil, which, as it is today, is worthless. We create it for ourselves but also for them; by drainage for example, by stamping out malaria."

"At this point our honorable opponent thinks he is playing his trump card." A high degree of intellectual satisfaction shone on Dov's face, pain-fraught as the subject and the argument were to him. "For he says, 'Even though we render arable more ground for this and the next generation than was available before, we nevertheless take from the third or perhaps from the tenth generation of Arabs the soil that is here and contract their reserves. We do this not to the Arabs of today, but to their children or perhaps their children's children. But against this, too, they are bound to defend themselves.' Now look, Shaul, I've found a higher trump than this trump—one which overcomes that dazzling and morbidly conscientious train of thought."

From one of his blue pasteboard boxes Dov took out a long notation and read as follows: " 'Labrador. The largest North American peninsula projecting into Hudson Bay. Area almost 1,000,000 square kilometers, not counting the area of the inland waters. Number of inhabitants: 20,000, that is, 75 square kilometers per capita. The actual indigenous inhabitants, Eskimos and Indians, constitute only one-fifth of the population. The others are recent arrivals.' Of course, I took this out of a pretty old encyclopedia. It's dated 1895. Now if we apply the argument of our opponent to the case of Labrador, we must come to the conclusion that the 4,500 natives had the right to resist the immigration of Europeans and Americans even at that time in the interests of a future colonization exclusively by natives. Carrying this argument to its logical conclusion, a single Eskimo family on that vast peninsula would suffice to claim for itself and its descendants to the hundredth or, if you like, to the thousandth generation the sole right to the land reserves of Labrador." Dov Popper sighed. It was as though that gleam of beauty was to settle permanently upon his grotesque face. He said, "If you think that what I have just read you makes me happy, you're mistaken. Justice is a difficult matter, a very difficult matter. It is my belief that one can never do justice to one's neighbor by seeking to be merely just. We will have to love the Arabs. Then only will we begin to practice justice toward them. There is no other way."

After a long and thoughtful silence Helfin said, "At least you will admit that there have been but few ruined water towers in besieged villages in all the earth and throughout all of history in which people weighed the rights of their enemies as sensitively as we do here and now."

"I do admit that," Dov replied, yet retaining his careworn aspect. "And that does suffice for the state of war. In respect of the peace, if I live to see it, I stick to my program; we must come to love the Arabs. It will be difficult. It must not be otherwise."

Another *chaver*, a member of the settlement, came in to fetch Dov Popper to *shmira*, guard duty. Helfin accompanied the two as far as the olive grove. Above the water tower stood the constellation of divine justice, as high above human justice as divine love is above human love. Distant firing sounded in the valley and from the mountains. "Just be careful to confine yourself to defensive action," Helfin cried out to Dov. "Don't you attack the Arabs. And don't fall in love with them yet. It's too early for that."

On his way back through the star-clear summer night, which was agreeably cool at this elevation, Helfin reflected that one did not judge people like Dov fairly if one sought to explain them by the constituents of past experience. These constituents existed but they had no connection with the essence. Formerly Dov had been a journalist; he still scribbled. He used to be a mighty debater; he still flamed in the fire of argument and counterargument. So it would appear. The same façade showed. But behind it appeared, quite as in the case of the man from Shanghai or the girl soldier Rina, a wholly changed human being. One must see this new human being and give it a new name. One must not try to piece together one's knowledge of the new from the stones that went to build the old; that method failed. The philosophizing which took place in this ruined water tower might remind one externally of a European seminar. But the point was that there was nothing abstract about it; it was no intel-

lectual game. Its issue concerned instantaneous death or life. As
he was falling asleep, a comparison occurred to him: There is the
sound which is symbolized in English by *sh* and in German by *sch*.
There should be a separate phonetic symbol for this sound, as
there is in the Slavic languages and in Hebrew. For if we put together an *s* and an *h*, the result is not in the least the sound that is
uttered. Obviously an attempt was made to wring the new from
the old. The consequence is absurd. If we analyze other well-
known phonetic phenomena we find the same poverty-stricken
substitutes. Why not admit that something has come into being
which did not formerly exist? Why not admit that threads of
cotton, however differently combined, will not give us silk?

4.

Sundry other days and nights passed. The dread increased. The
conviction grew that all resistance upon this bit of the beloved
earth was vain. Again a plane circled above Zur-Yaakov and threw
down sacks. This time they contained mail. Many settlers had
not heard in months from their evacuated families. "Everything
is O.K." It was a letter for him too. From Gad Reis. His nephew
had written him to his former military station. From there it
had been forwarded to Rosh Pinah and finally arrived. He was
sure that the letter was of no importance. Only unimportant
things, it seemed to him in his present mood, clicked so well, the
while convoys and one's dearest friends met with disaster. . . .

It turned out that the letter did contain more than a mere
greeting. Gad wrote in a mild variety of despair unskillfully hidden by a mischievous jocosity which did not suit him. Atida had
abandoned him; she had definitely put an end to their relationship. She herself had not even written. Her friend Shlomit had
written. And it was all the fault of Miss Bianca Petry. How?
Helfin stopped reading at this point. Impossible! He rubbed his
forehead. Had he taken in the meaning; wasn't that definitely
contrary to their agreement, to the rules of the game; was it in
Bianca's power to thrust through the layer of isolation which
lay between the two forms of his existence? It was certainly a
symptom of her abnormal energy to be able to accomplish something wholly unpermitted. She was evidently able to talk the

Devil himself into a small concession. Oddly enough, although her energy had often seemed fascinating and even in a way admirable to him in that aspect of his being which he sometimes called his minus-life, now in that life which was morally plus, the whole thing impressed him as contemptible, as involuntarily comic. But he didn't dwell long on this impression. What stirred him deeply and exclusively was the matter of Gad and Atida, which threatened to take so unpleasant a turn on account of the intervention of this self-important creature with the reconstructed nose. In the end this matter might really be disastrous. He read on. Bianca was really concerned only as a sort of machine part, or else as a *diabolus ex machina*. She had no independent function. Nor did she arouse any trace of emotion in Helfin. What a different type of femininity was represented by the girl soldier Rina. But Rina was something to be admired from afar, to be regarded with undesirous joy in the fact that such a creature existed. Rina was nothing more to him, nor was she to be. But precisely at a distance she was a dreamlike consolation—even as an old sailor on the high seas is consoled by a vision of his flowery homeland when at night he stretches himself out wearily on the deck between the rope coils and their stench of dirt and salt.

And so Gad—as the letter informed him—had gone to a movie with Bianca. Faintly, Helfin remembered that this incident contravened a command he had given and a promise he had received. But he did not care to pursue this side issue. Far more important was the circumstance that Shlomit, Atida's friend, had seen Bianca and Gad in the theater. Well, they hadn't been there alone. Baruch and Jonah had been with them. Unfortunately bad luck would have it that on the very next evening Shlomit had again seen Gad and Bianca together—or had believed to have seen them—sitting on a bench on the Shore Promenade, snuggled to each other. Gad had sworn by all that was sacred to him that it had not been he. He knew—thus he wrote—that his uncle had some sort of affection for that vain creature. Not that he had ever understood that, begging his uncle's pardon. As far as he was concerned, Bianca seemed to him neither good-looking nor agreeable. But be that as it may, that was not the point. According to Shlomit's description the man with Bianca on that bench had

not in the least resembled Helfin, either; he had been consider-
ably shorter than the lady. Of course Gad was not able to judge
in how far the excellent Shlomit, though wanting to be accurate, had been able to estimate the height of the two people, especially in view of their passionate gestures. The man, at all
events, had worn a tropical helmet. Needless to say, Helfin reflected with some amusement, it was that mushroomy Josefovitch. Even while he continued to read he also continued his
inner commentary. His nephew, the impertinent boy, was somehow turning the knife in his uncle's wound. It amused Helfin
immensely. It was the proof that Gad had no feeling for Bianca
outside of a rather humorous interest. Otherwise he could not
even have pretended to write so merrily. And that Bianca had
made no hit at all with Gad was satisfactory to Helfin, not pri-
marily on his own account, but because he really regarded the
love of Atida and Gad with profound sympathy and hoped that
the estrangement between them would not be serious and prove
itself to be temporary. Well, he hoped for the best. As for that
wound of his in which the knife was supposed to have been
turned—it seemed completely anesthetized. What did annoy him
was that Gad, who could not possibly have guessed his condition, used the vigorous ruthlessness of his generation. This was
the only disturbing element to Helfin as he finished the letter.

What did the boy expect him to do? Now, of course, the
uncle was supposed to help, after the young know-it-all had
stirred the wasp's nest. "I hear," the letter said, "that you will be
transferred to staff duty at Rosh Pinah within the next few days.
Couldn't you arrange to have me stationed there for a little
while too? There's nothing doing here at Lud. We're waiting for
the end of the armistice. We've got a little surprise for Achmed.
Until then—as you know, Mansura-el-Cheit is not far from Rosh
Pinah and I could make myself useful. I could make a chart of the
vicinity. I was trained to do that. Atida wrote me in our good
days that no such attempt had yet been made, and that for anyone who is an expert at that kind of thing there is a lot of work
at Mansura. I think that if I could just see her, just talk to
her . . ." And this went on with all the spiritual wholeness and
secret anxiety of youth.

Of course the boy had not been able to foresee that this letter would reach his uncle in a place besieged, starving, facing death.

Helfin was just about to try at least to clarify his changed situation by a letter, even though this letter would have little chance of reaching his correspondent, when an event ensued which completely changed the direction of all that had been taking place.

The High Command radioed a message: "The settlement of Zur-Yaakov is to be evacuated. Arye is to conduct the operation. A group will be sent out from the *Kibbutz* Birya, which is familiar with the almost inaccessible paths through the swamps around Safed—the same group which smuggled food through the Arab lines during the siege of Safed. The evacuation is to take place the following night, that is to say, within twenty-four hours."

It was a serious shock, especially to the fighters, when Arye read them the message. What an end to all their combat and their sacrifices! Yet they all knew that it was probably correct according to a broader view of the entire campaign to choose this way out as that of the lesser evil. They knew it with their heads, not with their hearts. Dull resignation appeared on all faces. Only Arye's delicate countenance, which seemed so young in the framework of his thick blond beard, was tense with the prospect of action.

He had no time to grieve. He had to communicate the decisions for the execution of the plan to his helpers. He had to see to it that all necessary details would be taken care of. He had no room for other thoughts. For the whole thing was desperate, almost suicidal. Yet among all the kinds of suicide, among which the small garrison could choose, this was evidently the only one which had a chance of saving them. They were most worried about their three sick patients, the old men, the baby, and the two-year-old Chaya, and the pregnant woman. And it had to happen, too, that, the day before, one of the fighters had sustained a double fracture of the leg. The orders for the transport were given out. They had stretchers, but too few. The doctor picked the worst cases to be carried. How about the others? They would be helped along. Additional stretchers would be woven of branches. The thing must be done. Necessity produced measures to the very border of the possible.

No civilian was permitted to take more than the contents of a small suit case. It went without saying that the three scrolls of the Torah would not be left behind. No one even thought of that, in spite of the fact that most of the soldiers had no relationship to the inner truth of religion and were fond of calling themselves unbelievers, materialists, atheists. It would not have occurred to anyone to abandon to pagan hands the *Sifre-Thora* which had been saved from the destroyed congregations of Lithuania and Volhynia. It is a venerable custom of every *Kibbutz* that the young settlers have the right of bringing over their parents and taking care of them at communal expense. It was these elders who had brought the Torah scrolls from Poland and Russia, these sacred heritages of the tradition. On that night the three scrolls were destined to wander with the people uphill and downdale, even as they had accompanied it through the centuries.

First of all it was necessary to destroy the settlement. This was their grievous task. Hitherto they had cleared the earth, had planted trees, had sown seed. Now they were forced to destroy with the same thoroughness with which that which existed had been slowly and painfully built up. They had to use the same fantastic carelessness of self and had to be bound by the same iron discipline. Only now all this had to be burned, as it were, against their own flesh.

All that had preceded had been easier, even those final months of combat and hunger. The people went to accomplish the hateful work in every room. They wished that they could have blown up everything in a single explosion. That would have been easier, in any case quicker. But one dared not excite the attention of the besiegers; the withdrawal could be successful only as a stealthy surprise. Thus it was necessary to shred the remaining garments. Weeping the women cut up their bed linen. Furniture was split up into fagots. Little souvenirs, bric-a-brac, carrying long associations of wish and fulfillment, all were crushed bit by bit. The medical station and the operating table were rendered useless. Penicillin, a gift from America, and other compact medicaments could be packed. But the beloved piano in the dining hall, together with the chairs and tables, had to be reduced to splinters. Even the quite useless armored car was taken to pieces and the pieces burned. The few chickens that remained were slaughtered. This resulted in a festive meal in which, however, no one took pleasure, much as each one needed the added strength.

Helfin was hastening past the room of the old gentleman from Shanghai. He stood at the center of a little heap of broken wood and glass and furnishings, destroying his radio with a hatchet. Helfin could not bear to look at him. It seemed to him as though he should be ashamed, having been somehow responsible. He was about to rush on. But the old man stopped him with quite a cheerful cry. To Helfin's amazement he was not discouraged. "Out in the world I could not have endured it a third time. But here I'm sure that the Land will make it up to me. I'm not the only one who has to begin all over again." He lifted his hatchet and clenched his left fist and brought his hatchet down mechanically to the right and to the left with a grim smile on his face. With loud cries he whipped up his own courage. His half-paralyzed eyelid quivered at every blow and the whole thing looked like a dream image of annihilation frightened at itself. Helfin could not take his eyes from the old man. Two thousand years of Jewish suffering seemed here to perform a wild dance along a quivering line, comparable to a tightrope, running along the narrow, dark frontier which divides hope from despair.

It was very quiet in the reading room under the ruined water tower. Dov Popper was going over the notes he had made toward his long-planned "History of the Settlement of Galilee". He had obviously found a system according to which he could separate the important from the unimportant. Perhaps he had long prepared for such a selective process. He never hesitated. He placed some of the groups of notes on the side or on the ground; others he put in his suit case which, to be sure, was pretty full already. Now he stooped and took some shirts and a pair of shoes out of the trunk, thus creating additional space for his source material.

A bad business was the poisoning of the watchdog. No one wanted anything to do with that. But his barking would undoubtedly have betrayed the withdrawal. So it had to be done.

In the pharmacy there was a fairly large jug filled with opium. Figaro didn't make the thing difficult for his friends. He licked up a plateful of the opium with relish. Then he was a little drunk and his eyes watered and he went to sleep. Soon he breathed no more. The rest of the opium was given to the three mules and the horse.

The young men from Birya who were to guide the settlers through the swamp arrived at the first gleam of dawn. No one in Zur-Yaakov had slept. Finally the searchlight picked up the group mounting the hillside. Sweat streamed from their faces. The five young men, who were strong, well nourished, armed to the teeth, were ready to drop with weariness. This showed the character of the road which would have to be traveled. Well, the remaining hours before daybreak were useless for so difficult an expedition in any event. It could not be thought of until the following nightfall.

The new arrivals were led to the communal house, where there were still straw sacks. The settlers, too, lay down on the bare floors of their ruined rooms in order to rest until evening and husband their strength. A few took care to see to it that the work of destruction had been completed. Rage, grief, sleep, these three presiding spirits of the world of shades ruled the final hours of Zur-Yaakov.

Toward evening the few cigarettes that still remained were distributed. They were smoked to the last fragment of tobacco; it looked as though the lips themselves emitted smoke. Nervousness seized upon everyone. Yesterday they had been calmly determined. Rumors arose: The Arabs had observed the preparations and had increased their outposts since the afternoon. An attack was feared. Even if it were to be repulsed there would not be enough ammunition left for the breakthrough.

There were some who quite unmotivatedly began to say that perhaps the High Command would retract the evacuation order at the last moment. How would one then, lacking all supplies, be able to hold the self-destroyed settlement? To one who babbled such stuff, Rina said sharply, "Tomorrow in Birya I'm going to have you tried by a military court and condemned to a lifelong repetition of such silly gossip!"

At the communal house, groups of ten were formed. Outposts, protectors at each side, and rear guards were also grouped by tens. Helfin belonged to those who had to march with the civilians, with the ailing and the children. He waited in the doctor's office, which had a strong odor of valerian. The physician gave the two small children who were to be carried morphine injections. They screamed. Now the arrangement of the escorts was complete. They waited for the word of command. The five from Birya stood ready in the lead.

One group had to remain in the settlement for another hour, so as to feign a continuance of life and activity. Two radios were to play at full strength. The searchlights were to continue to play over hills and chasms. Here and there a few reports were to issue from one of the pill boxes and singing and tumult were to be raised to a maximum for this one hour within the lanes of the ghostly village. Then these last settlers, too, would depart.

Everything was in readiness. The march could begin.

There was no farewell; there was no sentimentality. One after another they marched toward the valley through the dark. They hoped that it would not occur to the Arabs to make an assault on the almost empty settlement. The merry incessant radio music, like a bad film, faded more and more into the distance behind them, and the desolateness of the mountain night filled that space which seemed mysteriously to increase under the feet of the wanderers. As all boundaries seemed to melt, so the rising mist increased. The beams of the searchlights glided toward the opposite direction, seeming there, too, to pierce the infinitude of the landscape.

Unnatural silence prevailed. All had drawn socks over their boots. Here and there a valise struck a stone or one of the two children whimpered in its sleep. Otherwise no sound was uttered. Thus the path went through a field of grain, the while above, on the mountain, to the accompaniment of the howling of a pack of jackals, Zur-Yaakov and its last lights faded away behind a protruding cliff.

They had passed through the dry bed of the stream. Now the winding road mounted. On the neighboring hill lay a well-fortified Arabic village. An attack from there was a threatening possibility. The enemy had mortars and machine guns and an attack from that quarter could have utterly destroyed the entire caravan. It would have sufficed to meet a single outpost to alarm the whole section.

The leaders insisted on haste, in spite of the difficulties of the stretcher bearers amid the rocks and cliffs. Now and then a brief repose was permitted so that the civilians might catch their breath. Then the pitiless march continued. Unhappily the wind had ceased. Now every little stone loosened by a foot rolled audibly. The most dangerous moment would be that during which the highway had to be crossed. Naturally this was to be accomplished at an inhospitable and therefore unprotected section, where the declivities, almost impassable, fell away toward the road. But how easy it would have been to have met, say, an Arab bicyclist at the decisive moment. Then everything would have been discovered. However, the moon receded behind clouds; the highway was crossed; a slight feeling of security supervened.

Suddenly, to the horror of everyone, little Chaya began to weep. Her tiny voice increased in energy until the weeping of a child seemed to echo through the night from all the hills.

She had awakened in the knapsack in which she was being carried. It had amazed her to find herself like an Eskimo baby slung across the back of a strange man, instead of being in her crib. The long line of wanderers crouched. Arye and the physician went into swift consultation. The child had to be quieted at any price. Its silence meant the lives of seventy people. Morphine! But the doctor declared that in the darkness he could not measure the dose and would have to risk killing the child. Furthermore the effect of the injection would not be instantaneous and the introduction of the needle would only increase the child's howling. Helfin took Chaya from her bearer. He pressed the warm, trembling little body to his heart, cheek to cheek. He exerted his entire will to calm Chaya, talking to her softly and insistently. It did no good. The decision had to be made at once. Perhaps even this minute had been too long. Helfin saw Dov Popper approach with something thick and soft, a cloth or a woolen jacket, which he threw over Helfin's head and over the child in his arms. The muffling did not suffice. The child struggled and tugged at the cloth with its hand. The weeping resounded more piercingly. The physician approached with his syringe. There was no choice. Desperately Helfin pressed the child against his face. At that moment its little mouth found Helfin's ear lobe and began to suck it. The sucking put the child gradually to sleep. In a few moments there was silence. They all arose. Helfin's body was covered with perspiration. He had the feeling that he had just experienced the most terrible moments of his life, perhaps in expiation of some far, forgotten guilt. Dov Popper seemed to crush his hand in his own.

From this point on his consciousness was clouded. Only his legs moved mechanically over stones and rubble, hour after hour— an endless nightmare. They climbed up pathless cliffs; they sought support; they found none and slid back. The moon had set at last. Now path and wanderer were indistinguishable in the darkness.

Was the column still assembled? Had some parts lost touch with others? Some of the people were evidently stronger than Helfin, younger than he; they preserved their entire awareness and did not lose sight of the whole group. He himself saw nothing more than the back of the man in front of him which swayed up and down. For moments at a time he thought he was asleep. Then he would stumble and that would awaken him and there, again, was that dark, human back two paces ahead of him. To cling to this bit of darkness, to follow its movement as it preceded him like a pillar of fog—more than that he could not grasp, for more than that he could not be responsible. Someone spoke to him. In the first gray streak of dawn the village of Birya emerged in the distance with its little white houses. His comrades pointed it out to him. To Helfin it still seemed immeasurably, hopelessly far. He felt no joy. Indeed it was now that his weariness reached an excess which was no longer bearable. That intensification had been unimaginably swift. To break down was the only thing that he could still do, of which he was still capable. No other evidence of life could be expected of him. But in the very face of this stormy despair he trudged on. He had been turned into a gasping trudging machine—a machine invented for no discoverable purpose; he was incomprehensible to himself and no longer human. He had forgotten how to be. Nevertheless he observed that the stretcher bearers had to be changed often, much oftener than before. Now, too, Arabs seemed to have been alerted and to have observed the procession. Shots were heard. No one paid attention to them. Onward, onward! The pace was slightly increased, as were the intervals between the groups. There were still individuals who felt that they must issue orders. Here and there a sharp word or a curse was heard. The chief thing was to keep the entire line in motion. Forward! No relaxation! Suddenly, wholly surprised, Helfin knew himself to be marching at a swift tempo into the great open gate of Birya. He leaned against the wall of a house. He was thirsty. There was a burning in his feet which seemed to bear witness not only to the rough surface of this region over which he had trodden but to the heaviness of the whole earth in its fiery anguish. He sat down on a box. Someone gave him a piece of chocolate and a glass of orange juice.

5.

A few days later he awakened with a feeling of dull indifference. His return to life did not lead through a triumphal arch, as he had perhaps at one time fancied whenever that return had seemed possible to him. Rather did it drag him through a lane of misery, a whole coil of such lanes; through a kind of reaction and hangover, as though he had been wallowing in forbidden indulgence. Thus it would seem that there are sufferings forbidden to human nature because they are not conformable to it and these, like excessive indulgences, are followed by a similar reaction.

The settlers, who had lived on wretched hunger rations much longer than he, remained in the hospital. Everything was plentiful here—milk, cheese, fragrant bread. But the settlers could eat only very small portions at a time. Lack of prudence was followed by wretched sickness. Only gradually did their bodies accustom themselves to the normal intake of nourishment. Helfin recovered rapidly. A car was to take him at the very earliest moment up to Rosh Pinah.

The evacuation had taken place without loss of life. But this, too, caused almost no joy. The only gleam of light in the whole thing was the fact that the last group which had remained behind in Zur-Yaakov had reached Birya a few hours later on the same morning. And it was felt to be a kind of a joke at the heart of this tragedy that the two radios had gone on thundering after the last soul had left the settlement.

Next came Rosh Pinah. This was a real little city with houses of stone and red tile roofs. No more barracks of wood. In the streets of this old market town, which nestles at the foot of the mountain on which Safed is built, there was an amazingly calm and peacefully ordered life. Here there were women with their market bags, and open shops. Carpet beaters were busy on balconies, and lilting women's voices audible at windows. Here the armistice was a fact. It was not until he reached the main road below that Helfin met any soldiers. In the town life was normal. Fruits were sold from a wooden truck; a cobbler tapped at heels; three old men, engaged in lively conversation, strolled along the street. In spite of the intense heat they wore their fur-brimmed hats. They were pious men according to the strictest rite. One had a huge black-covered book under his arm. Their shoes had no heels. A bearded young man modestly joined the group.

The impression that one received was always the same. Human beings didn't will war, not one. They wanted to live and rejoice and work at what pleased them and take walks. No one even thought of force. And one should use one's imagination and realize that it was not otherwise in Damascus, in Beyrouth, in Cairo. There, too, the bazaars were busy, bales were uncorded, there was enough to do and the people were glad to do it and be left in peace. Here as there the war must seem to an unprejudiced observer as something wildly artificial, monstrous, impossible, which had been forced upon the people against its will the while it desired to be contented with the labor and the joy of its common day. Simultaneously Helfin saw the tranquillity here but also the quiet contentedness beyond the frontiers, in the towns of the enemy. It was a confusing picture. How solve the riddle of the many centuries? No one wanted war and it continued to be waged. Why? He determined not to forget certain fundamentals. Firstly: We had been attacked. The guilt for that lay with the Arabs, still more with Bevin and his minions. He was not ready to say with the English people or to identify that people with its immediate, accidental leadership. Secondly: In the process of defense we, too, had committed excesses which must be atoned for at the earliest moment. Thirdly and generally: Our state must be a pure state, or else it would be none. It must be a state of justice, a state which, as Dov expressed it, must love its minority. Else everything had been meaningless.

While he was pondering thus, he caught sight of his nephew.

Amazed he went to meet him. It was in the square in front of the city hall, which was covered with directive placards and red arrows:— "Parking Forbidden," "Station for the Wounded," "Bomb Shelter," "Visa Office." In the midst of soldiers and cars, beside a pillar in the hall in which formerly there had been the customs office of the Lebanese frontier—among this rush and tumult, Gad passed him by and did not recognize him. The experience of semistarvation must have changed him, he thought. Then he called to the lad.

Gad was moved and embraced him. He had already heard how his uncle had escaped the extremity of danger.

"Well, and how is it with you?" Helfin asked.

"At Latrun the war is practically over. The armistice is taken fairly seriously. Our trenches and those of the Arabs are only about a hundred paces from each other. Early in the morning the Arabs cry out to us, '*Boker tov*, good morning!' And '*Ma achalta Yankele?* What have you eaten, Yankele?'"

"Why precisely Yankele?"

"They heard us use the name. And eating is always their chief interest. They're like children. But like evil children whom one dare not trust. In the morning they greet us in Hebrew. By noon they begin to throw stones. Toward nightfall they get bored and begin to shoot. Of course we return the fire. In the end they use cannons. In the communiqués the whole thing is then called an artillery duel."

"And what are you doing up here in Rosh Pinah?"

"Just for the moment I've got to attend to a few formalities. Several days ago I was transferred to Mansura-el-Cheit. Until the end of the armistice. As a cartographer. I wrote you. I didn't find out until later why you didn't answer. So I found another way.

After all, this is my *Kibbutz*, to which I properly belong."

"And how about Atida?"

It turned out that Gad regretted the transfer which he had so passionately desired. He had been too impatient to await the quiet development of things. Atida had by no means calmed down. She had, on the contrary, received him with extreme reluctance and had steadily refused to see him alone. In the life of the *Kibbutz* such an occasion was difficult to avoid, but the proud girl had used every possible device in order to prevent ever being alone with him. It was a melancholy conflict, in which he proved to be the weaker. He suffered so much that he had even considered begging for a transfer back. "And I have so much to say to her," he cried passionately. "I could furnish her with irrefutable proof. But no sooner do I begin to talk about that whole matter than she rushes away. I can't, after all, pull her back by her skirt."

"No, you can't do that." An odd feeling, half of melancholy and half of jocular insight came over Helfin. He was amused that this skirmishing of the sexes did not cease even amid the conflicts of war, but that it seemed to develop a special intensity at the front and to vie victoriously with the very founding of a state. But even while he smiled at this reflection, his paternal heart was moved. He understood Gad; he understood the boy's grief and felt as though he were a party to it and would so gladly have helped. He recalled the similar confusions of his own youth. Though these had been but sparks, wild conflagrations could so easily be caused by such in inexperienced hearts.

"The worst of it is that Shlomit sticks to her slanderous statements. She insists that it was I who was on that damned bench on the Promenade."

"Maybe Shlomit has some special interest in the matter?"

"I don't believe it," Gad said swiftly with a warm and radiant glance. "That would be quite uncomradely."

"Didn't you tell me yourself that Shlomit's brother is in love with Atida?"

"Who isn't? She's the prettiest girl in the *Kibbutz*." He seemed proud, though in a rather sad way, of this superiority of his beloved, for he sighed, "Unluckily she knows it too." Then he was all eagerness. "But you're all wet with your suspicion of

Shlomit. Such things don't happen among us. Shlomit is a hell of a fine girl." Helfin knew well with what high ideals these young people treated their companionship and how intolerant they were of any defection from these ideals. He believed, too, that he had a quite clear insight into their notions of purity and wholeness.

Perhaps, as he was to perceive immediately, not as clear as he thought. For what Gad now began to tell him was not only alien in character but displeasing as well. A new generation had grown up with its hardness and its forthrightness. Thus it had, perhaps, to be as a counterpressure against the inhumanity of the age. Helfin knew, also, that he had always been too soft and yielding. Nevertheless there were limits which he could have desired this generation to use as a test of its hardness only in the nobler sense and not in an oafish one. Doubtless the many generations of the dispersion had been too much given to analysis and to talk. So here one had emerged which was almost too silent, which insisted upon the deed alone. This was well, but far from perfect. In other days we were almost throttled by our problems. This generation was being throttled by its negation of the problematic. He was willing to risk the thought that the danger in sight was stupidity.

This impression became intensified as Gad continued his rather random account. What he and the fellows should have done to Bianca was to push her teeth down her throat—this filthy old maid who played the part of naïveté when it suited her and then again pretended to be as sophisticated as all getout. That wasn't all. His comrades, Baruch and Jonah, had had a bone to pick with her ever since Paris. That was the main thing. She had long played for a poke in the nose. To deliver this at the proper moment the boys had formed a little club which they called the Z.M. club, standing for the Hebrew letters *Zayin, Mem*. They had whispered to him that, of course, he must be a member of the club. This had been the purpose of the visit to the theater, aside from the fact that Jonah had had a good bout of petting with the broad. Oh well, hell. *Mele*—it'll all come out in the wash. As far as he had been concerned the whole thing had been revolting to him, *pashut*, just revolting and funny at the same time, and really and truly he had had nothing more to do with it than a fish has with the desert. All he wanted to do was to explain that to Atida. It was just as a comrade of his comrades that he had joined the conspiracy against Bianca. "Bianca fell for the thing at once. Secret society—a-ha, that was quite to her taste. We told her that whoever among the younger people wanted to have a career in the new state would have to belong to the Z.M. First she thought it had something to do with front fighting. We told her O.K., that too, but later. First we had something else in mind. We would have a meeting at midnight at the Inn *Sheva Tachanot*, the Seven Mills. This was to be a test of courage and a condition of membership.

She turned up all alone along the desolate bank of the Yarkon far beyond Tel Aviv among the orange groves. We had someone to watch her unseen and to report. There are Arabs around there; occasionally there is firing; you can hear the groan of an irrigation pump in the distance. She was to take all that. She was to be all dressed up and come to the deserted mooring place and step on the old landing bridge, balancing herself across the planks to a motor boat. All the while she was to sing a folk song and carry across her shoulder the heavy spade which is the symbol of agriculture. And we told her a lot of additional nonsense. Well, at the stroke of midnight she did turn up. We three were lying in the reeds. She really balanced herself on the planks, singing like mad, and carrying the spade. We slipped the plank away from under her and, all dressed up as she was, she slid into the water. The most comical part of it was that she didn't at first grasp the fact that she had fallen for a lot of crap. How could anything like that happen to a great star like her? She never dreamed of that. On the contrary she pulled herself agilely out of the brook and tried quite seriously and proud as any rooster to march on to the motor boat. She probably thought that this had been the test. It wasn't until we began to scream with laughter and to take one flashlight photograph of her after another that she began to raise hell. And that's the way we took pictures of her, standing there in her soaked evening dress with the spade, like a thin, bedraggled scarecrow, scolding and weeping. 'Attention! We are taking you!' Jonah yelled—*Zehirut mekalmim!*' That, you see, was the point of our two letters *Zayin, Mem*. And so, in the end, she understood what she had been let in for."

"That was a very crude thing to do," Helfin said, "and quite ungentlemanly."

"Healthy for her, all right."

"Ugly and ill bred. Not even funny."

"You probably don't know that she spied for the Gestapo in Paris. We should have shot her. We were far too decent to her."

Helfin refused to enter upon such arguments. "If there is ground for such suspicions, bring her to trial. That's all!"

Gad's expression was first hurt and next knowing. He had found the confirmation of what was currently said among the members of his age group: No use telling the older generation anything. No understanding was to be expected.

Helfin easily read the lad's thoughts. "What you are now thinking," he said ironically, "may be not incorrect at times. But don't fool yourself and depend upon it altogether."

Gad shook his head in admiration. "It makes life difficult to have so clever an uncle."

"Yes, you're very much to be pitied on my account, aren't you?"

Gad quickly took his hand. "Oh no, I'm not, not really." And the reconciliation was almost complete.

Over a game of chess which they were playing in the parlor of the inn after a good and simple meal, Helfin returned to his criticism. He didn't, of course, expect his nephew to repeat the old-fashioned promise of the naughty child, that he wouldn't do it again. He wouldn't have minded something similar. He waved away the troublesome flies with a gesture of probably inordinate annoyance. For Gad looked up from the chessboard with a sad expression.

"I admit that I went too far," he said after a pause and made a very thoughtful move. "But Atida goes too far too. The idea of keeping on being angry with me on account of a piece of silliness. I admit that it was silly. But Atida ought to see that there was no question of the slightest disloyalty. But she refuses to listen. She has the feeling that she has been soiled. That is the only message which she sent me."

He lost the game although he was, as a rule, the better player.

Sympathetically Helfin considered how the breach could be healed. He said so, and this drew from Gad quite a number of suggestions, none of which were any good at all, as Helfin easily recognized and proved on the basis of reflection and experience. There was just one device that was any good and that was also very disagreeable to Helfin. He was to tell the girl that it was he who on that night had been Bianca's companion on the bench. "A lie?" Helfin said. "A ruse of war," the nephew entreated. Curious, what presumptuous demands could be made by a nephew upon an uncle *in statu parentis*. He would never have asked a thing like that of his real father.

In the heat of the next afternoon Helfin was driving in a military truck which was giving him a lift to Mansura-el-Cheit. Gad had not yet completed the formalities attendant on his transfer. It was just as well, too, that he remained behind in Rosh Pinah. Meanwhile, accompanied by his nephew's blessings, the advocate proceeded to his task.

The heat was withering. His uniform stuck to his skin. Past lines of trucks and wooden barracks the truck rumbled through a dusty eucalyptus grove and finally came out into the open. Soon thereafter they crossed an enormous flying field. On that broad, desolate open space stood random white walls, tall masts, and cabins, of which the purpose was clear only to experts. These apparently useless things created a dreamlike impression; the enormous waste of space was in itself fantastic. But what would not have affected one dreamily in the soporific heat? Since the end of the Mandate, the flying field had not been used; it was too near the Syrian frontier. Neglected buildings at great intervals were falling into decay. It was an organized void. It was something like the precise contrary of a well-built-up temple area. There was a hollowness about this space of air, of flat earth rudely prepared with an indication of paths into the pathless. In the distance rose the mountains. Otherwise a void. But one can get lost even in the void. The chauffeur tried several directions and finally knew not whither to turn. Suddenly there appeared two Arabs from behind a ruined wall. Perhaps they were shepherds. With hoarse noises in their throats they indicated a direction.

Gradually the land, which had seemed for a while to have been lost from creation, assumed form again. There was a hill; there was the grave of a sheik under a group of trees. There was something like the adumbration of a field of grain. Now the thistles in it were as high as a man. These white thistle fields are the most conspicuous feature of the Galilean landscape. The thistles are white and the plants look like small, slender trees or, rather, like the skeletons of trees, bony skeletons, from the thorns of which the flesh has fallen. There are whole fields of these upright white skeletons. For centuries the earth of this plateau has not known a plow. It produces sun-parched grasses, wasps, stones, dust. The silence is so deep that even the soughing of the wind does not really break it.

The chauffeur apologized to Helfin. Daily he drove the truck which brought supplies from Rosh Pinah to Mansura; yet it would happen to him from time to time that he lost his sense of direction in this solitude. The young officer who accompanied them and whom Helfin had met in the "Little Forest of the Fifty" pointed out the positions of the enemy. A few kilometers to the north lay Mishmar-Hayarden, the only point on this side of the Jordan which the Syrians had taken. A big transport car which came to meet them, visible from afar, might very well have been a hostile vehicle. When would the shooting begin? But the vigorous blond lad who suddenly leaped out of the jolting car greeted them with a gay *Shalom*. He was on his way to Tuba, the deserted Arab village on the plateau. Now they were not far from Mansura. The young settler showed them the way.

Yehuda, the young officer who accompanied them, had orders to communicate to the *mukhtar*, the head man of the settlement. For here the military front and a new colony coincided. Military labor immediately became visible. Youths, stripped to the waist, worked with all their strength in this breathless heat under this merciless sky. They were working with a drill, that frightfully noisy vibrating and rattling mechanism with which holes are bored into the stony crags. They were preparing a trench. The machine makes the impression not as though you were using it but as though it were using you, leading you, shaking you, causing your entire body to vibrate.

Eli, one of these workers, was the *mukhtar* here. In spite of his dignified title he was barely twenty—sinewy, blackened by the sun, with great dark, merry eyes. After the officer had executed his commission, the two guests were conducted through the settlement. What they found here was a treeless plateau, sloping down toward the valley of the Jordan in broad-curved, gray-green declivities. The area cut off the farther view like a tongue of land or a peninsula until you approached its rim. The abandoned Arab village on the height consisted of black stone huts. Black basalt was the characteristic stone in these parts. The white lines of mortar between the black stones, of which all buildings were built here, produced an agreeable pattern in the walls. These human habitations looked well enough from without. They were frightful inside. There was but a single room, which the families shared with their beasts, with the filth of generations, with mighty swarms of vermin which resisted even the most thorough treatment of powerful insecticides. Only one of these houses had hitherto been put to use by the settlers as a *machsan*, a storage shed. No one had yet dared enter the others, although these massive structures with their little windows might have offered shelter from the heat. It had seemed preferable to sleep in the new wooden huts, hot as they were, or under the open sky in tents.

A table under a board roof, open on all sides, such was the dining hall. Cool water in porcelain cups was handed to the guests. It seemed a mystery how on this land, where any motion induced extreme fatigue, it was possible to do the heaviest work under the burning sun. And the new settlers, all quite young, had been driven by their pioneering enthusiasm from Belgium, France, North Africa, and had blended in comradeship with the *Sabras*, the home-born. In addition to Hebrew, a good deal of French was spoken here. "*Ve-shavu banim li-gvulam,*" thus did the *mukhtar*, Eli, quote from the prophet Jeremiah: "And the children shall return to their boundaries." He smiled tranquilly, while two girls with typical Parisian figures ran by chatting. Thus, in this brave present, there were blended the immemorial and the immediate day.

"How about the Arabs?" Helfin asked.

"The village was usually occupied for only a part of the year. The nomads came from the South with their herds, when these had grazed off the fields. Two important tribes used to gather here—the Sheck Abu Yussef and the Arab al Cheib. The trouble was that there was an old blood feud between them. They didn't flee from us. When the English left they were scared of each other."

"Will they come back?"

"Who can tell? We don't mind. There would be room enough for all of us, if they were to settle down and cultivate the earth. Of course, they wouldn't recognize the land again. Wait till our irrigation system works."

"Is there water here?"

"Water can be pumped from the Jordan. Not while the war is on, because the enemy is over there. What we are doing is to build pipes out of Tuba, where there is a good well. That's what we're doing now, as you can see. We've got to drag the pipes over the hills on our backs because there is yet no proper road. But once we have water, you must come back and take a look. The soil here is excellent; we can plant pear trees and plum trees and apple trees. It will be beautiful. We'll have olives, too, and figs, and some of our people are dreaming of bananas. We'll have forests, too, of eucalyptus and cypress." He added coolly in order that Helfin might not consider him too romantic, "The cypresses, you see, make the best telegraph poles. It's a very profitable business."

They passed a wooden structure which had been erected in the center of the village. They had hung up the casing of a missile; it looked like a gong, and from it hung a tiny horseshoe. It seemed the most primitive kind of monument, such as one would expect in an African village. "It's our souvenir," the *mukhtar* explained. "A Syrian aerial bomb. Happily it didn't explode."

The goal of their walk was one of the black houses at the edge of the village. They climbed up broken steps to the flat roof.

On a field stool, under a piece of matting, sat the *djara*, the lookout, a broad-shouldered, vigorous, dark-skinned girl. Next to her she had an Arab jug of water. She wore the regulation blue blouse, and brief shorts; her legs were bare. She was watching the enemy positions and her instrument was an ordinary small opera glass. One could see that the military equipment here was still fairly primitive. And it was profoundly touching in this wilderness to see the slender hands of a girl use this instrument which she had probably once used for purposes so different. It needs to be said that at this front the armistice was fairly well respected.

From the edge of the roof there opened a broad, inclusive view. Deep below, the Jordan showed its narrow, glittering green ribbons curling through the valley down to Lake Kinereth. Not far from here, on one of these dove-gray slopes which seemed not so much mountains as the petrified folds of some primordial garment, an impassioned youth once proclaimed anew the ancient wisdom of his people, reteaching it with deeply moving love and consecration in the sentences of the Sermon on the Mount.

From such a distance the Jordan did not look very impressive. But this showed how high up Mansura was situated. For, in fact, the river is at this point an impassable barrier. South of the only bridge which, since time immemorial, both Jews and Arabs call the "Bridge of the Daughters of Jacob," the river is eight meters in breadth and several meters deep and its current is of torrential force. On the other side of the frontier, even as on our side, the rounded slopes form an extensive plateau, the immense brown Syrian territory of Golan. In the far horizon a series of hilltops form a semicircle. From the air the whole territory must make the impression as of a landscape of the moon, like one of those broad craters, lined by a gigantic circle of mountain walls.

"How big is the Syrian territory that we see from here?" Helfin asked.

The young officer was of the opinion that they were surveying about 500 square kilometers.

"And all this huge area is almost uncultivated, almost empty?"

"In all this territory that we see," the *mukhtar* said, "there are only four Syrian villages with a maximum population of a thousand souls." They stepped back into the shadow of the hut, seeking shelter from the glow of noon, which is scarcely tolerable in spite of smoked glasses. One of the new huts was serving as a laundry. At its door one girl was ironing, a second was mending linen, a third was arranging the linen in heaps. Helfin recognized the third girl to be Atida.

She was prettier than ever, more grownup, too. She was far less childlike. She greeted Helfin and walked beside him for a little. She wanted to show him how well everything was arranged here. Oh, it was all *mequyan, nehedar*, excellent, splendid. If he were to see her parents in Tel Aviv, he must report to them. "They worry and worry uselessly. There's no shooting here. There used to be a little; that interfered with the harvesting. The feed isn't all gathered yet. But we'll do the last bits this week." He was to tell her parents that she had never been so happy, that all her wishes were fulfilled. Her parents couldn't imagine it, but it was so. He was to be sure to tell them that she was terribly grateful to them for having finally given her her way. "Tell them I am perfectly happy!"

"And how about Gad?" Helfin asked casually.

Her beautiful, smooth, gracefully curved forehead under the bright, wind-blown hair, tried to wrinkle. It really didn't work. But into the deep blue eyes there came a warning gleam. "Well, what about him?"

Helfin found it undeniably difficult to try to tell this little lady with her frank yet penetrating glance about a love affair of his own on a bench on the Promenade. It would make him look too ridiculous. Worse still, the story hadn't even happened. An inspiration came to him. There was that second alibi of Gad's. Suddenly he found himself telling her the tale of that practical joke on the shore of the Yarkon River. He told her about Gad's share in this rather unpleasant trick which had been played on the puffed-up vanity of the actress. He found himself entering into the spirit of the anecdote and related it in all its color and crudeness.

While he was talking, Atida stood on the threshold of her hut with her back against the doorpost. She had crossed her arms behind her. One of her legs was bent at the knee so that her sole was lightly placed against the wooden wall. There was something defensive in this attitude, as though behind her, in the house, Atida had something that she wanted to guard. Her expression was not an unfriendly one; one could even perceive the beginnings of a smile. Yet this very tranquillity, this easy self-assurance seemed to keep the speaker within certain limits. At last she said, "Why do you interfere?" Her tone was thoughtful as she looked into Helfin's eyes. There was a matter-of-fact familiarity blended with sternness in her words. It seemed to Helfin that there was an element of unconscious humor in this sixteen-year-old girl's addressing a man of his age in quite this fashion. At bottom, however, he had to confess that she was right and within her rights.

It was not easy for him to explain his pseudo-paternal relationship to Gad.

"So what?" Atida was both pert and frank. "What you told me didn't please me a bit. I think it's *pashut nora*, simply disgusting."

Helfin could not help admiring her reaction. She was a good child. He hoped that she would live up to her name of "The Future One"; that she would prove to be the representative of the coming generation. If that were so one could rejoice in the instinctive delicacy and rectitude of that next generation. The whole thing delighted Helfin, though at the same time and with the other half of his heart he wanted so much to advocate the cause of his poor nephew.

What was most curious was this, that Helfin, who ordinarily was able to think and to adjust himself intellectually with extreme swiftness, found no appropriate word and no counter-argument. This little girl had put him in an embarrassing situation.

"What an ugly piece of revenge," said the clever child. "It sounds as though somebody had been turned down in his amatory hopes."

"That least of all!" Helfin assured her. The very insistence of his words made them seem less credible.

She took the offensive. "How can you be so sure?" She was really forcing him into the story which he had been told to tell and which he had suppressed out of embarrassment.

He had to come out with it in the end. He had to explain about himself and the bench and the Promenade, and it took all his self-control not to stammer and halt. In spite of that, the effect was second rate. Atida curved her beautiful lips. He couldn't deny that after the Yarkon story his confession sounded artificial enough. It might all have been more convincing the other way around. His false shame had blunted the edge. He strolled off, quite ashamed of himself, and left Atida apparently implacable.

The only thing left him to do, seeing that he had muffed this chance, was to have a thorough explanation with Atida's friend. He was quite emphatic with Shlomit. He tried to stir her conscience. That conscience, by the way, was without strain. She really believed that she had served the truth. She had had no ax to grind; she had merely wanted to clarify the position of her friend. Goddammit, Helfin reflected, these kids are stubborn. But he did in the end convince her, as he had not convinced Atida. After a long conversation she shared his view of Gad's entire innocence and loyalty.

Night had fallen in the meantime and the truck, the only communication with the hinterland, had long left for Rosh Pinah. That mattered little. Helfin slept in a tent.

He was to be called for early in the morning. He was awakened in time and soon after dawn made a round of the cool, fragrant, dewy village. Once more he climbed the roof for that wide view. He looked away from the Jordan and quite near him beheld an image as of the days of Ruth and Boaz. Ruth in the dawn, in the legendary beauty of the first awakening of the rosy light, in the lovely blowing of the morning breeze. . . . Harvesters, girls and boys, in the field of grain, vigorously at their task. And on these fields with their high plants, like stalks of maize, the harvesting was being done by hand, according to the most ancient of ways, and not with the modern machines used on the Jewish farms. These were Arab fields, irregularly sown in Arab fashion. But the Arabs had fled, and the harvest had to be brought in by the new settlers.

They proceeded in lines which took in the whole fields, in groups of three. In each group there were working two girls and a boy. The girls proceeded to the right and to the left with implements that looked like garden shears. Then the boy would follow in the middle between the two, a step or two behind them, gathering the cut stalks in a heavy sack which, from time to time, he dragged over to a waiting wagon.

The harvesters went ahead in long, steady lines, like battle lines, and Helfin reflected that these battle lines of harvesters were the only ones worthy of the dignity of man. Such were his thoughts in this rare mood, lit by the dawn light, delicate and bright. If he could only always have nourished this mood. At that moment he perceived that one of the groups of three consisted of Shlomit, Atida, and his nephew Gad. He remembered now Gad's telling him that this was one of the recurrent occasions which the *Kibbutz* offered of Atida and himself being together, but that recently Atida had refused to communicate with him even on these occasions. He was annoyed at the thought that he had probably accomplished nothing and continued for a while to watch the slowly approaching harvesters. It was too far to call out to them. And what, to be exact, was he to say? Alas, he would have to return with the whole thing mismanaged. He would have to leave it to the young people themselves, fearing that further confusion would ensue.

At that moment Shlomit gave a cry. She had hurt her foot against a stone. He could see that from her gestures. She limped aside and sat down on the edge of the field. At that moment Helfin could also see how his nephew began to talk very insistently to Atida without, however, interrupting his work. And now Atida could not but listen. She was forced to do so. It was considered improper to cease from work if one had taken no hurt. For the broad front of the harvesters was meant to proceed regularly. Each was assigned a place. Each, therefore, moved along as in a common wave. Thus she and Gad were firmly wedged into the systematic rows of the harvesters and released from the operation of their own wills.

Atida attacked the stalks violently with her shears. But she could neither run away nor fail to listen. The lad took thorough advantage of the situation. He took out photographs, evidently of that farcical practical joke. Helfin was not too much astonished to hear a merry laugh across the distance from the girl. What she had deprecated when he told about it seemed now to find some favor in her eyes. Perhaps Shlomit had just feigned to have that little accident? In that case his persuasion of her last night had, perhaps, not been wholly in vain.

When Helfin's car was ready to leave, Gad and Atida presented themselves to him. They were both radiant. Shlomit came to tell him goodbye too. Meaningfully she shook hands with him. It goes without saying that she wasn't limping in the least.

CHAPTER SEVEN

Which confirms the biblical saying that "the land will spew them out," but in which, nevertheless, hope has the last word to say.

1.

So far as Helfin's friends and acquaintances knew, his life continued integrally and without interruptions. Only in his own consciousness did it sway confusedly between two scenes which alternated. The others, naturally, saw him only either in Galilee or in Tel Aviv. In both sequences the happenings that constituted his life proceed without gaps. In reality the two chains of experience occurred simultaneously, since Helfin remained under the spell of the magic of the red switch, the little stage, and that fat adviser, and hence existed in a double fashion. The whole matter was incomprehensible. Nevertheless it was a given fact which had to be accepted. It was only as a matter of convenience that the two chains of events were kept apart, that in alternate strata of a single week or, as in this last instance, of three weeks, they seemed to follow each other. But this was due to his lack of practice. So there had been a three weeks' period in Tel Aviv and a similar one in Galilee. The fat man seemed to have foreseen a different regulation for the future. The separation of the two simultaneous existences into an appearance of succession was only a temporary device. More experienced partakers of the magic were undoubtedly able to fit the two chains of events into their actual simultaneity. Perhaps that would come later. For the present one thing was utterly clear to Helfin, namely, that to save himself from a choice between the two courses of life, he had taken upon himself both and at the same time. The trouble was that the old proverb was reversed in his case: He who does not pay the piper cannot call the tune. For it appeared gradually that he who had avoided the act of choosing by means of the ingenious Unambo apparatus found his misery not diminished but increased. In place of that Either-Or with which our earthly life constantly threatens us, there had been substituted an apparently friendlier formula: "Either-and-Or." But this formula turned out to be a pure poison, searing the heart.

Another hurt which Helfin expected did not ensue. No one of his fingers became transparent or threatened to wither. Perhaps the fat man had used this threat in order to gain the attention of his victim and to divert it from more serious matters. No, his fingers were whole. But a much deeper spiritual devastation set in. It was his soul, not his finger, that gradually withered.

How to bear the heavy burden of the twofold torment apportioned to him, this was Helfin's personal secret, accessible to no one else. As far as others were concerned, his life went smoothly on. To them he was as they were and destined to no dark separateness from man's common fate. Take the neat girl who had received him in the Josefovitch offices in that top story of the office building of glass and steel. As far as she was concerned he had normally walked into her boss's reception room and had there waited for the speculator for fifteen minutes and hadn't had the least contact with a horse's head leaping out of the wall. For Josefovitch had turned up, and half an hour later Helfin had come back out of the reception room rather red-faced after the difficult consultation, which had entailed a violent dispute. What that neat young lady did not know and what, moreover, didn't interest her in the least, was the circumstance that during that last half hour Helfin had, though with intense resistance, finally signed the contract, including the hateful paragraph, and had thus succumbed to Bianca's machinations. As for this little secretary with whom, since we needed her as an example, we have been dealing at a quite improper length and of whom we now take our permanent leave—to her the whole procedure had had no tinge of the uncommon. She had seen Helfin come and wait and go, as many others had done in the course of business hours, who had also departed more or less cheated and taken in. It is most probable, indeed, that she did not individualize Helfin among these others, or indeed notice him at all.

At precisely the same hour at which Helfin had been waiting for Josefovitch, he had also been playing a farewell game of chess with Gad at Rosh Pinah. Gad had made a powerful move quite by accident with a Knight and the little chess figure had suddenly had eyes that came to life and looked at Helfin with sharp and threatening glances. Red sparks leaped from the pupils and the lids winked. It was well that Gad was oblivious of this. Helfin understood the signal; he knew that he was again facing that barrier which the horse's head, this time in the miniature form of a chess figure, signified. He knew that he was being thrown out.

Resistance, he knew, was quite useless. It was his deserved punishment to be forced to leave this clean world of youth and hope in which, in spite of tragic incidents, he had fared so well. This only he determined—to return to this life as quickly as possible and to seek with all his strength to shorten the week which he was doomed to pass in that other existence.

In mind and will he now set the apparatus to a three-day interval. He knew by now that this operation of the will was effective. Thereupon, having lost the game of chess, he went out into the streets of Rosh Pinah on the pretext of mailing a letter in the box in front of the inn. Opening the door, he found himself, quite as he had expected, not on the street of Rosh Pinah, but on the thickly carpeted reception room of the Josefovitch office. Here he sat a while at the luxurious oaken table, turning the pages of pamphlets and waiting for the mighty one. This sounds not a little overwhelming but is in accordance with the simple facts. Much as the teller of this tale regrets it, he cannot spare the reader the necessity of familiarizing himself with the double course of events and with making a real effort to grasp this somewhat unusual partition of time into two lengthwise strands. Indeed, the reader must be asked to exert his imagination to the effect—and on this occasion the chronicler demands no more—that Helfin, aside from the fact that he did wait for Josefovitch and did sign the degrading contract, simultaneously came back from the street of the little town into the inn parlor and soon thereafter took leave of his nephew, whereupon he himself sought his station in the so-called grove, while Gad, now in the best of spirits, returned to the sunshine of Mansura.

Next day, which was the eighth of July, the Egyptians launched a major attack in the Negev, which was repulsed with heavy enemy losses. Officially the armistice did not come to an end until July 9. But the enemy could not wait for its expiration. Suddenly, at noon on July 10, came the news that the Jewish army had conquered the important air field at Lydda. And now began a series of victories which utterly changed the entire situation. Prior to the armistice we had been happy that the improvised Jewish army had been able to repel the attacks of well-armed and incomparably more numerous forces. What now set in was a counteroffensive which succeeded in proving within a few days the superiority of the reorganized army of Israel. Its air force no longer consisted of "primus stoves" and museum pieces. It had been thoroughly overhauled and was now able to reply to the numerous and continuous air attacks on Tel Aviv with raids on Cairo and Damascus. Now, too, the Jewish army was well supplied with fighter planes and bombers and tanks and armored vehicles. The mighty heroism of the young fighters was confirmed in victory. The big Arab cities of Lydda and Ramle fell to us in quick succession. In the North, Nazareth was occupied. Its many churches and monasteries came under the effectual protection of the Jewish High Command. In the South the Jerusalem corridor was extended and Ein-Kerem was taken. A vigorous attack was delivered at Latrun, where the old highway was still being blocked. Now it came to pass that the United Nations, which, in May, after the founding of the state, had watched the bitter need of Israel with comparative equanimity, found it necessary to insist upon a new armistice in order to save the Arab aggressors and invaders from complete destruction. It was clear that, had the war not been interrupted at the end of ten days, the whole of Galilee and the whole of the Negev and perhaps also the Old City of Jerusalem would have fallen into Jewish hands and that thus the campaign would have been brought to an end once and for all. This was not permitted and on July 18 a second armistice settled down on the Land. It was welcomed in Tel Aviv, which had been attacked not less than nine times within the preceding two days and nights and where many people had been killed and wounded. It was generally welcomed, too, as a step toward permanent peace, although it put an end to that victorious and triumphant activity of our army against a beaten enemy which the Jews of the Land had not dared to hope for even in their dreams.

These matters were of interest to Helfin in only one of his two existences, namely, in the positive variation of experience. In this phase he himself shared in the stubborn battles around Latrun; his unit had been thrown thither and its attack was cheated of final victory only by the renewed cease fire. Simultaneously his negative life took an entirely different course. The yoke of Bianca in Tel Aviv became ever more painful and fateful. He hardly observed the air attacks on the city, so deeply was he enmeshed in that adventure, so frantically did he seek to disentangle himself from its net. In order to escape he conceived the plan of dividing his two lives into briefer intervals, to pass through the barrier of the horse's head more and more frequently, whenever possible day by day. This method was, of course, exhausting. The subtlest and most experienced of narrators might well be dismayed by an effort to delineate this constant oscillation between Tel Aviv and Latrun. This chronicler, however, is content to relate as simply as possible that which actually took place. His is not the ambition to enter into a conflict with the narrative difficulties involved and to overcome these. For this reason he has been able to decide to contract coherent portions of experience into large masses, without considering the fact when and how often Helfin in his despair tore asunder the continuity of happenings and switched from one of his lives to the other. These interruptions and switchings did not exist, as should be remembered, for those with whom his life was passed. He himself, too, gradually mastered the art of his simultaneous double existence and attained such skill in it that quite soon only the crass culminations of his parallel existences seemed to him to have any singularity, while all ordinary matters were to him but as the contrapuntal treble and bass of a musical composition which accompanied each other when they did not, as happened now and then, flow together into one.

The contract returned by Josefovitch was accepted by Bianca with cool approval. She had gained her every point, even the elimination, if she wanted it, of her former comrades. She had used her bad humor to achieve her ends. It is impossible to have about one a beloved human being with the feeling that that being is constantly depressed and unhappy when it is in one's own power to return that being to life, to gaiety, to pleasantness, so that the light which one causes to radiate from one's friend streams back upon oneself. And how could one fail of the action which made all this possible? Helfin, at least, was not the man for that.

He tried to persuade himself that his yielding had not been quite inexcusable. For the moment his young friends were at the front and could not work in the studio in any event. Nor had Bianca as yet exercised the veto provided for in the contract. Finally, he was sure that, when work actually started, he would be able to reconcile the conflict of interests. He tried to persuade himself of that, though he was at the same time deeply shamed by the thought that he had obviously deserted the path of rectitude and loyalty. What would his young friends say when they heard of that ominous paragraph which placed their fate into the power of such a creature? Nor did he doubt that Bianca would spread the news abroad and that she would at least make her power threateningly apparent to her colleagues. But in consequence of a strangely dense, though inexplicable, nebulousness of mind he was less concerned with the effect on his young friends than with Bianca's gratitude, which she did not fail appropriately to express. Perhaps she would now give tangible evidence of her appreciation of the fact that all discussions had ended in her favor, that he had finally let her opinion and her advantage prevail over his very conscience. And he remembered how at the beginning of their common life in Tel Aviv he had entertained the fear that her delicate and difficult soul might arrive at a point in which it would be a hardship for her to separate her love and her gratitude, to prove to him that she did not love him as a matter of gratitude but purely, as the meaning of true love requires.

Perhaps that moment of conflict had now been reached.

It was astonishing how simply Bianca solved that problem. On the following day he got a letter from her informing him that she had decided not to meet him for some time because their constant disputes diverted her from her own work. "It's healthy for neither one of us," she wrote. "You've said often enough that in certain matters we don't understand each other nor ever can. And so it seems best to make an end."

In rising rage he muttered to himself that this was easy now, seeing that the contract had been signed. This was the first clear thought which he entertained after the brief inner storm that drove the blood rushing to his head.

But he went further, into the heart of the matter. Would an eternity suffice to grasp the incredible moral foulness involved? Could she not have used a single friendly word, a single expression of regret? What spiritual stinginess and inhuman coldness! This cool element in her which had hitherto been an element of her special attractiveness suddenly revealed its origin in a region of the world or of hell in which the most modest germ of life was doomed to death. That such a woman could breathe within that icy air—that was at once her advantage and her curse.

Dvora had brought the letter to his bed. Mechanically he got up and got dressed, while his pulses throbbed so violently that his temples ached. He felt as though he would never be rid of that ache and that it would be best to die. It would be horrible to go on living with such an ache. And now suddenly a visionary picture appeared before his eyes in all the fragmentariness characteristic of dreams and visions. The gate of a graveyard arose suddenly out of the earth. The grillwork of the gate was secured by heavy locks of golden-brown metal and chains of darker hue and thus resembled the vault of a bank. But that locked gate, it was borne in upon him, meant: Finality. Something irrevocable had taken place. His access to that land in which he and Bianca had been lovers was denied as ultimately as though it had never been, as though it were a graveyard. And perhaps, thus the reflection rushed through his skull, perhaps it had never existed, perhaps the whole thing had been a lie and the mere creation of his fancy. Had he not long ago in Paris set down a clear analysis of the loveless and purely calculating character of this woman to be a warning to him in the future? It hadn't done him any good. Yet the statement was there and every word in it had proved itself overwhelmingly true. And while feelings and reflections of this kind rushed past his soul, reflections which seemed most important at one moment and wholly meaningless the next, he kept his eyes on the graveyard gate of this continuing vision. He had never had a vision before. He didn't know how one took such an event. He had the feeling that he was being guided and drawn onward by superhuman forces. And so he stared rigidly at that gate of marble and metal. And now he observed a thing that pained him, pained him boundlessly, though this pain could not alter the impression he received: all over this graveyard there arose other such gates of metal and marble, each one provided with chains and gigantic locks—an army of such gates, frequent as headstones in an ordinary cemetery, but so constructed that the grillwork of each enclosed that of the next. What hurt him in this symbolism was that the inaccessibility of the grave-yard, though sufficiently assured by that first locked gate, was increased and rendered utterly irrevocable by the protection of others gates within still further gates. And Helfin's soul cried that all this display was superfluous and in the nature of an affront, because he would not try to break through even the first of those barriers. Was he a child? There was no need, there was no need. . . .

And while his soul was crying thus, the distance of earth as far as eye could reach was covered with further gates and other locks. Then, suddenly, the vision vanished in a black mist.

He dressed himself. In his clothes closet he came upon Bianca's white nurse's costume. He stared at it longer than he wanted to.

He decided that the matter was worth a final interview. All the graveyard gates in the world weren't going to keep him from that. He set out on the way to the agreeable pension in which he had housed her. He knocked at her door and heard her bid him enter. Not only was her voice astonishingly unchanged with its beautiful, dark viola note, but there was an objective kind of encouragement in it. She was sitting by the window at a tiny table, bent over the Hebrew grammar which they had so often used together. He placed her letter on the polished table top next to the book: "What is the meaning of this?"

"You can't expect anything to last forever." There was a cer-tain pleasant willingness in her voice and a gleam of the desire to understand in her glance, as though a fit moment for some general discussion had arrived. "You don't have to be so excited," she added in the tone of a physician who was being consulted. She had evidently perceived the excitement in his face, although he had tried to utter his few words calmly. He fell silent. Otherwise he would have had to roar.

After a little she spoke. "These things happen every day. Even in very nice marriages. It's quite unimportant."

"I wish you'd explain to me—"

"There's nothing much to explain. It just happens that one doesn't want to go on. The erotic attraction has vanished. And, as you ought to know, I'm no person for half-measures."

She really talked on this difficult theme as they had done in their quite objective debates in Paris. She had liked such talk well enough but had always somewhere made the observation that one shouldn't talk about such things.

He thought that all that was needed now was that she should talk about the infallibility of her instincts, of the judgment of the senses from which there was no appeal, and similar trash.

"But why precisely now? At this moment? Yesterday all right; not today."

She smiled. "There are things that one shouldn't talk about. Maybe even yesterday it was no fun; maybe it hasn't been for quite a while. Things like that grow clear in a flash. They are retroactive. You know that as well as I."

He restrained himself from saying, though it was on the tip of his tongue, that the coincidence of her feeling with the signing of the contract was odd enough. Odd enough! And suspicious enough. But how prove the suspicion? Bianca always made her arrangements so that no suspicion could ever be proved. And we're all egoists, he reflected, sloppy egoists whose actions are random ones. In addition, however, there exist these precise egoists of the Bianca type. Their egoism is reckoned out with the precision of logarithmic tables. . . . It had all been a swindle, a pretense of nonexistent affection. Not otherwise was this brutal breach to be explained. And all this noble reserve, seeing that there had been nothing to keep in reserve, because there had been no feeling present—all this had been a swindle and a piece of the grossest charlatanism. A parallel dance of constellations! Ha! He could not help remembering those words of hers which marked some of their common experiences. "If one has you, one has everything in the world." And he remembered the bench in Joseph Street, in the noon-day tumult of Allenby Road, and the newsboys calling out the evening papers. And that book, that book which she was going to write to explain how she had gotten the better of men, because she herself would have desired to be a man, a conqueror, a revenger. But that she would not want to revenge herself upon him, who was different from all others, who was an exception. . . .

He didn't know how long he had stood silently beside that polished little table, whose gleaming surface seemed to hypnotize him and to evoke from him a feeling of profound and unfathomable misery. Suddenly it occurred to him that he was really being insulted. "You didn't even ask me to sit down."

"Oh please, do."

He sat down. She began to talk about things that seemed so indifferent. How beautiful the sea was today. She pointed to it beyond her window. It had a new aspect every day. Calmly she described some of these varying aspects.

So there were people who hated using big words, but not out of a feeling of inadequacy, as would be proper enough, but on account of their own inner emptiness. Since they had nothing within that corresponded to these words except some swindling pretense, they knew that one must use those words with some prudence. And when someone insisted on being objective in that scientific manner, there was always room for two entirely different interpretations. Either he didn't want to exhibit his emotion or else he had none. He knew that this wisdom came to him rather late. As a matter of fact, though, he had always known; there was nothing new. What was happening for the first time in this hour and would probably give his life a new direction, a downward direction, was something that he didn't want to admit to himself. That was the reason why he let all these drifting notions pass through his poor head. He could have done that without her. Indeed, that would have been better. For that he didn't need to sit here. So why didn't he go quietly home? Home, at all events, whether quietly or not. But it was just this thing that seemed unthinkable and impossible. He found it hard to estimate how long he had been sitting there.

"If you like," he heard Bianca say as through a wall, "we can continue to be friends. We can see each other from time to time. But no more."

These words helped him to rise from his chair. It was as though he had been thrust from it. He left the room without a further glance at her.

He did not calm down during the succeeding days. Gnawingly he was forced to rehearse to himself the whole story of his disillusion from beginning to end. Had he not tried to get rid of the woman? She had run after him, not he after her. She had thrust herself upon him. But it helped him little to recall her double assault upon him in his Parisian hotel or the vision of her in her sensual self-abasement. And all her further attempts in Paris. During his second sojourn there he had carefully avoided her. But in Tel Aviv she had hunted him down. She had refused to be shaken off. Perhaps the moment had now come when her hunter's instinct had been satiated and so her interest had died. So perhaps it was not calculation but a physiological process which entailed the extinction of the lust for booty when the game had been bagged. So perhaps there was a kind of honesty in her breaking with him now. The trouble was that her gesture coincided with the very day on which she had gained all her material wishes and had no further use for him. This was attributable only to calculation, not to some vital instinct. He would have liked to have forgiven her; he could not believe that she had never done anything but pretend. Surely there had been intervals during which her feeling must have been genuine. That day when she had kissed him on Allenby Road, for instance, or once at the theater during a representation of *The Dybuk*, when Chemerinsky, cast in the part of the aged rabbi, said with such infinite tranquillity: "*Nu, nu, nu*" ("Well, well, well"). At the extreme simplicity and naturalness of the actor's expression she had taken his hand and had pressed it. Doubtless that had been a moment of true union for them. He rejected the thought that everything about her was falsified, not only the color of her hair, her nose, her name, her origin, her age—but everything. To assume that would have been, he thought, an exaggeration evoked by a feeling of vengefulness or by the insult done to his male vanity. He truly desired to guard against such feelings and not to condemn her frivolously. But through this passion for justice, if one wants to call it so, he always drove himself anew into an emotional crisis.

Those months of a true binding between them, were they as nothing? He had resisted her assertion that there was no such thing as a metaphysical binding between human beings. He had asserted that not everything arose from self-regardingness; that there existed, however rarely, the emergence of a spiritual world without falseness or lies, within which we are allied to truth and to some eternal element and within that ultimate truth do truly belong to each other. Pursued by these thoughts he could not but remember—and wondered that he had not done so before—the not infrequent hours in which he had truly loved Bianca. Had she forgotten how often the flaming up from them of a simultaneous opinion or observation had made them feel a deep togetherness, especially in the aspirations of their work and of their common plans, which had divided them so beautifully from that sordid clique at the Hotel Layla just when they had been forced to make common cause with it. If not love, then at least this common pride in cleanly workmanship had constituted a bond between them. Had that been nothing? Was that forgotten too? Had he not honorably nursed the notion of making a great actress of her? Had he not remained convinced of her extraordinary talent and its possibilities of development in periods during which her evil and destructive inclinations had made themselves felt? Had he not had the hope of cleansing her of her fragility and developing within her whatever was noble and authentic? This hope had become a part of his very life, its prominent part, his greatest joy, the meaning of his existence, as he was now bound in retrospect to perceive. And was all that to be over? An abyss gaped at his feet when he tried to imagine a world without this task, this effort—without Bianca. It was unbearable! This emptiness was the worst thing that could have happened to him. Suddenly he realized that no vital preoccupation was waiting for him any more. There was a morass of hours and he had to wade through that disconsolate, green, and nauseous morass. He was appalled at the possibility of such a future which seemed to stretch into the infinite. So that was what happened when love died. All that one had done had had the beloved as its goal; all strivings had been connected more or less directly with Bianca. If she now disappeared and the right were taken from him to be concerned with her, to center all his thoughts upon her, why think? Of what good was the world, of what good his work? There was emptiness and that difficult senseless wading through the greenish morass. In his terror that this was to be his fate, indeed was assuredly his fate, there arose before him a second image, not so clear as that first vision of the graveyard gate, but palpable and close for all that. Revolting, too. Like a painting by Hieronymus Bosch. In this vision love appeared in the form of a broad, bright knife, the blade of which was penetrating his body, and he was glad of that penetration. The slow introduction of the alien steel into his flesh was almost imperceptible. But so far as it was perceptible it was something good and delightful and pleasant. But once the beloved had thrust the knife beyond a certain depth she suddenly ceased to be careful and considerate. Now she had her object in her power. Now she could use the knife as a saw and penetrate deeper and deeper, and she did so. It bled and pained, but that did not deter her. Merrily she butchered on. And there was no way of resisting as had been possible when first the smooth knife penetrated the skin. Now it was too late. The battle was lost and the conquest complete and the object in her power. But that was unendurable; terror rebelled in him, and pride, some last small remnant of pride and vitality that was still left him. He seemed, too, in that vision to be pleading that she had truly given him a great deal, that, nevertheless, he could still be useful to her; that it was probably not well for her, either as an artist or a woman, to separate herself from him and to underestimate him. She could still learn much of him that might be important to her future work. She should consider that, consider it before a final decision which could no more be revoked.

This final notion seemed to him important in his state of confusion. He recorded it in a letter to her. This only: "You may still have need of me." This was a cry he uttered before sinking into the green morass.

He wrote. He wrote for a whole hour. That single sentence was expanded explicitly and wildly, a mixture of accusation and pleading. When he reread it, it seemed feeble to him. Full of empty phrases, of circumlocution. Veraciously felt but not so expressed. "Don't underestimate me!" That was actually childish. "You have given me much!" What had she really given him when you looked at it soberly? A series of powerful erotic sensations. Nothing else. Nothing else? Not really? That was not exactly true either. And wasn't even that a great deal, a very great deal? Nothing else? This was an oversimplification. It was a decay of thought to reduce life to such naked contradictions. Life was a play of infinitely varying colors. It was not black and white. Only weaklings were unaware of that.

He sent the letter, although he had his doubts of it.

He rather expected a harsh reply. How often had Bianca not assured him that her decisions in matters of this kind were irrevocable and that the use of many words was utterly futile. But the result of his move was more annihilating than any possible notion of it. He got a letter from her. When he opened the envelope he found his own letter unopened.

This was the final blow. It was an insult too grotesque. He had not deserved that of her and was not disposed to endure it. To put an end to a relationship which, at the very least, and aside from all other matters, had been a genuine comradeship, and to put an end to it with unnecessary brutality, displayed an evil and malevolent heart. Yet even here on the very edge of the morally possible his inner ear heard a contrary reason: If one wants to end a thing, it is better to do it swiftly and fundamentally. To use a scalpel. It hurts less than a long, hesitating handling of the wounded place. But he rejected this argument. He had had quite enough of Bianca's surgical skill. When, some days later, he met her on the street, he took no notice of her.

2.

To his amazement this failure to greet her or show any awareness of her existence had placed a weapon of unexpected effectiveness into his hands. He met Bianca not infrequently in the studio. His heart contracted at each meeting until he got hold of himself.

There were consultations and preliminary planning, at which Bianca had to be present together with the committee of directors, Uri Waritzki and the younger Josefovitch. It escaped no one that Helfin did not greet Bianca, nor look at her, nor ever address her. No one mentioned the fact. But since everyone knew that they had been extremely good friends, people necessarily speculated about the reasons. And these speculations were by no means favorable to Bianca. For of Helfin's honorable character everyone was convinced, in spite of criticism in particular matters. Even as the continuous attacks of the "yapper" had by no means shaken the respect in which he was held, so, too, the evident break between Bianca and himself reflected on Bianca and not on him. There were those who turned up their noses when she was mentioned.

He would gladly have given up the meager satisfaction provided him in exchange for her reversing her vulgar and calculated behavior. But there was no way of turning events back. That was beyond all possibility. He even thought of getting out of her way, of leaving the country. It would be unendurable to him in the long run to have to be seeing her as the mistress of Josefovitch, which she undoubtedly was.

So he was going to be a deserter? Even during the war? So he was going to illustrate the scriptural warning that the Land would spew out the sinner?

It came to him like a mysterious monition that just at this time the new state issued a stamp on which appeared the symbol of a flying scroll. This referred to the curse of which the prophet Zechariah had spoken. It did so for him, at least. Actually the design of the stamp had used the antique symbol not to convey a curse but a blessing. Nevertheless, it was that flying scroll. And the prophet had said that in the house of him who had departed from righteousness the curse would settle which the flying scroll bore over the Land, and that his house of wood or stone would fall into ruins.

It was at this period that Helfin did his best to avoid everything that took place around Bianca and sought to concentrate all his spiritual forces upon that other life of his. He could not wholly escape; all he could do was to alter the scene of his existence. He now sought out passionately the horse's head which he had formerly feared, only, of course, in a single direction, in the direction of his post amid the hills of Latrun. There he passed the barrier gladly and breathing freely. When he was thrown into the opposite direction he felt throttled and rebelled.

On one occasion, on the road, he met a milk delivery wagon with two horses. In one of the two horses, which seemed to trot along not more mysteriously than the other, he recognized by a malicious gleam of the eye and a vibrating stamping of the iron hoof that this was the satanic horse out of the subterranean laboratory of Manshiyeh. He suddenly lost all control of himself and in a state of insane rage lunged toward the horse and began to beat its head with the butt of his gun.

Naturally the driver cursed and lifted his whip. A crowd gathered and Helfin was arrested. There was a hearing, there was a great shaking of heads, there were expert medical opinions and a military sentence was passed. Amid all this confusion it was Helfin's tacit hope that the whole thing, which he could no longer endure, would come to light. He hoped that the framework which held him would be shattered. Had not the fat man affirmed that the machine would be shattered against the rock of reality whenever unsolvable contradictions were to arise between the two existences as the simple consequence of given facts? Surely, he thought, the point had been reached. He simply could not continue this bizarre existence. When he performed sentinel duty along the "Burma Road," when, as had recently happened, he suddenly met Gad, whose regiment was stationed there now, since he was no longer needed at Mansura, when he went with patrols through the night in order to secure the way to Jerusalem, which must be saved—then all was well with him. Then Bianca and her deadly insults were as though they had no existence; or only a shadowy existence. But that was it—it was only a shadow and yet it was there. He could not wholly give himself to that which uplifted his heart, which his soul delighted in, the protection of the Holy City on its hill from hunger and thirst—to this blessed forgetfulness of self. Not wholly. For Bianca lay in wait somewhere in a niche on the horizon, awaiting his return in order to plunge into his side and tug back and forth the knife delineated by Hieronymus Bosch. But these ghostly presences were bearable in comparison to the wretched life which seized upon him so soon as the horse's head sent him in the other direction, the horse's head which suddenly started into life out of a battle picture in a book or from the pattern of wallpaper or from a coin or from a cloud in the afterglow, or even from lines scribbled on the margin of a letter or from the curves of a signature which incomprehensibly, in the space of a moment, coalesced into the galloping figure of the fatal beast. That sufficed. He had to go where he did not want to be. And in that life about Bianca, Gad was not a mere shadowy presence but sought him out with a certain importunity, even though they met but rarely. But on those occasions he clung. Not with a bodily clinging. For there was no bodily exchange between the two spheres of existence. But in his thoughts the matter was so, that he was keenly aware of Gad while dwelling in the swamps of Bianca. He was clearer to him and somehow more palpable than Bianca ever was in his life at the front. The Gad, however, who made his appearance in the world of Bianca had no kindly attitude to Helfin nor did he act like a nephew standing in a son's stead. He was changed. Helfin didn't even always recognize him. Rather was the lad like one sent out in pursuit, like a myrmidon or jailer. That was the impression. It was that image which drove him to mad acts, such as the idiotic assault upon a harmless milkman's nag. The interpretation must be that his reality was in a state of revolt against the life upon that artificial double stage. The unnaturalness of it all became ever more perceptible. A resistance arose within him that must at last bring to an end the accursed wizardry. Had not the fat man promised this? Alas, whoever has ever depended on the promises of the devil has ever, according to all accounts, been cheated and deceived.

It could, of course, be otherwise. Perhaps there was in him the resistance of a higher order which desired the flying scroll of the curse to crash against a crag.

Or he might perhaps just die of exhaustion, since this twofold life, which was no splitting of life, but a doubling of life, might use up a twofold supply of vital energy and thus exhaust the sources of his strength. There must be a final repercussion to so ruthless and extravagant an expenditure of resources. So much the worse for him. Ah no, so much the better.

3.

The stony slopes of the "Burma Road" to Jerusalem were the right landscape for the entertaining of such trains of thought. Gray and white chalk formations, cliffs and terraces as in the Dolomites, sparsely covered here and there with sunburned grass and bushes—a desert rendered more solitary by the birds of prey which now and then flew across the hot blue sky.

Helfin had been ordered to watch the road between Dir Muheisin and Beit Djis. The Arab villages were empty and deserted; not till you reached the main road of the plain near the monastery of Emaus could you catch sight of the enemy's army. The large, handsomely built Trappist cloister with its red roof was clearly visible from the mountain road. From its hill it commanded the entire plain of Ajalon in which first Joshua and later Judah Maccabi and many others had engaged in bloody battles. The so-called "Burma Road" by-passed this strong Arab position and constituted the main artery of the corridor toward Jerusalem. Farther toward the south a new road was now being built. It was no longer an improvisation; it was properly constructed of asphalt, dark, broad, convenient. During the last battles the corridor had been immensely broadened, so that the new road was no longer at the mercy of hostile artillery.

In the oasis-like palm garden, the *bustan*, a soldier was drinking from the pump and joined Helfin on his march. Helfin was wearing about his neck a picturesque red-checkered *kefiyeh*, an Arab kerchief, evidently a piece of booty. Jonah had given it to him. How had Jonah gotten hold of it? Helfin had not inquired; the kerchief pleased him.

The strange soldier began to discuss the war, especially the cease fire in Jerusalem which was no cease fire. Daily the Arabs used artillery, daily there were casualties on both sides. From his conversation it was evident that he was by no means a fanatical warrior. A *kibbutznik*, a specialist in the fisheries, he asked nothing better than to be able to return to his carp pools at Zichron-Yaakov. "Well, duty is duty. At one time you dig pools and at another you shoot. There is a time for everything. *Lakol zeman ve-eth*, as it is written in Kohelet, the Preacher.

"And where are you bound for?"

It appeared that the soldier had paid a visit to an Arab teacher in Jaffa. Now he was returning to his post. A passing car had given him a lift to this point. He would now continue on foot. They strolled on together.

"What kind of a teacher is that?"

Before the war the Arab teacher and the soldier had been very friendly. They had exchanged scientific books and loaned each other technical journals. They had first met in an adult education course for the breeding of fish. The soldier had used a brief furlough to assure his Arab colleague that he had not forgotten their stimulating intercourse. Under the changed conditions of today it might have been possible, too, that some intervention with the authorities could have been useful to the Arab scholar. He had stood in no such need. But he had been deeply pleased by the good will of his Jewish friend; he had thanked him for his visit as for a great gift and had assured him that he now felt less isolated.

"Merciful sons of the merciful," Helfin quoted the traditional saying.

"Mercy?" the soldier exclaimed. "It's nothing of the kind. It's our duty. It isn't even that; it's just sound politics. We'll have to live with a world of Arabs about us. We can't make friends with them a moment too soon. Of course, if we had the grace to feel an authentic sympathy . . ." Then he asked where Helfin had obtained his kerchief. "Can you buy those?"

Silently Helfin took it off. "You're right," he said. "We shouldn't wear anything like that. It's funny, isn't it? A kind of Wild West romanticism. And yet, why not? Little trophies like that have always and everywhere been used in war."

"And be like the other peoples, eh?" the soldier said inquiringly and leaned his back against the cliffside, as though he was suddenly very tired of walking in the heat, in the desert wind, the *chamsin*, which causes certain autumn days to be even more trying than the settled glow of summer. Helfin remarked on this. "The end of the summer is even harder to bear than the summer itself. Thus our sages said. And the climate has gotten worse since their day. Not until we have accomplished a complete reforestation of the land—"

"Quite like the other peoples?" the soldier asked again in that stubborn way. "So two thousand years of exile have taught us nothing?" An almost iron earnestness lay on the face of the wanderer; his eyes were pallid and yet glowing. At this moment he reminded Helfin of Dov Popper. Only this boy was younger and his face was smooth and his lips well molded. "The greatest misfortune which the Jewish people has had to bear in this year came to pass yesterday," the stranger continued in a suddenly changed voice. Was he about to weep? His voice vibrated. "We have fought honorably; we have defended ourselves against craft and force. Nor are we responsible for the deed of a few isolated mad men. Yet it cuts into our own marrow. Don't you know? Haven't you heard of the catastrophe—the assassination of an ambassador, of the mediator, of Count Bernadotte? The men who did that no longer belong to us. But the point is that such a thing could happen among us at all! It is sad, it is terribly sad; this is no time for trophies or for fine words or for red kerchiefs."

Who was this man who spoke in this fashion? His voice had risen from sentence to sentence and rolled forth at last with such power that, doubled by the echo of the mountains round about, it seemed about to loosen avalanches, to roll into the valley. In the glare of the light, which was like a curtain of radiance, a curtain of glittering pearls of glass which both dazzled and veiled the sight, the stranger had suddenly vanished.

Helfin stared at the mountain wall against which his companion had been leaning. It was smooth. No fissure or door led into it. Yet it was as though it had received and swallowed up the soldier.

Not far away Helfin now observed a few green military tents. Perhaps the man had walked over to one of these while Helfin, shocked by his words, had sunk into absent-minded, half-conscious contemplation, such as had often overtaken him recently.

Again a change of scene. The tent into which Helfin made his way in order to look for the young man and to inquire further concerning the surprising and dismaying event was transformed at the very moment of his drawing the flap aside into the bar of the Hotel Layla. The ritual of the horse's head had evidently been abandoned. It had become superfluous in this constant, swifter alternation of the scenes of his life.

The news had evidently not yet reached this place. Later Helfin found out that his meeting with the strange young soldier had taken place only a few hours after the assassination. At this time the fact was known to but a very few. It remained inexplicable how the information had reached the lad on the "Burma Road," seeing that the news had not yet been officially released even though abroad special editions of newspapers announced it.

Precisely as our waking days are joined together without a rift, while we ignore the intervening nights with their dreams, so that on every morning we take up life at the very point at which sleep had interrupted it, even so Helfin had long ceased to be surprised at the fact that each transition from one phase of his existence to another started him off at the exact moment at which the transformation had occurred the last time. And not only did he continue whatever activity had been interrupted by the intermezzo, but all feelings, desires, anxieties, preceded from what had gone before as though no interruption had taken place. In direction, strength, depth they streamed continuously onward and carried in their current all the stimuli which had moved him before.

Thus, when Helfin drew aside the flap of that tent but entered the hotel bar instead of the tent, he was immediately absorbed by the interests which had normally brought him thither. The conversation on the "Burma Road" and the conscience stirred by it faded. Instead he looked greedily about to see whether he could find Bianca and the younger Josefovitch. For once he wanted to observe, without being observed, what the relationship between those two was. Were they reconciled? How intimate were they?

He saw them at a corner table. They now took all their meals together. At bottom there could be no doubt about the character of their relationship. Moreover, Helfin had received a letter from Gad, in which there had been all kinds of evidence about an incident on a bench of the Promenade. But this letter had reached him weeks ago in his positive life in Galilee. And experiences were not really transferable from one phase to another, even though they were, in a sense, remembered. Such memories had something vague and dull in that other environment, into which they seemed illicitly to enter, and entailed nothing obligatory. But this remembering did not release him from the necessity of repeating the experience in that variation of his existence to which it belonged. This happened to Helfin now in the Tel Aviv phase. Now, too, the thing had its right accent, so that he was convinced of it as of something assured, palpable, and actually known.

Remaining at the door, Helfin stared at the couple but did not greet them. Quite involuntarily he had extended his refusal to recognize Bianca to anyone who happened to be with her. At that moment Goldgarten, who wanted to get in and whose way he was barring, addressed him.

"How are you, Professor?" the elegant gentleman said softly. He looked as though he had something sour in his mouth. But then he always looked that way. The flickering shadows which flitted across his face from his American lenses never subdued this strangely empty expression, which seemed to reject the world and all its ways. "Did you hear about it? The whole of Tel Aviv is in a state! The Terrorists in Jerusalem killed Bernadotte." Helfin was deeply shaken. He'd heard the news once before. But according to the law to which he was so mysteriously subjected it affected him almost as something new, at least ninety-nine percent new, the final one percent being occupied by a dull, faint presage, a kind of shadowy *déjà vu, déjà entendu*. Goldgarten walked on toward Philip Josefovitch while Helfin continued to stand at the door. But he heard the small man's cynical observation to his manager, "I know, I know. You won't see me putting on mourning."

Goldgarten joined Helfin and they went into the second dining room. "The news is unconfirmed as yet," said the manager, "but these Hebrews are capable of anything. I've always said, we're a small people but a nasty people."

286

Helfin could not regain control of himself swiftly enough for an appropriate answer. Furthermore he had become accustomed to the fact that in the circles frequenting this hotel and other similar places everything that was Jewish was deprecated in a bitterish spirit. The soldier with the narrow lips and the glowing eyes had spoken after another fashion. He, too, had condemned, but warningly, threateningly, out of the earnestness of deeply wounded love. Here, on the other hand, a gay satisfaction came to salute everything that might justify hatred, any hatred, including the hatred of oneself. Goldgarten's observations, in addition, were uttered in a very special tone, quite different from the general jocosity of the business gentlemen here and, if possible, even more revolting in its pedantic gravity. It was true that in a raid on a café the police had found a package of marijuana in the pocket of a little lad. Goldgarten seemed to derive some satisfaction from the circumstance. "It was smuggled in from Lebanon. Right across the military front. What did I tell you? We'll do anything for money."

"Forgive me, Mr. Goldgarten. How can you talk so? Aren't you a Jew yourself?" "That's just my misfortune." The bitterish gentleman sighed over his menu, from which he was selecting the items of an opulent meal.

At bottom Helfin was amazed that Goldgarten seemed so indifferent to the rumor of the assassination. He was equally astonished that he himself was not more powerfully stirred, that he did not rush to the telephone to make further inquiries. It was not the doubleness of his life that blunted the shock. It was rather the style of this luxury hotel. Here he seemed capable of thinking only of Bianca, of attributing importance to nothing else.

He hadn't, in fact, listened very carefully to what Goldgarten had said, although the man really constituted a special case. He hated the rich. But if he spoke of one of these people among whom he himself belonged, both by his standing and by his habits, he never forgot to add, "He made his money by sheer fraud. That's the only way it can be done here." He had formerly been in business for himself. Now, after a bankruptcy which had been hushed up, he worked for Schäftel who paid him a salary appropriate to his expert knowledge. Yet he hated Schäftel for having, as he expressed it, "reduced him to slavery by dishonorable machinations." Ejected from his capitalistic supremacy to a managerial position, he acted the part of an affronted prima donna, in spite of his extraordinarily high salary. He plotted vengeance because he had been excluded from the top rank of the gamblers. Meanwhile he lived exceedingly well and seemed at times to dispose of very large sums from additional sources. When his mood was bright he vied with his boss in the telling of anecdotes. Preferably, though, he retired into a bitter silence, accompanied by that slow rubbing together of his palms and the critical observation of all about him. If he made any remark in a larger company, it was always in the form of an anecdote. "The anecdote is our folksong; we have no other," he declared to Helfin with a contemptuous smile. "You are mistaken," Helfin replied. "We have a very rich and very authentic literature of folksongs. You've probably not paid any attention to them." "Oh, you're thinking of those syncopated Russian songs. I dislike them intensely."

It was odd that he was accustomed to converse more intimately with Helfin than with others. At first, too, Helfin had felt a certain confidence in him. But this initial impulse had not lasted long. There was something uncanny about the man. On the other hand, the very fact that he uttered his criticism so openly was rather likable. The least that could be said of him was this, that he didn't so thoughtlessly sink into the swamp of comfort and self-admiration as did the other plutocrats of the Hotel Layla, whose words were ironical, even when they spoke of themselves, but whose real complacency and self-satisfaction were never shaken. About Goldgarten, on the other hand, there had been built something similar to a basin of icy water, immersed in which he himself frostily quivered. And it was precisely the radiation of this shuddering discomfort which attracted Helfin. Applied to himself discomfort was too feeble a word. Horror shook him when he thought of Bianca and his disappointment. And when did he not do that? Birds of a feather! And so Helfin, the dismayed, the somber, told the story of his woe to the equally somber businessman who openly displayed his ill will to the world. When, still at this time, he summoned up the strength to speak at all, he labored under the compulsion to analyze the story of Bianca and himself anew again and again, to discuss her insolent deception, the crafty calculatedness of her scarcely believable procedure, which, often as he returned to it, never lost the acute shrillness of its false effectiveness. He never, however, failed to present the mitigating arguments from which it appeared that a genuine feeling, too, had broken forth from profound female instincts of unfaith and of changeableness in this demonic human being. Evil but incalculable instincts. And he did this because such an explanation seemed to him more bearable than that of her mere calculating craftiness. It would, at least, not so revoltingly soil the memory of all that had been between them and might leave him some little refuge of feeling not wholly defiled. It was a subject of unlimited extent. He never got to the end of the pros and cons. He brought out innumerable details of which he was not sure whether they proved or disproved anything and demanded of his partner that he should give an opinion on the inferences to be drawn from this happening or that. In the last analysis these conversations were no more than a meaningless attempt to re-establish somehow the presence of the beloved object, to summon her up bodily, an exertion which seemed undignified to him, of which he was ashamed, which could lead to nothing but the worship of an idol turned into its contrary, and which therefore, even had it succeeded, could have led to nothing but a horrendous station of cold misery. He talked and talked and could not get rid of the disgust which chilled his breast. It was certainly this icy feeling which united him with Goldgarten and Goldgarten's vengeful and vast indifference. If he could only have talked away these icy walls from his own heart! It was hopeless. And yet he continued to become involved in these conversations as though they were a long, long avenue at the dusky termination of which Bianca might perhaps be standing and waiting for him.

She was not waiting for him. He knew it well. Nevertheless he continued his vigorous way along the avenue, since his very tread upon it caused him momentarily to forget the meaninglessness of the whole undertaking and so gave him a little ease. It was like a shot of something into his soul, an opiate that gave no

hope, but did not wholly deny hope either, something tormenting and maimed and all-powerful.

"I talked the thing over with Miss Petry the other day,"
Goldgarten interrupted him this time.

Now this was something new. He found that he had expected
nothing of the kind. He had resigned himself to be dragged
through a changeless, unchangeable and therefore quite sterile
mass of matter to the end. If a man has for weeks and weeks gone
through the same repulsive material—like a schoolboy who is told
to learn by heart a long poem and can't retain it—then the unexpected emergence of a new turning point has something frightening. It may cause a sort of horror. By a silent gesture he invited
the manager to tell what he knew. He had the feeling, not as a
matter of metaphor, that his bodily temperature dropped by
several degrees. He had had, in fact, no suspicion that Goldgarten
was well acquainted with Bianca. Had he known that, he might
have picked himself another confidant.

"Well, it's not surprising that she sees the whole matter in a
different light."

"She does? Just how?" Helfin stammered.

"The fact that you ignore her she does explain as a consequence
of the breach between you. But she says that you, and you alone,
caused the breach."

"Well, now I'm really curious."

"She says she once asked you to lend her a small sum. For just a
few days. She said that on the first of every month she was receiving from her rich sister in Buenos Aires an ample income
which covered all her expenses. But the postal service, like everything else here, was in bad shape. So her income was delayed. And
her rent was due."

"And you believed that? Go on, go on!"

"And on that occasion you had made a proposition to her, Mr.
Helfin. I really don't like to go into the terms of the proposition.
Let's not talk about that. Let's talk about something else."

"Look, since you've started now, please go on."

"You said that you were willing to advance her the money provided that she would come and spend a night with you. This she
had indignantly refused to do."

"Indignantly refused," Helfin mechanically repeated. "All right. Now I ask you, do you believe that tripe?"

"Not a word. She's known to be a liar. She says it herself. She tells anyone who will listen."

"For that very reason people believe her. Understandably enough. I mean to say, pardon my abruptness, that her whole behavior in this matter is thoroughly understandable. Somehow or other she has to explain the fact that I ignore her. It's doing her no good. So she turns the spit around. In general people think that her lies concern trivialities, that they are a harmless exercise of fancy. I myself thought that at one time. A slander as foul as this surprises even me. And considering the subject matter, it tends to make a man powerless."

He stared into nothingness. It seemed to him that he must determine upon some line of action. What line? And then it came to him with a sense of relief that there was no immediate necessity for action.

He seemed almost to lose consciousness for a little while. Goldgarten was too busy with his own reflections to observe any change in Helfin. Swiftly the latter pulled himself together. When he was capable of listening again, it was Bianca who was being discussed. And, of all things, in terms of praise. This appeared to Helfin as an exaggerated objectivity or else cold indifference on the part of Goldgarten. He would have welcomed a grain of comfort, a confirmation of his rights, of his credibility. Perhaps Goldgarten had said some such thing during the moments of Helfin's absent-mindedness. Even now he found it difficult to pay the right attention. What he heard was a story of elaborate forgeries. This woman, the manager said, was a person of the most extraordinary skill. When she sat down and made a real effort her forgeries could scarcely be distinguished from the original. Not even a handwriting expert could do so. Her intuition got the better of science. It was extraordinary!

Now Helfin listened intently. Hadn't Bianca once forged a love letter for his young friend Baruch? Hadn't that had further consequences? Hadn't this trick led indirectly to her contact with Gad? And she had been very proud of it. What, he wondered, was the object of her forgeries now?

Helfin did not receive any enlightenment on that evening. It was to come later. Goldgarten evidently considered him not yet ripe for the information. During several further weeks he supplied him with plentiful news concerning the shameless slanders with which Bianca undermined his reputation. And she evidently had some success. Helfin observed a growing coolness in certain quarters. Finally Josefovitch informed him that Miss Petry would refuse to collaborate with him and that she seemed to have excellent reasons.

"You got her her job. And for that she pushes you out. Same thing happened to me. That's the way these Hebrews are, and their women too," Goldgarten observed with grim solemnity. "That's the way they all are, that's the way this whole state is. It won't last. You'll see, it won't last."

After the Egyptians had for months refused free passage for convoys to the isolated settlements in the Negev, the Jewish army took the offensive in the middle of October. The United Nation's observers demanded free passage for the convoys again and again. The Egyptians paid no attention. Now the Jewish army broke through and cleared the roads, without the assent of the enemy, whose positions collapsed in an astonishingly short time. In these circumstances Beer-Sheba, the city which has been the crossroads of all the desert paths in the South since the time of Abraham, fell into Jewish hands. The losses in this battle had been heavy. Almost without casualties and in an even briefer period similar events took place a few days later in western Galilee, that is, in the northern part of the Land. Here, too, the invaders fled, having failed to carry out the least of their bombastic threats, and with a feeling of profound relief our people were able to repeat the biblical definition of the Land of the Jews, stretching from "Dan to Beer-Sheba."

And yet there was no peace. Diplomatic intrigues prolonged an armistice which imposed oppressive burdens on the land of Israel and no less inflicted grievous hurts upon the Arabs, hurts which the Arab potentates tried to hide from their peoples by a mask of empty verbiage. Unsuccessfully. Here and there in Damascus, in Bagdad, in Cairo the hungry masses protested. These accusations of the poor against their feudal governments were understandably blended with the accents of Mohammedan fanaticism. This furnished a new pretext for Bevin and his followers not to attempt to allay the tumult by social reforms, but to attribute all responsibility to the Jews. The Jews were winning victories; therefore this uproar in the entire Middle East. To begin with, at the outbreak of the war, the political line had been that the Jews were too weak. Therefore one could not grant even their just demands. Now the slogan was: The Jews are too strong; therefore—there was no change of inference—therefore one cannot grant even their just demands. All the while, in spite of the war, the new state developed quite respectably, consolidated itself, received tens of thousands of new immigrants, founded new settlements, and though bearing all these heavy burdens, exhibited some measure of economic health. Even the fever of speculation on the exchanges in Tel Aviv did not prevent a considerable decrease in the price of gold after the victories in the Negev and in Galilee. And those fine gentlemen who had speculated on the misfortunes of their people lost considerable portions of their capital.

Meanwhile the United Nations, meeting in Paris, had gone in for endless debates and the taking of complicated votes. No doubt that some men there were honorably intent upon a solution. Others talked irrelevancies for world consumption; still others were filled with resentment and ill will. Upon the whole it was depressing enough to observe how feebly the cause of justice was represented, how the conspiracies of imperial interests always coldly beat down any honorable attempt at agreement. The helplessness of this gigantic international apparatus reminded one of the image of a whale washed up on dry land. It is said that whales sometimes commit suicide by voluntarily permitting themselves to be swept from sea to earth.

What, next to the intrepidity of our youth, shone like a star above these days was the fact that the war itself had fulfilled chief Jewish demands, above all, the demand for unrestricted immigration. From all the countries of the dispersion, from the camps in Germany, in which scandalously there were still homeless Jews three years after the ending of the war, from all the places of the oppression, the homeland brought its hostages home. Only their booty in Cyprus was not released by the British. Without a shadow of legal or moral right ten thousand Jews who for years had wanted nothing but to go home, were still imprisoned behind wire entanglements there. It was a politically meaningless piece of vengeance against these unhappy people, for Israel utilized its absorptive capacity by the reception of others. Only those who waited longest were not yet permitted to come. That was painful as well as senseless.

In his other, essential life Helfin had shared the battles at Hartuf. His division had crossed the railroad which mounts toward Jerusalem over the Judean hills. His column had reached the Arab village which is called Nebi Zachariye. It reminded him strangely enough of the prophet with the flying scroll. For the Arabic word *Nebi*, the cognate of the Hebrew *Navi*, means prophet. And, indeed, the Arabs assert that the prophet Zechariah lies buried under the mosque of their village. And so the village was taken, for the fleeing enemy had left the entire territory from here to the southern frontier and beyond Beer-Sheba.

On his return from the village of Zachariye, Helfin encountered one evening that young soldier with the handsome, narrow lips and the radiant, precise face. The army units to which they both belonged were resting in a police fortress below Hartuf, at the foot of the old Jewish settlement which had been completely destroyed. That night under the starry sky these two soldiers took a walk along the road. Now both the days and the nights were beautiful. Now the tormenting heat was gone. Now, at this season, one could attain to a true consciousness of this land's paradisal beauty. He who sees the Land only in summer does not know it and departs with a distorted image.

"The constellation of Scorpio stops rising at this season," the soldier said. "It remains below the horizon. In fall and winter its red eye is no longer to be seen in our nocturnal sky."

Helfin looked up in astonishment. He wondered how the young man knew how baleful was his connection with the aspect of that constellation.

"How do you feel nowadays? Are you better satisfied than

when we walked together in the summer?" Helfin asked and looked searchingly into that clear and handsome countenance, which bore an edge of pain under the curving black brows.

"Unfortunately, I'm always dissatisfied," the stranger said, though his smile was friendly. He seemed suddenly to show another and a milder aspect. "It seems very hard to content me," he continued. "And there's no reason why anyone should take the trouble to do so."

"Don't be so sure," said Helfin, who was attracted by what seemed to him a strange community of feeling with this young man. It was difficult to him to keep up with the other's impetuous striding. "Anyhow, it would interest me greatly if you were to tell me what satisfies you, and what fails to satisfy you, as things are today."

The strange young man immediately plunged into the center of things. "Our cause is well regarded in the U.N. That is real progress. A little earlier or a little later our state, which has long been a fact, will be recognized and accepted into the family of nations. What hurts me is the circumstance that we owe this progress not to our clear right, not to reason or righteousness, but exclusively to the success of our arms. Had we been beaten, no one would stir a hand in our behalf. So it was once more force that prevailed—prevailed for once on our side, after it had almost always in all history prevailed against us. But is that, seen from some true tribunal of humanity, a genuine victory? We are far enough from the days of the Messiah."

"I myself," said Helfin, "have always considered this period of ours as the worst and most detestable among all ages. We, and with us all mankind in its present condition, are farther than ever from the days of the Messiah."

"One should never say that. How can we tell? That which is great sometimes appears at the end of long preparations, sometimes it comes overnight. In this matter there are no iron laws. Indeed, it may come overnight. It was so in the matter of our state when that vote was taken at Lake Success on November 29. The miracle had come overnight."

"And what did that have to do with the days of the Messiah? Would you kindly tell me that?" Helfin was irritated. "It is my conviction that the purpose of the Jewish state is to put an end after two thousand years to the misery and humiliation of the persecuted Jews all over the world. More I do not expect of it. And that suffices—quite suffices."

"It does not suffice," the other answered in a tranquil voice. "It may be that in addition our state signifies the taking of one step, however small, in the direction of the Kingdom of Heaven."

"It doesn't look that way." Helfin stuck stubbornly to his doubt.

The other assumed no visionary attitude. Indeed, his aspect was a little more careworn. He was no less firm. "It doesn't look that way," he said calmly. "But we really can't tell. One thing is certain: we must do our utmost to take that little step, at the least that little messianic step."

Helfin felt the powerful glance of the stranger upon him. The man continued, "It is within our power to take this effort upon us. Success is not assured us, but the effort is ours. And that means much."

Goldgarten had a very simple plan. The trouble with it was that it rested upon rather complicated premises. These he sought to explain to the somewhat amazed Helfin, whom he had invited to his apartment.

"The state of Israel is not viable," he explained. "It can't disappear fast enough. The Jews are not a politically constructive people and have never been one." Goldgarten proceeded to show how this fact arose indisputably from the history of Palestine. It had been demonstrated repeatedly by a great number of serious historians from the time of Mommsen on. One didn't have to argue the point. After the aberration of the Balfour Declaration, the English had found this out for themselves and had therefore switched their support to the somewhat unprogressive Arabs to whom, nevertheless, the future belonged. On numerous occasions leading personalities in the Foreign Office at London had instructed him to that effect. He had had no need of that instruction. He knew it all from personal observation. He was thoroughly acquainted with these Hebrews here, to whom he had sacrificed his fortune and his health. He had, in a word, purchased his expert knowledge at a high price.

He shifted his lenses up and down; the sharp shadows flitted over his lids and cheeks. Helfin looked at him sidewise with a keen discomfort, as though he were afraid that this expert gentleman with his cool, impenetrable assurance could assume a golden covering at the next moment and turn himself into a Chinese idol which, crouching, would stare at him from a niche in the wall instead of from that chair beside the desk. Not a Buddha, far rather a counterimage and contradiction of everything divine, soaked in vanity, in hatred, in all unholy activities. The man spoke with a dignity as though he had the authority to order the affairs of earth according to his approval and his unerring insight. He seemed to expand with every word. Soon invisible priestly choirs would be heard from the walls to do him honor. He was accuser and judge in one and the same person. "It seems to me to be the duty of every honorable person," thus he issued his order, "to collaborate with the swift liquidation of this absurd illusion which calls itself a Jewish state. I don't know what your opinion is, Professor, but it seems to me that you must be fed up with this riffraff too. The usury practiced by the men is the same in kind as the egoism and the insane and slanderous campaign of Miss Petry. . . . Maybe you don't even know what the Petry woman has been telling her boon companions recently for their amusement. She says that you're still trying to force yourself upon her. You have, for instance, sent her a poem about a graveyard gate and about a knife in the style of the painter Hieronymus Bosch."

"But that's impossible," Helfin exclaimed. "That's the very essence of madness."

"She shows the poem and reads it to people in her melancholy whisper."

Helfin was about to jump up. Goldgarten took his hand and felt his pulse. "Go slow, go slow! Don't get so excited. Most of us are destined to die from a stroke. But why invite it prematurely? There's no reason anyhow. Obviously Bianca forged your letter. She probably wrote the poem, too. It isn't that the louse has no talent."

"But how can she possibly know? I never spoke of my private visions . . ."

"We're all mind readers, we of the Secret Service," the idol said with a false tone of soothing, which was really meant to sting. "But it's truly astonishing how good Bianca is at this 'white work.' That's our term for this forging of letters. It's a very effective means of wheedling information out of people. For instance, out of these foreign officers with whom Bianca associates a good deal. She has already found out a lot about a delivery of planes from Czechoslovakia. You show a man like that a letter from a friend, in which all kinds of things are indiscreetly expressed. How do you get hold of the handwriting of the friend? Well, maybe you've cultivated an intimate contact with the chap and taken from his wallet some notation about a very different matter. Bianca studies the letters one by one—there are her instinct and her intuition—and then she uses these letters to write what she likes up to the point of high treason. This document is shown to the colleague. The fellow sees that we know everything and so he begins to talk at random. We're generous. A small share in drug smuggling which we control means independence for life."

Recently, however, Goldgarten went on to explain, there had been difficulties with Bianca, so that finally it had seemed desirable to get rid of her. "This is the point at which we are, and since we believe that you have a score to settle with this fine lady we have picked you. You see, I'm being perfectly frank with you. I'm giving you all the reasons. I've been observing you very closely for some weeks, Professor, and I've come to the conclusion that you're a hell of a decent fellow. No use trying any funny business with you. That wouldn't suit you. So I'm putting all of my cards on the table and calling every spade a spade. All right. This is the situation. Bianca has done you dirt enough; she will continue to persecute you without mercy. I know her. She has the feeling that her security is threatened by you. Whether it's true or not doesn't matter. She considers you an irreconcilable enemy." Helfin nodded. "So she's going to try to harm you as much as she can. She still has various subtle tricks up her sleeve which you probably don't suspect. Nothing is left us then but to draw her fangs. It's necessary for you, Professor, and equally for us." With coarse directness Goldgarten pointed out that Helfin, once he had been provided with the identifications of a member of the Secret Service, could spend what nights he wanted with the lady before giving her up to the police. He smiled. "This additional premium has its agreeable aspects." To Helfin's enraged protest he replied calmly, "Well, you don't have to if you don't want to."

Now only did Helfin quite recover his self-control and he proceeded to express his utter astonishment at what he was told.

Goldgarten listened indulgently, as though Helfin had used only a conventional formula in his assertion that he had had no suspicion of Bianca's activities as a spy. All right. There were those who thought that this pretense was a necessity, and far be it from him to be discourteous and say, "Don't go on so!" On the contrary. He was all for letting these baby-faces have their little fun. But one mustn't overdo it either. In the end one had to come to the point. After all, Helfin could not have been ignorant of the fact that Bianca had worked for the Gestapo in Paris. He was evidently calculating that this hint would abbreviate the debate and make out Helfin to have been a fellow conspirator for a long time. He emphasized the further fact that Helfin, though he was fully informed as to the lady's history, had cordially recommended her to Josefovitch. At this point there was an implicit threat. Had not Helfin assisted Bianca to settle in the Land? He hadn't exactly imported her, but he had gotten her a job, although—how would the authorities of the state of Israel like that?—he had known what a dangerous character she was.

"I never knew," Helfin said firmly.

"You knew," Goldgarten replied. Confidentially he continued. He was almost familiar. "You don't have to be scared of me." He now made it perfectly clear that he had long been with the British Intelligence Service. As a matter of conviction. They were stingy enough. For purely historical reasons and an honest enthusiasm for the British Empire, as he had already explained. Nor had he been able to make up his mind to discontinue this activity after the end of the Mandate. On the contrary, it had seemed to him more necessary than ever. Of course his present employers, the Arabs, didn't manage their affairs in as orderly a fashion as the British had done. As was well known, there were two parties in the Arab camp, as hostile to each other as both were to the Jews, perhaps even more so. Recently Bianca had allied herself with one of these groups, which was the wrong group. This had been indubitably proved by the Secret Service central office. It was necessary therefore to lure her into a trap, to provide her with the proper material and to give proper notice at the right moment to the Israeli authorities. That would blow up the lady properly. It would lead to an investigation on criminal charges.

Helfin reflected. Criminal charges? The thoughts whirled through his head. They no longer had specific contours. They were like the cloud-streaked red disk of the sun before it dips into the sea. Yes, he thought, she is a criminal. But not after this fashion as far as I'm concerned. There are things that one doesn't do. Forbidden things. Spiritually impossible things. I have been weak. But weakness has its limits.

"I don't understand you, Mr.—" Helfin seemed unable to articulate the name. The word "idol" floated through his mind. "How can you attempt still further to wound this unhappy people with its back to the wall, finding its last refuge here as an alternative to destruction? I don't understand how a creature can be so dehumanized. You will fail, too. This people will stand sturdily on its feet and yield no inch of its heritage."

"You let me worry about that," Goldgarten said with his air of an expert. "It may take more than a year; it may take a decade or two."

Helfin began to tremble before the cold look in those monstrous eyes. He wondered whether one shouldn't cast oneself upon one's knees before this idol beseeching mercy for oneself, for one's people. Those two looked at each other in silence. A watch on the desk ticked audibly.

The interval of silence passed. The imperturbable expert placed before Helfin a flight ticket. To Latin America, to Rio de Janeiro, accompanied by a visa, an exit permit—all necessary documents. A careful preparation had evidently been undertaken. But precisely this meticulous care used in his case strengthened all of Helfin's inhibitions. He pushed the ticket from him. "I have no intention of leaving the country."

"It isn't on account of the Israel authorities," said Goldgarten. "They'll have every reason to be grateful to you, and they will be, for taking care of this lady. Nothing against your early return, either. I may be able to use you here later. But I would advise a temporary absence. That Petry woman has a couple of muscle men who swear by her. There might be real danger."

"I'm not afraid of danger, and vengeance is never handsome. But I am in such a miserable condition that perhaps only vengeance will restore me to myself. So I have nothing against vengeance. I know that that road is a foul one. Yet I would like to pursue it to the end. It all began with vengeance against a seventh-rate journalist; let it end with vengeance on a larger scale. But, though vengeance is unclean in itself, the accompanying circumstances must be clean."

"How are you going to keep the two apart?" the expert cried with a bright, hitherto unheard note of triumph in his voice. And at once, before Helfin was quite aware of it, secret documents were spread out on the table. He was given instructions. He was told by what method news of arms shipments, of troop movements behind the front, of technical innovations were gathered and by what channels these were being communicated to the enemy. He was given an insight into the organizations which plotted against the new state in Rome, in Athens, all over Europe. "Now you can go and denounce me to the Israeli authorities," said Goldgarten. "In fact, that's your duty. If you don't do it, you're an accessory to the crime. But if you do do it, that won't be so profitable either. We have quite a dossier about you. Bianca herself has added to it. The whole thing started with a curious visit to a subterranean laboratory in Manshiyeh that you once told her about. This laboratory has been investigated and has been found to be a secret Arab storage place for arms."

When Helfin slowly returned home from this interview, with whirling head, he took the way of the shore road. He trod through the sand and passed a hill on which an Arab cemetery was situated. The autumnal sea foamed and roared. Long did Helfin

301

pace up and down to quiet his heart. Twilight fell. He was glad to have agreed to nothing. He had left the ticket on the table and had run out without a word.

Suddenly he noticed someone walking beside him. It was Gad. Without raising his eyes he knew that it was Gad. The lad wore a black mask over the upper half of his face. He had followed him like the emissary of a secret tribunal. Now he had caught up with him. He still betrayed the evidences of swift pursuit.

It must have been an error. Gad could not belong to this world of Bianca. Gad had no place here.

In his thoughts Helfin had, in fact, dwelt upon his nephew in this phase of his existence, too, with its vengeance and its moral horrors. He had clung to the boy, no longer in his semipaternal capacity but rather as one who himself seeks instruction. But this had taken place only in his thoughts. Hitherto Gad had never corporeally intruded upon this minus-world; he had belonged exclusively to the other, better life. Once, only once, in the very beginning, to be sure, had Gad rung the doorbell and stood at the head of the stairs with his knapsack halfway to the floor. But on that occasion Helfin had refused him entrance. Since then he had never again entered this sphere. Bianca had spoken of him. He had felt this very fact to be illicit and scabrous. Later Helfin had prevented Gad's further penetration into this world as something inadmissible. Or, at least, he had made every effort in this direction. If I breathe upon him now, Helfin thought, he will vanish. I breathed then and he appeared no more. Later, during that harvest scene in Galilee, everything was well again. . . .

These memories came to him as from far-off days. So much had happened since, that he could not gather it into one view. Those earlier times had, at least, been times in which an order, though an unblessed order, prevailed by virtue of the Unambo apparatus. There was still something to which one could cling. Now anarchy and chaos prevailed. Gad's figure had the effect of a cut-out photograph dubbed into a new photograph. He did not know in which of the two worlds he was. The two montages seemed to have flowed together. The transference had taken place without a signal. The absence of the horse's head as a sign of the barrier had been agreeable enough on several occasions. That added nervous shock had seemed futile. But the lack of any marking of way or phase had its disadvantages too. Unexpectedly one glided from one form of being to another. One lost all supervisory control and had to be more prepared for surprises than before.

"What have you to tell me, Gad?" Helfin cried in a loud voice, so as to be heard above the thunder of the surf.

Gad did not answer. When Helfin looked more closely he now observed that it was not Gad at all. It was the young soldier with whom he had had those two conversations in the field and who assuredly had no place either in this world of shame. Beneath the velvet mask which covered the face only from forehead to the end of the nose, he recognized clearly that well-formed, thin-lipped mouth. The lips remained closed. Only the eyes gleamed white through the slits in the mask. Silently that figure strode on and overtook Helfin and did not turn back again. Yet at that moment when he passed him, the stranger had once more looked somewhat like Gad.

Helfin rendered himself no accounting concerning the number of times he had gone to see Goldgarten since then. Maybe two or three times. He was given commissions but executed none. He was ill; his heart beat irregularly. Now one evening Gad seemed indubitably to be calling on him. That is to say, it seemed so for a moment in the dusk of the anteroom. Then at once the guest seemed again rather to resemble the strange soldier. The aspect alternated. It proceeded from an uninterrupted iridescence over the lines of the face. Nor could Helfin tell from the voice which of these beloved young people was in his presence. It was a blended figure which assumed now one of the two contours, now the other, to crystallize now as the one and then again for a little while as the other. But there was no permanence in either aspect. The figure would address him with a curious formality. "By your visits to Mr. Goldgarten, whom we are watching, you have thrown suspicion upon yourself. Perhaps you would be good enough to relate to us the contents of your conversation with him. So far as we know, you have been an excellent citizen heretofore. But recently you seem to have been careless in your choice of acquaintances."

All that Helfin could do at best was to say something about his plans for a film, which had long been interrupted, by the way, and his visitor, who had evidently undertaken this mission with extreme reluctance, contented himself with a sharp warning. The visitor had stayed but briefly. He had displayed evident signs of disgust.

That evening Helfin heard in the Layla bar that quite unexpectedly Bianca Petry had abandoned her job and had flown to Paris. The rumor added that the brothers Josefovitch had been arrested. It was further added that Bianca had gotten away at the last possible moment. She had just heard that legal action was being taken against her. For an infinitesimal moment Helfin, who didn't put two and two together at once, felt something like regret. He was amazed, and yet it was a real regret. He thought of her as a restless spirit, restless and disquieted, who had failed again. At bottom she was an unhappy being who deserved pity, for none of her stumbling and glittering brought her anything but suffering. A brilliant and intriguing mind which always came to grief. Could there be a thing more lamentable? Once more he listened. In connection with Bianca's flight there was mentioned a rather unobtrusive person, to whom no one had paid particular attention, a horrid old pessimist, a thoroughly nasty creature. "No one will regret his absence," said Uri Waritzki, "unless it's his boss, Mr. Schäftel, for whom he did do some very effective work."

"Regret whom?" Helfin asked.

"That very strange fellow, that Goldgarten. Haven't you heard the news? He was found dead in his apartment. A couple of young fellows made their way into it at noon today and simply shot him down. No details are known. The neighbors pretend they heard nothing. Maybe they had been intimidated."

They were the same fellows, undoubtedly, who by night had lain in ambush near Helfin's apartment and fired in his direction. "Regards from Bianca," one of them had cried. None of the bullets had reached him.

Helfin had the ticket to Rio in his pocket. During one of

their last conversations Goldgarten had pressed him hard. Now Helfin went home once more only to pack his suitcase, into which he stuffed his many manuscripts and diaries. He took leave of no one, not even of Dvora; he drove directly to the airport.

But in that other, simultaneous variation of his life Helfin had not left the Land at all. He continued to belong to the guardians of the "Burma Road." Here he met Gad, who knew nothing of any machinations in Tel Aviv.

Needless to say that he addressed his uncle with the familiarity of old. Helfin accused him of having been rude to him recently. But Gad considered this a joke. He didn't know what Helfin was talking about. They embraced each other and determined to play a game of chess as soon as possible. Helfin observed that his heart was in thoroughly good order. It was probably sick only in his Brazilian embodiment. Here he beheld the future spreading out before him beautiful and hale, his own as well as that of the Land. The black-out had just now been discontinued in all the cities and villages. For the first time in a long while did the friendly lights arise by night and at the same time came the news of tentative negotiations toward peace. Now all would be well, he thought. We will return to the building up of the Land; we will also have neighbors again with whom we can live on decent terms. Ah, the dead will not come back. But if we could just take that brief step into a messianic age, in that case, as the prophets assure us, the estate of the dead will be different too.

Everything will be different. Helfin asked himself whether that could be true of himself as well. Was he not in worse estate than if he were dead? Was he not thrust out of any orderly human community, whether of the living or of the dead? Had he not taken upon himself the most abominable of all adventurous destinies—that of being two? He was living neither here nor there. He had two existences but both tainted with magic, unsufficing, ghostly shades. Now he was torn asunder between Brazil and the "Burma Road." This was the nadir. He was angry at himself. Yet he felt unexpectedly well. That may have been on account of his excellent health. Or it may have been caused by the thought that soon the machine would be shattered, shattered against its own inherent madness, against its contradiction of the simple facts of life. Perhaps it would not be shattered by reason of these corporeal obstacles. Against himself it would be shattered, against his rebellion. For a new light shone which rejected the bypassing of decision, the accursed Either-and-Or.

The narrator is unwilling to add anything to the last report furnished by Gad.

Gad's account was as follows:

"My uncle and I had stood on sentinel duty all night. Early in the morning we wanted to return to Bet-Susin. All night long the Arabs had been quite active. Again and again, singly or in small groups, they tried to seep through our corridor, as they had attempted to do in previous nights. It was in vain. Not a one got through. But it was understandable that after the loss of their roads of communication in the Negev they laid great value upon the possibility of gaining some advantages for their positions near Latrun as a means of connecting with their front at Bet-Lechem. In spite of the armistice and rumors of peace there was a good deal of firing from time to time. This particular sector of the front was exceptionally active. At the break of dawn, when others had come to take our place and we were marching along the road happily enough, we suddenly ran into a couple of these maddened Arabs who had skillfully climbed up the mountainside. At once we crouched in the grass behind a cliff and returned their fire. All would have been well, for we kept them at a distance. They began to climb back, pursued by our men. At that moment an enemy plane appeared above us. It dived and thundered. There was no protection against it in the open field on the dry grass. Its machine gun rattled. With a mighty thrust Helfin threw me to the ground, plunged himself over me, and pressed me into the earth. 'Be still! It'll be over in a moment.' I felt the weight of his body over me. His arms were about my neck. His breath touched my hair. 'Lie still! Don't be afraid.' The bullets riddled him. He died instantly. We buried him with full military honors."

From the "Burma Road" Gad brought back a curious object which he had found on the road near the scene of the skirmish. "I don't know," Gad said, "why it made me think of him who died that I might live. But a kind of voice told me to pick it up and bring it to you."

I recognized the framework of the little machine, fragments of a red switch, a couple of bluish-green tatters of organdy and a broken tube. As a mechanism the whole thing was extraordinarily primitive. And this trifling object had caused and evoked such mighty tempests and transformations in the tragic struggles of a human life to which, in spite of its errors, perhaps because of its errors, no one will refuse his sympathy.

I was too deeply moved to explain to Gad the connection which I suspected. The little machine had evidently been shattered against that strong willing of Helfin's to be again, despite the black magic, a single and integral human being. It had taken an enormous moral exertion and a profound recovery of power. In life the fusion of the two forms of existence was irrecoverable. Not so easily does that subterranean one release the victims who have once pacted with him. Another way had to be trodden. This difficult way was possible only by means of radical renunciation, the renunciation of the self for a beloved fellow being, by means of death. The oneness which was no longer possible in life, seeing that the corruption had proceeded too far, this oneness was re-established by the redemption of death.

"He loved you very much," I said to Gad, who understood me without further speech.

Several weeks later I received a package from Brazil. It contained Helfin's diaries, which I have utilized in this narration. They were tied up with a thin string of that same bluish-green material which I knew so well. The package was accompanied by a letter from an unknown gentleman with an undecipherable signature. In this letter there was communicated to me Helfin's desire that I proceed to the writing of this chronicle in his justification and in his place. Just before his death he had emphatically and on several occasions expressed this desire. He had died quite painlessly of heart failure. His last thoughts had been for the Land of Israel.

I scrutinized the date of the letter. It had been written on the very day on which Helfin had met his death on the "Burma Road."

Perhaps in this circumstance lay that grace for which Helfin had yearned. The two forms of his life had been simultaneously extinguished. It could have been possible for him to survive for a period in the evil version of his life and to continue to suffer. That had been spared him. I am, of course, not at all inclined to make any assertion of a kind which might ascribe a meaningful issue at the very end to events which seemed to fly into the face of nature and its laws. I merely indicate a possibility. Beyond that I limit myself to the facts which I myself experienced or which I learned, by word of mouth or through writing, from Helfin himself or from those close to him.

From the conversations which I had with Gad, I may finally communicate some significant details. "Do you believe that Helfin was unhappy during those last days?"

The answer was direct and clear. "He was not unhappy at all. He loved the 'Burma Road.' He was delighted to have been stationed where he had started his military service. I never saw him happier than during those last days in the hills of Jerusalem. He was accustomed to say that this work of peace in the midst of war was precisely to his taste; that it was as though specially chosen for him; that, by virtue of it, he might return to oneness. Of course, I never quite understood what he meant by oneness, probably something romantic. The kind of thing I don't like. And yet my friends and I had an excellent understanding with him. Just the other day Atida wrote me that no one among the older people seemed so close to us as he; maybe he had wanted to take our point of view entirely, which was not altogether possible, of course. But maybe it was this that he meant by that remark which he repeated so often during his last days."

"To be at one with the youth of the Land," I said hesitatingly. "Don't you believe that in a certain sense he was just that, at least in his very last moments?"

Gad tossed the brown lock from his forehead. "That's a romantic notion. You, my dear sir, belong to the romantic generation too. We late-born people know little or nothing of that. I would rather say this: in those last days my uncle was more tranquil than he had ever been before. He was full of confidence. Formerly he always used to say that life tormented him too much and he used to tell the story of the iron steer of the tyrant Phalaris. Recently he said none of these things. It seemed to me sometimes as though he had become a different person really, as though he agreed with most of what he saw. Not with everything, of course. He remained critical even though he didn't like being so and was fond of being enthusiastic, sometimes too fond. He remained critical, in spite of that. But finally he did seem to be fairly well satisfied with the turn of events. He didn't say that in so many words. But when he talked about the future and about his great hopes, in spite of an element of fear, and of the light which Israel might be to the whole of humanity, then one felt that he was altogether with us. And to be altogether on the side of hope, that's youthful, isn't it?"

I made such an exact notation of these remarks of Gad because, at that time—it was the beginning of December—news of a real termination of hostilities in Jerusalem was confirmed. The first serious negotiations with the enemy began. There was hope in that. It could easily portend an early end of the war.